THE VAMPIRE

AN ANTHOLOGY

arranged and selected by
ORNELLA VOLTA and VALERIA RIVA

Foreword by
ROGER VADIM

English adaptation by
MARGARET CROSLAND

UNABRIDGED

PAN BOOKS LTD : LONDON

First published 1963 by Neville Spearman Ltd.
This edition published 1965 by Pan Books Ltd.,
33 Tothill Street, London, S.W.1.

ISBN 0 330 20112 3

2nd Printing 1971

PUBLISHER'S NOTE

This book is the adaptation, with some additional material, of an anthology *I Vampiri tra Noi*, first published by Feltrinelli in Milan, 1960. The compilers would like to thank all those who have assisted them in their research, particularly Enrico Fulchignoni, Jean Boullet, Robert Benayoun, Fereidoun Hoveida, Mario Praz, Roland Villeneuve, Franco Cagnetta, Jacques Bergier, Ulrike Neumann, Roger Cornaille 'Minotaure', Elena and Alda Croce, Franco Venturini, Victor Mitz, Dr Hunwald, Standford Greenburger, Wanda Patroni-Griffi, Nicole Ménant, Michel and Laryse Zimbacca, Njuyene Manh Khan, John Atkins, Bruno Tasso and Biana Maria Ramorino.

PRINTED AND BOUND IN ENGLAND BY
HAZELL WATSON AND VINEY LTD
AYLESBURY, BUCKS

THE VAMPIRE

'. . . like the vampire, she has been dead many times, and learned the secrets of the grave.'

Walter Pater, *The Renaissance*

'Vampire. 1734.
[adjective French, adaptation of Magyar *vampir*, a word of Slavonic origin; perhaps ultimately formed on Turkish *uber*, witch.]
1. A preternatural being of malignant nature (in the original and usual form of the belief, a reanimated corpse), supposed to seek nourishment, or do harm, by sucking the blood of sleeping persons; a man or woman endowed with similar habits.'

The Shorter Oxford English Dictionary

ROGER VADIM, the French actor-writer-director, was born Roger Vadim Plemiannikow in 1928. He is scarcely less celebrated for his marriages to Brigitte Bardot, Catherine Deneuve and Jane Fonda, three of the most beautiful women in the world, than for such successful films as *Les Liasons Dangereuses*, *La Ronde* and *Barbarella*.

CONTENTS

ACKNOWLEDGEMENTS

Acknowledgements are made to the following for permission to reprint the stories contained in this volume:

Carnival from *Balthazar*. Lawrence Durrell. 1958. Faber & Faber, Ltd.

Chriseis from *Doctors Wear Scarlet*. Simon Raven. 1960. Anthony Blond, Ltd.

The Horla. Guy de Maupassant. Translated by Marjorie Laurie. T. Werner Laurie, Ltd.

Mrs Amworth from *Visible and Invisible*. E. F. Benson. 1923. Hutchinson & Co. (Publishers), Ltd.

The Adventure of the Sussex Vampire from *The Case Book of Sherlock Holmes*. The Trustees of the estate of Sir Arthur Conan Doyle. John Murray, Ltd.

Fresh Guy. E. C. Tubb. Nova publications, Ltd.

The Cloak. Robert Bloch. Nova publications, Ltd.

Viy. Nicolai Gogol. Translated by Constance Garnett. Chatto & Windus, Ltd.

The Man Upstairs. Ray Bradbury. 1956. Rupert Hart-Davis, Ltd.

FOREWORD

On a December day in 1959 I was sitting with a few friends in a *trattoria* in Rome. I was telling one of them, who was a brilliant writer and a recent Goncourt prizewinner, about a striking dream I had had the previous night. R. V. (his initials are the same as mine) is an uncompromising rationalist who always enjoys finding some Freudian significance in dreams.

Myself: 'I was in a theatre. The seats had been pulled up and piled into an untidy pyramid in the middle of the auditorium. The floor was strewn with scraps of metal. I was fighting with a friend. I fell, then got up again. I looked at my hands and noticed that the little finger was missing from the left one. I had cut it clean off without noticing.'

R. V.: 'Castration complex!'

. . . I never learnt what unsuspected developments could follow from interpreting a dream by someone like myself in this way. I think that the *spaghetti alla carbonara* arrived just at that moment.

The same evening I was invited at the last moment to a cocktail party and a man whom I had never seen before was introduced to me. I shall remember him for a long time: the little finger was missing from his left hand. He had lost it in Japan during the war.

Had I had a premonition? Or should I accept R. V.'s explanation and believe it was a coincidence?

Sometimes, a strange, complex, undefined universe projects into the fringe of our lives. Some of us, without knowing why, discern it or sense its existence for a brief moment. Without mentioning the supernatural, this may be merely one unexplored aspect, inconceivable today, of that material domain which is known to us for such a short time. Mankind has defined this domain in three dimensions and every day it breaks the rules which for a brief moment seem to be rigid.

Occultists have attempted to regulate this marginal universe just as scientists have regulated the movements of the stars and codified energy: but in principle the viewpoints of these two groups are essentially opposed to each other.

Poets however have often derived their inspiration from both sources.

Among the poetic manifestations of the occult world the vampire myth is the most fascinating. It seems to have originated in Bohemia and Moravia three centuries ago, based on stories about witches and quarrels among peasants. It certainly did not start with Dom Calmet's famous book on the subject.

The secrets of this strange survival have also been attributed to a group of Christians who are said to have solved the mysteries of Christ's resurrection and who, more than a thousand years later, were driven out of Palestine and emigrated to Central Europe, where they became despotic rulers. This would explain the unwillingness of the peasants to take part in the rite of renewing blood, for they already found sufficient cause for antipathy in hard work and taxes.

The Egyptians also had their vampires and, further back still, so did the Chinese – they were called by different names.

Tracing the history of vampires is a dubious enterprise; let us devote ourselves instead to stories about them.

I do not believe in vampire stories, but I believe in what inspired them.

ROGER VADIM
January, 1960.

AUGUSTIN CALMET

THE VAMPIRES OF HUNGARY AND SURROUNDING COUNTRIES

Translated by Rosemary Dinnage

EVERY AGE, every country, and every district has its own fashions, customs and habits that successively engage the interest of the population, and frequently the fashion of one age is a laughing-stock to the next. In some ages, certain modes of study or devotion have been very widespread. For more than a century it was the fashion throughout Europe to make the pilgrimage to Jerusalem; kings, princes, nobles, priests and monks all flocked there. At other times the pilgrimage to Rome was very popular. Now all that has passed. At certain times whole districts have been overrun by flagellants, and now there are none left save in certain fraternities of penitents that survive in a few places.

In our own country tumblers and dancers were once seen everywhere, performing in the streets and squares and even in the churches. Their counterparts today are the convulsionaries. Posterity will surely wonder why we found them so diverting. At the end of the sixteenth century and the beginning of the seventeenth, witchcraft was a subject of scandal in Lorraine; but now for many years it has been forgotten. When the philosophy of Monsieur Descartes first appeared, what a vogue it had! The foundations of the old philosophy were shaken, and the talk was all of physics, of new systems and discoveries. Now Mr Newton has appeared and created a new sensation. The theories of Mr Law and his bank-notes, the outbreaks in the Rue de Quincampoix: what havoc they caused throughout the country! The whole nation seemed to be seized by a sort of convulsion.

In our times another drama has been enacted for sixty years or more in Hungary, Moravia, Silesia and Poland; it is said that men who died months or years before walk and talk again, haunt men and beasts, overrun the villages, suck the blood of their relatives till they sicken and die, and that there is but one way to rid the people of this dangerous affliction: the bodies must be dug up, impaled on a spike, decapitated, the heart cut out, or the corpse burnt. These spectres are called oupires or vampires, and such tales are told of them, so singular in their details and likely in all their circumstances, that we are almost forced to accept the current beliefs that these creatures do indeed rise from their graves.

These ghosts or vampires of Hungary are men who died some time past and rise from their graves to haunt the living, suck their blood, clamour at their doors or in their houses, and in the end often drive them to death.

Many explanations have been put forward for these apparitions. It has been said that they are no more than a delusion, arising from the ignorance and prejudice of the population in these countries.

Others maintain that these are really living people who have been buried alive and escaped from their tombs.

Others maintain that they are indeed dead, but that God has permitted them or commanded them to return to the world and re-enter their bodies again for a time; for when they are taken from the ground, their bodies are found intact, their blood bright red and liquid, and their limbs still flexible.

Others argue that it is the Devil who causes the apparitions and works evil to men and beasts through them.

I have heard from the late Monsieur de Vassimont, Chief Financial Adviser in Bar, that when he was sent to Moravia by the late Duke Leopold of Lorraine to mind the affairs of his brother, Monseigneur Prince Charles, Bishop of Olmutz and Osnaburgh, he was told that it was common knowledge in these parts that a man, dead for some time past, might suddenly make an appearance at a meal and sit down among his friends without a word, nodding his head perhaps at one of the company, who would then invariably sicken and die a few days later. This occurrence was confirmed by several persons, among them a priest who had seen it happen more than once.

The bishops and priests of the country consulted Rome about these singular occurrences, but they received no reply, for it was held that they were delusions or popular superstitions. Later they were advised to exhume the bodies of the men who had haunted them and to burn them, or destroy them in some other manner. Thus they were delivered from the importunities of the apparitions, which are now much less common in these parts; so said the priest.

A little book has been written about these apparitions entitled *Magia Posthuma*, by Charles Ferdinand de Schertz, printed at Olmutz in 1706 and dedicated to Prince Charles of Lorraine, Bishop of Olmutz and Osnaburgh. The author relates that in a certain village a woman was buried in the cemetery in the normal manner, after receiving the sacraments at her death. Four days later, the villagers heard a great uproar and clamouring, and many of them saw an apparition which first took the form of a dog and then of a man: striking them, catching them by the throat, squeezing them in the stomach till they nearly suffocated; they were bruised all over and reduced to a pitiable condition, pale, thin and exhausted. The apparition attacked animals as well, and cows were discovered bruised and half-dead; sometimes they would be tied together by the tail. The horses would be found lying as though they were weak with exhaustion, heated, sweating, and gasping, covered with lather as though they had run a hard race. These calamities lasted for several months.

The aforesaid author is expert in the law, and he examines the facts of the case scrupulously. He reports many examples of similar apparitions and the disasters that followed their appearance: such as the case of the shepherd in the village of Blow near the town of Kadam in Bohemia, who appeared more than once and named several persons, who straightaway died within the week. The peasants disinterred his body and transfixed it to the ground by a stake. But he laughed at his tormentors from this position, and thanked them for giving him a stick with which to beat the dogs. He got up again that same night and terrified many persons by his appearance, and suffocated some of them, even more than the previous time. The gravedigger took him then and wheeled him out of the village on a cart to be burnt. The corpse shrieked like a madman, and waved its arms and legs as though it were still alive; and when it was transfixed again by stakes it screamed very loud and its blood was bright red and very profuse. At last it was burnt, and the villagers were no more molested by apparitions.

The same procedure has been followed in other places where the folk were troubled by apparitions, and when the bodies were taken from the earth they were found to be flushed, with all the limbs soft and pliable, and free from worms and putrefaction, though not without a very rotten stench. The author of this book cites many other writers who confirm all that he says about these apparitions, which still appear, he says, in the mountains of Silesia and Moravia. They are seen both by day and night, and sometimes their former possessions are seen to move from one place to another without any visible agency. The only remedy against these hauntings is to cut off the head and burn the corpse of the vampire.

In all cases, a regular form of justice is followed; witnesses are heard, the bodies are examined for the betraying marks of vampirism, such as the looseness of the joints, liquefaction of the blood, and incorruption of the flesh. When these signs are found, the bodies are taken away to be burnt. Sometimes it comes about that the spectres appear again only three or four days after the burning. At times certain corpses that are suspect are kept for six or seven weeks before burial. If they do not rot, and their limbs remain soft and flexible as in a living body, they are burnt. It is attested beyond doubt that the clothing on these bodies is seen to move without any living agency; and recently, our author relates, an apparition was seen at Olmutz that threw stones and caused great distress to the inhabitants.

Some fifteen years ago a soldier, billeted in a peasant's house on the Hungarian frontier, was sitting down to a meal with his hosts when a stranger joined them at the table. The master of the house and his family appeared strangely alarmed. The soldier was puzzled, not realizing who the man was. But by morning the master of the house was dead, and the soldier learnt the identity of the visitor. He was told that he was the father of his host, dead and buried ten years ago, who had appeared among them and caused his son's death.

The soldier informed his regiment of this happening, and they informed the higher officers, who commissioned the

Comte de Cabreras, captain of the Alandetti Infantry, to inquire into it further. He travelled to the village in the company of other officers, a surgeon and a recorder; they heard the depositions of all the members of the household, who agreed unanimously that the apparition was the host's father and that the soldier's account was true in every respect. This was also confirmed by all the villagers.

They dug up the body of this creature, and it was found as whole as if he had died yesterday, the blood as fresh as if he were still alive. The Comte de Cabreras had the head cut off and the body was reburied. He was given information about other apparitions, among them a man who had been dead for more than thirty years, who reappeared in his house three times just as the meal was served; the first time he sucked blood from his own brother's throat, the second time from one of his sons, and the third time from a servant, and all three fell dead on the instant.

After taking this deposition the Comte ordered the man to be exhumed; when he was found in the same condition as the other one, with the blood still fresh, the Comte ordered that an iron bar be driven through his head, and the body was then reburied. Yet a third one was burnt; he had been dead for more than sixteen years, and had killed two of his sons by sucking their blood. The report on these extraordinary occurrences was passed to the Emperor, who decreed that a party of officers, lawyers, physicians, surgeons and scholars should make an inquiry into their causes on the spot.

In the village of Kisilova, three leagues from Gradisch, an old man of 62 died in September; three days after the funeral he appeared before his son in the night and asked for food. His son gave him some and he disappeared. The next day the son told his neighbours what had happened. That night the old man did not appear; but the following night he appeared and demanded food; no one knows whether his son gave it to him or not, but in the morning the son was found dead in his bed, and on that same day five or six others in the village suddenly fell ill, and they died one after the other a few days later. The governor of the district forwarded a report to the Tribunal in Belgrade, and they sent two officials and an executioner to deal with the matter. The governor who first reported it travelled from Gradisch to see with his own eyes what had happened. All the bodies that had been buried for the last six weeks were disinterred; when they reached the body of the old man, they found his eyes were open and of a red colour, and the respiration was normal, though he was quite still and dead. From this they concluded that he was an undoubted vampire. The hangman drove a stake through his heart. A great fire was made, and the corpse was reduced to ashes. It is said that 'none of the marks of vampirism was found on the body of the son, nor on any of the others.'

About five years ago in Medreïga a certain Haïdouk, or Hungarian soldier, called Arnold Paul, was killed when a cartload of hay fell on top of him. Thirty days after his death four persons died suddenly in the manner that was traditionally ascribed to vampirism. It was recalled that this same Arnold Paul had often related how he had been tormented by a Turkish vampire, near Cassova on the frontiers of Turkish Serbia; for he too believed that those who had been passive vampires in life became active ones after death, that is to say those who had been sucked would suck in their turn; but that he had cured himself by eating earth from the vampire's grave and rubbing himself with its blood, yet this precaution had not prevented him from becoming one after death, for when he was exhumed forty days after his burial he showed all the marks of an arch-vampire. His body was flushed; his hair, nails and beard had grown, and his veins were full of liquid blood that had splashed all over his winding-sheet. The *Hadnagy* or governor of the district, who was well versed in the ways of vampires, was present at the exhumation, and he ordered that a sharp stake be driven right through the body as was customary, whereupon the corpse emitted a fearful shriek as though it were still living. Next the head was cut off and the body burnt. After this, the same procedure was followed with the four other persons who had died at the vampire's hands, lest they should cause more deaths. All this dispatch was to no purpose, for towards the end of last year, five years after the original occurrences, these terrible events recommenced, and several inhabitants of the same village perished miserably. Within the space of three months seventeen persons of both sexes and all ages died of vampirism, some without any illness, others after two or three days of illness. Among others, a certain Stanoska, daughter of the Haïdouk Jotuitzo, is reported to have gone to bed in good health and to have awakened trembling and shrieking in the middle of the night, saying that the son of Millo, who had died nine weeks before, had nearly strangled her in her sleep. She sickened from this moment and died three days later. This woman's accusation was the first sign that Millo's son was a vampire; he was exhumed, and found to be one indeed. The governors of the district, and the doctors and surgeons, demanded how it was that vampirism had reappeared after all the precautions they had taken several years before.

After careful inquiries they discovered that the deceased Arnold Paul had not only killed these four persons but also several animals, which the new vampires had eaten, among them Millo's son. Therefore they undertook to exhume all the recent dead. Seventeen of them were found with the signs of vampirism; so they were transfixed with the stake, decapitated, burnt and the ashes thrown into the river.

All these inquiries and executions were legally and impartially carried out and witnessed by several of the officers garrisoned in the district, by the regimental surgeons, and many respected local inhabitants. A copy of the proceedings was sent to the Imperial Council of War in Vienna at the end of last January, and they instituted a military commission to investigate the true facts of the case.

In the public records for the years 1693 and 1694 there is a description of vampires or apparitions that were seen in Poland and Russia. They appear between midday and midnight to suck the blood of men and live animals in such abundance that frequently it runs out of their mouth, nose and ears; sometimes they are floating in blood inside their coffins. They are said to have a sort of hunger that makes them eat their winding-sheets. These ghosts or vampires or disguised demons issue from their graves at night to embrace their friends or relatives and suck their blood till they weaken and die. The persecution never stops at one member of the family unless the course of events is interrupted by piercing the heart and cutting off the head of the vampire, whose body is found to be soft, pliable, plump and flushed in its coffin, even though dead for a long time. A great quantity of blood issues from the body, which some people mix with flour to make bread; when this has been eaten they are generally free from the persecution of the spirit, who never reappears.

The following is a letter written to an acquaintance of mine regarding the apparitions in Hungary:

'In response to the questions of Monsieur l'Abbé Dom Calmet regarding vampires, the author has the honour to assure him that there is nothing more true and indisputable than the accounts that he has doubtless read in the published gazettes of every European country; but as well as these public records Monsieur l'Abbé must consider the indisputable evidence of the deputation of Belgrade, ordered by his late Imperial Majesty Charles VI, of glorious memory, and directed by his late Serene Highness, Duke Charles Alexander of Wurtemburg, then vice-regent or governor of the kingdom of Serbia; but I cannot at the present moment cite the year, the month, or the date without my papers, which are not with me at the moment.

'The Prince sent a deputation from Belgrade consisting of both civil and military officials, with the Public Prosecutor of the kingdom, to a village where a notorious vampire, dead many years since, was ravaging his kinsmen; for it is notable that the bloodsuckers only seek to destroy their own families. This deputation was composed of respected persons, both civil and military, well known for their experience and respectability; they were put on oath, and accompanied by a lieutenant of the Grenadiers of Prince Alexander of Wurtemburg's regiment and twenty-four of his men.

'Many reputable citizens accompanied the deputation, even the Duke himself, who happened to be in Belgrade at the time, in order to have visible proof of the strange occurrences.

'When they reached the village they discovered that the vampire had already dispatched three of his nieces and nephews and one of his own brothers within the past fortnight. He had just commenced on his fifth victim, his young and beautiful niece, and had sucked blood twice when the tragedy was arrested in the following manner.

'At dusk some members of the deputation went to the grave in the presence of a crowd of people. My informant was unable to tell me precisely at what time the previous victims were sucked nor the details. The pangs are so violent that after his blood has been sucked the victim remains in a pitiful state of weakness and lassitude. The vampire had been buried three years ago; now they saw a light over his tomb like a flickering lamp.

'The grave was opened and a man was revealed, as whole and apparently as healthy as anyone present; his hair, and the hair of his body, his nails, teeth and eyes (which were half-open) were all firmly attached as in life, and his heart was beating.

'He was taken from his coffin; the body was not truly flexible, but no particle of bone or flesh was missing; his heart was then pierced through with a species of sharp iron bar: a whitish fluid issued, mixed with blood, but the blood predominating, and the whole without any bad odour; next the head was cut off with a sort of axe such as is used in England for executions: the same fluid and blood issued as before, but more abundantly.

'The body was put into the ground, covered with quicklime to consume it as rapidly as possible, and from this time onwards the girl who had been sucked twice began to recover. A bluish patch forms on the spot where these people have been sucked; but the spot is not precise, it shows in different places at different times.'

On 17th October, 1746, a kinsman of the same officer wrote to me that his brother, who had spent twenty years in Hungary and was well acquainted with the local beliefs about ghosts, acknowledged that these people were exceptionally credulous and superstitious and ascribed all their misfortunes to witchcraft; that the moment they suspected that one of the dead was bewitching them they submitted the matter to the magistrate, and if a few witnesses could be found to testify, he would open the grave; the corpse would be decapitated with a spade and if the least drop of blood were found, they would conclude that it must have been sucked from the sick person. But my correspondent does not seem to be swayed by these local superstitions.

These examples and arguments in favour of vampirism may be said to show that the apparitions in Hungary, Moravia, Poland, etc, are not really dead at all, that the fresh scarlet blood, the flexibility of their limbs, their shrieks when pierced through the heart or decapitated, prove that they were in truth entombed alive, but without movement or respiration. This indeed might be possible; but how could they issue from their graves and return to them without disturbing the earth; and how appear in their own clothes, and find food? Why return to their graves? Why not stay among the living? Why harass and torment those who should be dearest to them and have never caused them any harm? If all this is a delusion of the victims, how is it that the vampires are found uncorrupted in their graves, still soft and full of blood, that their feet are muddy soon after they have appeared in the village, and that nothing of the sort is found on the other corpses buried at the same time in the same cemetery? Why do the visitations cease after the bodies have been burnt or impaled on a stake? Might this too be due simply to superstition, if the peasants are reassured by the executions? How is it that these events are so frequent in this part of the world, and that the superstitions do not abate but increase with the familiarity of the experience?

It is widely held in Germany that certain persons after death chew in their graves and demolish anything that is near them, and that they can even be heard munching like pigs with a muffled grunting and snorting.

A German author called Michel Raufft has written a book entitled *De Masticatione Mortuorum in Tumulis* (that dead men chew in their coffins). He assumes without question that certain corpses have devoured their winding-sheets and anything else close to their mouths, even their own flesh. He relates that in certain parts of Germany a lump of earth is placed under the corpse's chin in the coffin, to prevent him from biting, and in other parts of the country a small piece of silver and a stone are placed in the mouth, which is then tightly gagged with a handkerchief.

He might also have related the story of Henry, Comte de Salm, who was accidentally buried alive; during the night shrieks were heard coming from the church of the Abbey of Haute-Seille where he was buried, and the next day when his tomb was opened he was found lying face downwards, although he had been placed in the coffin on his back. Some years ago, at Bar-le-Duc, after a man had been buried in the cemetery, sounds were heard coming from his grave; he was exhumed the next day and was discovered to have eaten the flesh of his own arms; this was attested by several witnesses. He had passed into a stupor after drinking *eau-de-vie* and was buried alive. Raufft mentions a woman in Bohemia who ate half her winding-sheet in the year 1345. In the time of Luther a man and a woman buried at the same time gnawed out each other's vitals. In Moravia a dead man devoured the winding-sheet of the woman buried next to him.

The most remarkable case he describes is a certain Pierre Plogojowits in a Hungarian village called Kissolova; ten weeks after his burial this man appeared to some of the villagers at night and shook them by the throat so violently that they died within twenty-four hours; nine persons, young and old, died within the space of eight days; the widow of the aforesaid Plogojowits declared that her husband had appeared and demanded his shoes, which frightened her so much that she left the village and settled elsewhere.

The villagers therefore determined to exhume the body of Plogojowits and burn it, to free themselves from his malice. They applied to the local representative of the Emperor and to the Curé of the district for permission to exhume the body; both were reluctant to allow it. But the peasants declared that they knew this to be an undoubted vampire (as they call the apparition), and they would be obliged to abandon the village if permission to destroy the corpse was refused.

The official who related these events, realizing that he could not force the peasants to stay by threats or enticements, travelled to Kissolova with the Curé; when the body was exposed, it was found to have no bad smell at all and to be intact as a living body, except for the tip of the nose, which appeared to be somewhat withered and dried; the hair and beard were abundant, and where his fingernails had dropped off, new ones had grown; beneath his old skin, which was pale and withered, there appeared to be a new one, healthy and flesh-coloured, also his feet and hands were whole as in a living man. They remarked a spot of fresh blood on his mouth, which induced the people to believe that he had sucked his victims to death.

The Emperor's official and the Curé examined all these matters carefully; in the meantime the peasants' anger grew, and their conviction that they had found the true cause of their fellows' death; so they fetched a sharp stake and plunged it in his breast, and a quantity of fresh scarlet blood issued, and from the nose and mouth as well; more issued from that part of his body which decency forbids me to name. Finally the peasants put the body on a bonfire and reduced it to ashes.

Many explanations for these occurrences have been advanced. Firstly, some people have declared them to be miracles. Secondly, others have considered them to be no more than the results of a restless imagination or a powerful superstition. Thirdly, others offer a simple and natural explanation; these persons were still alive. Fourthly, others have claimed that this was the work of the Devil; some of these people distinguish harmless devils, authors of practical jokes, from the race of malicious and evil demons, who are the cause of sin and crime and all our woes. Fifthly, others maintain that it is not the dead who eat their own flesh or their winding-sheets, but snakes, rats, moles, wolves, or other voracious beasts, or even what the pagans called *Striges*, which are birds that devour animals and men and suck their blood. Some authors have argued that these cases mostly concern women, and occur chiefly in times of pestilence. But there are examples of apparitions of both sexes, more men than women; though indeed those who died of plague, poison, cholera, or drunkenness are more likely to appear and haunt people, doubtless because sometimes they are buried still alive, for fear that they will spread infection if they are left unburied.

It is also maintained that these vampires are only reported in certain countries, such as Hungary, Moravia and Silesia, where pestilence is common and the people suffer from hunger and bad weather, ignorance and superstition. As for the belief that the dead chew like pigs in their grave, this is manifestly nonsensical and can only be a superstition.

As I have already said, it is indeed hard to believe that

the vampires could move in and out of their graves without disturbing the earth; this has never been accounted for, and never can be. To say that the Devil dematerializes the vampires' bodies is irrational and unwarranted.

The redness and fluidity of the vampires' blood and the pliability of their limbs are nothing extraordinary, nor are the growth of their nails and hair and the failure of their flesh to decay. It is common to see bodies that have not decayed at all and have retained a flushed complexion after death. This may occur after a very sudden death without illness, or after certain illnesses, well known to physicians, which leave the blood liquid and the limbs pliant.

Regarding the growth of the hair and the nails in bodies that have not decayed, this is a natural occurrence. The humours of the body still circulate gradually and cause them to grow, just as bulbs can commonly be seen to continue sprouting without any moisture or nourishment from the earth. The same is true of flowers, and indeed of the vegetative system of both animals and plants.

The belief of the ancient Greeks in the return of departed spirits was no more rational than the belief in ghosts and vampires. Ignorance, prejudice and fear nourished this foolish fantasy and nourish it still.

The reports of the dead chewing in their graves are so pitifully puerile that they do not deserve serious consideration.

It is widely known that all too often bodies are buried while there is still some life in them. There are examples, too many of them, in ancient times and modern. The discourse of Monsieur Winflou and the additional remarks by Monsieur Bruhier prove beyond doubt that there are no signs of death apart from the commencement of putrefaction and odour. There are numberless cases of persons believed dead who have revived, even after burial. In many illnesses the patient may lie for long unconscious, without speaking, moving, or apparently breathing; sometimes a drowned man has been taken for dead, and then revived by bleeding and careful nursing.

This is common knowledge, and it suffices to explain how vampires have been dragged from the grave and made to speak, shout, scream and bleed: they were still alive. They were killed by decapitation, perforation, or burning, and this has been a great wrong; for the allegation that they returned to haunt and destroy the living has never been sufficiently proved to authorize such inhumanity, or to permit innocent beings to be dishonoured and ignominiously killed as a result of wild and unproved accusations. For the stories told of these apparitions, and all the distress caused by these supposed vampires, are totally without solid proof. I am not surprised that the Sorbonne has condemned the bloody and violent retribution wrought on these corpses; but it is astonishing that the magistrates and secular bodies have not employed their authority and legal force to put an end to it.

This is a mysterious and difficult matter, and I leave bolder and more proficient minds to resolve it.

LAWRENCE DURRELL

CARNIVAL

from Balthazar

THE CARNIVAL in Alexandria is a purely social affair – having no calendar relationship to the other religious festivals of the city. I suppose it must have been instituted by the three or four great Catholic families of the place – perhaps vicariously they enjoyed through it a sense of identity with the other side of the Mediterranean, with Venice and Athens. Nevertheless, there is today no rich family which does not keep a cupboard full of velvet dominoes against the three days of folly – be it Copt, Moslem or Jewish. After New Year's Eve it is perhaps the greatest Christian celebration of the year – for the ruling spirit of the three days and nights is – utter anonymity; the anonymity conferred by the grim black velvet domino which shrouds identity and sex, prevents one distinguishing between man and woman, wife and lover, friend and enemy.

The maddest aberrations of the city now come boldly forward under the protection of the invisible lords of Misrule who preside at this season. No sooner has darkness fallen than the maskers begin to appear in the streets – first in ones and twos and then in small companies, often with musical instruments or drums, laughing and singing their way to some great house or to some nightclub where already the frosty air is bathed in the nigger warmth of jazz – the cloying grunting intercourse of saxophones and drums. Everywhere they spring up in the pale moonlight, cowled like monks. The disguise gives them all a gloomy fanatical uniformity of outline which startles the white-robed Egyptians and fills them with alarm – the thrill of a fear which spices the wild laughter pouring out of the houses, carried by the light offshore winds towards the cafés on the sea-front; a gaiety which by its very shrillness seems to tremble always upon the edge of madness.

Slowly the bluish spring moon climbs the houses, sliding up the minarets into the clicking palm-trees, and with it the city seems to uncurl like some hibernating animal dug out of its winter earth, to stretch and begin to drink in the music of the three-day festival.

The jazz pouring up from the cellars displaces the tranquil winter air in the parks and thoroughfares, mingling as it reaches the sealine with the drumming perhaps of a liner's screws in the deepwater reaches of the estuary. Or you may hear and see for a brief moment the rip and slither of fireworks against a sky which for a moment curls up at the edges and blushes, like a sheet of burning carbon paper: wild laughter which mixes with the hoarse mooing of an old ship outside the harbour bar – like a cow locked outside a gate.

'The lover fears the carnival,' says the proverb. And with the emergence of these black-robed creatures of the night everywhere, all is subtly altered. The whole temperature of life in the city alters, grows warm with the subtle intimations of spring. *Carni vale* – the flesh's farewell to the year, unwinding its mummy wrappings of sex, identity and name, and stepping forward naked into futurity of the dream.

All the great houses have thrown open their doors upon fabulous interiors warm with a firelight which bristles upon china and marble, brass and copper, and upon the black-leaded faces of the servants as they go about their duties. And down every street now, glittering in the moonlit gloaming, lounge the great limousines of the brokers and gamblers, like liners in dock, the patient and impressive symbols of a wealth which is powerless to bring true leisure or peace of mind for it demands everything of the human soul. They lie webbed in a winter light, expressing only the silence and power of all machinery which waits for the fall of man, looking on at the maskers as they cross and recross the lighted windows of the great houses, clutching each other like black bears, dancing to the throb of nigger music, the white man's solace.

Snatches of music and laughter must rise to Clea's window where she sits with a board on her knees, patiently drawing while her little cat sleeps in its basket at her feet. Or perhaps in some sudden lull the chords of a guitar may be plucked to stay and wallow in the darkness of the open street until they are joined by a voice raised in remote song, as if from the bottom of a well. Or screams, cries for help.

But what stamps the carnival with its spirit of pure mischief is the velvet domino – conferring upon its wearers the disguise which each man in his secret heart desires above all. To become anonymous in an anonymous crowd, revealing neither sex nor relationship nor even facial expression – for the mask of this demented friar's habit leaves only two eyes, glowing like the eyes of a Moslem woman or a bear. Nothing else to distinguish one by; the thick folds of the blackness conceal even the contours of the body. Everyone becomes hipless, breastless, faceless. And concealed beneath the carnival habit (like a criminal desire in the heart, a temptation impossible to resist, an impulse which seems preordained) lie the germs of something: of a freedom which man has seldom dared to imagine for himself. One feels free in this disguise to do whatever one likes without prohibition. All the best murders in the city, all the most tragic cases of mistaken identity, are the fruit of the yearly carnival; while most love affairs begin or end during these three days and nights during which we are delivered from the thrall of personality, from the bondage of ourselves. Once inside that velvet cape and hood, and wife loses husband, husband wife, lover the beloved. The air becomes crisp with the saltpetre of feuds and follies, the fury of battles, of agonizing night-long searches, of despairs. You cannot tell whether you are dancing with a man or a woman. The dark tides of Eros, which demand full secrecy if they are to overflow the human soul, burst out during carnival like something long dammed up and raise the forms of strange primeval creatures – the perversions which are, I suppose, the psyche's aliment – in forms which you would think belonged to the Brocken or to Ebis. Now hidden satyr and maenad can rediscover each other and unite. Yes, who can help but love carnival when in it all debts are paid, all crimes expiated or committed, all illicit desires sated – without guilt or premeditation, without the penalties which conscience or society exact?

But I am wrong about one thing – for there is one distinguishing mark by which your friend or enemy may still identify you: hands. Your lover's hands, if you have ever noticed them at all, will lead you to her in the thickest press of maskers. Or by arrangement she may wear, as Justine does, a familiar ring – the ivory intaglio taken from the tomb of a dead Byzanteni youth – worn upon the forefinger of the right hand. But this is all, and it is only just enough. (Pray that you are not as unlucky as Amaril who found the perfect woman during carnival but could not persuade her to raise her hood and stand identified. They talked all night, lying in the grass by the fountain, making love together with their velvet faces touching, their eyes caressing each other. For a whole year now, he has gone about the city trying to find a pair of human hands, like a madman. But hands are so alike! She swore, this woman of his, that she would come back next year to the same place, wearing the same ring with its small yellow stone. And so tonight he will wait trembling for a pair of hands by the lily pond – hands which will perhaps never appear again in his life. Perhaps she was after all an *afreet* or a vampire – who knows? Yet years later, in another book, in another context, he will happen upon her again, almost by accident, but not here, not in these pages too tangled already by the record of ill-starred loves. . . .)

So then you walk the dark streets, serene as a murderer unidentified, all your traces covered by the black cowl, feeling the fresh wintry airs of the city upon your eyelids. The Egyptians you pass look askance at you, not knowing whether to smile or be afraid at your appearance. They hover in an indeterminate state of mind when carnival comes on – wondering how it should be taken. Passing, you give them a burning stare from the depths of your cowl, glad to see them flinch and avert their faces. Other dominoes like yourself emerge from every corner, some in groups laughing and singing as they walk towards some great house or to neighbouring night-clubs.

Walking like this towards the Cervonis', across the network of streets by the Greek Patriarchate you are reminded of other carnivals, perhaps even in other cities, distinguished by the same wildness and gaiety which is the gift of lost identities. Strange adventures which befell you once. At one corner in the Rue Bartout last year the sound of running feet and cries. A man presents a dagger to your throat, crying like a wounded animal, 'Helen, if you try and run away tonight I swear I'll kill . . .' but the words die as you raise your mask and show your face, and he stammers an apology and he turns away only to burst into sobs and throw himself against an iron railing. Helen has already disappeared, and he will search for her the whole night through!

At a gate into a yard, weirdly lit by the feeble street-lamps, two figures in black are grappling each other, fighting with a tremendous silent fury. They fall, rolling over and over from darkness into light and then back into darkness. Without a word spoken. At the Étoile there is a man hanging from a beam with his neck broken; but when you get close enough you see that it is only a black domino hanging from a nail. How strange that in order to free oneself from guilt by a disguise one should choose the very symbol of the Inquisitor, the cape and hood of the Spanish Inquisition.

But they are not all in domino – for many people are superstitious about the dress and, besides, it can be hot to wear in a crowded room. So you will see many a harlequin and shepherdess, many an Antony and Cleopatra as you walk the streets of the city, many an Alexander. And as you turn into the great iron gates of the Cervonis' house to present your card and climb into the warmth and light and drunkenness within, you will see outlined upon the darkness the feared and beloved shapes and outlines of friends and familiars now distorted into the semblance of clowns and zanies, or clothed in the nothingness of black capes and hoods, infernally joined in a rare and disoriented gaiety.

As if under pressure the laughter squirts up to the ceiling or else, like feathers from a torn quilt, drifts about in clumps in that fevered air. The two string bands, muted by the weight of human voices, labour on in the short staggered rhythms of a maniac jazz – like the steady beating of an airpump. Here on the ballroom floor a million squeakers and trumpets squash and distort the sound while already the dense weight of the coloured paper streamers, hanging upon the shoulders of the dancers, sways like tropical seaweed upon rock-surfaces and trails in ankle-high drifts about the polished floors.

On the night in question, the first night of carnival, there was a dinner-party at the great house. On the long hall sofas the dominoes waited for their tenants while the candlelight still smouldered upon the faces of a Justine and Nessim now framed among the portaits which lined the ugly but imposing dining-room. Faces painted in oils matched by human faces lined by preoccupations and maladies of the soul – all gathered together, made one in the classical brilliance of candlelight. After dinner Justine and Nessim were to go together to the Cervoni ball according to the yearly custom. According to custom too, Narouz at the last moment had excused himself. He would arrive upon the stroke of ten, just in time to claim a domino before the whole party set off, laughing and chattering, for the ball.

As always, he himself had preferred to ride into the city on his horse and to stable it with his friend the carpenter, but as a concession to the event he had struggled into an ancient suit of blue serge and had knotted a tie at his collar. Undress did not matter, since he too would later be wearing a domino. He walked lightly, swiftly across the ill-lit Arab quarter, drinking in the familiar sights and sounds, yet eager for the first sight of the maskers as he reached the end of Rue Rouad and found himself on the confines of the modern town.

At one corner stood a group of shrill-chattering women in domino bent upon mischief. From their language and accent he could detect at once that they were society women, Greeks. These black harpies caught hold of every passer-by to shout jests at him and to pluck at his hood if he were masked. Narouz too had to run the gauntlet: one caught hold of his hand and pretended to tell his fortune; another whispered a proposition in Arabic, setting her hand upon his thigh; the third cackled like a hen and shouted 'Your wife has a lover' and other unkindnesses. He could not tell if they recognized him or not.

Narouz flinched, shook himself and burst smiling through their number fending them off good-naturedly and roaring with laughter at the sally about his wife. 'Not tonight, my doves' he cried hoarsely in Arabic, thinking suddenly of Clea; and as they showed some disposition to capture him for the evening, he began to run. They chased him a little way, shouting and laughing incoherently down the long dark street, but he easily outdistanced them, and so turned the corner to the great house, still smiling but a little out of breath, and flattered by these attentions which seemed to set the key for the evening's enjoyment. In the silent hall his eye caught the black dominoes and he put one on before edging open the door of the drawing-room behind which he could hear their voices. It disguised his shabby suit. The cape lay back upon his shoulders.

They were all there by the fire, waiting for him, and he took their cries of welcome greedily and seriously, making his round to kiss Justine on the cheek and to shake hands with the rest in an agony of awkward silence. He put on an artificially sincere expression, looking with distaste into the myopic eyes of Pierre Balbz (he hated him for the goatee and spats) and those of Toto de Brunel (an old lady's lap-dog); but he liked the overblown rose, Athena Trasha, for she used the same scent as his mother; and he was sorry for Drusilla Banubula because she was so clever that she hardly seemed to be a woman at all. With Pursewarden he shared a smile of easy complicity. 'Well,' he said, expelling his breath at last in relief. His brother handed him a whisky with mild tenderness, which he drank slowly but all in one draught, like a peasant.

'We were waiting for you, Narouz.'

'The Hosnani exile,' glittered Pierro Balbz ingatiatingly.

'The farmer,' cried little Toto.

The conversation which had been interrupted by his sudden appearance closed smoothly over his head once more and he sat down by the fire until they should be ready to leave for the Cervoni house, folding his strong hands one upon the other in a gesture of finality, as if to lock up once and for all his powers. The skin at Nessim's temples appeared to be stretched, he noticed, an old sign of anger or strain. The fullness of Justine's dark beauty in her dress (the colour of hare's blood) glowed among the ikons, seeming to enjoy the semi-darkness of the candlelight – to feed upon it and give back the glitter of her barbaric jewellery. Narouz felt full of a marvellous sense of detachment, of unconcern; what these small portents of trouble or stress meant, he did not know. It was only Clea who flawed his self-sufficiency, who darkened the edges of his thought. Each year he hoped that when he arrived at his brother's house he would find she had been included in the party. Yet each year she was not, and in consequence he was forced to drift about all night in the darkness, searching for her as aimlessly as a ghost, not even really hoping to encounter her: and yet living upon the attenuated wraith of this fond hope as a soldier upon an iron ration.

They had been talking that night of Amaril and his unhappy passion for a pair of anonymous hands and a carnival voice, and Pursewarden was telling one of his famous stories in that crisp uninflected French of his which was just a shade too perfect.

'When I was twenty, I went to Venice for the first time at the invitation of an Italian poet with whom I had been corresponding, Carlo Negroponte. For a middle-class English youth this was a great experience, to live virtually by candlelight in this huge tumbledown palazzo on the Grand Canal with a fleet of gondolas at my disposal–not to mention a huge wardrobe of cloaks lined with silk. Negroponte was generous and spared no effort to entertain a fellow-poet in the best style. He was then about fifty, frail and rather beautiful, like a rare kind of mosquito. He was a prince and a diabolist, and his poetry happily married the influence of Byron and Baudelaire. He went in for cloaks and shoes with buckles and silver walking-sticks and encouraged me to do the same. I felt I was living in a Gothic novel. Never have I written worse poetry.

'That year we went to the carnival together and got separated though we each wore something to distinguish each other by; you know of course that carnival is the one time of the year when vampires walk freely abroad, and those who are wise carry a pig of garlic in their pockets to drive them off – if by chance one were to be encountered. Next morning I went into my host's room and found him lying pale as death in bed, dressed in the white nightshirt with lace cuffs, with a doctor taking his pulse. When the doctor had gone he said: 'I have met the perfect woman, masked; I went home with her and she proved to be a vampire.' Then drawing up his nightshirt he showed me with exhausted pride that his body was covered with great bites, like the marks of a weasel's teeth. He was utterly exhausted but at the same time excited – and frightening to relate, very much in love. 'Until you have experienced it,' he said, 'you have no idea what it is like. To have one's blood sucked in darkness by someone one adores.' His voice broke. 'De Sade could not begin to describe it. I did not see her face, but I had the impression she was fair, of a northern fairness; we met in the dark and separated in the dark. I have only the impression of white teeth, and a voice – never have I heard any woman say the things she says. She is the very lover for whom I have been waiting all these years. I am meeting her again tonight by the marble griffin at the Footpads' Bridge. O my friend, be happy for me. The real world has become more and more meaningless to me. Now at last, with this vampire's love, I feel I can live again, feel again, write again!' He spent all that day at his papers, and at nightfall set off, cloaked, in his gondola. It was not my business to say anything. The next day once more I found him, pale and deathly tired. He had a high fever, and again these terrible bites. But he could not speak of his experience without weeping – tears of love and exhaustion. And it was now that he had begun his great poem which begins – you all know it —

> Lips not on lips, but on each other's wounds
> Must suck the envenomed bodies of the loved
> And through the tideless blood draw nourishment
> To feed the love that feeds upon their deaths. . . .

'The following week I left for Ravenna where I had some studies to make for a book I was writing and where I stayed two months. I heard nothing from my host, but I got a letter from his sister to say that he was ill with a wasting disease which the doctors could not diagnose and that the family was much worried because he insisted on going out at night in his gondola on journeys of which he would not speak but from which he returned utterly exhausted. I did not know what to reply to this.

'From Ravenna, I went down to Greece and it was not until the following autumn that I returned. I had sent a card to Negroponte saying I hoped to stay with him, but had no reply. As I came down the Grand Canal a funeral was setting off in choppy water, by twilight, with the terrible plumes and emblems of death. I saw that they were coming from the Negroponte Palazzo. I landed and ran to the gates as the last gondola in the procession was filling up with mourners and priests. I recognized the doctor and joined him in the boat, and as we rowed stiffly across the canal, dashed with spray and blinking at the stabs of lightning, he told me what he knew. Negroponte had died the day before. When they came to lay out the body, they found the bites: perhaps of some tropical insect? The doctor was vague. "The only such bites I have seen," he said, "were during the plague of Naples when the rats had been at the bodies. They were so bad we had to dust him down with talcum powder before we could let his sister see the body." '

Pursewarden took a long sip from his glass and went on wickedly. 'The story does not end there; for I should tell you how I tried to avenge him, and went myself at night to the Bridge of the Footpads – where according to the gondolier this woman always waited in the shadow. . . . But it is getting late, and anyway, I haven't made up the rest of the story as yet.'

There was a good deal of laughter and Athena gave a well-bred shudder, drawing her shawl across her shoulders. Narouz had been listening open-mouthed, with reeling senses, to this recital: he was spellbound. 'But,' he stammered, 'is all this true?' Fresh laughter greeted his question.

'Of course it's true,' said Pursewarden severely, and added: 'I have never been in Venice in my life.'

SHERIDAN LE FANU

CARMILLA

I. AN EARLY FRIGHT

IN STYRIA, we, though by no means magnificent people, inhabit a castle, or schloss. A small income, in that part of the world, goes a great way. Eight or nine hundred a year does wonders. Scantily enough ours would have answered among wealthy people at home. My father is English, and I bear an English name, although I never saw England. But here, in this lonely and primitive place, where everything is so marvellously cheap, I really don't see how ever so much more money would at all materially add to our comforts, or even luxuries.

My father was in the Austrian service, and retired upon a pension and his patrimony, and purchased this feudal residence, and the small estate on which it stands, a bargain.

Nothing can be more picturesque or solitary. It stands on a slight eminence in a forest. The road, very old and narrow, passes in front of its drawbridge, never raised in my time, and its moat, stocked with perch, and sailed over by many swans, and floating on its surface white fleets of water-lilies.

Over all this the schloss shows its many-windowed front; its towers, and its Gothic chapel.

The forest opens in an irregular and very picturesque glade before its gate, and at the right a steep Gothic bridge carries the road over a stream that winds in deep shadow through the wood.

I have said that this is a very lonely place. Judge whether I say truth. Looking from the hall door towards the road, the forest in which our castle stands extends fifteen miles to the right, and twelve to the left. The nearest inhabited village is about seven of your English miles to the left. The nearest inhabited schloss of any historic associations, that of old General Spielsdorf, nearly twenty miles away to the right.

I have said 'the nearest *inhabited* village,' because there is only three miles westward, that is to say in the direction of General Spielsdorf's schloss, a ruined village, with its quaint little church, now roofless, in the aisle of which are the mouldering tombs of the proud family of Karnstein, now extinct, who once owned the equally-desolate château which, in the thick of the forest, overlooks the silent ruins of the town.

I must tell you now, how very small is the party who constitute the inhabitants of our castle. My father, who is the kindest man on earth, but growing old; and I, at the date of my story, only nineteen. Eight years have passed since then. I and my father constituted the family at the schloss. My mother, Styrian lady, died in my infancy, but I had a good-natured governess, who had been with me from, I might almost say, my infancy. I could not remember the time when her fat, benignant face was not a familiar picture in my memory. This was Madame Perrodon, a native of Berne, whose care and good nature in part supplied to me the loss of my mother, whom I do not even remember, so early I lost her. She made a third at our little dinner party. There was a fourth, Mademoiselle De Lafontaine, a lady such as you term, I believe, a 'finishing governess.' She spoke French and German, Madame Perrodon French and broken English, to which my father and I added English, which, partly to prevent its becoming a lost language among us, and partly from patriotic motives, we spoke every day.

The first occurrence in my existence, which produced a terrible impression upon my mind, which, in fact, never has been effaced, was one of the very earliest incidents of my life which I can recollect. Some people will think it so trifling that it should not be recorded here. You will see, however, by and by, why I mention it. The nursery, as it was called, though I had it all to myself, was a large room in the upper story of the castle, with a steep oak roof. I can't have been more than six years old, when one night I awoke, and looking round the room from my bed, failed to see the nursery-maid. Neither was my nurse there; and I thought myself alone. I was not frightened, for I was one of those happy children who are studiously kept in ignorance of ghost stories, of fairy tales, and of all such lore as makes us cover up our heads when the door creaks suddenly, or the flicker of an expiring candle makes the shadow of a bedpost dance upon the wall, nearer to our faces. I was vexed and insulted at finding myself, as I conceived, neglected, and I began to whimper, preparatory to a hearty bout of roaring; when to my surprise, I saw a solemn, but very pretty face looking at me from the side of the bed. It was that of a young lady who was kneeling, with her hands under the coverlet. I looked at her with a kind of pleased wonder, and ceased whimpering. She caressed me with her hands, and lay down beside me on the bed, and drew me towards her, smiling; I felt immediately delightfully soothed, and fell asleep again. I was wakened by a sensation as if two needles ran into my breast very deep at the same moment, and I cried loudly. The lady stared back, with her eyes fixed on me, and then slipped down upon the floor, and, as I thought, hid herself under the bed.

I was now for the first time frightened, and I yelled with all my might and main. Nurse, nursery-maid, housekeeper, all came running in, and hearing my story, they made light of it, soothing me all they could meanwhile. But, child as I was, I could perceive that their faces were pale with an unwonted look of anxiety, and I saw them look under the bed, and about the room, and peep under tables and pluck open cupboards; and the housekeeper whispered to the nurse: 'Lay your hand along that hollow in the bed; some one *did* lie there, so sure as you did not; the place is still warm.'

I remember the nursery-maid petting me, and all three examining my chest, where I told them I felt the puncture, and pronouncing that there was no sign visible that any such thing had happened to me.

I was very nervous for a long time after this. A doctor was called in, he was pallid and elderly. How well I remember his long saturnine face, slightly pitted with smallpox, and his chestnut wig. For a good while, every second day, he came and gave me medicine, which of course I hated.

The morning after I saw this apparition, I was in a state of terror, and could not bear to be left alone, daylight though it was, for a moment.

I remember my father coming up and standing at the bedside, and talking cheerfully, and asking the nurse a number of questions, and laughing very heartily at one of the answers; and patting me on the shoulder, and kissing me, and telling me not to be frightened, that it was nothing but a dream and could not hurt me.

But I was not comforted, for I knew the visit of the strange woman was *not* a dream; and I was *awfully* frightened.

I was a little consoled by the nursery-maid's assuring me that it was she who had come and looked at me, and then lain down beside me in the bed, and that I must have been half-dreaming not to have known her face. But this, though supported by the nurse, did not quite satisfy me.

I remember, in the course of that day, a venerable old man, in a black cassock, coming into the room with the nurse and housekeeper, and talking a little to them, and very kindly to me; his face was very sweet and gentle, and he told me they were going to pray, and joined my hands together, and desired me to say, softly, while they were praying, 'Lord, hear all good prayers for us, for Jesus' sake.' I think these were the very words, for I often repeated them to myself, and my nurse used for years to make me say them in my prayers.

I remember so well the thoughtful sweet face of that white-haired old man, in his black cassock, as he stood in that rude, lofty, brown room, with the clumsy furniture of a fashion three hundred years old, about him, and the scanty light entering its shadowy atmosphere through the small lattice. He kneeled, and the three women with him, and he prayed aloud with an earnest quavering voice for, what appeared to me, a long time. I forgot all my life preceding that event, and for some time after it is all obscure also; but the scenes I have just described stand out vivid as the isolated pictures of the phantasmagoria surrounded by darkness.

II. A GUEST

I am now going to tell you something so strange that it will require all your faith in my veracity to believe my story. It is not only true, nevertheless, but truth of which I have been an eyewitness.

It was a sweet summer evening, and my father asked me, as he sometimes did, to take a little ramble with him along that beautiful forest vista which I have mentioned as lying in front of the schloss.

'General Spielsdorf cannot come to us so soon as I had

hoped,' said my father, as we pursued our walk.

He was to have paid us a visit of some weeks, and we had expected his arrival next day. He was to have brought with him a young lady, his niece and ward, Mademoiselle Rheinfeldt, whom I had never seen, but whom I had heard described as a very charming girl, and in whose society I had promised myself many happy days.

'And how soon does he come?' I asked.

'Not till autumn. Not for two months, I dare say,' he answered. 'And I am very glad now, dear, that you never knew Mademoiselle Rheinfeldt.'

'And why?' I asked, both mortified and curious.

'Because the poor young lady is dead,' he replied. 'I quite forgot I had not told you, but you were not in the room when I received the General's letter this evening.'

We sat down on a rude bench, under a group of magnificent lime trees. The sun was setting with all its melancholy splendour behind the sylvan horizon, and the stream that flows beside our home, and passes under the steep old bridge I have mentioned, wound through many a group of noble trees, almost at our feet, reflecting in its current the fading crimson of the sky. General Spieldorf's letter was so extraordinary, so vehement, and in some places so self-contradictory, that I read it twice over – the second time aloud to my father – and was still unable to account for it, except by supposing that grief had unsettled his mind.

It said, 'I have lost my darling daughter, for as such I loved her. During the last days of dear Bertha's illness I was not able to write to you. Before then I had no idea of her danger. I have lost her, and now learn *all*, too late. She died in the peace of innocence, and in the glorious hope of a blessed futurity. The fiend who betrayed our infatuated hospitality has done it all. I thought I was receiving into my house innocence, gaiety, a charming companion for my lost Bertha. Heavens! what a fool have I been! I thank God my child died without a suspicion of the cause of her sufferings. She is gone without so much as conjecturing the nature of her illness, and the accursed passion of the agent of all this misery. I devote my remaining days to tracking and extinguishing a monster. I am told I may hope to accomplish my righteous and merciful purpose. At present there is scarcely a gleam of light to guide me. I curse my conceited incredulity, my despicable affectation of superiority, my blindness, my obstinacy – all – too late. I cannot write or talk collectedly now. I am distracted. So soon as I shall have a little recovered, I mean to devote myself for a time to inquiry, which may possibly lead me as far as Vienna. Some time in the autumn, two months hence, or earlier if I live, I will see you – that is, if you permit me; I will then tell you all that I scarce dare put upon paper now. Farewell. Pray for me, dear friend.'

The sun had now set, and it was twilight by the time I had returned the General's letter to my father.

It was a soft clear evening, and we loitered, speculating upon the possible meanings of the violent and incoherent sentences which I had just been reading. We had nearly a mile to walk before reaching the road that passes the schloss in front, and by that time the moon was shining brilliantly. At the drawbridge we met Madame Perrodon and Mademoiselle De Lafontaine, who had come out, without their bonnets, to enjoy the exquisite moonlight.

We heard their voices gabbling in animated dialogue as we approached. We joined them at the drawbridge, and turned about to admire with them the beautiful scene.

The glade through which we had just walked lay before us. At our left the narrow road wound away under clumps of lordly trees, and was lost to sight amid the thickening forest. At the right the same road crosses the steep and picturesque bridge, near which stands a ruined tower, which once guarded that pass; and beyond the bridge an abrupt eminence rises, covered with trees, and showing in the shadow some grey ivy-clustered rocks.

No softer, sweeter scene could be imagined. The news I had just heard made it melancholy; but nothing could disturb its character of profound serenity, and the enchanted glory and vagueness of the prospect.

My father, who enjoyed the picturesque, and I, stood looking in silence over the expanse beneath us. The two good governesses, standing a little way behind us, discoursed upon the scene, and were eloquent upon the moon.

Madame Perrodon was fat, middle-aged, and romantic, and talked and sighed poetically. Mademoiselle De Lafontaine – in right of her father, who was a German, assumed to be psychological, metaphysical, and something of a mystic – now declared that when the moon shone with a light so intense it was well known that it indicated a special spiritual activity. The effect of the full moon in such a state of brilliancy was manifold. It acted on dreams, it acted on lunacy, it acted on nervous people; it had marvellous physical influences connected with life.

'I have got into one of my moping moods tonight,' said my father, after a silence, and quoting Shakespeare, whom, by way of keeping up our English, he used to read aloud, he said:

> 'In truth I know not why I am so sad:
> It wearies me; you say it wearies you;
> But how I got it – came by it.

'I forget the rest. But I feel as if some great misfortune were hanging over us. I suppose the poor General's afflicted letter has had something to do with it.'

At this moment the unwonted sound of carriage wheels and many hoofs upon the road, arrested our attention.

They seemed to be approaching from the high ground overlooking the bridge, and very soon the equipage emerged from that point. Two horsemen first crossed the bridge, then came a carriage drawn by four horses, and two men rode behind.

It seemed to be the travelling carriage of a person of rank; and we were all immediately absorbed in watching that very unusual spectacle. It became, in a few moments, greatly more interesting, for just as the carriage had passed the summit of the steep bridge, one of the leaders, taking fright, communicated his panic to the rest, and, after a plunge or two, the whole team broke into a wild gallop together, and dashing between the horsemen who rode in front, came thundering along the road towards us with the speed of a hurricane.

The excitement of the scene was made more painful by the clear, long-drawn screams of a female voice from the carriage window.

We all advanced in curiosity and horror; my father in silence, the rest with various ejaculations of terror.

Our suspense did not last long. Just before you reach the castle drawbridge, on the route they were coming, there stands by the roadside a magnificent lime tree, on the other stands an ancient stone cross, at sight of which the horses, now going at a pace that was perfectly frightful, swerved so as to bring the wheel over the projecting roots of the tree.

I knew what was coming. I covered my eyes, unable to see it out, and turned my head away; at the same moment I heard a cry from my lady friends, who had gone on a little.

Curiosity opened my eyes, and I saw a scene of utter confusion. Two of the horses were on the ground, the carriage lay upon its side, with two wheels in the air; the men were busy removing the traces, and a lady, with a commanding air and figure, had got out, and stood with clasped hands, raising the handkerchief that was in them every now and then to her eyes. Through the carriage door was now lifted a young lady, who appeared to be lifeless. My dear old father was already beside the elder lady, with his hat in his hand, evidently tendering his aid and the resources of his schloss.

I approached; the young lady was apparently stunned, but she was certainly not dead. My father, who piqued himself on being something of a physician, had just had his fingers to her wrist and assured the lady, who declared herself her mother, that her pulse, though faint and irregular, was undoubtedly still distinguishable. The lady clasped her hands and looked upward, as if in a momentary transport of gratitude; but immediately she broke out again in that theatrical way which is, I believe, natural to some people.

She was what is called a fine-looking woman for her time of life, and must have been handsome; she was tall, but not thin, and dressed in black velvet, and looked rather pale, but with a proud and commanding countenance, though now agitated strangely.

'Was ever being so born to calamity?' I heard her say, with clasped hands, as I came up. 'Here am I, on a journey of life and death, in prosecuting which to lose an hour is possibly to lose all. My child will not have recovered sufficiently to resume her route for who can say how long. I must leave her; I cannot, dare not, delay. How far on, sir, can you tell, is the nearest village? I must leave her there; and shall not see my darling, or even hear of her till my return, three months hence.'

I plucked my father by the coat, and whispered earnestly in his ear, 'Oh! papa, pray ask her to let her stay with us – it would be so delightful. Do, pray.'

'If Madame will entrust her child to the care of my daughter, and of her good *gouvernante*, Madame Perrodon, and permit her to remain as our guest, under my charge, until her return, it will confer a distinction and an obligation upon us, and we shall treat her with all the care and devotion which so sacred a trust deserves.'

'I cannot do that, sir, it would be to task your kindness and chivalry too cruelly,' said the lady, distractedly.

'It would, on the contrary, be to confer on us a very great kindness at the moment when we most need it. My daughter has just been disappointed by a cruel misfortune, in a visit from which she had long anticipated a great deal of happiness. If you confide this young lady to our care it will be her best consolation. The nearest village on your route is distant, and affords no such inn as you could think of placing your daughter at; you cannot allow her to continue her journey for any considerable distance without danger. If, as you say, you cannot suspend your journey, you must part with her tonight, and nowhere could you do so with more honest assurances of care and tenderness than here.'

There was something in this lady's air and appearance so distinguished, and even imposing, and in her manner so engaging, as to impress one, quite apart from the dignity of her equipage, with a conviction that she was a person of consequence.

By this time the carriage was replaced in its upright position, and the horses, quite tractable, in the traces again.

The lady threw on her daughter a glance which I fancied was not quite so affectionate as one might have anticipated from the beginning of the scene; then she beckoned slightly to my father, and withdrew two or three steps with him out of hearing; and talked to him with a fixed and stern countenance, not at all like that with which she had hitherto spoken.

Two or three minutes at most, I think, she remained thus employed, then she turned, and a few steps brought her to where her daughter lay, supported by Madame Perrodon. She kneeled beside her for a moment and whispered, as Madame supposed, a little benediction in her ear; then hastily kissing her, she stepped into her carriage, the door was closed, the footmen in stately liveries jumped up behind, the outriders spurred on, the postilions cracked their whips, the horses plunged and broke suddenly into a furious canter that threatened soon again to become a gallop, and the carriage whirled away, followed at the same rapid pace by the two horsemen in the rear.

III. WE COMPARE NOTES

We followed the *cortège* with our eyes until it was swiftly lost to sight in the misty wood; and the very sound of the hoofs and wheels died away in the silent night air.

Nothing remained to assure us that the adventure had not been an illusion of a moment but the young lady, who just at that moment opened her eyes. I could not see, for her face was turned from me, but she raised her head, evidently looking about her, and I heard a very sweet voice asking complainingly, 'Where is mamma?'

Madame answered all her questions in so far as she understood them; and gradually the young lady remembered how the misadventure came about, and was glad to hear that no one in, or in attendance on, the carriage was hurt; and on learning that her mamma had left her here, till her return in about three months, she wept.

My father in the meantime had sent a servant on horseback for the physician, who lived about two leagues away; and a bedroom was being prepared for the young lady's reception.

The stranger now rose, and leaning on Madame's arm, walked slowly over the drawbridge and into the castle gate.

In the hall, servants waited to receive her, and she was conducted forthwith to her room.

The room we usually sat in as our drawing-room is long, having four windows, that looked over the moat and drawbridge, upon the forest scene I have just described.

It is furnished in old carved oak, with large carved cabinets, and the chairs are cushioned with crimson Utrecht velvet. The walls are covered with tapestry, and surrounded with great gold frames, the figures being as large as life, in ancient and very curious costume, and the subjects represented are hunting, hawking, and generally festive.

We sat here this night, and with candles lighted, were talking over the adventure of the evening.

Madame Perrodon and Mademoiselle De Lafontaine were both of our party. The young stranger had hardly lain down in her bed when she sank into a deep sleep; and those ladies had left her in the care of a servant.

'How do you like our guest?' I asked, as soon as Madame entered. 'Tell me all about her.'

'I like her extremely,' answered Madame, 'she is, I almost think, the prettiest creature I ever saw; about your age, and so gentle and nice.'

'Did you remark a woman in the carriage, after it was set up again, who did not get out,' inquired Mademoiselle, 'but only looked from the window?'

No, we had not seen her.

Then she described a hideous black woman, with a sort of coloured turban on her head, who was gazing all the time from the carriage window, nodding and grinning derisively towards the ladies, with gleaming eyes and large white eye-balls, and her teeth set as if in fury.

'Did you remark what an ill-looking pack of men the servants were?' asked Madame.

'Yes,' said my father, who had just come in, 'ugly, hang-dog looking fellows, as ever I beheld in my life. I hope they mayn't rob the poor lady in the forest. They are clever rogues, however; they got everything to rights in a minute.'

'I dare say they are worn out with too long travelling,' said Madame. 'Besides looking wicked, their faces were so strangely lean, and dark, and sullen. I am very curious, I own; but I dare say the young lady will tell us all about it tomorrow, if she is sufficiently recovered.'

'I don't think she will,' said my father, with a mysterious smile, and a little nod of his head, as if he knew more about it than he cared to tell us.

This made me all the more inquisitive as to what had passed between him and the lady in the black velvet, in the brief but earnest interview that had immediately preceded her departure.

We were scarcely alone, when I entreated him to tell me. He did not need much pressing.

'There is no particular reason why I should not tell you. She expressed a reluctance to trouble us with the care of her daughter, saying she was in delicate health, and nervous, but not subject to any kind of seizure – she volunteered that – nor to any illusion; being, in fact, perfectly sane.'

'How very odd to say all that!' I interpolated. 'It was so unnecessary.'

'At all events it *was* said,' he laughed, 'and as you wish to know all that passed, which was indeed very little, I tell you. She then said, "I am making a long journey of *vital* importance" – she emphasized the word – "rapid and secret; I shall return for my child in three months; in the meantime, she will be silent as to who we are, whence we come, and whither we are travelling." That is all she said. She spoke very pure French. When she said the word "secret", she paused for a few seconds, looking sternly, her eyes fixed on mine. I fancy she makes a great point of that. You saw how quickly she was gone. I hope I have not done a very foolish thing, in taking charge of the young lady.'

The doctor did not arrive till nearly one o'clock; but I could no more have gone to my bed and slept, than I could have overtaken, on foot, the carriage in which the princess in black velvet had driven away.

When the physician came down to the drawing-room, it was to report very favourably upon his patient. She had sustained no injury, and the little shock to her nerves had passed away quite harmlessly. There could be no harm certainly in my seeing her, if we both wished it.

Our visitor lay in one of the handsomest rooms in the schloss. It was, perhaps, a little stately. There was a sombre piece of tapestry opposite the foot of the bed, representing Cleopatra with the asps to her bosom; and other solemn classic scenes were displayed, a little faded, upon the other walls.

There were candles at the bedside. She was sitting up; her slender pretty figure enveloped in the soft silk dressing-gown, embroidered with flowers, and lined with thick quilted silk, which her mother had thrown over her feet as she lay upon the ground.

What was it that, as I reached the bedside and had just begun my little greeting, struck me dumb in a moment, and made me recoil a step or two from before her? I will tell you.

I saw the very face which had visited me in my childhood at night, which remained so fixed in my memory, and on which I had so many years so often ruminated with horror, when no one suspected of what I was thinking.

It was pretty, even beautiful; and when I first beheld it, wore the same melancholy expression.

But this almost instantly lighted into a strange fixed smile of recognition.

There was a silence of fully a minute, and then at length *she* spoke; *I* could not.

'How wonderful!' she exclaimed. 'Twelve years ago, I saw your face in a dream, and it has haunted me ever since.'

'Wonderful indeed!' I repeated, overcoming with an effort the horror that had for a time suspended my utterances. 'Twelve years ago, in vision or reality, *I* certainly saw you. I could not forget your face. It has remained before my eyes ever since.'

Her smile had softened. Whatever I had fancied strange in it, was gone, and it and her dimpling cheeks were now delightfully pretty and intelligent.

I was a little shy, as lonely people are, but the situation made me eloquent, and even bold. She pressed my hand, she laid hers upon it, and her eyes glowed, as, looking hastily into mine, she smiled again, and blushed.

She answered my welcome very prettily. I sat down beside her, still wondering; and she said:

'I must tell you my vision about you; it is so very strange that you and I should have had, each of the other so vivid a dream, that each should have seen, I you and you me, looking as we do now, when of course we both were mere children. I was a child, about six years old, and I awoke from a confused and troubled dream, and found myself in a room, unlike my nursery, wainscoted clumsily in some dark wood, and with cupboards and bedsteads, and chairs, and benches placed about it. The beds were I thought, all empty, and the room itself without any one but myself in it; and I, after looking about me for some time, and admiring especially an iron candlestick, with two branches, which I should certainly know again, crept under one of the beds to reach the window; but as I got from under the bed, I heard someone crying;

and looking up, while I was still upon my knees, I saw *you* – most assuredly you – as I see you now; a beautiful young lady, with golden hair and large blue eyes, and lips – your lips – you, as you are here. Your looks won me; I climbed on the bed and put my arms about you, and I think we both fell asleep. I was aroused by a scream; you were sitting up screaming. I was frightened, and slipped down upon the ground, and, it seemed to me, lost consciousness for a moment; and when I came to myself, I was again in my nursery at home. Your face I have never forgotten since. I could not be misled by mere resemblance. You *are* the lady whom I then saw.'

It was now my turn to relate my corresponding vision, which I did, to the undisguised wonder of my new acquaintance.

'I don't know which should be most afraid of the other,' she said, again smiling. 'If you were less pretty I think I should be very much afraid of you, but being as you are, and you and I both so young, I feel only that I have made your acquaintance twelve years ago, and have already a right to your intimacy; at all events, it does seem as if we were destined, from our earliest childhood, to be friends. I wonder whether you feel as strangely drawn towards me as I do to you; I have never had a friend – shall I find one now?' She sighed, and her fine dark eyes gazed passionately on me.

Now the truth is, I felt rather unaccountably towards the beautiful stranger. I did feel, as she said, 'drawn towards her', but there was also something of repulsion. In this ambiguous feeling, however, the sense of attraction immensely prevailed. She interested and won me; she was so beautiful and so indescribably engaging.

I perceived now something of languor and exhaustion stealing over her, and hastened to bid her good night.

She held me close in her pretty arms for a moment and whispered in my ear, 'Good night, darling, it is very hard to part with you, but good night; tomorrow, but not early, I shall see you again.'

She sank back on the pillow with a sigh, and her fine eyes followed me with a fond and melancholy gaze, and she murmured again, 'Good night, dear friend.'

Next day came and we met again. I was delighted with my companion; that is to say, in many respects.

Her looks lost nothing in the daylight – she was certainly the most beautiful creature I had ever seen, and the unpleasant remembrance of the face presented in my early dream, had lost the effect of the first unexpected recognition.

She confessed that she had experienced a similar shock on seeing me, and precisely the same faint antipathy that had mingled with my admiration of her. We now laughed together over our momentary horrors.

IV. HER HABITS – A SAUNTER

I told you that I was charmed with her in most particulars.

There were some that did not please me so well.

She was above the middle height of women. I shall begin by describing her. She was slender, and wonderfully graceful. Except that her movements were languid – *very* languid – indeed, there was nothing in her appearance to indicate an invalid. Her complexion was rich and brilliant; her features were small and beautifully formed; her eyes large, dark, and lustrous; her hair was quite wonderful, I never saw hair so magnificently thick and long when it was down about her shoulders; I have often placed my hands under it, and laughed with wonder at its weight. It was exquisitely fine and soft, and in colour a rich very dark brown, with something of gold. I loved to let it down, tumbling with its own weight, as, in her room, she lay back in her chair talking in her sweet low voice, I used to fold and braid it, and spread it out and play with it. Heavens! If I had but known all!

I said there were particulars which did not please me. I have told you that her confidence won me the first night I saw her; but I found that she exercised with respect to herself, her mother, her history, everything, in fact connected with her life, plans, and people, an ever-wakeful reserve. I dare say I was unreasonable, perhaps I was wrong; I dare say I ought to have respected the solemn injunction laid upon my father by the stately lady in black velvet. But curiosity is a restless and unscrupulous passion, and no one girl can endure, with patience, that hers should be baffled by another. What harm could it do anyone to tell me what I so ardently desired to know? Had she no trust in my good sense or honour?

There was a coldness, it seemed to me, beyond her years, in her smiling melancholy persistent refusal to afford me the least ray of light.

What she did tell me amounted, in my unconscionable estimation – to nothing.

It was all summed up in three very vague disclosures:

First – Her name was Carmilla.

Second – Her family was very ancient and noble.

Third – Her home lay in the direction of the west.

She would not tell me the name of her family, nor their armorial bearings, nor the name of their estate, nor even that of the country they lived in.

You are not to suppose that I worried her incessantly on these subjects. I watched opportunity, and rather insinuated than urged my inquiries. Once or twice, indeed, I did attack her more directly. But no matter what my tactics, utter failure was invariably the result. Reproaches and caresses were all lost upon her.

She used to place her pretty arms about my neck, draw me to her, and laying her cheek to mine, murmur with her lips near my ear, 'Dearest, your little heart is wounded; think me not cruel because I obey the irresistible law of my strength and weakness; if your dear heart is wounded, my wild heart bleeds with yours. In the rapture of my enormous humiliation I live in your warm life, and you shall die – die, sweetly die – into mine. I cannot help it; as I draw near to you, you, in your turn, will draw near to others, and learn the rapture of that cruelty, which yet is love; so, for a while, seek to know no more of me and mine, but trust me with all your loving spirit.'

And when she had spoken such a rhapsody, she would press me more closely to her trembling embrace, and her lips in soft kisses gently glow upon my cheek.

In these mysterious moods I did not like her. I experienced a strange tumultuous excitement that was pleasurable, ever and anon, mingled with a vague sense of fear and disgust. I had no distinct thoughts about her while such scenes lasted, but I was conscious of a love growing into adoration, and also of abhorrence. This I know is paradox, but I can make no other attempt to explain the feeling.

I now write, after an interval of more than ten years, with a trembling hand, with a confused and horrible recollection of certain occurrences and situations, in the ordeal through which I was unconsciously passing; though with a vivid and very sharp remembrance of the main current of my story. But, I suspect, in all lives there are certain emotional scenes, those in which our passions have been most wildly and terribly roused, that are of all others the most vaguely and dimly remembered.

Sometimes after an hour of apathy, my strange and beautiful companion would take my hand and hold it with a fond pressure, renewed again and again; blushing softly, gazing in my face with languid and burning eyes, and breathing so fast that her dress rose and fell with the tumultuous respiration. It was like the ardour of a lover; it embarrassed me; it was hateful and yet overpowering; and with gloating eyes she drew me to her, and her hot lips travelled along my cheek in kisses; and she would whisper, almost in sobs, 'You are mine, you *shall* be mine, and you and I are one for ever.' Then she has thrown herself back in her chair with her small hands over her eyes, leaving me trembling.

'Are we related,' I used to ask; 'what can you mean by all this? I remind you perhaps of someone whom you love; but you must not, I hate it; I don't know you – I don't know myself when you look so and talk so.'

She used to sigh at my vehemence, then turn away and drop my hand.

Respecting these very extraordinary manifestations I strove in vain to form any satisfactory theory – I could not refer them to affectation or trick. It was unmistakably the momentary breaking out of suppressed instinct and emotion.

In some respects her habits were odd. She used to come down very late, generally not till one o'clock, she would then take a cup of chocolate, but eat nothing; we then went out for a walk, which was a mere saunter, and she seemed, almost immediately, exhausted, and either returned to the schloss or sat on one of the benches that were placed, here and there, among the trees. This was a bodily languor in which her mind did not sympathize. She was always an animated talker, and very intelligent.

She sometimes alluded for a moment to her own home, or mentioned an adventure or situation, or an early recollection, which indicated a people of strange manners, and described customs of which we knew nothing. I gathered from these chance hints that her native country was much more remote than I had at first fancied.

As we sat thus one afternoon under the trees a funeral passed us by. It was that of a pretty young girl, whom I had often seen, the daughter of one of the rangers of the forest. The poor man was walking behind the coffin of his darling; she was his only child, and he looked quite heart-broken. Peasants walking two-and-two came behind, they were singing a funeral hymn.

I rose to mark my respect as they passed, and joined in the hymn they were very sweetly singing.

My companion shook me a little roughly, and I turned surprised.

She said brusquely, 'Don't you perceive how discordant that is?'

'I think it very sweet, on the contrary,' I answered, vexed at the interruption, and very uncomfortable, lest the people who composed the little procession should observe and resent what was passing.

I resumed, therefore, instantly, and was again interrupted. 'You pierce my ears,' said Carmilla, almost angrily, and stopping her ears with her tiny fingers. 'Besides, how can you tell that your religion and mine are the same; your forms wound me, and I hate funerals. What a fuss! Why, *you* must die – *everyone* must die; and all are happier when they do. Come home.'

'My father has gone on with the clergyman to the churchyard. I thought you knew she was to be buried today.'

'*She?* I don't trouble my head about peasants. I don't know who she is,' answered Carmilla, with a flash from her fine eyes.

'She is the poor girl who fancied she saw a ghost a fortnight ago, and has been dying ever since, till yesterday, when she expired.'

'Tell me nothing about ghosts. I shan't sleep tonight if you do.'

'I hope there is no plague or fever coming; all this looks

very like it,' I continued. 'The swineherd's young wife died only a week ago, and she thought something seized her by the throat as she lay in her bed, and nearly strangled her. Papa says such horrible fancies do accompany some forms of fever. She was quite well the day before. She sank afterwards, and died before a week.'

'Well, *her* funeral is over, I hope, and *her* hymn sung; and our ears shan't be tortured with that discord and jargon. It has made me nervous. Sit down here, beside me; sit close; hold my hand; press it hard – hard – harder.'

We had moved a little back, and had come to another seat.

She sat down. Her face underwent a change that alarmed and even terrified me for a moment. It darkened, and became horribly livid; her teeth and hands were clenched, and she frowned and compressed her lips, while she stared down upon the ground at her feet, and trembled all over with a continued shudder as irrepressible as ague. All her energies seemed strained to suppress a fit, with which she was then breathlessly tugging; and at length a low convulsive cry of suffering broke from her, and gradually the hysteria subsided. 'There! That comes of strangling people with hymns!' she said at last. 'Hold me, hold me still. It is passing away.'

And so gradually it did; and perhaps to dissipate the sombre impression which the spectacle had left upon me, she became unusually animated and chatty; and so we got home.

This was the first time I had seen her exhibit any definable symptoms of that delicacy of health which her mother had spoken of. It was the first time, also, I had seen her exhibit anything like temper.

Both passed away like a summer cloud; and never but once afterwards did I witness on her part a momentary sign of anger. I will tell you how it happened.

She and I were looking out of one of the long drawing-room windows, when there entered the courtyard, over the drawbridge, a figure of a wanderer whom I knew very well. He used to visit the schloss generally twice a year.

It was the figure of a hunchback, with the sharp lean features that generally accompany deformity. He wore a pointed black beard, and he was smiling from ear to ear, showing his white fangs. He was dressed in buff, black, and scarlet, and crossed with more straps and belts than I could count, from which hung all manner of things. Behind, he carried a magic lantern, and two boxes, which I well knew, in one of which was a salamander, and in the other a mandrake. These monsters used to make my father laugh. They were compounded of parts of monkeys, parrots, squirrels, fish, and hedgehogs, dried and stitched together with great neatness and startling effect. He had a fiddle, a box of conjuring apparatus, a pair of foils and masks attached to his belt, several other mysterious cases danging about him, and a black staff with copper ferrules in his hand. His companion was a rough, spare dog, that followed at his heels, but stopped short, suspiciously at the drawbridge, and in a little while began to howl dismally.

In the meantime, the mountebank, standing in the midst of the courtyard, raised his grotesque hat, and made us a very ceremonious bow, paying his compliments very volubly in execrable French, and German not much better. Then, disengaging his fiddle, he began to scrape a lively air, to which he sang with a merry discord, dancing with ludicrous airs and activity, that made me laugh, in spite of the dog's howling.

Then he advanced to the window with many smiles and salutations, and his hat in his left hand, his fiddle under his arm, and with a fluency that never took breath, he gabbled a long advertisement of all his accomplishments, and the resources of the various arts which he placed at our service, and the curiosities and entertainments which it was in his power, at our bidding, to display.

'Will your ladyships be pleased to buy an amulet against the oupire, which is going like the wolf, I hear, through these woods,' he said, dropping his hat on the pavement. 'They are dying of it right and left, and here is a charm that never fails; only pinned to the pillow, and you may laugh in his face.'

These charms consisted of oblong slips of vellum, with cabalistic ciphers and diagrams upon them.

Carmilla instantly purchased one, and so did I.

He was looking up, and we were smiling down upon him, amused; at least, I can answer for myself. His piercing black eye, as he looked up in our faces, seemed to detect something that fixed for a moment his curiosity.

In an instant he unrolled a leather case, full of all manner of odd little steel instruments.

'See here, my lady,' he said, displaying it, and addressing me, 'I profess, among other things less useful, the art of dentistry. Plague take the dog!' he interpolated. 'Silence, beast! He howls so that your ladyships can scarcely hear a word. Your noble friend, the young lady at your right, has the sharpest tooth – long, thin, pointed, like an awl, like a needle; ha, ha! With my sharp and long sight, as I look up, I have seen it distinctly; now if it happens to hurt the young lady, and I think it must, here am I, here are my file, my punch, my nippers; I will make it round and blunt, if her ladyship pleases; no longer the tooth of a fish, but of a beautiful young lady as she is. Hey? Is the young lady displeased? Have I been too bold? Have I offended her?'

The young lady, indeed, looked very angry as she drew back from the window.

'How dares that mountebank insult us so? Where is your father? I shall demand redress from him. My father would have had the wretch tied up to the pump, and flogged with a cart-whip, and burnt to the bones with the castle brand!'

She retired from the window a step or two, and sat down, and had hardly lost sight of the offender, when her wrath subsided as suddenly as it had risen, and she gradually recovered her usual tone, and seemed to forget the little hunchback and his follies.

My father was out of spirits that evening. On coming in he told us that there had been another case very similar to the two fatal ones which had lately occurred. The sister of a young peasant on his estate, only a mile away, was very ill, had been, as she described it, attacked very nearly in the same way, and was now slowly but steadily sinking.

'All this,' said my father, 'is strictly referable to natural causes. These poor people infect one another with their superstitions, and so repeat in imagination the images of terror that have infested their neighbours.'

'But that very circumstance frightens one horribly,' said Carmilla.

'How so?' inquired my father.

'I am so afraid of fancying I see such things; I think it would be as bad as reality.'

'The doctor said he would come here today,' said my father, after a silence. 'I want to know what he thinks about it, and what he thinks we had better do.'

'Doctors never did me any good,' said Carmilla.

'Then you have been ill?' I asked.

'More ill than ever you were,' she answered.

'Long ago?'

'Yes, a long time. I suffered from this very illness; but I forgot all but my pain and weakness, and they were not so bad as are suffered in other diseases.'

'You were very young then?'

'I dare say; let us talk no more of it. You would not wound a friend?' She looked languidly in my eyes, and passed her arm round my waist lovingly, and led me out of the room. My father was busy over some papers near the window.

'Why does your papa like to frighten us?' said the pretty girl, with a sigh and a little shudder.

'He doesn't, dear Carmilla, it is the very furthest thing from his mind.'

'Are you afraid, dearest?'

'I should be very much if I fancied there was any real danger of my being attacked as those poor people were.'

'You are afraid to die?'

'Yes, everyone is.'

'But to die as lovers may – to die together, so that they may live together. Girls are caterpillars while they live in the world, to be finally butterflies when the summer comes; but in the meantime there are grubs and larvae, don't you see – each with their peculiar propensities, necessities and structure. So says Monsieur Buffon, in his big book, in the next room.'

Later in the day the doctor came, and was closeted with papa for some time. He was a skilful man, of sixty and upwards, he wore powder, and shaved his pale face as smooth as a pumpkin. He and papa emerged from the room together, and I heard papa laugh, and say as they came out:

'Well, I do wonder at a wise man like you. What do you say to hippogriffs and dragons?'

The doctor was smiling, and made answer shaking his head —

'Nevertheless, life and death are mysterious states, and we

know little of the resources of either.'

And so they walked on, and I heard no more. I did not then know what the doctor had been broaching, but I think I guess it now.

V. A WONDERFUL LIKENESS

This evening there arrived from Gratz the grave, dark-faced son of the picture-cleaner, with a horse and cart laden with two large packing-cases, having many pictures in each. It was a journey of ten leagues, and whenever a messenger arrived at the schloss from our little capital of Gratz, we used to crowd about him in the hall, to hear the news.

This arrival created in our secluded quarters quite a sensation. The cases remained in the hall, and the messenger was taken charge of by the servants till he had eaten his supper. Then with assistants, and armed with hammer, ripping chisel, and turnscrew, he met us in the hall, where we had assembled to witness the unpacking of the cases.

Carmilla sat looking listlessly on, while one after the other the old pictures, nearly all portraits, which had undergone the process of renovation, were brought to light. My mother was of an old Hungarian family, and most of these pictures, which were about to be restored to their places, had come to us through her.

'There is a picture that I have not seen yet,' said my father. 'In one corner, at the top of it, is the name, as well as I could read, "Marcia Karnstein," and the date "1698"; and I am curious to see how it has turned out.'

I remembered it; it was a small picture, about a foot and a half high, and nearly square, without a frame; but it was so blackened by age that I could not make it out.

The artist now produced it, with evident pride. It was quite beautiful; it was startling; it seemed to live. It was the effigy of Carmilla!

'Carmilla, dear, here is an absolute miracle. Here you are, living, smiling, ready to speak, in this picture. Isn't it beautiful, papa? And see, even the little mole on her throat.'

My father laughed, and said, 'Certainly it is a wonderful likeness,' but he looked away, and to my surprise seemed but little struck by it, and went on talking to the picture-cleaner, who was also something of an artist, and discoursed with intelligence about the portraits or other works, which his art had just brought into light and colour, while *I* was more and more lost in wonder the more I looked at the picture.

'Will you let me hang this picture in my room, papa?' I asked.

'Certainly, dear,' said he, smiling, 'I'm glad you think it so like. It must be prettier even than I thought it, if it is.'

The young lady did not acknowledge this pretty speech, did not seem to hear it. She was leaning back in her seat, her fine eyes under their long lashes gazing on me in contemplation, and she smiled in a kind of rapture.

'And now you can read quite plainly the name that is written in the corner. It is not Marcia; it looks as if it was done in gold. The name is Mircalla, Countess Karstein, and this is a little coronet over it, and underneath A.D. 1698. I am descended from the Karsteins; that is, mamma was.'

'Ah!' said the lady, languidly, 'so am I, I think, a very long descent, very ancient. Are there any Karsteins living now?'

'None who bear the name, I believe. The family were ruined. I believe, in some civil wars, long ago, but the ruins of the castle are only about three miles away.'

'How interesting!' she said, languidly. 'But see what beautiful moonlight!' She glanced through the hall door, which stood a little open. 'Suppose you take a little ramble round the court, and look down at the road and river.'

'It is so like the night you came to us,' I said.

In silence, slowly we walked down to the drawbridge, where the beautiful landscape opened before us.

'And so you were thinking of the night I came here?' she almost whispered. 'Are you glad I came?'

'Delighted, dear Carmilla,' I answered.

'And you ask for the picture you think like me, to hang in your room,' she murmured with a sigh, as she drew her arm closer about my waist, and let her pretty head sink upon my shoulder.

'How romantic you are, Carmilla,' I said. 'Whenever you tell me your story, it will be made up chiefly of some one great romance.'

She kissed me silently.

'I am sure, Carmilla, you have been in love; that there is,

at this moment, an affair of the heart going on.'

'I have been in love with no one, and never shall,' she whispered, 'unless it should be with you.'

How beautiful she looked in the moonlight!

Shy and strange was the look with which she quickly hid her face in my neck and hair, with tumultuous sighs, that seemed almost to sob, and pressed in mine a hand that trembled.

Her soft cheek was glowing against mine. 'Darling, darling,' she murmured, 'I live in you; and you would die for me, I love you so.'

I started from her.

She was gazing on me with eyes from which all fire, all meaning had flown, and a face colourless and apathetic.

'Is there a chill in the air, dear?' she said drowsily. 'I almost shiver; have I been dreaming? Let us come in. Come, come; come in.'

'You look ill, Carmilla; a little faint. You certainly must take some wine,' I said.

I was beginning to take alarm, lest she should have been stricken with the strange epidemic that they said had invaded the country about us.

'Papa would be grieved beyond measure,' I added, 'if he thought you were ever so little ill, without immediately letting us know. We have a very skilful doctor near this, the physician who was with papa today.'

'I'm sure he is. I know how kind you all are; but, dear child, I am quite well again. There is nothing ever wrong with me, but a little weakness. I can scarcely walk as far as a child of three years old; and every now and then the little strength I have falters, and I become as you have just seen me. But after all I am very easily set up again; in a moment I am perfectly myself. See how I have recovered.'

So, indeed, she had; and she and I talked a great deal, and very animated she was; and the remainder of that evening passed without any recurrence of what I called her infatuations. I mean her crazy talk and looks, which embarrassed, and even frightened me.

But there occurred that night an event which gave my thoughts quite a new turn, and seemed to startle even Carmilla's languid nature into momentary energy.

VI. A VERY STRANGE AGONY

When we got into the drawing-room, and had sat down to our coffee and chocolate, although Carmilla did not take any, she seemed quite herself again, and Madame, and Mademoiselle De Lafontaine, joined us, and made a little card party, in the course of which papa came in for what he called his 'dish of tea'.

When the game was over he sat down beside Carmilla on the sofa, and asked her, a little anxiously, whether she had heard from her mother since her arrival.

She answered 'No.'

He then asked her whether she knew where a letter would reach her at present.

'I cannot tell,' she answered, ambiguously, 'but I have been thinking of leaving you; you have been already too hospitable and too kind to me. I have given you an infinity of trouble, and I should wish to take a carriage tomorrow, and post in pursuit of her; I know where I shall ultimately find her, although I dare not yet tell you.'

'But you must not dream of any such thing,' exclaimed my father, to my great relief. 'We can't afford to lose you so, and I won't consent to your leaving us, except under the care of your mother, who was so good as to consent to your remaining with us till she should herself return. I should be quite happy if I knew that you heard from her; but this evening the accounts of the progress of the mysterious disease that has invaded our neighbourhood, grow even more alarming; and my beautiful guest, I do feel the responsibility unaided by advice from your mother, very much.'

'Thank you, sir, a thousand times for your hospitality,' she answered, smiling bashfully. 'You have all been too kind to me; I have seldom been so happy in all my life before, as in your beautiful château, under your care, and in the society of your dear daughter.'

So he gallantly, in his old-fashioned way, kissed her hand, smiling, and pleased at her little speech.

I accompanied Carmilla as usual to her room, and sat and chatted with her while she was preparing for bed.

'Do you think,' I said, at length, 'that you will ever confide fully in me?'

She turned round smiling, but made no answer, only continued to smile on me.

'You won't answer that?' I said. 'You can't answer pleasantly; I ought not to have asked you.'

'You were quite right to ask me that, or anything. You do not know how dear you are to me, or you could not think any confidence too great to look for. But I am under vows, no nun half so awfully, and I dare not tell my story yet, even to you. The time is very near when you shall know everything. You will think me cruel, very selfish, but love is always selfish; the more ardent the more selfish. How jealous I am you cannot know. You must come with me, loving me, to death; or else hate me, and still come with me, and *hating* me through death and after. There is no such word as indifference in my apathetic nature.'

'Now, Carmilla, you are going to talk your wild nonsense again,' I said hastily.

'Not I, silly little fool as I am, and full of whims and fancies; for your sake I'll talk like a sage. Were you ever at a ball?'

'No; how you do run on. What is it like? How charming it must be.'

'I almost forgot, it is years ago.'

I laughed.

'You are not so old. Your first ball can hardly be forgotten yet.'

'I remember everything about it – with an effort. I see it all, as divers see what is going on above them, through a medium, dense, rippling, but transparent. There occurred that night what has confused the picture, and made its colours faint. I was all but assassinated in my bed, wounded *here*,' she touched her breast, 'and never was the same since.'

'Were you near dying?'

'Yes, very – a cruel love – strange love, that would have taken my life. Love will have its sacrifices. No sacrifices without blood. Let us go to sleep now; I feel so lazy. How can I get up just now and lock my door?'

She was lying with her tiny hands buried in her rich wavy hair, under her cheek, her little head upon the pillow, and her glittering eyes followed me wherever I moved, with a kind of shy smile that I could not decipher.

I bid her good night, and crept from the room with an uncomfortable sensation.

The precautions of nervous people are infectious, and persons of a like temperament are pretty sure, after a time, to imitate them. I had adopted Carmilla's habit of locking her bedroom door, having taken into my head all her whimsical alarms about midnight invaders and prowling assassins. I had also adopted her precaution of making a brief search through her room, to satisfy herself that no lurking assassin or robber was 'ensconced.'

I had a dream that night that was the beginning of a very strange agony.

I cannot call it a nightmare, for I was quite conscious of being asleep. But I was equally conscious of being in my room, and lying in bed, precisely as I actually was. I saw, or fancied I saw, the room and its furniture just as I had seen it last, except that it was very dark, and I saw something moving round the foot of the bed, which at first I could not accurately distinguish. But I soon saw that it was a sooty-black animal that resembled a monstrous cat. It appeared to me about four or five feet long, for it measured fully the length of the hearthrug as it passed over it; and it continued to-ing and fro-ing with the lithe sinister restlessness of a beast in a cage. I could not cry out, although as you may suppose, I was terrified. Its pace was growing faster, and the room rapidly darker and darker, and at length so dark that I could no longer see anything of it but its eyes. I felt it spring lightly on the bed. The two broad eyes approached my face, and suddenly I felt a stinging pain as if two large needles darted, an inch or two apart, deep into my breast. I waked with a scream. The room was lighted by the candle that burnt there all through the night, and I saw a female figure standing at the foot of the bed, a little at the right side. It was in a dark loose dress, and its hair was down and covered its shoulders. A block of stone could not have been more still. There was not the slightest stir of respiration. As I stared at it, the figure appeared to have changed its place, and was now nearer the door, then, close to it, the door opened, and it passed out.

I was now relieved, and able to breathe and move. My first thought was that Carmilla had been playing me a trick, and that I had forgotten to secure my door. I hastened to it, and found it locked as usual on the inside. I was afraid to open it – I was horrified. I sprang into my bed and covered my head up in the bedclothes, and lay there more dead than alive till morning.

VII. DESCENDING

I could not bear next day to be alone for a moment. I should have told papa, but for two opposite reasons. At one time I thought he would laugh at my story, and I could not bear its being treated as a jest; and at another, I thought he might fancy that I had been attacked by the mysterious complaint which had invaded our neighbourhood. I had myself no misgivings of the kind, and as he had been rather an invalid for some time, I was afraid of alarming him.

I was comfortable enough with my good-natured companions, Madame Perrodon, and the vivacious Mademoiselle Lafontaine. They both perceived that I was out of spirits and nervous, and at length I told them what lay so heavy at my heart.

Mademoiselle laughed, but I fancied that Madame Perrodon looked anxious.

'By the by,' said Mademoiselle, laughing, 'the long lime-tree walk, behind Carmilla's bedroom window, is haunted!'

'Nonsense!' exclaimed Madame, who probably thought the theme rather inopportune, 'and who tells that story, my dear?'

'Martin says that he came up twice, when the old yard gate was being repaired before sunrise, and twice saw the same female walking down the lime-tree avenue.'

'So he well might, as long as there are cows to milk in the river fields,' said Madame.

'I dare say; but Martin chooses to be frightened, and never did I see a fool *more* frightened.'

'You must not say a word about it to Carmilla, because she can see down that walk from her room window,' I interposed, 'and she is, if possible, a greater coward than I.'

Carmilla came down rather later than usual that day.

'I was so frightened last night,' she said, so soon as we were together, 'and I am sure I should have seen something dreadful if it had not been for that charm I bought from the poor little hunchback whom I called such hard names. I had a dream of something black coming round my bed, and I awoke in a perfect horror, and I really thought, for some seconds, I saw a dark figure near the chimney piece, but I felt under my pillow for my charm, and the moment my fingers touched it, the figure disappeared, and I felt quite certain, only that I had it by me, that something frightful would have made its appearance, and, perhaps, throttled me, as it did those poor people we heard of.'

'Well, listen to me,' I began, and recounted my adventure, at the recital of which she appeared horrified.

'And had you the charm near you?' she asked, earnestly.

'No, I had dropped it into a china vase in the drawing-room, but I shall certainly take it with me tonight, as you have so much faith in it.'

At this distance of time I cannot tell you, or even understand, how I overcame my horror so effectually as to lie alone in my room that night. I remember distinctly that I pinned the charm to my pillow. I fell asleep almost immediately, and slept even more soundly than usual all night.

Next night I passed as well. My sleep was delightfully deep and dreamless. But I wakened with a sense of lassitude and melancholy, which, however, did not exceed a degree that was almost luxurious.

'Well, I told you so,' said Carmilla, when I described my quiet sleep, 'I had such delightful sleep myself last night; I pinned the charm to the breast of my nightdress. It was too far away the night before.'

'And what do you think the charm is?' said I.

'It has been fumigated or immersed in some drug, and is an antidote against the malaria,' she answered.

'Then it acts only on the body?'

'Certainly; you don't suppose that evil spirits are frightened by bits of ribbon, or the perfumes of a druggist's shop? No, these complaints, wandering in the air, begin by trying the nerves, and so infect the brain; but before they can seize upon you, the antidote repels them. That I am sure is what the charm has done for us. It is nothing magical, it is simply natural.'

I should have been happier if I could quite have agreed with Carmilla, but I did my best, and the impression was a little losing its force.

For some nights I slept profoundly; but still every morning I felt the same lassitude, and a languor weighed upon me all day. I felt myself a changed girl. A strange melancholy was stealing over me, a melancholy that I would not have interrupted. Dim thoughts of death began to open, and an idea that I was slowly sinking took gentle, and, somehow, not unwelcome possession of me. If it was sad, the tone of mind which this induced was also sweet. Whatever it might be, my soul acquiesced in it.

I would not admit that I was ill, I would not consent to tell my papa, or to have the doctor sent for.

Camilla became more devoted to me than ever, and her strange paroxysms of languid adoration more frequent. She used to gloat on me with increasing ardour the more my strength and spirits waned. This always shocked me like a momentary glare of insanity.

Certain vague and strange sensations visited me in my sleep. The prevailing one was of that pleasant, peculiar cold thrill which we feel in bathing, when we move against the current of a river. This was soon accompanied by dreams that seemed interminable, and were so vague that I could never recollect their scenery and persons, or any one connected portion of their action. But they left an awful impression, and a sense of exhaustion, as if I had passed through a long period of great mental exertion and danger. After all these dreams there remained on waking a remembrance of having been in a place very nearly dark, and of having spoken to people whom I could not see; and especially of one clear voice, of a female's, very deep, that spoke as if at a distance, slowly, and producing always the same sensation of indescribable solemnity and fear. Sometimes there came a sensation as if a hand was drawn softly along my cheek and neck. Sometimes it was as if warm lips kissed me, and longer and more lovingly as they reached my throat, but there the caress fixed itself. My heart beat faster, my breathing rose and fell rapidly and full drawn; a sobbing, that rose into a sense of strangulation, supervened, and turned into a dreadful convulsion, in which my senses left me, and I became unconscious.

My father asked me often whether I was ill; but, with an obstinacy which now seems to me unaccountable, I persisted in assuring him that I was quite well.

In a sense this was true. I had no pain, I could complain of no bodily derangement. My complaint seemed to be one of the imagination, or the nerves, and, horrible as my sufferings were, I kept them, with a morbid reserve, very nearly to myself.

It could not be that terrible complaint which the peasants call the oupire, for I had now been suffering for three weeks, and they were seldom ill for much more than three days, when death put an end to their miseries.

One night, instead of the voice I was accustomed to hear in the dark, I heard one, sweet and tender, and at the same time terrible, which said, 'Your mother warns you to beware of the assassin.' At the same time a light unexpectedly sprang up, and I saw Carmilla, standing, near the foot of my bed, in her white nightdress, bathed, from her chin to her feet, in one great stain of blood.

I wakened with a shriek, possessed with the one idea that Carmilla was being murdered. I remember springing from my bed, and my next recollection is that of standing on the lobby, crying for help.

Madame and Mademoiselle came scurrying out of their rooms in alarm; a lamp burned always on the lobby, and seeing me, they soon learned the cause of my terror.

I insisted on our knocking at Carmilla's door. Our knocking was unanswered. It soon became a pounding and an uproar. We shrieked her name, but all was vain.

We all grew frightened, for the door was locked. We hurried back, in panic, to my room. There we rang the bell long and furiously. If my father's room had been at that side of the house, we would have called him up at once to our aid. But, alas! he was quite out of hearing, and to reach him involved an excursion for which we none of us had courage.

Servants, however, soon came running up the stairs; I had got on my dressing-gown and slippers meanwhile, and my companions were already similarly furnished. Recognizing the voices of the servants on the lobby, we sallied out together; and having renewed, as fruitlessly, our summons at Carmilla's door, I ordered the men to force the lock. They did so, and we stood, holding our lights aloft, in the doorway, and so stared into the room.

We called her by name; but there was still no reply. We looked round the room. Everything was undisturbed. It was exactly in the state in which I left it on bidding her good night. But Carmilla was gone.

VIII. SEARCH

At sight of the room, perfectly undisturbed except for our violent entrance, we began to cool a little, and soon recovered our senses sufficiently to dismiss the men. It had struck Mademoiselle that possibly Carmilla had been wakened by the uproar at her door, and in her first panic had jumped from her bed, and hid herself in a press, or behind a curtain, from which she could not, of course, emerge until the major-domo and his myrmidons had withdrawn. We now recommenced our search, and began to call her by name again.

It was all to no purpose. Our perplexity and agitation increased. We examined the windows, but they were secured. I implored of Carmilla, if she had concealed herself, to play this cruel trick no longer – to come out, and to end our anxieties. It was all useless.

It was past four o'clock, and I preferred passing the remaining hours of darkness in Madame's room. Daylight brought no solution of the difficulty.

The whole household, with my father at its head, was in a state of agitation next morning. Every part of the château was searched. The grounds were explored. Not a trace of the missing lady could be discovered. The stream was about to be dragged; my father was in distraction; what a tale to have to tell the poor girl's mother on her return. I, too, was almost beside myself, though my grief was quite of a different kind.

The morning was passed in alarm and excitement. It was now one o'clock, and still no tidings. I ran up to Carmilla's room, and found her standing at her dressing-table. I was astounded. I could not believe my eyes. She beckoned me to her with her pretty finger, in silence. Her face expressed extreme fear.

I ran to her in an ecstasy of joy; I kissed and embraced her again and again. I ran to the bell and rang it vehemently, to bring others to the spot, who might at once relieve my father's anxiety.

'Dear Carmilla, what has become of you all this time? We have been in agonies of anxiety about you,' I exclaimed. 'Where have you been? How did you come back?'

'Last night has been a night of wonders,' she said.

'For mercy's sake, explain all you can.'

'It was past two last night,' she said, 'when I went to sleep as usual in my bed, with my doors locked, that of the dressing-room, and that opening upon the gallery. My sleep was uninterrupted, and, so far as I know, dreamless; but I awoke just now on the sofa in the dressing-room there, and I found the door between the rooms open, and the other door forced. How could all this have happened without my being wakened? It must have been accompanied with a great deal of noise, and I am particularly easily wakened; and how could I have been carried out of my bed without my sleep having been interrupted, I whom the slightest stir startles?'

By this time, Madame, Mademoiselle, my father, and a number of the servants were in the room. Carmilla was, of course, overwhelmed with inquiries, congratulations, and welcomes. She had but one story to tell, and seemed the least able of all the party to suggest any way of accounting for what had happened.

My father took a turn up and down the room, thinking. I saw Carmilla's eye follow him for a moment with a sly, dark glance.

When my father had sent the servants away he came to Carmilla thoughtfully, took her hand very kindly, led her to the sofa, and sat down beside her.

'Will you forgive me, my dear, if I risk a conjecture, and ask a question?'

'Who can have a better right?' she said. 'Ask what you please, and I will tell you everything. But my story is simply one of bewilderment and darkness. I know absolutely nothing. Put any question you please. But you know, of course, the limitations mamma has placed me under.'

'Perfectly, my dear child. I need not approach the topics on which she desires our silence.'

Carmilla was leaning on her hand dejectedly. Madame and I were listening breathlessly.

'Now, my question is this. Have you ever been suspected of walking in your sleep?'

'Never since I was very young indeed.'

'But you did walk in your sleep when you were young?'

'Yes; I know I did. I have been told so often by my old nurse.'

My father smiled and nodded.

'Well, what has happened is this. You got up in your sleep, unlocked the door, not leaving the key as usual, in the lock, but taking it out and leaving it on the outside; you again took the key out and carried it away with you to some one of the five and twenty rooms on this floor, or perhaps upstairs or downstairs. There are so many rooms and closets, so much heavy furniture, and such accumulations of lumber, that it would require a week to search this old house thoroughly. Do you see, now, what I mean?'

'I do, but not all,' she answered.

'And how, papa, do you account for her finding herself on the sofa in the dressing-room, which we had searched so carefully?'

'She came there after you had searched it, still in her sleep, and at last awoke spontaneously, and was as much surprised to find herself where she was as anyone else. I wish all mysteries were as easily and innocently explained as yours, Carmilla,' he said, laughing.

Carmilla was looking charmingly. Nothing could be more beautiful than her tints. Her beauty was, I think, enhanced by that graceful languor that was peculiar to her. I think my father was silently contrasting her looks with mine, for he said:

'I wish my poor Laura was looking more like herself,' and he sighed.

So our alarms were happily ended, and Carmilla restored to her friends.

IX. THE DOCTOR

As Carmilla would not hear of an attendant sleeping in her room, my father arranged that a servant should sleep outside her door, so that she could not attempt to make another such excursion without being arrested at her own door.

That night passed quietly; and next morning early, the doctor, whom my father had sent for without telling me a word about it, arrived to see me.

I told him my story, and as I proceeded he grew graver and graver.

After a minute's reflection, he asked Madame if he could see my father.

He was sent for accordingly, and as he entered, smiling, he said:

'I dare say, doctor, you are going to tell me that I am an old fool for having brought you here; I hope I am.'

But his smile faded into shadow as the doctor, with a very grave face, beckoned him to him.

He and the doctor talked for some time in the same recess where I had just conferred with the physician. It seemed an earnest and argumentative conversation. The room is very large, and I and Madame stood together, burning with curiosity, at the farther end. Not a word could we hear, however, for they spoke in a very low tone, and the deep recess of the window quite concealed the doctor from view, and very nearly my father, whose foot, arm, and shoulder only could we see; and the voices were, I suppose, all the less audible for the sort of closet which the thick wall and window formed.

After a time my father's face looked into the room; it was pale, thoughtful, and, I fancied, agitated.

'Laura dear, come here for a moment. Madame, we shan't trouble you, the doctor says, at present.'

My father held out his hand to me as I drew near, but he was looking at the doctor, and he said:

'It certainly *is* very odd; I don't understand it quite. Laura, come here, dear; now attend to Doctor Spielsberg, and recollect yourself.'

'You mentioned a sensation like that of two needles piercing the skin, somewhere about your neck, on the night when you experienced your first horrible dream. Is there still any soreness?'

'None at all,' I answered.

'Can you indicate with your finger about the point at which you think this occurred?'

'Very little below my throat – *here*,' I answered.

I wore a morning dress, which covered the place I pointed to.

'Now you can satisfy yourself,' said the doctor. 'You won't mind your papa lowering your dress a very little. It is necessary, to detect a symptom of the complaint under which you have been suffering.'

I acquiesced. It was an inch or two below the edge of my collar.

'God bless me! – so it is,' exclaimed my father, growing pale.

'You see it now with your own eyes,' said the doctor, with a gloomy triumph.

'What is it?' I exclaimed, beginning to be frightened.

'Nothing, my dear young lady, but a small blue spot, about the size of the tip of your little finger; and now,' he continued, turning to papa, 'the question is what is best to be done?'

'Is there any danger?' I urged, in great trepidation.

'I trust not, my dear,' answered the doctor. 'I don't see why you should not recover. I don't see why you should not begin *immediately* to get better. That is the point at which the sense of strangulation begins?'

'Yes,' I answered.

'And – recollect as well as you can – the same point was a kind of centre of that thrill which you described just now, like the current of a cold stream running against you?'

'It may have been; I think it was.'

The doctor called Madame to him, and said:

'I find my young friend here far from well. It won't be of any great consequence, I hope; but it will be necessary that some steps be taken, which I will explain by and by; but in the meantime, Madame, you will be so good as not to let Miss Laura be alone for one moment. This is the only direction I need give for the present. It is indispensable.'

'We may rely upon your kindness, Madame, I know,' added my father.

Madame satisfied him eagerly.

'And you, dear Laura, I know you will observe the doctor's direction.'

'I shall have to ask your opinion upon another patient, whose symptoms slightly resemble those of my daughter, that have just been detailed to you – very much milder in degree, but I believe quite the same sort. She is a young lady

– our guest; but as you say you will be passing this way again this evening, you can't do better than take your supper here, and you can then see her. She does not come down till the afternoon.'

'I thank you,' said the doctor. 'I shall be with you, then, at about seven this evening.'

The doctor did not return. I saw him mount his horse there, take his leave, and ride away eastward through the forest. Nearly at the same time I saw the man arrive from Dranfeld with the letters, and dismount and hand the bag to my father.

About half an hour after my father came in – he had a letter in his hand – and said:

'This letter had been delayed; it is from General Spielsdorf. He might have been here yesterday, he may not come till tomorrow, or he may be here today.'

He put the open letter into my hand; but he did not look pleased, as he used to when a guest, especially one so much loved as the General, was coming. On the contrary, he looked as if he wished him at the bottom of the Red Sea. There was plainly something on his mind which he did not choose to divulge.

'Does the doctor think me very ill?'

'No, dear; he thinks, if right steps are taken, you will be quite well again, at least on the high road to a complete recovery, in a day or two,' he answered, a little dryly. 'I wish our good friend, the General, had chosen any other time; that is, I wish you had been perfectly well to receive him.'

'But do tell me, papa,' I insisted, '*what* does he think is the matter with me?'

'Nothing; you must not plague me with questions,' he answered, with more irritation than I ever remember him to have displayed before; and seeing that I looked wounded, I suppose, he kissed me, and added, 'You shall know all about it in a day or two; that is, all that *I* know. In the meantime, you are not to trouble your head about it.'

He turned and left the room, but came back before I had done wondering and puzzling over the oddity of all this; it was merely to say that he was going to Karnstein, and had ordered the carriage to be ready at twelve, and that I and Madame should accompany him; he was going to see the priest who lived near those picturesque grounds, upon business, and as Carmilla had never seen them, she could follow, when she came down, with Mademoiselle, who would bring materials for what you call a picnic, which might be laid for us in the ruined castle.

At twelve o'clock, accordingly, I was ready, and not long after, my father, Madame and I set out upon our projected drive. Passing the drawbridge we turn to the right, and follow the road over the steep Gothic bridge, westward, to reach the deserted village and ruined castle of Karnstein.

No sylvan drive can be fancied prettier. The ground breaks into gentle hills and hollows, all clothed with beautiful wood, totally destitute of the comparative formality which artificial planting and early culture and pruning impart.

The irregularities of the ground often lead the road out of its course, and cause it to wind beautifully round the sides of broken hollows and the steeper sides of the hills, among varieties of ground almost inexhaustible.

Turning one of these points, we suddenly encountered our old friend, the General, riding towards us, attended by a mounted servant. His portmanteaus were following in a hired wagon, such as we term a cart.

The General dismounted as we pulled up, and, after the usual greetings, was easily persuaded to accept the vacant seat in the carriage, and send his horse on with his servant to the schloss.

X. BEREAVED

It was about ten months since we had last seen him; but that had sufficed to make an alteration of years in his appearance. He had grown thinner; something of gloom and anxiety had taken place of that cordial serenity which used to characterize his features. His dark blue eyes, always penetrating, now gleamed with a sterner light from under his shaggy grey eyebrows. It was not such a change as grief alone usually induces, and angrier passions seemed to have had their share in bringing it about.

We had not long resumed our drive, when the General began to talk, with his usual soldierly directness, of the bereavement, as he termed it, which he had sustained in the death of his beloved niece and ward; and he then broke out in a tone of intense bitterness and fury, inveighing against the 'hellish arts' to which she had fallen a victim, and expressing with more exasperation than piety, his wonder that Heaven should tolerate so monstrous an indulgence of the lusts and malignity of hell.

My father, who saw at once that something very extraordinary had befallen, asked him, if not too painful to him, to detail the circumstances which he thought justified the strong terms in which he expressed himself.

'I should tell you all with pleasure,' said the General, 'but you would not believe me.'

'Why should I not?' he asked.

'Because,' he answered testily, 'you believe in nothing but what consists with your own prejudices and illusions. I remember when I was like you, but I have learned better.'

'Try me,' said my father; 'I am not such a dogmatist as you suppose. Besides which, I very well know that you generally require proof for what you believe, and am, therefore, very strongly predisposed to respect your conclusions.'

'You are right in supposing that I have not been led lightly into a belief in the marvellous – for what I have experienced *is* marvellous – and I have been forced by extraordinary evidence to credit that which ran counter, diametrically, to all my theories. I have been made the dupe of a preternatural conspiracy.'

Notwithstanding his professions of confidence in the General's penetration, I saw my father, at this point, glance at the General, with, as I thought, a marked suspicion of his sanity.

The General did not see it, luckily. He was looking gloomily and curiously into the glades and vistas of the woods that were opening before us.

'You are going to the Ruins of Karnstein?' he said. 'Yes, it is a lucky coincidence; do you know I was going to ask you to bring me there to inspect them. I have a special object in exploring. There is a ruined chapel, ain't there, with a great many tombs of that extinct family?'

'So there are – highly interesting', said my father. 'I hope you are thinking of claiming the title and estates?'

My father said this gaily, but the General did not recollect the laugh, or even the smile, which courtesy exacts for a friend's joke; on the contrary, he looked grave and even fierce, ruminating on a matter that stirred his anger and horror.

'Something very different,' he said gruffly. 'I mean to unearth some of those fine people. I hope, by God's blessing, to accomplish a pious sacrilege here, which will relieve our earth of certain monsters, and enable honest people to sleep in their beds without being assailed by murderers. I have strange things to tell you, my dear friend, such as I myself would have scouted as incredible a few months since.'

My father looked at him again, but this time not with a glance of suspicion – with an eye, rather, of keen intelligence and alarm.

'The house of Karnstein,' he said, 'has been long extinct: a hundred years at least My dear wife was maternally descended from the Karnsteins. But the name and title have long ceased to exist. The castle is a ruin; the very village is deserted; it is fifty years since the smoke of a chimney was seen there; not a roof left.'

'Quite true. I have heard a great deal about that since I last saw you; a great deal that will astonish you. But I had better relate everything in the order in which it occurred,' said the General.

'You saw my dear ward – my child, I may call her. No creature could have been more beautiful, and only three months ago none more blooming.'

'Yes, poor thing! when I saw her last she certainly was quite lovely,' said my father. 'I was grieved and shocked more than I can tell you, my dear friend; I knew what a blow it was to you.'

He took the General's hand, and they exchanged a kind pressure. Tears gathered in the old soldier's eyes. He did not seek to conceal them. He said:

'We have been very old friends; I knew you would feel for me, childless as I am. She had become an object of very dear interest to me, and repaid my care by an affection that cheered my home and made my life happy. That is all gone. The years that remain to me on earth may not be very long; but by God's mercy I hope to accomplish a service to mankind before I die, and to subserve the vengeance of Heaven upon the fiends who have murdered my poor child in the spring of her hopes and beauty!'

By this time we had reached the point at which the Drunstall road, by which the General had come, diverges from the road which we were travelling to Karnstein.

'How far is it to the ruins?' inquired the General, looking anxiously forward.

'About half a league,' answered my father. 'Pray let us hear the story you were so good as to promise.'

XI. THE STORY

'With all my heart,' said the General, with an effort; and after a short pause in which to arrange his subject, he commenced one of the strangest narratives I ever heard.

'My dear child was looking forward with great pleasure to the visit you had been so good as to arrange for her to your charming daughter.' Here he made me a gallant but melancholy bow. 'In the meantime we had an invitation to my old friend the Count Carlsfeld, whose schloss is about six leagues to the other side of Karnstein. It was to attend the series of fêtes which, you remember, were given by him in honour of his illustrious visitor, the Grand Duke Charles.'

'Yes; and very splendid, I believe, they were,' said my father.

'Princely! The night from which my sorrow dates was devoted to a magnificent masquerade. The grounds were thrown open, the trees hung with coloured lamps. There was such a display of fireworks as Paris itself had never witnessed. And such music – music, you know, is my weakness – such ravishing music! The finest instrumental band, perhaps, in the world, and the finest singers who could be collected from all the great operas in Europe. As you wandered through these fantastically illuminated grounds, the moon-lighted château throwing a rosy light from its long rows of windows, you would suddenly hear these ravishing voices stealing from the silence of some grove, or rising from boats upon the lake.

'When the fireworks were ended, and the ball beginning, we returned to the noble suite of rooms that were thrown open to the dancers. A masked ball, you know, is a beautiful sight; but so brilliant a spectacle of the kind I never saw before.

'My dear child was looking quite beautiful. She wore no mask. Her excitement and delight added an unspeakable charm to her features, always lovely. I remarked a young lady, dressed magnificently, but wearing a mask, who appeared to me to be observing my ward with extraordinary interest. I had seen her, earlier in the evening, in the great hall, and again, for a few minutes, walking near us, on the terrace under the castle windows, similarly employed. A lady, also masked, richly and gravely dressed, and with a stately air, like a person of rank, accompanied her as a chaperon. Had the young lady not worn a mask, I could, of course, have been much more certain upon the question whether she was really watching my poor darling. I am now well assured that she was.

'We were now in one of the *salons*. My poor dear child had been dancing, and was resting a little in one of the chairs near the door; I was standing near. The two ladies I have mentioned had approached, and the younger took the chair next my ward; while her companion stood beside me, and for a little time addressed herself, in a low tone, to her charge.

'Availing herself of the privilege of her mask, she turned to me, and in the tone of an old friend, and calling me by my name, opened a conversation with me, which piqued my curiosity a good deal. She referred to many scenes where she had met me – at Court, and at distinguished houses. She alluded to little incidents which I had long ceased to think of, but which, I found, had only lain in abeyance in my memory, for they instantly started into life at her touch.

'In the meantime the young lady, whom her mother called by the odd name of Millarca, when she once or twice addressed her, had, with the same ease and grace, got into conversation with my ward.

'She introduced herself by saying that her mother was a very old acquaintance of mine. She spoke of the agreeable audacity which a mask rendered practicable; she talked like a friend; she admired her dress, and insinuated very prettily her admiration of her beauty. She was very witty and lively when she pleased, and after a time they had grown very good friends, and the young stranger lowered her mask, displaying a remarkably beautiful face. I had never seen it before, neither had my dear child. But though it was new to us, the features were so engaging, as well as lovely, that it was impossible not to feel the attraction powerfully.

'In the meantime, availing myself of the licence of a masquerade, I put not a few questions to the elder lady.

'"You have puzzled me utterly," I said, laughing. "Is that not enough? Won't you, now, consent to stand on equal terms, and do me the kindness to remove your mask?"

'"Can any request be more unreasonable?" she replied. "Ask a lady to yield an advantage! Beside, how do you know you should recognize me? Years make changes."

'"As you see," I said, with a bow, and, I suppose, a rather melancholy little laugh.

'"As philosophers tell us," she said; "and how do you know that a sight of my face would help you?"

'"I should take chance for that," I answered. "It is vain trying to make yourself out an old woman; your figure betrays you."

'"Years, nevertheless, have passed since I saw you, rather since you saw me, for that is what I am considering. Millarca, there, is my daughter; I cannot then be young, even in the opinion of people whom time has taught to be indulgent, and I may not like to be compared with what you remember me. You have no mask to remove. You can offer me nothing in exchange."

'"My petition is to your pity, to remove it."

'"And mine to yours, to let it stay where it is," she replied.

'"At all events, you won't deny this," I said, 'that being honoured by your permission to converse, I ought to know how to address you. Shall I say Madame la Comtesse?"

'"As to that," she began; but she was interrupted, almost as she opened her lips, by a gentleman, dressed in black, who looked particularly elegant and distinguished, with this drawback, that his face was the most deadly pale I ever saw, except in death. He was in no masquerade – in the plain evening dress of a gentleman; and he said, without a smile, but with a courtly and unusually low bow:

'"Will Madame la Comtesse permit me to say a very few words which may interest her?"

'The lady turned quickly to him, and touched her lip in token of silence; she then said to me, "Keep my place for me, General; I shall return when I have said a few words."

'And with this injunction, playfully given, she walked a little aside with the gentleman in black, and talked for some minutes, apparently very earnestly. They then walked away slowly together in the crowd, and I lost them for some minutes.

'I spent the interval in cudgelling my brains for conjecture as to the identity of the lady who seemed to remember me so kindly, and I was thinking of turning about and joining in the conversation between my pretty ward and the Countess's daughter, but at this moment she returned, accompanied by the pale man in black, who said:

'"I shall return and inform Madame la Comtesse when her carriage is at the door."

'He withdrew with a bow.'

XII. A PETITION

'"Then we are to lose Madame la Comtesse, but I hope only for a few hours," I said, with a low bow.

'"It may be that only, or it may be a few weeks. It was very unlucky his speaking to me just now as he did. Do you now know me?"

'I assured her I did not.

"'You shall know me," she said, "but not at present. We are older and better friends than, perhaps, you suspect. I cannot yet declare myself. I shall in three weeks pass your beautiful schloss about which I have been making inquiries. I shall then look in upon you for an hour or two, and renew a friendship which I never think of without a thousand pleasant recollections. This moment a piece of news has reached me like a thunderbolt. I must set out now, and travel by a devious route, nearly a hundred miles, with all the dispatch I can possibly make. My perplexities multiply. I am only deterred by the compulsory service I practise as to my name from making a very singular request of you. My poor child has not quite recovered her strength. Her horse fell with her, at a hunt which she had ridden out to witness, her nerves have not yet recovered the shock, and our physician says that she must on no account exert herself for some time to come. We came here, in consequence, by very easy stages – hardly six leagues a day. I must now travel day and night, on a mission of life and death – a mission the critical and momentous nature of which I shall be able to explain to you when we meet, as I hope we shall, in a few weeks, without the necessity of any concealment."

'She went on to make her petition, and it was in the tone of a person from whom such a request amounted to conferring, rather than seeking a favour. It was simply that I would consent to take charge of her daughter during her absence.

'This was, all things considered, a strange, not to say, an audacious request. She in some sort disarmed me, by stating and admitting everything that could be urged against it, and throwing herself entirely upon my chivalry. At the same moment, by a fatality that seems to have predetermined all that happened, my poor child came to my side, and, in an undertone, besought me to invite her new friend, Millarca, to pay us a visit. She had just been sounding her, and thought, if her mamma would allow her, she would like it extremely.

'At another time I should have told her to wait a little, until, at least, we knew who they were. But I had not a moment to think in. The two ladies assailed me together, and I must confess the refined and beautiful face of the young lady, about which there was something extremely engaging, as well as the elegance and fire of high birth, determined me; and quite overpowered, I submitted, and undertook, too easily, the care of the young lady, whom her mother called Millarca.

'The Countess beckoned to her daughter, who listened with grave attention while she told her, in general terms, how suddenly and peremptorily she had been summoned, and also of the arrangement she had made for her under my care, adding that I was one of her earliest and most valued friends.

'The gentleman in black returned, and very ceremoniously conducted the lady from the room.

'The demeanour of this gentleman was such as to impress me with the conviction that the Countess was a lady of very much more importance than her modest title alone might have led me to assume.

'Her last charge to me was that no attempt was to be made to learn more about her than I might have already guessed, until her return. Our distinguished host, whose guest she was, knew her reasons.

' "But here," she said, "neither I nor my daughter could safely remain for more than a day. I removed my mask imprudently for a moment, about an hour ago, and, too late, I fancied you saw me. So I resolved to seek an opportunity of talking to you. Had I found that you *had* seen me, I should have thrown myself on your high sense of honour to keep my secret for some weeks. As it is, I am satisfied that you did not see me; but if you now *suspect*, or, on reflection, *should* suspect, who I am, I commit myself, in like manner, entirely to your honour. My daughter will observe the same secrecy, and I well know that you will, from time to time, remind her, lest she should thoughtlessly disclose it."

'She whispered a few words to her daughter, kissed her hurriedly twice, and went away, accompanied by the pale gentleman in black, and disappeared in the crowd.

' "In the next room," said Millarca, "there is a window that looks upon the hall door. I should like to see the last of mamma, and to kiss my hand to her."

'We assented, of course, and accompanied her to the window. We looked out, and saw a handsome old-fashioned carriage, with a troop of couriers and footmen. We saw the slim figure of the pale gentleman in black, as he held a thick velvet cloak, and placed it about her shoulders and threw the hood over her head. She nodded to him, and just touched his hand with hers. He bowed low repeatedly as the door closed, and the carriage began to move.

' "She is gone," said Millarca, with a sigh.

' "She is gone," I repeated to myself, for the first time – in the hurried moments that had elapsed since my consent – reflecting upon the folly of my act.

' "She did not look up," said the young lady, plaintively.

' "The Countess had taken off her mask, perhaps, and did not care to show her face," I said; "and she could not know that you were in the window."

'She sighed and looked in my face. She was so beautiful that I relented. I was sorry I had for a moment repented of my hospitality, and I determined to make her amends for the unavowed churlishness of my reception.

'The young lady, replacing her mask, joined my ward in persuading me to return to the grounds, where the concert was soon to be renewed. Millarca became very intimate with us, and amused us with lively descriptions and stories of most of the great people whom we saw upon the terrace. I liked her more and more every minute.

'This ball was not over until the morning sun had almost reached the horizon. It pleased the Grand Duke to dance till then, so loyal people could not go away, or think of bed.

'We had just got through a crowded saloon, when my ward asked me what had become of Millarca. I thought she had been by her side, and she fancied she was by mine. The fact was, we had lost her.

'All my efforts to find her were vain. I feared that she had mistaken, in the confusion of a momentary separation from us, other people for new friends, and had, possibly, pursued and lost them in the extensive grounds which were thrown open to us.

'Morning broke. It was clear daylight before I gave up my search. It was not till two o'clock next day that we heard anything of my missing charge.

'At about that time a servant knocked at my niece's door, to say that he had been earnestly requested by a young lady, who appeared to be in great distress, to make out where she could find the General Baron Spielsdorf and the young lady, his daughter, in whose charge she had been left by her mother.

'There could be no doubt, notwithstanding the slight inaccuracy, that our young friend had turned up; and so she had. Would to Heaven we had lost her!

'She told my poor child a story to account for her having failed to recover us for so long. Very late, she said, she had got into the housekeeper's bedroom in despair of finding us, and had then fallen into a deep sleep which, long as it was, had hardly sufficed to recruit her strength after the fatigues of the ball.

'That day Millarca came home with us. I was only too happy, after all, to have secured so charming a companion for my dear girl.

XIII. THE WOOD-MAN

'There soon, however, appeared some drawbacks. In the first place, Millarca complained of extreme languor – the weakness that remained after her late illness – and she never emerged from her room till the afternoon was pretty far advanced. In the next place, it was accidentally discovered, although she always locked her door on the inside, that she was undoubtedly sometimes absent from her room in the very early morning, and at various times later in the day, before she wished it to be understood that she was stirring. She was repeatedly seen from the windows of the schloss, in the first faint grey of the morning, walking through the trees, in an easterly direction, and looking like a person in a trance. This convinced me that she walked in her sleep. But this hypothesis did not solve the puzzle. How did she pass out from her room, leaving the door locked on the inside? How did she escape from the house without unbarring door or window?

'In the midst of my perplexities, an anxiety of a far more urgent kind presented itself.

'My dear child began to lose her looks and health, and that in a manner so mysterious, and even horrible, that I became thoroughly frightened

'She was at first visited by appalling dreams; then, as she fancied, by a spectre, sometimes resembling Millarca, sometimes in the shape of a beast, indistinctly seen, walking round the foot of her bed, from side to side. Lastly came sensations. One, not unpleasant, but very peculiar, she said, resembled the flow of an icy stream against her breast. At a later time, she felt something like a pair of large needles pierce her, a little below the throat, with a very sharp pain. A few nights after, followed a gradual and convulsive sense of strangulation; then came unconsciousness.'

You may guess how strangely I felt as I heard my own symptoms so exactly described in those which had been experienced by the poor girl who, but for the catastrophe which followed, would have been at that moment a visitor at my father's château. You may suppose, also, how I felt as I heard him detail habits and mysterious peculiarities which were, in fact, those of our beautiful guest, Carmilla!

A vista opened in the forest; we were on a sudden under the chimneys and gables of the ruined village, and the towers and battlements of the dismantled castle, round which gigantic trees are grouped, overhung us from a slight eminence.

In a frightened dream I got down from the carriage, and in silence, for we had each abundant matter for thinking; we soon mounted the ascent, and were among the spacious chambers, winding stairs, and dark corridors of the castle.

'And this was once the palatial residence of the Karnsteins!' said the old General at length, as from a great window he looked out across the village, and saw the wide, undulating expanse of forest. 'It was a bad family, and here its bloodstained annals were written,' he continued. 'It is hard that they should, after death, continue to plague the human race with their atrocious lusts. That is the chapel of the Karnsteins, down there.'

He pointed down to the grey walls of the Gothic building, partly visible through the foliage, a little way down the steep. 'And I hear the axe of a wood-man,' he added, 'busy among the trees that surround it; he possibly may give us the information of which I am in search, and point out the grave of Mircalla, Countess of Karnstein.'

'We have a portrait, at home, of Mircalla, the Countess Karnstein; should you like to see it?' asked my father.

'Time enough, dear friend,' replied the General. 'I believe that I have seen the original; and one motive which has led me to you earlier than I at first intended, was to explore the chapel which we are now approaching.'

'What! see the Countess Mircalla,' exclaimed my father; 'why, she has been dead more than a century!'

'Not so dead as you fancy, I am told,' answered the General.

'I confess, General, you puzzle me utterly,' replied my father, looking at him, I fancied, for a moment with a return of the suspicion I detected before. But although there was anger and detestation, at times, in the old General's manner, there was nothing flighty.

'There remains to me,' he said, as we passed under the heavy arch of the Gothic church – for its dimensions would have justified its being so styled – 'but one object which can interest me during the few years that remain to me on earth, and that is to wreak on her the vengeance which, I thank God, may still be accomplished by a mortal arm.'

'What vengeance can you mean?' asked my father, in increasing amazement.

'I mean, to decapitate the monster,' he answered, with a fierce flush, and a stamp that echoed mournfully through the hollow ruin, and his clenched hand was at the same moment raised, as if it grasped the handle of an axe, while he shook it ferociously in the air.

'What!' exclaimed my father, more than ever bewildered.

'To strike her head off.'

'Cut her head off!'

'Aye, with a hatchet, with a spade, or with anything that can cleave through her murderous throat. You shall hear,' he answered, trembling with rage.

The General called to the wood-man, who had been removing some boughs which leaned upon the old walls; and, axe in hand, the hardy old fellow stood before us.

He could not tell us anything of these monuments; but there was an old man, he said, a ranger of this forest, at present sojourning in the house of the priest, about two miles away who could point out every monument of the old Karnstein family; and, for a trifle, he undertook to bring him back with him, if we would lend him one of our horses, in little more than half an hour.

'Have you been long employed about this forest?' asked my father of the old man.

'I have been a wood-man here,' he answered in his *patois*, 'under the forester, all my days; so has my father before me, and so on, as many generations as I can count up. I could show you the very house in the village here, in which my ancestors lived.'

'How came the village to be deserted?' asked the General.

'It was troubled by *revenants*, sir; several were tracked to their graves, there detected by the usual tests, and extinguished in the usual way, by decapitation, by the stake, and by burning; but not until many of the villagers were killed.

'But after all these proceedings according to law,' he continued – 'so many graves opened, and so many vampires deprived of their horrible animation – the village was not relieved. But a Moravian nobleman, who happened to be travelling this way, heard how matters were, and being skilled – as many people are in his country – in such affairs, he offered to deliver the village from its tormentor. He did so thus: There being a bright moon that night, he ascended, shortly after sunset, the tower of the chapel here, from whence he could distinctly see the churchyard beneath him; you can see it from that window. From this point he watched until he saw the vampire come out of his grave, and place near it the linen clothes in which he had been folded, and glide away towards the village to plague its inhabitants.

'The stranger, having seen all this, came down from the steeple, took the linen wrappings of the vampire, and carried them up to the top of the tower, which he again mounted. When the vampire returned from his prowlings and missed his clothes, he cried furiously to the Moravian, whom he saw at the summit of the tower, and who, in reply, beckoned him to ascend and take them. Whereupon the vampire, accepting his invitation, began to climb the steeple, and so soon as he had reached the battlements, the Moravian, with a stroke of his sword, clove his skull in twain, hurling him down to the churchyard, whither, descending by the winding stairs, the stranger followed and cut his head off, and next day delivered it and the body to the villagers, who duly impaled and burnt them.

'This Moravian nobleman had authority from the then head of the family to remove the tomb of Mircalla, Countess Karnstein, which he did effectually, so that in a little while its site was quite forgotten.'

'Can you point out where it stood?' asked the General, eagerly.

The forester shook his head and smiled.

'Not a soul living could tell you that now,' he said; 'besides, they say her body was removed; but no one is sure of that either.'

Having thus spoken, as time pressed, he dropped his axe and departed, leaving us to hear the remainder of the General's strange story.

XIV. THE MEETING

'My beloved child,' he resumed, 'was now growing rapidly worse. The physician who attended her had failed to produce the slightest impression upon her disease, for such I then supposed it to be. I called in an abler physician, from Gratz. Several days elapsed before he arrived. Having seen my poor ward together, they withdrew to my library to confer and discuss. I, from the adjoining room, where I awaited their summons, heard these two gentleman's voices raised in something sharper than a strictly philosophical discussion. I knocked at the door and entered. I found the old physician from Gratz maintaining his theory. His rival was combating it with undisguised ridicule, accompanied with bursts of laughter. This unseemly manifestation subsided and the altercation ended on my entrance.

'"Sir," said my first physician, "my learned brother seems to think that you want a conjuror, and not a doctor."

'"Pardon me," said the old physician from Gratz, looking displeased, "I shall state my own view of the case in my own way another time. I grieve, Monsieur le Général, that by my skill and science I can be of no use. Before I go I shall do myself the honour to suggest something to you."

'He seemed thoughtful, and sat down at a table, and began to write. Profoundly disappointed, I made my bow, and as I turned to go, the other doctor pointed over his shoulder to his companion who was writing, and then, with a shrug, significantly touched his forehead.

'This consultation, then, left me precisely where I was. I walked out into the grounds, all but distracted. The doctor from Gratz, in ten or fifteen minutes, overtook me. He apologized for having followed me, but said that he could not conscientiously take his leave without a few words more. He told me that he could not be mistaken; no natural disease exhibited the same symptoms; and that death was already very near. There remained, however, a day, or possibly two, of life. If the fatal seizure were at once arrested, with great care and skill her strength might possibly return. But all hung now upon the confines of the irrevocable. One more assault might extinguish the last spark of vitality which is, every moment, ready to die.

'"And what is the nature of the seizure you speak of?" I entreated.

'"I have stated all fully in this note, which I place in your hands, upon the distinct condition that you send for the nearest clergyman, and open my letter in his presence, and on no account read it till he is with you; you would despise it else, and it is a matter of life and death. Should the priest fail you, then, indeed, you may read it."

'The ecclesiastic was absent, and I read the letter by myself. At another time, or in another case, it might have excited my ridicule. But into what quackeries will not people rush for a last chance, where all accustomed means have failed, and the life of a beloved object is at stake?

'Nothing, you will say, could be more absurd than the learned man's letter. It was monstrous enough to have consigned him to a madhouse. He said that the patient was suffering from the visits of a vampire! The punctures which she described as having occurred near the throat, were, he insisted, the insertion of those two long, thin, and sharp teeth which, it is well known, are peculiar to vampires; and there could be no doubt, he added, as to the well-defined presence of the small livid mark, which all concurred in describing as that induced by the demon's lips, and every symptom described by the sufferer was in exact conformity with those recorded in every case of a similar visitation.

'Being myself wholly sceptical as to the existence of any such portent as the vampire, the supernatural theory of the good doctor furnished, in my opinion, but another instance of learning and intelligence oddly associated with some one hallucination. I was so miserable, however, that, rather than try nothing, I acted upon the instructions of the letter.

'I concealed myself in the dark dressing-room, that opened upon the poor patient's room, in which a candle was burning, and watched there till she was fast asleep. I stood at the door, peeping through the small crevice, my sword laid on the table beside me, as my directions prescribed, until, a little after one, I saw a large black object, very ill-defined, crawl, as it seemed to me, over the foot of the bed, and swiftly spread itself up to the poor girl's throat, where it swelled, in a moment, into a great palpitating mass.

'For a few moments I had stood petrified. I now sprang forward, with my sword in my hand. The black creature suddenly contracted towards the foot of the bed, glided over it, and, standing on the floor about a yard below the foot of the bed, with a glare of skulking ferocity and horror fixed on me, I saw Millarca. Speculating I know not what, I struck at her instantly with my sword; but I saw her standing near the door, unscathed. Horrified, I pursued, and struck again. She was gone! and my sword flew to shivers against the door.

'I can't describe to you all that passed on that horrible night. The whole house was up and stirring. The spectre Millarca was gone. But her victim was sinking fast, and before the morning dawned, she died.'

The old General was agitated. We did not speak to him. My father walked to some little distance, and began reading the inscriptions on the tombstones; and thus occupied, he strolled into the door of a side chapel to prosecute his researches. The General leaned against the wall, dried his eyes, and sighed heavily. I was relieved on hearing the voices of Carmilla and Madame, who were at that moment approaching. The voices died away.

In this solitude, having just listened to so strange a story, connected, as it was, with the great and titled dead, whose monuments were mouldering among the dust and ivy round us, and every incident of which bore so awfully upon my own mysterious case – in this haunted spot, darkened by the towering foliage that rose on every side, dense and high above its noiseless walls – a horror began to steal over me, and my heart sank as I thought that my friends were, after all, not about to enter and disturb this triste and ominous scene.

The old General's eyes were fixed on the ground, as he leaned with his hand upon the basement of a shattered monument.

Under a narrow, arched doorway, surmounted by one of those demoniacal grotesques in which the cynical and ghastly fancy of old Gothic carving delights, I saw very gladly the beautiful face and figure of Carmilla enter the shadowy chapel.

I was just about to rise and speak, and nodded smiling, in answer to her peculiarly engaging smile; when with a cry, the old man by my side caught up the wood-man's hatchet, and started forward. On seeing him a brutalized change came over her features. It was an instantaneous and horrible transformation, as she made a crouching step backwards. Before I could utter a scream, he struck at her with all his force, but she dived under his blow, and unscathed, caught him in her tiny grasp by the wrist. He struggled for a moment to release his arm, but his hand opened, the axe fell to the ground, and the girl was gone.

He staggered against the wall. His grey hair stood upon his head, and a moisture shone over his face, as if he were at the point of death.

The frightful scene had passed in a moment. The first thing I recollect after, is Madame standing before me, and impatiently repeating again and again, the question, 'Where is Mademoiselle Carmilla?'

I answered at length, 'I don't know – I can't tell – she went there,' and I pointed to the door through which Madame had just entered; 'only a minute or two since.'

'But I have been standing there, in the passage, ever since Mademoiselle Carmilla entered; and she did not return.'

She then began to call 'Carmilla' through every door and passage and from the windows, but no answer came.

'She called herself Carmilla?' asked the General, still agitated.

'Carmilla, yes,' I answered.

'Aye,' he said; 'that is Millarca. That is the same person who long ago was called Mircalla, Countess Karnstein. Depart from this accursed ground, my poor child, as quickly as you can. Drive to the clergyman's house, and stay there till we come. Begone! May you never behold Carmilla more; you will not find her here.'

XV. ORDEAL AND EXECUTION

As he spoke one of the strangest-looking men I ever beheld, entered the chapel at the door through which Carmilla had made her entrance and her exit. He was tall, narrow-chested, stooping, with high shoulders, and dressed in black. His face was brown and dried in with deep furrows; he wore an oddly-shaped hat with a broad leaf. His hair, long and grizzled, hung on his shoulders. He wore a pair of gold spectacles, and walked slowly, with an odd shambling gait, with his face sometimes turned up to the sky, and sometimes bowed down towards the ground, seemed to wear a perpetual smile; his long thin arms were swinging, and his lank hands, in old black gloves ever so much too wide for them, waving and gesticulating in utter abstraction.

'The very man!' exclaimed the General, advancing with manifest delight. 'My dear Baron, how happy I am to see you, I had no hope of meeting you so soon.' He signed to my father, who had by this time returned, and leading the fantastic old gentleman, whom he called the Baron, to meet him. The stranger took a roll of paper from his pocket, and spread it on the worn surface of a tomb that stood by. He had a pencil case in his fingers, with which he traced imaginary lines from point to point on the paper, which I concluded to be a plan of the chapel. He accompanied, what I may term his lecture, with occasional readings from a dirty little book, whose yellow leaves were closely written over.

They sauntered together down the side aisle, opposite to the spot where I was standing, conversing as they went; then they began measuring distances by paces, and finally they all stood together, facing a piece of the side wall, which they began to examine with great minuteness; pulling off the ivy that clung over it, and rapping the plaster with the ends of their sticks, scraping here, and knocking there. At length they ascertained the existence of a broad marble tablet, with letters carved in relief upon it.

With the assistance of the wood-man, who soon returned, a monumental inscription, and carved escutcheon, were disclosed. They proved to be those of the long lost monument of Mircalla, Countess Karnstein.

The old General, though not I fear given to the praying mood, raised his hands and eyes to heaven, in mute thanksgiving for some moments.

'Tomorrow,' I heard him say; 'the commissioner will be here, and the Inquisition will be held according to law.'

Then turning to the old man with the gold spectacles, he

shook him warmly by both hands and said:

'Baron, how can I thank you? How can we all thank you? You will have delivered this region from a plague that has scourged its inhabitants for more than a century. The horrible enemy, thank God, is at last tracked.'

My father led the stranger aside, and the General followed. I knew that he had led them out of hearing, that he might relate my case, and I saw them glance often quickly at me, as the discussion proceeded.

My father came to me, kissed me again and again, and leading me from the chapel, said:

'It is time to return, but before we go home, we must add to our party the good priest, who lives but a little way from this; and persuade him to accompany us to the schloss.'

In this quest we were successful: and I was glad, being unspeakably fatigued, when we reached home. But my satisfaction was changed to dismay, on discovering that there were no tidings of Carmilla. Of the scene that had occurred in the ruined chapel, no explanation was offered to me, and it was clear that it was a secret which my father for the present determined to keep from me.

The sinister absence of Carmilla made the remembrance of the scene more horrible to me. The arrangements for that night were singular. Two servants and Madame were to sit up in my room that night; and the ecclesiastic with my father kept watch in the adjoining dressing-room.

The priest had performed certain solemn rites that night, the purport of which I did not understand any more than I comprehended the reason of this extraordinary precaution taken for my safety during sleep.

I saw all clearly a few days later.

The disappearance of Carmilla was followed by the discontinuance of my nightly sufferings.

You have heard, no doubt, of the appalling superstition that prevails in Upper and Lower Styria, in Moravia, Silesia, in Turkish Servia, in Poland, even in Russia; the superstition, so we must call it, of the vampire.

If human testimony, taken with every care and solemnity, judicially, before commissions innumerable, each consisting of many members, all chosen for integrity and intelligence, and constituting reports more voluminous perhaps than exist upon any one other class of cases, is worth anything, it is difficult to deny, or even to doubt the existence of such a phenomenon as the vampire.

For my part I have heard no theory by which to explain what I myself have witnessed and experienced, other than that supplied by the ancient and well-attested belief of the country.

The next day the formal proceedings took place in the Chapel of Karnstein. The grave of the Countess Mircalla was opened; and the General and my father recognized each his perfidious and beautiful guest, in the face now disclosed to view. The features, though a hundred and fifty years had passed since her funeral, were tinted with the warmth of life. Her eyes were open; no cadaverous smell exhaled from the coffin. The two medical men, one officially present, the other on the part of the promoter of the inquiry, attested the marvellous fact, that there was a faint but appreciable respiration, and a corresponding action of the heart. The limbs were perfectly flexible, the flesh elastic; and the leaden coffin floated with blood, in which to a depth of seven inches, the body lay immersed. Here then, were all the admitted signs and proofs of vampirism. The body, therefore, in accordance with the ancient practice, was raised, and a sharp stake driven through the heart of the vampire, who uttered a piercing shriek at the moment, in all respects such as might escape from a living person in the last agony. Then the head was struck off, and a torrent of blood flowed from the severed neck. The body and head were next placed on a pile of wood, and reduced to ashes, which were thrown upon the river and borne away, and that territory has never since been plagued by the visits of a vampire.

My father has a copy of the report of the Imperial Commission, with the signatures of all who were present at these proceedings, attached in verification of the statement. It is from this official paper that I have summarized my account of this last shocking scene.

XVI. CONCLUSION

I write all this you suppose with composure. But far from it; I cannot think of it without agitation. Nothing but your earnest desire so repeatedly expressed, could have induced me to sit down to a task that has unstrung my nerves for months to come, and reinduced a shadow of the unspeakable horror which years after my deliverance continued to make my days and nights dreadful, and solitude insupportably terrific.

Let me add a word or two about that quaint Baron Vordenburg, to whose curious lore we were indebted for the discovery of the Countess Mircalla's grave.

He had taken up his abode in Gratz, where, living upon a mere pittance, which was all that remained to him of the once princely estates of his family, in Upper Styria, he devoted himself to the minute and laborious investigation of the marvellously authenticated tradition of vampirism. He had at his fingers' ends all the great and little works upon the subject. *Magia Posthuma, Phlegon de Mirabilibus, Augustinus de curâ pro Mortuis, Philosophicae et Christianae Cogitationes de Vampiris,* by John Christofer Herenberg; and a thousand others, among which I remember only a few of those which he lent to my father. He had a voluminous digest of all the judicial cases, from which he had extracted a system of principles that appear to govern – some always, and others occasionally only – the condition of the vampire. I may mention, in passing, that the deadly pallor attributed to that sort of *revenants,* is a mere melodramatic fiction. They present, in the grave, and when they show themselves in human society, the appearance of healthy life. When disclosed to light in their coffins, they exhibit all the symptoms that are enumerated as those which proved the vampire life of the long dead Countess Karnstein.

How they escape from their graves and return to them for certain hours every day, without displacing the clay or leaving any trace of disturbance in the state of the coffin or the cerements, has always been admitted to be utterly inexplicable. The amphibious existence of the vampire is sustained by daily renewed slumber in the grave. Its horrible lust for living blood supplies the vigour of its waking existence. The vampire is prone to be fascinated by an engrossing vehemence, resembling the passion of love, by particular persons. In pursuit of these it will exercise inexhaustible patience and stratagem, for access to a particular object may be obstructed in a hundred ways. It will never desist until it has satiated its passion, and drained the very life of its coveted victim. But it will, in these cases, husband and protract its murderous enjoyment with the refinement of an epicure, and heighten it by the gradual approaches of an artful courtship. In these cases it seems to yearn for something like sympathy and consent. In ordinary ones it goes direct to its object, overpowers with violence, and strangles and exhausts often at a single feast.

The vampire is, apparently, subject, in certain situations, to special conditions. In the particular instance of which I have given you a relation, Mircalla seemed to be limited to a name which, if not her real one, should at least reproduce, without the omission or addition of a single letter, those, as we say, anagrammatically, which compose it. *Carmilla* did this; so did *Millarca.*

My father related to the Baron Vordenburg, who remained with us for two or three weeks after the expulsion of Carmilla, the story about the Moravian nobleman and the vampire at Karnstein churchyard, and then he asked the Baron how he had discovered the exact position of the long-concealed tomb of the Countess Millarca? The Baron's grotesque features puckered up into a mysterious smile; he looked down, still smiling, on his worn spectacle-case and fumbled with it. Then looking up, he said:

'I have many journals, and other papers, written by that remarkable man; the most curious among them is one treating of the visit of which you speak, to Karnstein. The tradition, of course, discolours and distorts a little. He might have been termed a Moravian nobleman, for he had changed his abode to that territory, and was beside, a noble. But he was, in truth, a native of Upper Styria. It is enough to say that in very early youth he had been a passionate and favoured lover of the beautiful Mircalla, Countess Karnstein. Her early death plunged him into inconsolable grief. It is the nature of vampires to increase and multiply, but according to an ascertained and ghostly law.

'Assume, at starting, a territory perfectly free from that pest. How does it begin, and how does it multiply itself? I will tell you. A person, more or less wicked, puts an end to himself. A suicide, under certain circumstances, becomes a vampire. That spectre visits living people in their slumbers; *they* die, and almost invariably, in the grave, develop into vampires. This happened in the case of the beautiful Mircalla, who was haunted by one of those demons. My ancestor, Vordenburg, whose title I still bear, soon discovered this, and in the course of the studies to which he devoted himself, learned a great deal more.

'Among other things, he concluded that suspicion of vampirism would probably fall, sooner or later, upon the dead Countess, who in life had been his idol. He conceived a horror, be she what she might, of her remains being profaned by the outrage of a posthumous execution. He has left a curious paper to prove that the vampire, on its expulsion from its amphibious existence, is projected into a far more horrible life; and he resolved to save his once beloved Mircalla from this.

'He adopted the stratagem of a journey here, a pretended removal of her remains, and a real obliteration of her monument. When age had stolen upon him, and from the vale of years he looked back upon the scenes he was leaving, he considered, in a different spirit, what he had done, and a horror took possession of him. He made the tracings and notes which have guided me to the very spot, and drew up a confession of the deception that he had practised. If he had intended any further action in this matter, death prevented him; and the hand of a remote descendant has, too late for many, directed the pursuit to the lair of the beast.'

We talked a little more, and among other things he said was this:

'One sign of the vampire is the power of the hand. The slender hand of Mircalla closed like a vice of steel on the General's wrist when he raised the hatchet to strike. But its power is not confined to its grasp; it leaves a numbness in the limb it seizes, which is slowly, if ever, recovered from.'

The following Spring my father took me on a tour through Italy. We remained away for more than a year. It was long before the terror of recent events subsided; and to this hour the image of Carmilla returns to memory with ambiguous alternations – sometimes the playful, languid, beautiful girl; sometimes the writhing fiend I saw in the ruined church; and often from a reverie I have started, fancying I heard the light step of Carmilla at the drawing-room door.

THÉOPHILE GAUTIER

THE BEAUTIFUL VAMPIRE

translated by Paul Hookham

YOU ASK me, brother, if I have loved; yes. It is a strange and terrible story, and although I am sixty-six years old, I scarcely dare to stir the ashes of that memory. I am reluctant to refuse any request of yours, but I would not tell such a story to any soul less tempered by experience.

The events are so strange that I cannot believe that they ever happened to me. For more than three years I was the victim of an extraordinary, diabolical obsession. I, a poor country priest, led every night in a dream (pray God it was a dream!) the life of a lost soul, a voluptuary, a Sardanapalus. One single glance thrown at a woman nearly cost me the loss of my soul; but in the end, with the help of God and my patron saint, I was able to drive out the malignant spirit that possessed me. My life was complicated with a nocturnal existence of quite a different nature. During the day I was a priest of the Lord, chaste, occupied in prayer and holy works; at night, from the moment I closed my eyes, I became a young nobleman, a connoisseur of women, dogs and horses, dicing, drinking, blaspheming; and when I awoke at daybreak, it seemed as if I fell asleep and dreamed I was a priest.

Of that nocturnal life I have preserved memories of things and of words which I cannot banish from my mind; and although I have never left the walls of my presbytery, one would say, to hear me talk, that I was a man who had tasted every experience and turned his back on the world, one who had sought refuge in religion and desired to end his troubled days in the bosom of the Church, rather than a humble priest grown old in an obscure parish in the depths of a wood, wholly cut off from the life of the day.

Yes, I have loved as no one in the world has loved, with a mad furious passion, so violent that I wonder it did not burst my heart. Ah! what nights! what nights!

From my earliest childhood I felt that the priesthood was

my vocation; all my studies were therefore directed to that end, and my life up to the age of twenty-four was nothing but a long novitiate. Having finished my theological training, I took all the minor orders in turn, and my superiors thought me fit, despite my youth, to receive the last and most serious degree. The day of my ordination was appointed for Easter week.

I had never gone into society; for me the world was bounded by the limits of college and seminary. I knew vaguely that there was something which was called woman, but I gave no thought to it; I was perfectly innocent. I saw my old and infirm mother twice a year only. That was the only link I had with the outside world.

I felt no regret, not the slightest hesitation, in face of this irrevocable pledge; I was full of joy and impatience. Never did a young bridegroom count the hours with more feverish eagerness; I could not sleep for thinking of it; I dreamt that I was saying mass. To be a priest seemed to me to be the most wonderful thing in the world; I would have refused to be a king or a poet. My ambition knew no higher flight.

I am telling you this to show you that I was the last person in the world to whom such a thing should have happened, and of what inexplicable fascination I was the victim.

When the great day came, I walked to the church with so light a step that I seemed to tread on air or to have wings on my shoulders. I felt as if I were an angel, and I was astonished at the serious and preoccupied faces of my companions; for there were several of us. I had passed the night in prayer and was in a frame of mind that bordered on ecstasy. The bishop, a venerable old man, seemed to be God the Father contemplating His eternity, and I saw heaven through the vaulted roof of the sacred building.

You know the details of the ceremony: the benediction, the communion, the anointing of the palms of the hands with the oil of the catechumens, and lastly the holy sacrifice offered together with the bishop. I will not dwell upon this. Oh! how right Job is when he says that the man is imprudent who does not close a bargain with his eyes!

I chanced to raise my head, which till then I had held bowed down, and saw her before me – so near that I could have touched her, although in reality she was some distance away and on the other side of the railing – I saw, I say, a young woman of rare beauty and dressed with regal splendour. It was as though scales had fallen from my eyes. I experienced the sensation of a blind man who suddenly recovers his sight. The bishop, so radiant a moment before, faded out all of a sudden; the tapers grew pale in their gold sconces like the stars at daybreak, and the whole church became quite dark. The lovely creature stood out against the background of shadow like an angelic vision; she seemed to be illuminated of herself, to create rather than to receive light.

I lowered my eyelids, firmly resolved not to lift them again, so as to be free from the influence of external objects; for my thoughts wandered more and more, and I hardly knew what I was doing.

A minute later I opened my eyes again, for through my lashes I saw her, glittering with all the colours of the prism, and in a roseate twilight, as when one looks at the sun.

Oh! how beautiful she was! The greatest painters, searching for ideal beauty in heaven and bringing down to earth the divine portrait of the Madonna, do not approach this fabulous reality. Neither poet's verse nor painter's palette can give an idea of it.

She was fairly tall, with the figure and carriage of a goddess. Her soft hair was parted and flowed over her temples like two waves of gold; a queen with her diadem, one might fancy; her forehead of a bluish, transparent whiteness, spread broad and serene over almost brown eyebrows, a peculiarity which still further enhanced the effect of sea-green eyes that shone with a sparkle and brilliance that were unbearable. What eyes! With one flash they decided the fate of a man; they had a life, a limpidity, a liquid brightness, which I have never seen in a human eye; rays like arrows darted from them straight to the heart. I know not whether the flame that illuminated them came from heaven or hell, but of a surety it came from one or the other. This woman was an angel or a demon, perhaps both: certainly she did not spring from the womb of Eve, the common mother. Teeth of purest Oriental pearl gleamed through the red of her smiling lips, and at each movement of her mouth little dimples showed in the roseate softness of her adorable cheeks. The nose was well-cut and of truly royal pride, and betokened the most noble descent. Bright agates wantoned on the smooth, shining skin of her half-revealed shoulders, and rows of large pearls, nearly as white as her neck, fell on her breast. From time to time she raised her head with the undulating motion of a snake or of a bridling peacock, which sent a movement through the high open-work ruff that encircled her throat like a silver trellis.

She wore a dress of red velvet, and from the broad ermine-trimmed sleeves emerged patrician hands of infinite delicacy, with long rounded fingers, so translucent that the light shone through them, like those of Aurora.

All these details are still as present to my eyes as if they dated from yesterday, for though my mind was extremely troubled, nothing escaped me: the minutest details, the tiny black spot on the side of the chin, the scarcely perceptible down at the corners of the lips, the velvet softness of the brow, the quivering shadow of the eyelashes on the cheeks – I took everything in with an astonishing clearness.

As I looked at her, I felt doors which hitherto had been closed open within me: it was as if little windows were unshuttered in every direction to open up unknown vistas; life appeared to me in a wholly new aspect. I had just been born into another world of thought and feeling. A frightful anguish gripped my heart; each minute that passed seemed a second and an age.

Meanwhile, the ceremony proceeded, and carried me far away from the world the entrance to which my growing desires were furiously besieging. I said yes when I wanted to say no, while everything in me revolted and protested against the wrong my tongue was doing to my soul; in spite of myself, some mysterious power tore the words from my throat. Thus it is, perhaps, that so many young women go to the altar with the fixed intention of refusing emphatically the husbands forced upon them, and not one carries out her project. It is thus, doubtless, that poor novices take the veil, for all their determination to tear it in shreds at the moment of uttering their vows. One dares not cause such a scandal in public, or disappoint the expectations of so many people; the wishes of all, the looks of all, seem to weigh on one like a casque of lead; and then the procedure has been so well arranged, everything so completely regulated in advance, in a manner so manifestly irrevocable, that thought yields to the weight of facts and becomes completely impotent.

The gaze of the beautiful stranger changed its expression as the ceremony proceeded. Tender and caressing at first, it took the air of disdain and dissatisfaction of one misunderstood.

I made an effort, violent enough to uproot a mountain, to cry out that I did not wish to be a priest; but I could not do it; my tongue clove to the roof of my mouth, and I could not translate my desire into the faintest movement of refusal. Wide awake, I was in a condition like that of nightmare, when you want to utter the word upon which your life depends, and cannot do it.

She seemed to be aware of the torture I was suffering, and, as if to give me courage, cast upon me a look full of divine promise. Her eyes were a poem, of which each look was a verse. They said:

'If you will be mine, I will make you happier than God Himself in His paradise; the angels will envy you. Tear off that funeral winding-sheet in which you are about to wrap yourself. I am Beauty, I am Youth, I am Life; come to me, and we will be Love. What could Jehovah offer you in exchange for that? Our life will glide by like a dream, and be but a kiss prolonged to eternity.

'Dash that cup from your lips, and you are free. I will transport you to unknown isles; you shall sleep upon my breast in a bed of pure gold under a canopy of silver. For I love you, and would take you from your God, before Whom so many noble hearts melt into floods of love that reach Him not.'

I seemed to hear these words in a rhythm of infinite sweetness; for her look all but had sound, and the sentences her eyes sent to me echoed in the depths of my heart as if invisible lips had breathed them into my soul. I felt myself ready to renounce God, yet my lips went mechanically through the formalities of the ceremony. The beautiful one flung me a second glance so beseeching, so despairing, that steel blades went through my heart, and I felt more darts in my breast than the Mother of Sorrows.

It was done; I was a priest.

Never did human countenance portray such poignant anguish. The girl who sees her betrothed die suddenly at her side, the mother beside the empty cradle of her child, Eve sitting on the threshold of Paradise, the miser who finds a stone in the place of his treasure, the poet who has dropped into the fire the only manuscript of his finest work – none of these could seem more prostrated by grief, more inconsolable. The blood fled from her lovely cheeks and she became as white as marble; her beautiful arms fell beside her body; as though the muscles had lost their power, and she leaned against a pillar as if her legs were weakening and slipping from under her.

As for me – livid, my forehead bathed in a bloodier sweat than that of Calvary, I tottered to the door of the church; I was suffocated; it seemed as if the vaulted roof above was falling upon my shoulders and that my head alone was supporting the whole weight of the dome.

As I was about to cross the threshold a hand suddenly grasped mine – a woman's hand! I had never touched one. It was cold as a snake's skin, and its impress remained, burning into my flesh like the brand of a red-hot iron. It was she. 'Unhappy man! unhappy man! what have you done?' she said to me in a low voice; then she disappeared in the crowd.

The old bishop passed by; he looked at me with a severe expression. My demeanour must have been strange; I paled, I flushed, my vision was clouded. One of my companions took compassion on me and led me away; alone, I could not have found my way back to the seminary. At a turn of a street, while the young priest's head was turned another way, a negro page, fantastically dressed, came towards me and handed me, without stopping, a little pocket-book with gilt-edged corners, signing to me to hide it.

I slipped it into my sleeve and kept it there until I was alone in my cell. I undid the clasp. There were but two leaves with the words: 'Clarimonde, Concini Palace.' I was then so little conversant with life that I had never heard of Clarimonde, in spite of her celebrity, and had no idea where the Concini Palace was. I made a thousand conjectures, each one more extravagant than the last, but to tell the truth, provided I could see her again, I cared little what she might be, great lady or courtesan.

This love, just born, had taken root imperishably; I did not even think of attempting to eradicate it. I felt so strongly that it was impossible. This woman had taken complete possession of me; one look had sufficed to work the change in me; she had breathed her will into me; my life was no more my own, but hers, drawing its breath from her. I committed a thousand extravagances; I kissed the place on my hand which she had touched, and repeated her name for hours together. I had only to close my eyes to see her as clearly as if she had really been present, and I kept repeating the words she had spoken at the church door: 'Unhappy man! unhappy man! what have you done?'

I realized all the horror of the situation, and the funereal and dreadful aspects of the state into which I had just been initiated were clearly revealed to me. To be a priest! That is to say, to be chaste, not to love, to make no distinction of sex or age, to turn aside from all beauty, to cower beneath the icy shadow of a monastery or a church, to see only the dying, to keep watch beside unknown corpses, to wear your own mourning in the shape of your black cassock, until at last your priest's robe shall be your own coffin-cloth!

And I felt life rising within me like an underground lake that fills and overflows; my blood throbbed violently in my arteries; my youth, so long repressed, burst out all at once like the aloe that takes a hundred years to flower and blossoms with a clap of thunder.

What should I do to see Clarimonde again? I had no pretext for leaving the seminary, knowing no one in the town; I was not even to remain there, was only waiting until the parish which was to be my charge should be allotted to me. I tried to loosen the bars of the window; but it was a fearful height, and descent without a ladder was not to be dreamed of. Besides, it could only be made at night; and how find my way in the intricate maze of the streets? All these difficulties, which would have been nothing to others, were immense to me, a poor seminarist, a lover without experience, without money, without clothes.

If I had not been a priest I might have seen her every day; I should have been her lover, her husband, I told myself in my infatuation. Instead of being wrapped in my dismal shroud, I should have clothes of silk and velvet, gold chains, a sword at my side and a feather in my cap, like handsome young cavaliers. My hair, instead of being spoilt by a large tonsure, would play about my neck in wavy curls. I should have a beautiful waxed moustache and be a gallant. But an hour passed before an altar, a few scarcely articulated words, had cut me off for ever from the number of the living; I had myself sealed the stone of my tomb, pushed with my own hand the bolt of my prison!

I went to the window. The sky was beautifully blue, the trees were clad in their spring dress; Nature seemed to make parade of an ironic gaiety. The square was full of people; they came and went; young sparks and young beauties, couple by couple, made their way towards gardens and arbours. Boon companions passed by arm-in-arm singing drinking-songs. There was movement, life, bustle; liveliness that contrasted sadly with my mourning and my loneliness. A young mother on the doorstep played with her child, kissed the rosy little mouth still beaded with drops of milk, teased it with a thousand of those divine childishneses which mothers alone can invent. The father, who stood at a distance, smiled quietly on the charming group, and with folded arms hugged his happiness to his heart. I could not bear the sight; I closed the windows and threw myself on my bed, my heart filled with hatred and fearful jealousy, gnawing my fingers and my blanket like a tiger that has hungered for three days.

I do not know how long I remained thus; but, turning with a convulsive movement, I saw the Abbé Sérapion standing in the middle of the room and watching me with fixed attention. I was overcome with shame, and letting my head fall on my breast, I covered my eyes with my hands.

'Romuald, my friend, something extraordinary is taking place in you,' said Sérapion, after a few minutes' silence; 'your behaviour is truly unaccountable! You, so pious, so calm, so gentle, you rage in your cell like a wild beast. Be on your guard, my brother, and do not listen to the promptings of the devil; the evil spirit, incensed because you are for ever consecrated to the Lord, is prowling round you like a ravenous wolf and making a last effort to draw you to him. Instead of letting yourself be downcast, my dear Romuald, make yourself a breastplate of prayers, a buckle of mortifications, and valiantly do battle with the enemy; you will conquer him. Virtue must be put to the test; gold comes out of the cupel finer than before. Do not be afraid or discouraged; the most watchful and steadfast souls have had moments such as these. Pray, fast, meditate, and the evil spirit will leave you.'

The words of the Abbé Sérapion recalled me to myself, and I regained something of my composure.

'I came,' he continued, 'to announce to you your nomination to the living of C —. The priest who had it has just died, and Monseigneur the Bishop has directed me to install you there; be ready to start tomorrow.'

I replied with a movement of the head that I would be ready, and the Abbé withdrew. I opened my missal and began to read prayers; but the lines soon became confused; the sequence of thoughts in my brain became tangled, and the book dropped from my hand without my noticing it.

I must leave tomorrow without seeing her again! Add another obstacle to all those that already lay between us! Lose for ever the hope of meeting her except by a miracle! Should I write to her? By whom could I send a letter? Considering the sacred character with which I was invested, to whom should I unbosom myself, in whom could I confide? I was distracted with doubts and fears. Then, what the Abbé Sérapion had said about the wiles of the devil came back to my mind. The strangeness of the adventure, the unearthly beauty of Clarimonde, the phosphorescent brilliance of her eyes, the burning impress of her hand, the trouble of mind into which she had thrown me, the sudden change which had taken place in me, my pious aspirations dispelled in a moment – all this proved clearly the presence of the devil, and that soft hand was perhaps only the glove with which he had sheathed his claw.

These ideas threw me into a great terror; I picked up the missal which had fallen from my knees and betook myself again to prayer.

The next day Sérapion came to fetch me. Two mules awaited us before the door laden with our scanty baggage; he mounted one and I the other. As we traversed the streets of the town I glanced at all the windows and balconies in the hope of seeing Clarimonde; but it was too early; and the town was not yet awake. My eyes tried to penetrate the blinds and curtains of all the mansions before which we passed. Sérapion, doubtless, attributed this curiosity to the admiration which the beauty of the architecture excited in me, for he slackened his mount's pace in order to give me time to look. At length we reached the town gate and began to climb the hill. When I was at the top, I turned to take a last look at the place where Clarimonde lived. The shadow of a cloud completely covered the town; its blue and red roofs were merged in a general half-tone over which the morning smoke floated here and there, like white wisps of foam. By a curious optical effect, one edifice stood out shining and golden under a single ray of light, a house higher than the buildings near it, which were completely lost in the mist; although more than a league distant, it seemed quite near. The smallest details could be distinguished – turrets, leads, windows, even its swallow-tailed weathercocks.

'What is that palace I see down there lit up by a sunbeam?' I asked Sérapion.

He shaded his eyes with his hand, and, looking towards it, answered:

'It is the ancient palace which the Prince Concini has given to the courtesan Clarimonde; fearful things take place there.'

At that moment – I do not know even now whether it was reality or an illusion – I thought I saw a slim white figure glide on to the terrace; it sparkled there for a moment and faded out. It was Clarimonde!

Oh! did she know that at that very moment, from the top of the steep road that was leading me away from her, and which I was never more to descend, I was gazing, ardent and troubled, on the palace where she lived, and which a mocking play of light seemed to ring close to me, as if to bid me enter it as master? Without doubt she knew it, for her soul was linked to mine in too intimate a sympathy not to feel its faintest vibrations; and it was this consciousness that had impelled her, still arrayed in her night-robe, to ascend the terrace in the shining dews of morning.

The shadow enveloped the palace, and there was now only a motionless sea of roofs and summits, in which nothing could be distinguished but an undulating expanse. Sérapion urged his mule forward, my own immediately fell into pace, and a bend in the road placed the town of S— for ever beyond my view, for I was never to return to it. After three days of travel through rather dreary country, we saw peeping out from among the trees the weather-cock of the church at which I was to officiate; and after passing along a few crooked roads between thatched cottages and crofts, we found ourselves before its front, which was not magnificent. A porch adorned with a few flutings and two or three roughly-sculptured columns of sandstone, a tiled roof and buttresses of the same sandstone as the pillars; to the left the churchyard, overgrown with rank herbage, with a large iron cross in the middle; to the right, overshadowed by the church, the presbytery. It was a dwelling of extreme simplicity and severe cleanliness.

We went in. Some fowls were pecking the ground in search of scantily strewn grains of oats; apparently accustomed to the black robes of priests, they were not at all disconcerted at our intrusion, and barely disturbed themselves to allow us to pass. A cracked and husky barking reached our ears, and we saw an old dog come running towards us.

It was my predecessor's dog. He had the dimmed eye, grey jowl, and all the signs of the most advanced age a dog can live to. I patted him gently, and he at once began to walk by my side with an air of inexpressible satisfaction. An oldish woman, who had been housekeeper to the old curé, also came out to meet us, and after showing us into a low-ceilinged room, asked me if it was my intention to keep her. I said that I would keep her, the dog, the fowls, and all the furniture that her master had left her at his death, which threw her into transports of joy; the Abbé Sérapion paid her on the spot the price she asked.

My installation complete, the Abbé Sérapion returned to the seminary. I was left alone with no one but myself to rely on. The thought of Clarimonde began again to obsess me, and, strive to banish it as I might, I did not always succeed. One evening, as I strolled along the box-bordered walks of my little garden, I fancied I saw through the trimmed hedge the figure of a woman, who was following all my movements, her two sea-green eyes shining through the leaves; but it was only an illusion, for on reaching the further end of the walk, I found nothing but a footprint on the sand, so small that one would have pronounced it the footmark of a child. The garden was surrounded by very high walls; I searched every nook and corner of it, but no one was there. I have never been able to explain this occurrence, which indeed was nothing compared with the strange things which were to happen to me.

I lived thus for a year, fulfilling punctually all the duties of my state, praying, fasting, exhorting, ministering to the sick, giving so much in alms as to be deprived of the most indispensable necessities. But I felt that all was barren within me, and that the fountains of grace had dried up. I did not enjoy the happiness that the fulfilment of a holy mission gives; my thoughts were elsewhere; and Clarimonde's words often returned to my lips like a kind of involuntary refrain. Brother, meditate well on this! For having once raised my eyes to a woman, for a fault apparently so trifling, I have suffered for years the most grievous torment; my whole life has been troubled, always and for ever.

I will not detain you longer with these secret defeats, the victories always followed by a deeper relapse, but will pass at once to a decisive event. One night the door-bell rang violently. The old housekeeper went to open it, and a man of swarthy appearance, richly but outlandishly dressed and wearing a long sword, stood revealed in the light of Barbara's lantern. Her first feeling was one of fear, but the man reassured her and told her that he must see me immediately on a matter that concerned me as a priest. Barbara brought him upstairs to me. I was just going to bed. The man informed me that his mistress, a very great lady, was at the point of death and wished to see a priest. I replied that I was ready to accompany him; I took with me the requisites for extreme unction, and went down as quickly as I could.

Before the door, two horses, black as night, their chests streaked with two long waves of foam, were impatiently pawing the ground. The man held the stirrup for me and helped me to mount one of them; then, resting his hand upon the pommel of the saddle, vaulted on to the other. He gripped his horse with his knees, gave it free rein, and it shot forward like an arrow. Mine, the bridle of which he held, set off at a gallop also, and kept exactly abreast of the other. We tore over the ground; the earth swept beneath us grey and streaked, and the dark outline of the trees fled past like a routed army. We passed through a forest of such dense and chilly darkness that I felt my flesh creep with a thrill of superstitious terror. The showers of sparks that our horses' hoofs beat from the stones left a trail of fire in our wake; and if anyone had seen my guide and me at that hour of the night, he would have taken us for two phantom horsemen careering through a nightmare. Will-o'-the-wisps crossed our path from time to time, and jackdaws squawked piteously in the depths of the wood, where the phosphorescent eyes of wild cats gleamed now and then. The manes of our horses streamed more and more wildly, the sweat poured down their sides, the breath came from their nostrils panting and laboured. But when he saw them failing, the groom, to rally them, uttered a guttural cry such as human lips never uttered, and the furious pace was resumed.

At last the whirlwind subsided; a black mass, dotted with a few points of light, rose suddenly before us; our horses' hoofs rang more sharply on an iron causeway, and we passed under a vaulted passage which opened its dark jaws between two gigantic towers. Great excitement prevailed in the castle; servants with torches in their hands were hurrying through the courtyard in all directions, and lights were going up and down from landing to landing. I had a confused view of a vast structure, columns, arcades, and stairways, an architectural splendour altogether regal and fantastic. A negro page, the same who had brought me Clarimonde's pocket-book, whom I recognized immediately, came to help me dismount, and a major-domo dressed in black velvet, with a gold chain about his neck and an ivory staff in his hand, advanced to meet me. Tears flowed from his eyes, and trickled down his cheeks on to his white beard.

'Too late!' he said, shaking his head. 'Too late, sir Priest! But if you have not been able to save her soul, come and watch by the poor body.'

He took my arm and led me to the chamber of death. I wept as bitterly as he, for I knew now that the dead woman was no other than Clarimonde, loved so much and so madly.

A *prie-Dieu* was placed at the bedside; a bluish flame flickering over a bronze cup threw a feeble and uncertain light through the room and brought into twinkling prominence here and there some projecting angle of furniture or moulding. On the table, in a vase of chased silver, was a faded white rose, whose petals, save one which still clung to its stem, had fallen at the foot of the vase like fragrant tears. A broken black mask, a fan, fancy dresses of every kind lay about on the chairs, and showed that Death had come into this sumptuous dwelling unexpected and unannounced. I knelt down without daring to look towards the bed, and began to recite psalms with fervour, thanking God for having placed the tomb between the thought of this woman and myself, so that I might add to my prayers her name, henceforth sanctified.

But little by little my enthusiasm abated, and my thoughts wandered. There was nothing of the death-chamber about this room. Instead of the fetid, corpse-infected atmosphere which I was accustomed to breathe in these funereal vigils, a languishing vapour of Eastern perfumes, an indefinable feminine, love-inspiring scent floated gently on the warm air. The pale light suggested rather a twilight arranged for voluptuous pleasure than the yellow rays of the night-light that flickers beside a corpse. I reflected on the strange chance by which I had found Clarimonde again at the moment when I was losing her for ever, and a sigh of regret escaped my breast. It seemed as if someone sighed behind me also, and I turned involuntarily. It was an echo. As I turned, my eyes fell upon the death-bed they had till then avoided. The red damask curtains, embroidered with large flowers and relieved by spiral fringes of gold, showed the dead woman lying at full length, her hands joined on her breast. It was covered with linen drapery of dazzling whiteness, a whiteness accentuated by the dark purple of the tapestry, and so fine in texture that it in no way concealed the exquisite form of the body, and permitted the eye to follow the beautiful outlines, undulous as a swan's neck, which death itself had not been able to stiffen. One would have said it was an alabaster statue, wrought by a clever sculptor for the tomb of a queen, or, still better, a young girl asleep with snow fallen on her.

I could contain myself no longer: the atmosphere intoxicated me, the feverish scent of half-faded roses went to my brain; and I strode up and down the room, pausing each time before the bed to look upon the beauty that lay dead under its transparent burial robe. Strange thoughts passed through my mind; I pictured to myself that she was not really dead at all, that it was only a stratagem which she had employed to draw me to her castle and tell me of her love. For a moment I even imagined that I saw her foot move under the whiteness of her coverings, and the straight folds of the shroud change their outline.

And then I said to myself: 'Is this really Clarimonde? What proof of it have I? May not that black page have entered the service of another woman? I must be mad so to distress and agitate myself.' But my beating heart replied: 'It is she, it is she!' I approached the bed again, and gazed with redoubted attention at the object of my uncertainty. Shall I confess it? That perfection of form, although purified and sanctified by the shadow of death, affected me more pleasurably than it should have done, and that repose was so like sleep as to deceive the onlooker.

I forgot that I had come to discharge a funereal rite, and imagined myself a young bridegroom entering the chamber of his bride, who hides her face in modesty and will not let her charms be seen. Torn with grief, mad with joy, shivering with fear and delight, I bent towards her and took hold of the corner of the sheet; I raised it gently, holding my breath for fear of waking her. My heart beat so wildly that I felt a rushing noise in my temples, and my forehead streamed with sweat as though I had moved a slab of marble.

It was indeed Clarimonde, as I had seen her in the church on the day of my ordination; she was just as charming, and death, with her, seemed but one form of coquetry the more. The pallor of her cheeks, the fuller rose of her lips, the long drooping lashes that made a brown fringe on the whiteness of the face, gave her an expression of melancholy chastity and pensive suffering that was inexpressively seductive; her long loosened hair, in which a few little blue flowers were still mingled, made a pillow for her head and covered her bare shoulders with its curls; her beautiful hands, purer, more transparent than the sacrificial wafer, were crossed in an attitude of pious repose and mute prayer – an attitude that counter-balanced the too great seduction, it might have been, even in death, of the exquisite moulding and ivory whiteness of her bare arms from which the bracelets of pearls had not been taken.

I remained for a long time absorbed in silent contemplation, and the longer I looked, the less could I believe that life had for ever deserted that beautiful body. I do not know if it was an illusion or a reflection from the lamp, but it seemed that the blood began to flow again under that dull pallor. I touched her arm lightly; it was cold, but no colder than was her hand on the day that it had touched mine under the portal of the church. I resumed my former position, bending my face over hers, and letting the warm dew of my tears rain upon her cheeks. Ah! what a bitter sensation of despair and impotence I felt! What an agony that vigil was! I should have liked to be able to gather together all my life that I might give it to her and breathe into those icy relics the fire that consumed me. The night was advancing; and feeling that the moment of eternal separation was at hand, I could not deny myself the last and supreme pleasure of leaving a kiss upon the dead lips of her who had all my love.

Oh, miracle! light breath mingled with my breath, and Clarimonde's mouth replied to the pressure of mine: her eyes opened and regained a little brilliance: she sighed, and uncrossing her arms, put them round my neck with a look of inexpressible bliss.

'Ah! it is you, Romuald,' she said, in a voice as languishing and sweet as the last vibration of a harp; 'what have you been doing? I have waited for you so long that I have died; but now that we are betrothed, I shall be able to see you and come to you. Farewell, Romuald, farewell! I love you; that is all I wished to tell you, and I give you back the life which you recalled in me for a minute by your kiss. Farewell, for a little while!'

Her head fell back, but she still held me in her arms as if to keep me with her. A furious gust of wind blew through the window and swept into the room; the last petal of the white rose quivered for a moment like a wing at the end of its stalk, then it broke away and flew out through the open window, bearing with it the soul of Clarimonde. The light went out, and I fell senseless on the bosom of the beautiful corpse.

When I came to myself I was lying on my bed in my little room at the presbytery, and the former curé's old dog was licking my hand, which lay outside the blanket. Barbara was busying herself about the room with the trembling movements of old age, opening and shutting drawers or stirring powders in glasses. On seeing me open my eyes, the old woman uttered a cry of joy, and the dog barked and wagged his tail; but I was so weak that I could not speak a word or make the least movement.

I learned afterwards that I had been in this condition for three days, giving no sign of life except an almost imperceptible breathing. Those three days were a blank in my life, and I do not know whither my spirit had gone during the whole of that time; I remember nothing at all about it. Barbara told me that the same man of swarthy aspect, who had come to fetch me in the night, had brought me back the next morning in a closed litter, and had immediately taken his departure. As soon as I could collect my thoughts, I went over in my mind all the events of that fatal night. At first I believed that I had been the plaything of a magical illusion; but actual and tangible circumstances soon demolished that supposition. I could not think that I had been dreaming, since Barbara as well as myself had seen the man with the two black horses and accurately described their trappings and appearance. At the same time, no one in the neighbourhood had any knowledge of a castle answering the description of the castle where I had found Clarimonde.

One morning the Abbé Sérapion entered my room. Barbara had sent to tell him that I was ill, and he had lost no time in coming to me. Although this promptitude was a proof of his affection and concern for me, his visit did not give me the pleasure that it ought to have given me. There was something searching and inquisitorial in the Abbé Sérapion's look that made me uncomfortable. I felt embarrassed and guilt-stricken in his presence. He had been the first to discover that something was preying on my mind, and I was angry with him for his perception.

Even while he was inquiring about my health in hypocritically honeyed tones, he fixed his two yellow lion's eyes on mine and plunged his gaze into my soul like a plummet. Then he asked me a few questions about the way I managed my parish, asked whether I took pleasure in my work, how I passed the time my duties left free, if I had made any acquaintances among the inhabitants of the place, what were my favourite books, and a thousand other details of the kind. I replied to all this as briefly as possible, and he, without waiting till I had finished speaking, passed on to something else. This conversation had evidently nothing to do with what he wished to say. Then, without the least preface, and as if he were giving me a piece of news which he had just remembered and was afraid of forgetting, he said, in a clear and ringing voice that sounded in my ears like the trumpets of the Last Judgment:

'The famous courtesan Clarimonde died lately, after an orgy that lasted eight days and eight nights. It was something hellishly splendid. The abominations of Balthazar's and Cleopatra's feasts were revived. Good God! in what an age we live! The guests were served by copper-complexioned slaves who spoke an unknown language, and who, I believe, were real demons; the livery of the lowest among them might have served as the gala dress of an emperor. There have always been very strange stories about this Clarimonde; and all her lovers have come to a miserable and violent end. The tale went that she was a ghoul, a female vampire; but I believe she was Beelzebub in person.'

He ceased speaking, and watched me more narrowly than ever to see the effect of his words upon me. I could not prevent myself from starting on hearing the name of Clarimonde, and this news of her death, besides the grief it caused me, by its strange coincidence with the night scene I had witnessed, threw me into a state of agitation and fear which was reflected in my face, do what I would to control it. Sérapion cast an anxious and severe glance on me; then he said:

'My son, I must do my duty and warn you that you are on the brink of a precipice; beware lest you fall. Satan has long claws, and tombs are not always secure. The stone that covers Clarimonde should be sealed with a triple seal; for according to what men say, this is not the first time she has died. May God watch over you, Romuald!'

When he had uttered these words, Sérapion went slowly to the door, and I did not see him again; for he set out for S— immediately.

I had now entirely recovered and had resumed my accustomed duties. The memory of Clarimonde and the old Abbé's words were always in my mind; however, no extraordinary event had occurred to confirm Sérapion's gloomy forebodings, and I began to think that his fears and my own terrors had been exaggerated; but one night I had a dream. I had hardly fallen asleep when I heard the rings of my bed-curtains slide along the rods with a loud clatter; I raised myself sharply upon my elbow and saw the shadowy form of a woman standing before me.

At once I recognized Clarimonde.

She held in her hand a small lamp like those which are placed in tombs, and its rays gave her slender fingers a rosy transparence which spread upward, fading by insensible degrees into the dull, milky white of her bare arm. She had no other garment than the linen shroud that covered her on her death-bed, the folds of which she held to her breast as if ashamed of being so scantily clothed, but her little hand was too small for the task; she was so pale that the colour of the drapery, under the faint rays of the lamp, was confused with that of her flesh. Wrapped in this fine tissue which revealed all the outlines of her body, she looked like a marble statue of an antique bather rather than a woman, endowed with life. Dead or living, statue or woman, shade or body, her beauty was always the same; only the green sparkle of her eyes was a little dulled, and her mouth, before so vermilion, was now only tinged with a soft faint rose almost as pale as that of her cheeks. The little blue flowers I had noticed in her hair were quite withered and had lost nearly all their petals; but none the less she was charming, so charming that, despite the strangeness of the adventure and the mysterious manner in which she had entered my room, I was not for one moment afraid.

She placed the lamp on the table and seated herself on the foot of my bed; then, leaning towards me, she spoke in that voice, at once silvery and soft as velvet, which I have never heard from any lips but hers:

'I have kept you waiting a long time, dear Romuald, and you must have thought that I had forgotten you. But I have come a very long way, from a place from which no one has ever yet returned; there is neither sun nor moon in the country I come from; nothing but space and shadow; neither road nor pathway; no earth for the foot, no air for the wings; and yet I am here, for love is stronger than death and will conquer it in the end. Ah! what gloomy faces, what terrible things I have seen on my journey! How difficult it has been for my soul, come back to this world by the power of my will, to find its body and take up its abode there! What efforts I had to make before I could lift the stone with which they had covered me! See! the inside of my poor hands is all bruised. Kiss them and heal them, dear love!'

She pressed the cold palms of her hands, in turn, to my lips; I did indeed kiss them again and again, and she watched me do so with a smile of inexpressible content.

I confess to my shame that I had wholly forgotten the Abbé Sérapion's advice and the sacred character I had assumed. I had fallen without resistance and at the first assault. I had not even made an effort to repel the tempter; the coolness of Clarimonde's hand penetrated mine, and I felt voluptuous shivers run over my body. Poor child! In spite of all that I have seen of her, I can still hardly believe that she was a demon; at least she had not the appearance of one, and never has Satan better hidden his claws and hoofs. She had tucked her heels under her and sat on the edge of my couch in an attitude full of unstudied coquetry. Now and again she passed her little hand through my hair and rolled it into curls, as if to try how new ways of arranging it would suit me. I submitted to this with a most guilty satisfaction, and she kept up an accompaniment of the most charming prattle.

It is remarkable that I felt no astonishment at such an extraordinary adventure, and with that faculty which one has in dreams of accepting the most bizarre events as quite ordinary, I saw in it nothing that was not perfectly natural.

'I loved you long before I saw you, dear Romuald, and sought you everywhere. You were my ideal, and when I saw you in the church at the fatal moment, I said at once "It is he!" I gave you a look into which I put all the love that I had, and that I was to have for you; a look to damn a cardinal, to bring a king to his knees at my feet before all his court. You remained obdurate and preferred your God to me.

'Ah! how jealous I am of God, Whom you loved and still

love better than me!

'How unhappy I am! I shall never have your heart for my very own; I, whom you recalled to life with a kiss; I, the dead Clarimonde, who, for your sake, has broken the doors of the tomb, and has come to devote to you the life which she has only resumed to make you happy!'

These words were broken by intoxicating caresses which benumbed my senses and my reason to such a point that I did not fear, in order to console her, to utter a frightful blasphemy and tell her that I loved her as much as God.

New life came into her eyes; they shone like chrysoprases.

'Truly? truly? as much as God!' she said, clasping me in her beautiful arms. 'If it is so, you will come with me, you will follow me where I wish. You will leave your ugly black robes. You will be the proudest, the most envied of cavaliers; you will be my lover. To be the acknowledged lover of Clarimonde, who has refused a Pope, think of it! Ah! the happy life, the golden existence that we shall lead! When shall we start, my gallant?'

'Tomorrow! Tomorrow!' I cried in my delirium.

'Tomorrow, then!' she replied. 'I shall have time to change my clothes, for these are a little scanty and not suited for travelling. I must also tell my servants, who believe me to be dead in good earnest and are broken-hearted. Money, clothes, carriages, everything will be ready. I will come and fetch you at this time tomorrow. Farewell, dear heart.'

She touched my forehead with her lips. The lamp went out, the curtains closed again, and I saw no more; a leaden, dreamless sleep weighed me down and held me torpid until next morning. I woke later than usual, and the recollection of that strange vision disturbed my mind throughout the day; I persuaded myself at last that it was a mere product of a heated imagination. Yet the sensations had been so vivid that it was difficult to believe that they were not real, and it was not without fear of what was going to happen that I went to bed, after praying God to banish evil thoughts from my mind and to watch over my sleep.

I was soon fast asleep, and my dream continued. The curtains were drawn apart, and I saw Clarimonde, not, as the first time, pale in her white shroud and with the hues of death upon her cheeks, but gay, lively and elegant, in a magnificent travelling-dress of green velvet edged with gold and looped up on one side to show a satin skirt. Her fair hair escaped in large curls under a large black felt hat trimmed with white feathers fancifully twisted; she held in her hand a little riding-whip, the handle of which ended in a golden whistle. She touched me lightly with it and said:

'Well, fair sleeper, is this how you make your preparations? I counted on finding you waiting. Get up quickly; we have no time to lose.'

I jumped out of bed.

'Come, dress and let us be off,' she said, pointing to a small parcel she had brought; 'the horses are impatient and are champing their bits at the door. We ought to be ten leagues from here already.'

I dressed myself in haste, and she herself handed me the articles of clothing, going into fits of laughter at my awkwardness and showing me how to put them on when I made mistakes. She dressed my hair with a light touch and, when this was done, put into my hand a little pocket mirror of Venetian crystal framed in silver filigree, saying:

'What do you think of yourself? Would you take me into your service as valet?'

I was no longer the same person. I did not recognize myself. I was no more like my old self than a finished statue is like a block of stone. The face I knew seemed but a coarse sketch of the face the mirror reflected. I was handsome; and my vanity was roused by the transformation. The fine clothes, the rich embroidered waistcoat, made quite another man of me; and I marvelled at the power of a few ells of cloth cut in a certain fashion. The spirit of my costume found its way under my skin, and in ten minutes I was a passable coxcomb.

I walked round the room several times to give myself an easy bearing. Clarimonde watched me with an air of motherly pride, and seemed well pleased with her work.

'Come, we have been childish long enough; we must be off, dear Romuald! We have far to go and we shall not get there in time.'

She took me by the hand and led me away. All the doors opened to her immediately she touched them, and we passed the dog without waking him.

At the door we found Margheritone, the groom who had already been my guide; he held by their bridles three horses, black like the first, one for me, one for himself, and one for Clarimonde. Those horses must have been Spanish jennets out of mares by Zephyr; for they went as fast as the wind, and the moon, which had risen at our departure to light us on our way, rolled through the sky like a wheel broken loose from its chariot; we saw it on our right leaping from tree to tree as if it lost breath in pursuit of us. Soon we came to a plain where, by a clump of trees, a carriage drawn by four powerful beasts was waiting for us; we got into it, and the postilions set off at a furious gallop. I had one arm round Clarimonde and I held one of her hands clasped in mine; she laid her head on my shoulder, and I felt her half-uncovered bosom against my arm. I had never known such perfect happiness. In that moment I forgot everything, and I no more remembered having been a priest than I remembered what I had done in my mother's womb, so great was the fascination the malignant spirit exercised over me.

From that night onward my nature was in some way doubled; there were within me two men, neither of whom knew the other. Sometimes I thought I was a priest who dreamed every night that he was a nobleman, sometimes that I was a nobleman who dreamed that he was a priest. I could no longer distinguish dreams from real life; I did not know where reality began and illusion ended. The dissolute, supercilious young lord jeered at the priest, and the priest abhorred the dissipations of the young lord. Two spirals, entwined and confused, yet never actually touching, would give a good idea of this two-headed existence of mine. Despite the strangeness of the situation, I do not believe that I was ever insane. I always retained quite clearly the perception of my two existences. Only, there was one absurd fact that I could never explain to myself; this was that the feeling of the same identity should exist in two such different men. It was an anomaly I could not account for, whether I believed myself to be the curé of the little parish of C — or Signor Romualdo, the acknowledged lover of Clarimonde.

I was always, or at least imagined myself to be, in Venice; even now I cannot properly disentangle illusion from reality in this bizarre adventure. We lived in a great marble palace on the Canaleio, full of frescoes and statues, with two Titians of the best period in Clarimonde's bedroom, a palace fit for a king. We had each our own gondola with gondoliers in our livery, our own music-room and our own poet.

Clarimonde understood life in the grand style; she had a little of Cleopatra in her nature. As for me, I adopted the airs of a prince's son, and was as arrogant as if I had been descended from one of the twelve apostles or the four evangelists of the Most Serene Republic; I would not have turned aside to make way for the Doges, and I do not believe that there has been anyone more insolent since Satan fell from heaven. I went to the Ridotto and played the devil's own game. I frequented the best society, sons of ruined noble houses, actresses, swindlers, parasites and cut-throats.

Yet, in spite of the dissipated life I led, I remained faithful to Clarimonde. I loved her to distraction. She would have awakened satiety itself from its slumbers, and kept inconstancy inconstant. To possess Clarimonde was to possess twenty mistresses, it was to possess all the women in the world, so versatile was she, so changeable, so unlike herself; a veritable chameleon! An infidelity you would have committed with someone else, she made you commit with her by completely assuming the character, the style and the type of beauty of the woman you seemed to admire.

She returned my love a hundredfold; and it was in vain that young nobles and even elders of the Council of Ten made her the most magnificent offers. A Foscari even went so far as to propose to marry her. She refused everything. She had money enough; she wanted nothing but love, a young love, a pure love, a love awakened by her, a love that must be the first and the last. I should have been perfectly happy but for an accursed nightmare that returned every night, in which I fancied myself a village curé mortifying the flesh and doing penance for my excesses of the day. Reassured by being with her, I hardly thought any more of the strange manner in which I had made her acquaintance. But the Abbé Sérapion's words still returned to my mind at times, and did not cease to make me uneasy.

For some time Clarimonde's health had not been so good; her colour faded day by day. The doctors who were sent for did not understand what her illness was or what treatment to give. They prescribed a few medicines that could do neither good nor harm, and did not come again. Meanwhile she grew visibly paler and became colder and colder. She was almost as white and as dead as on the memorable night in the mysterious castle. I was heartbroken to see her thus slowly fading away. Touched by my grief, she smiled upon me softly and sadly, with the resigned smile of those who know they are going to die.

One morning I was sitting at her bedside, eating my breakfast at a little table, so as not to leave her for a minute. As I was cutting some fruit, I happened to make a rather deep gash in my finger. The blood spurted out immediately in crimson jets, and some of the drops were sprinkled upon Clarimonde. Her eyes lit up, her features assumed an expression of fierce, wild joy that I had never seen in them before. She leapt out of bed with the agility of an animal, a monkey or a cat, flew at my wound, and began to suck it with an air of unspeakable delight. She swallowed the blood in small draughts, slowly and grudgingly, like an epicure tasting Xeres and Syracuse wine; she half closed her eyes, and the pupils of her green eyes became elongated instead of round. Now and again she stopped to kiss my hand, then she began again to press the wound with her lips, to coax out a few more red drops. When she saw that no more blood was coming, she stood up with moist and shining eyes, rosier than a May dawn, her face full, her hand warm and soft, lovelier than ever and in perfect health.

'I shall not die! I shall not die!' she cried, half mad with joy, and hanging on my neck; 'I shall be able to love you for a long time still. My life is in yours, and all that is me comes from you. A few drops of your rich and noble blood, more precious and more potent than all the elixirs in the world, have given me back my life.'

This scene made a deep impression upon me and filled me with strange doubts concerning Clarimonde; and that very evening, when sleep had taken me back to my presbytery, I saw the Abbé Sérapion, graver and more anxious than ever. He observed me attentively and said: 'Not content with destroying your soul, you wish to destroy your body also. Unhappy young man, into what a snare you are fallen!' The tone in which he uttered these words struck me sharply, but in spite of its vividness, the impression was soon dispelled, and a thousand other cares effaced it from my mind.

One evening, however, looking in my mirror, the treacherous position of which she had not taken count of, I saw Clarimonde drop a powder into the cup of spiced wine which she used to prepare after the meal. I took the cup and pretended to sip from it; then I put it down on a table as if to finish it later at my leisure, and taking advantage of a moment when her back was turned, I threw the contents under the table; after which I retired to my room and went to bed, resolved to keep awake and see what would happen. I had not long to wait; Clarimonde came in and, having taken off her wrap, lay down in bed by my side. When she felt sure that I was asleep, she bared my arm and drew a golden pin from her hair; then she began to murmur in a low voice:

'One drop, just one little red drop, a ruby on the point of my needle! . . . Since you love me still, I must not die. . . . Ah! poor love! his beautiful blood, so red, I am going to drink it! Sleep, my only treasure; sleep, my god, my child; I will not hurt you, I will only take from your life what I need to keep mine from going out. If I did not love you so much, I could bring myself to have other lovers, whose veins I would drain dry; but since I have known you, I have held all other men in abhorrence. . . . Ah! what a lovely arm! how round it is! how white it is! I shall never dare to prick that pretty blue vein.'

And as she said this she wept, and I felt her tears rain upon my arm as she held it. At length she decided to act; she made a little prick in my arm with her needle, and began to sip the blood that flowed from it. Before she had taken more than a few drops she was seized with the fear of exhausting me; she carefully bound my arm with a little bandage, after smearing the wound with an ointment that closed it at once.

I could no longer be in doubt, the Abbé Sérapion was right. But in spite of this conviction, I would not suppress my love for Clarimonde, and I would willingly have given her all the blood she needed to maintain her artificial existence. Besides, I was not really frightened; to me, the woman made up for the vampire, and what I had heard and seen reassured me; I had then rich veins that would not quickly be exhausted, and I was not bargaining away my life drop by drop. I would have opened my arm myself and said to her: 'Drink! let my love enter your body with my blood!' I avoided making the least allusion to the powder she had poured out for me, or to the scene with the needle, and we went on living in the most perfect harmony.

Nevertheless, my priest's scruples tormented me more than ever, and I was always seeking new penances to tame and mortify my flesh. Although all this visionary existence was involuntary, and my other self took no part in it, I dared not touch the Christ with hands so contaminated and a soul polluted by such debaucheries, real or imagined. To avoid falling into these fatiguing hallucinations, I tried to prevent myself from sleeping; I held my eyelids open with my fingers and stood upright against the wall, struggling against sleep with all my strength; but my eyes were soon full of drowsiness, and finding that the struggle was in vain, I let my arms fall in discouragement and weariness, and the tide swept me back towards the treacherous shores.

Sérapion remonstrated with me with the greatest vehemence, and reproached me bitterly for my supineness and lack of fervour. One day, when I had been more agitated than usual, he said to me:

'There is only one way to rid you of this obsession, and although it is an extreme measure, it must be taken; for desperate ills, desperate remedies. I know where Clarimonde was buried; we must dig up her body, and let you see in what a wretched state the object of your love now is; you will not be tempted to lose your soul for a filthy corpse, devoured by worms and ready to fall to dust; it will surely bring you to your right mind.'

For my own part, I was so worn out with this double life that I agreed, wishing to learn, once for all, whether the priest or the nobleman was the victim of an illusion; I was prepared to kill one of these two men who were in me for the benefit of the other, whichever it might be, or to kill them both, for such a life could not last. The Abbé Sérapion provided himself with a mattock, crow-bar and lantern, and at midnight we set out for the cemetery of —, the arrangement of which, below and above ground, he knew perfectly.

After turning the light of the dark lantern on the inscriptions on several tombstones, we came at last to a stone half buried in long grass and covered with moss and parasitic plants, on which we deciphered the beginning of an epitaph:

Here lies Clarimonde
Beautiful beyond
All that earth could . . .

. . .

'This is it,' said Sérapion, and placing the lantern on the ground, he slipped the crowbar into the interstice of the stone and began to lift it. The stone gave way, and he set to work with the mattock. I watched him, gloomier and more silent than the night itself; he himself, bent over his dismal work, dripped sweat and panted; his laboured breath sounded like a death-rattle.

It was a strange sight, and anyone who had seen us from outside would have taken us for sacrilegious shroud-stealers rather than for priests of God. There was something hard and savage in Sérapion's zeal that gave him the look more of a demon than that of an apostle or angel, and his face, with its large austere features accentuated by the rays of the lantern, was not reassuring. I felt an icy sweat gathering in beads on my limbs, and my hair stood up on my head with a tingling sensation; in my heart I looked upon the action of the pitiless Sérapion as an abominable desecration, and would have been glad if, from the flank of the dark clouds that rolled heavily over us, a triangle of flame had shot out and reduced him to ashes. The owls perched in the cypresses, disturbed by the light of the lantern, came flapping heavily against the glass with their dusty wings and uttering plaintive cries; foxes yelped in the distance, and a thousand sinister sounds broke the silence.

At length Sérapion's mattock struck against the coffin, the boards of which echoed with a hollow, sonorous sound, that awful sound which nothingness gives when touched; he lifted the lid, and I saw Clarimonde, pale as marble, with clasped hands; her white shroud made only one single fold from head to feet. A little red drop gleamed like a rose at the corner of her discoloured mouth.

Sérapion, on seeing this, burst into a fury:

'Ah! there you are, demon, shameless harlot, drinker of blood and gold!' and he sprinkled with holy water the corpse and the coffin also, tracing upon it the figure of a cross.

No sooner had poor Clarimonde been touched by the sacred dew than her lovely body crumbled into dust; nothing remained but a horrible, shapeless heap of ashes, flesh and half-calcined bones.

'Behold your mistress, my lord Romuald!' said the pitiless priest, pointing to the miserable relics. 'Will you ever again be tempted to go walking with your beautiful lady at Lido and Fusine?'

I bowed my head; a great change had taken place in me. I returned to my presbytery, and the lord Romuald, lover of Clarimonde, took leave of the poor priest with whom he had so long and so strangely kept company. I only saw Clarimonde once more; the following night she appeared and said to me, as at our first meeting under the portal of the church:

'Unhappy man! unhappy man! what have you done? Why did you listen to that idiot priest? Were you not happy? And what had I done to you, that you should violate my poor grave and strip bare the horror of my annihilation? All communication between our souls and our bodies is broken. Farewell, you will regret me.'

She vanished into the air like smoke, and I never saw her again.

Alas, she spoke the truth! I have regretted her more than once, and I still regret her. My soul's peace has been very dearly bought; the love of God was not too great a thing to replace hers.

There, brother, is the story of my youth. Never look on a woman, but go with your eyes fixed on the ground, for chaste and steadfast as you may be, one minute may make you lose Eternity.

EDGAR ALLAN POE

BERENICE

MISERY IS manifold. The wretchedness of earth is multiform. Overreaching the wide horizon as the rainbow, its hues are as various as the hues of that arch, as distinct too, yet as intimately blended. Overreaching the wide horizon as the rainbow! How is it that from beauty I have derived a type of unloveliness? from the convent of peace a simile of sorrow? But as in ethics, evil is a consequence of good, so in fact, out of joy is sorrow born. Either the memory of past bliss is the anguish of today, or the agonies which *are* have their origin in the ecstasies which *might* have been.

My baptismal name is Egaeus, that of my family I will not mention. Yet there are no towers in the land more time-honoured than my gloomy, grey, hereditary halls. Our line has been called a race of visionaries; and in many striking particulars – in the character of the family mansion, in the frescoes of the chief saloon, in the tapestries of the dormitories, in the chiselling of some buttresses in the armoury, but more especially in the gallery of antique paintings, in the fashion of the library chamber, and lastly, in the very peculiar nature of the library's contents – there is more than sufficient evidence to warrant the belief.

The recollections of my earliest years are connected with that chamber and with its volumes, of which latter I will say no more. Here died my mother. Herein was I born. But it is mere idleness to say that I had not lived before, that the soul has no previous existence. You deny it? let us not argue the matter. Convinced myself, I seek not to convince. There is, however, a remembrance of aerial forms, of spiritual and meaning eyes, of sounds, musical yet sad; a remembrance which will not be excluded, a memory like a shadow, vague, variable, indefinite, unsteady, and like a shadow, too, in the impossibility of my getting rid of it while the sunlight of my reason shall exist.

In that chamber was I born. Thus awakening from the

long night of what seemed, but was not nonentity, at once into the very regions of fairyland, into a palace of imagination, into the wild dominions of monastic thought and erudition, it is not singular that I gazed around me with a startled and ardent eye, that I loitered away my boyhood in books, and dissipated my youth in reverie; but it *is* singular, that, as years rolled away and the noon of manhood found me still in the mansion of my fathers, it *is* wonderful what stagnation there fell upon the springs of my life, wonderful how total an inversion took place in the character of my commonest thought. The realities of the world affected me as visions, and as visions only, while the wild ideas of the land of dreams became, in turn, not the material of my every-day existence, but in very deed that existence utterly and solely in itself.

Berenice and I were cousins, and we grew up together in my paternal halls. Yet differently we grew – I, ill of health and buried in gloom, she, agile, graceful, and overflowing with energy; hers the ramble on the hillside, mine the studies of the cloister; I, living within my own heart, and addicted, body and soul to the most intense and painful meditation, she, roaming carelessly through life with no thought of the shadows in her path, or the silent flight of the raven-winged hoars. Berenice! I call upon her name, Berenice! and from the grey ruins of memory a thousand tumultuous recollections are startled at the sound! Ah, vividly is her image before me now, as in the early days of her lightheartedness and joy! O, gorgeous yet fantastic beauty! O, sylph amid the shrubberies of Arnheim! O, Naiad among its fountains! And then, then all is mystery and terror, and a tale which should not be told. Disease, a fatal disease, fell like the simoom upon her frame; and even while I gazed upon her, the spirit of change swept over her, pervading her mind, her habits, and her character, and in a manner the most subtle and terrible, disturbing even the identity of her person! Alas! the destroyer came and went! and the victim, where is she? I knew her not, or knew her no longer as Berenice!

Among the numerous train of maladies superinduced by that fatal and primary one which effected a revolution of so horrible a kind in the moral and physical being of my cousin, may be mentioned as the most distressing and obstinate in its nature, a species of epilepsy not unfrequently terminating in *trance* itself – trance very nearly resembling positive dissolution, and from which her manner of recovery was, in most instances, startlingly abrupt. In the meantime, my own disease – for I have been told that I should call it by no other appellation – my own disease, then, grew rapidly upon me, and assumed finally a monomaniac character of a novel and extraordinary form – hourly and momently gaining vigour – and at length obtaining over me the most incomprehensible ascendancy. This monomania, if I must so term it, consisted in a morbid irritability of those properties of the mind in metaphysical science termed the *attentive.* It is more than probable that I am not understood; but I fear, indeed, that it is in no manner possible to convey to the mind of the merely general reader an adequate idea of the nervous *intensity of interest* with which, in my case, the powers of meditation (not to speak technically) busied and buried themselves, in the contemplation of even the most ordinary objects of the universe.

To muse for long unwearied hours, with my attention riveted to some frivolous device on the margin or in the typography of a book; to become absorbed, for the better part of a summer's day, in a quaint shadow falling aslant upon the tapestry or upon the floor; to lose myself, for an entire night, in watching the steady flame of a lamp, or the embers of a fire; to dream away whole days over the perfume of a flower; to repeat monotonously some common word, until the sound, by dint of frequent repetition, ceased to convey any idea whatever to the mind; to lose all sense of motion or physical existence, by means of absolute bodily quiescence long and obstinately persevered in: such were a few of the most common and least pernicious vagaries induced by a condition of the mental faculties, not, indeed, altogether unparalleled, but certainly bidding defiance to anything like analysis or explanation.

Yet let me not be misapprehended. The undue, earnest, and morbid attention thus excited by objects in their own nature frivolous, must not be confounded in character with that ruminating propensity common to all mankind, and more especially indulged in by persons of ardent imagination. It was not even, as might be at first supposed, an extreme condition, or exaggeration of such propensity, but primarily and essentially distinct and different. In the one instance, the dreamer or enthusiast, being interested by an object usually *not* frivolous, imperceptibly loses sight of this object in a wilderness of deductions and suggestions issuing therefrom, until at the conclusion of a daydream *often replete with luxury,* he finds the *incitamentum,* or first cause of his musings, entirely vanished and forgotten. In my case, the primary object was *invariably frivolous,* although assuming, through the medium of my distempered vision, a refracted and unreal importance. Few deductions, if any, were made; and those few pertinaciously returning in upon the original object as a centre. The meditations were *never* pleasurable; and, at the termination of the reverie, the first cause, so far from being out of sight, had attained that supernaturally exaggerated interest which was the prevailing feature of the disease. In a word, the powers of mind more particularly exercised were, with me, as I have said before, the *attentive,* and are with the daydreamer, the *speculative.*

My books, at this epoch, if they did not actually serve to irritate the disorder, partook, it will be perceived, largely, in their imaginative and inconsequential nature, of the characteristic qualities of the disorder itself. I well remember, among others, the treatise of the noble Italian, Cœlius Secundus Curio, *'De Amplitudine Beati Regni Dei'*; St Austin's great work, *The City of God*; and Tertullian's *De Carne Christi,* in which the paradoxical sentence, *'Mortuus est Dei filius; credibile est quia ineptum est; et sepultus resurrexit; certum est quia impossibile est,'* occupied my undivided time, for many weeks of laborious and fruitless investigation.

Thus it will appear that, shaken from its balance only by trivial things, my reason bore resemblance to that ocean-crag spoken of by Ptolemy Hephaestion, which steadily resisting the attacks of human violence, and the fiercer fury of the waters and the winds, trembled only to the touch of the flower called Asphodel. And although, to a careless thinker it might appear a matter beyond doubt, that the alteration produced by her unhappy malady, in the *moral* condition of

Berenice, would afford me many objects for the exercise of that intense and abnormal meditation whose nature I have been at some trouble in explaining, yet such was not in any degree the case. In the lucid intervals of my infirmity, her calamity, indeed, gave me pain, and, taking deeply to heart that total wreck of her fair and gentle life, I did not fail to ponder frequently and bitterly upon the wonder-working means by which so strange a revolution had been so suddenly brought to pass. But these reflections partook not of the idiosyncrasy of my disease, and were such as would have occurred under similar circumstances to the ordinary mass of mankind. True to its own character, my disorder revelled in the less important but more startling changes wrought in the *physical* frame of Berenice – in the singular and most appalling distortion of her personal identity.

During the brightest days of her unparalleled beauty, most surely I had never loved her. In the strange anomaly of my existence, feelings with me *had never been* of the heart, and my passions *always were* of the mind. Through the grey of the early morning – among the trellised shadows of the forest at noonday – and in the silence of my library at night – she had flitted by my eyes, and I had seen her – not as the living and breathing Berenice, but as the Berenice of a dream; not as being of the earth, earthy, but as the abstraction of such a being; not as a thing to admire, but to analyse; not as an object of love, but as the theme of the most abstruse although desultory speculation. And *now* – now I shuddered in her presence, and grew pale at her approach; yet, bitterly lamenting her fallen and desolate condition, I called to mind that she had loved me long, and, in an evil moment, I spoke to her of marriage.

And at length the period of our nuptials was approaching, when, upon an afternoon in the winter of the year – one of these unseasonably warm, calm, and misty days which are the nurse of the beautiful Halcyon,[1] – I sat (and sat, as I thought, alone), in the inner apartment of the library. But, uplifting my eyes, I saw that Berenice stood before me.

Was it my own excited imagination – or the misty in-

[1] For as Jove, during the winter season, gives twice seven days of warmth, men have called this clement and temperate time the nurse of the beautiful Hálcyon – *Simonides.*

fluence of the atmosphere – or the uncertain twilight of the chamber – or the grey draperies which fell around her figure – that caused in it so vacillating and indistinct an outline? I could not tell. She spoke no word; and I – not for worlds could I have uttered a syllable. An icy chill ran through my frame; a sense of insufferable anxiety oppressed me; a consuming curiosity pervaded my soul; and, sinking back upon the chair, I remained for some time breathless and motionless, with my eyes riveted upon her person. Alas! its emaciation was excessive, and not one vestige of the former being lurked in any single line of the contour. My burning glances at length fell upon the face.

The forehead was high, and very pale, and singularly placid; and the once jetty hair fell partially over it, and overshadowed the hollow temples with innumerable ringlets, now of a vivid yellow, and jarring discordantly, in their fantastic character, with the reigning melancholy of the countenance. The eyes were lifeless, and lustreless, and seemingly pupilless, and I shrank involuntarily from their glassy stare to the contemplation of the thin and shrunken lips. They parted; and in a smile of peculiar meaning, the *teeth* of the changed Berenice disclosed themselves slowly to my view. Would to God that I had never beheld them, or that, having done so, I had died!

The shutting of a door disturbed me, and, looking up, I found that my cousin had departed from the chamber. But from the disordered chamber of my brain had not, alas! departed, and would not be driven away, the white and ghastly *spectrum* of the teeth. Not a speck on their surface – not a shade on their enamel – not an indenture in their edges – but what that brief period of her smile had sufficed to brand it upon my memory. I saw them *now* even more unequivocally than I beheld them *then*. The teeth! – the teeth! – they were here, and there, and everywhere, and visibly and palpably before me; long, narrow, and excessively white, with the pale lips writhing about them, as in the very moment of their first terrible development. Then came the full fury of my *monomania*, and I struggled in vain against its strange and irresistible influence. In the multiplied objects of the external world I had no thoughts but for the teeth. For these I longed with a frenzied desire. All other matters and all different interests became absorbed in their single contemplation. They – they alone were present to the mental eye, and they, in their sole individuality, became the essence of my mental life. I held them in every light. I turned them in every attitude. I surveyed their characteristics. I dwelt upon their peculiarities. I pondered upon their conformation. I mused upon the alteration in their nature. I shuddered as I assigned to them, in imagination, a sensitive and sentient power, and, even when unassisted by the lips, a capability of moral expression. Of Mademoiselle Salle it has been well said, '*Que tous ses pas étaient des sentiments,*' and of Berenice I more seriously believed *que tous ses dents étaient des idées. Des idées!* – ah, here was the idiotic thought that destroyed me? *Des idées* – ah, *therefore* it was that I coveted them so madly! I felt that their possession could alone ever restore me to peace, in giving me back to reason.

And the evening closed in upon me thus – and then the darkness came, and tarried, and went – and the days again dawned – and the mists of a second night were now gathering around – and still I sat motionless in that solitary room – and still I sat buried in meditation – and still the *phantasma* of the teeth maintained its terrible ascendancy, as, with the most vivid and hideous distinctness, it floated about amid the changing lights and shadows of the chamber. At length there broke in upon my dreams a cry as of horror and dismay; and thereunto, after a pause, succeeded the sound of troubled voices, intermingled with many low moanings of sorrow or of pain. I arose from my seat, and throwing open one of the doors of the library, saw standing out in the ante-chamber, a servant maid, all in tears, who told me that Berenice was no more! She had been seized with epilepsy in the early morning, and now, at the closing in of the night, the grave was ready for its tenant, and all the preparations for the burial were completed.

I found myself sitting in the library, and again sitting there alone. It seemed that I had newly awakened from a confused and exciting dream. I knew that it was now midnight, and I was well aware that since the setting of the sun Berenice had been interred. But of that dreary period which intervened I had no positive, at least no definite comprehension. Yet its memory was replete with horror – horror more horrible from being vague, and terror more terrible from ambiguity. It was a fearful page in the record of my existence, written all over with dim, and hideous, and unintelligible recollections. I strived to decipher them, but in vain; while ever and anon, like the spirit of a departed sound, the shrill and piercing shriek of a female voice seemed to be ringing in my ears. I had done a deed – what was it? I asked myself the question aloud, and the whispering echoes of the chamber answered me – *'What was it?'*

On the table beside me burned a lamp, and near it lay a little box. It was of no remarkable character, and I had seen it frequently before, for it was the property of the family physician; but how came it *there* upon my table, and why did I shudder in regarding it? These things were in no manner to be accounted for, and my eyes at length dropped to the open pages of a book, and to a sentence underscored therein. The words were the singular but simple ones of the poet Ebn Zaiat: *'Dicebant mihi sodales, si sepulchrum amicae visitarem, curas meas aliquantulum fore levatas.'* Why, then, as I perused them, did the hairs of my head erect themselves on end, and the blood of my body become congealed within my veins?

There came a light tap at the library door – and, pale as the tenant of a tomb, a menial entered upon tiptoe. His looks were wild with terror, and he spoke to me in a voice tremulous, husky, and very low. What said he? – some broken sentences I heard. He told of a wild cry disturbing the silence of the night – of the gathering together of the household – of a search in the direction of the sound; and then his tones grew thrillingly distinct as he whispered me of a violated grave – of a disfigured body enshrouded, yet still breathing – still palpitating – *still alive!*

He pointed to my garments; they were muddy and clotted with gore. I spoke not, and he took me gently by the hand; it was indented with the impress of human nails. He directed my attention to some object against the wall. I looked at it for some minutes: it was a spade. With a shriek I bounded to the table, and grasped the box that lay upon it. But I could not force it open; and, in my tremor, it slipped from my hands, and fell heavily, and burst into pieces; and from it, with a rattling sound, there rolled out some instruments of dental surgery, intermingled with thirty-two small, white, and ivory-looking substances that were scattered to and fro about the floor.

SIMON RAVEN

CHRISEIS

from Doctors Wear Scarlet

'The place must have been a Venetian stronghold,' said Piers.

We were outside looking at the low, square tower, with its narrow pointed windows and crenellated walls, which the light of morning revealed. The wind was still strong; but it had stopped raining now, and there was promise that the blanket of white cloud above us might later yield to the sun.

'They must have had a troop of soldiers here,' Piers went on, 'keeping watch over the mountains.'

'I hope,' I said, 'that they were frequently relieved. One night in the place is enough.'

'We shan't be able to move Richard for a day or two,' said Roddy, who on account of some slight experience in the field was acknowledged by us as a kind of crude medical expert.

'Just how bad is he?' I asked.

'Very weak,' said Roddy with a puzzled look. 'As far as I can tell he just needs rest and food. Building up. But it will be some time before he can take much of anything solid.'

'So long as we can keep that woman away from him,' Piers said, 'he will be all right.'

Roddy looked at him thoughtfully.

'Will she come back?'

'Oh yes.'

'She bolted fast enough when we appeared last night.'

'She was taken unawares. But soon she will pull herself together, and she will wait for her opportunity, and then she will . . .' His voice trailed away.

'Will what?' said Roddy.

'. . . will return, for Richard.'

'The three of us should be able to manage her.'

'She will have . . . resources,' Piers said.

For a time we were silent. The towering peaks crowded about us, but there was a gap between two of the mountains through which I glimpsed a green plain far below. Familiarity, I thought, security: home.

'We'd best go in and look to Richard.'

When we returned into the fort, Richard, for the first time, was awake. He was still as white as marble and he looked desperately weak; but he smiled softly at us and said, without apparent surprise —

'So you got here all right. Piers . . . Anthony . . . and you, Roddy. It was good of you to come.'

'We came as soon as we could.'

'Where did you sleep?'

'Here. With you.'

'No blankets,' said Richard, turning his head with effort and looking round the inside of the fort. 'You must have been cold.'

'Never mind that,' said Roddy; 'don't worry about us. Sleep.'

'Yes,' said Piers, 'you must sleep.'

But Richard was still gazing, restless and anxious, round the bare stone walls.

'Where is . . . Chriseis?' he said at length.

'She went away last night when we came.'

'We will take care of you now.'

'You must watch for her,' said Richard. 'She will come back. She . . . is . . . clever.'

Then his eyes closed and he fell asleep.

But later that day, early in the afternoon, he awoke once more. We gave him some yoghurt, which he swallowed with difficulty, and a little wine. And then he seemed disposed to talk.

'You must watch for Chriseis. If she comes back, I shall not be able to fight her. Neither, perhaps, will you. Even when I was well and strong . . . when I first met her months ago in Corinth . . . I could not fight her. But then, of course, I thought she was something different . . . liberation, escape.

'A dreary town, Corinth. Modern and hard. How should such a creature come from those everyday streets, the bright shops, the neat houses? But she was there, and she found me, and I thought she loved me. And indeed I loved her. For herself and the escape I thought she offered. But even then I couldn't . . . I couldn't . . .'

He broke off and looked despairingly at Piers, who put out

a hand and began to stroke the tumbled hair back from his forehead.

'Never mind, my dear, never mind. We understand. Don't force yourself to tell us.'

'But I want to tell you. You must all know.'

His voice was becoming urgent and he raised his head from the pillow.

'I couldn't . . . make love . . . like a man.'

His head sank back and he seemed much relieved.

'But Chriseis, she said it didn't matter, there were other things. And so there were – fearful, ugly things. But I went with her, dazed, not really knowing what I did, but helping her all the same, because, you see, I felt I had betrayed her by my lack of manhood, and now she meant so much I couldn't leave her. And so together we did these things.'

He gave a soft moan and looked at Piers once more.

'And then,' he went on, 'I had to leave Corinth for a time, to go to Athens and then to Delphi, where I had work. Some of the way she came with me, but after a time she had to return to Corinth. For a while I missed her desperately, but then it got better, and I began to realize that what I really needed was to forget her, was to have my own proper friends once more. That was when I wrote to Piers to ask him to come in the summer.'

He stretched out a hand to Piers, who took it lightly and rubbed it between his own to warm it.

'But later,' said Richard, 'when I had done my work and returned to Corinth, she came to me again. I had hoped she wouldn't . . . that she would have forgotten me and found someone else. But within a week of my return to Corinth – I had more work there, you see, and had to go back – within a week, she came to me. And it was then that something different began between us. We no longer went out and did . . . the things we used to. She turned herself entirely on to me, and thenceforth all the suffering was mine. You know what I mean, Piers. I can see it in your eye. But you, Anthony? And Roddy?'

A frustrated look appeared on Roddy's face. He opened his mouth as if to ask a question, but thought better of it when he saw Piers shake his head.

'You will find out, Roddy, as time goes on,' said Richard,

who had apparently noticed this exchange. 'You will find out. For the present you must just understand that she made me suffer and began to make me ill. I tried to get away. Although I wanted her to go on making me suffer, at that time I was still strong enough to want to escape from her also, and in the end I decided to leave for Crete several weeks before I had planned. I found the strength to leave without telling her; but she followed me to Athens and found me. Do you know, I was *glad* to be found. But I was also desperate, because I now knew that she was going to kill me. Sooner or later she would have taken everything she could, and then I would be dead. So from Athens I wrote to Anthony, begging him to bring you and follow me to Crete; because I was still strong enough and clear enough to know that I must have help, and that you, who were my friends, would help me. And now you have come. . . .

'Now you have come, but there is still danger. For I know she is not far from here, and soon she will come back. . . .'

He broke off, and then returned to the story of his love.

'So when we got to Crete, I became less and less clear, but all the time I knew that you would come. But somehow Chriseis knew too, and persuaded me to come with her to Hydra, thinking to elude you. The police were interested in us, she said, and we must go where we were not known. And then the monks in Hydra would make me strong. They would make me so strong that she would be able to love me, in her vile way, for ever, and yet I would never again get weak. So I listened to her lies and believed them; but although she tried to prevent me I left a clue for you, so that you could follow. I managed to speak to the old man, Arnold, though even then her influence was so strong that I found myself speaking in riddles, and whether I was trying to cheat her or trying to cheat you I shall never know. Still, it was a simple riddle, so I suppose you understood. . . .

'By the time we had gone to Mount Ida and then on to Hydra, I was very ill. So ill that I cannot remember how I was brought there. But the monks made me well. In a few days they made me so strong that I could stand up to her; and then I insisted that we went back to Crete. Because I was terrified that you would not find Arnold, or would not understand my riddle, and in any case all this was still in

June: so that at this time you had yet to come to Crete; and by going there straight away I might hope to find you. And in the end Chriseis gave way. She let me charter a caique owned by a German, and we came round to the coast near Sphakion. I wanted to go to Heraclion and wait there for you; but she didn't want this, because she hated you and was also afraid, or so she said, that there might be trouble with the police. And since I was already beginning to get weaker again, I gave in to her and let her bring me to Sphakion. From there she took me to several villages, while I was growing weaker all the time; but always the villagers seemed to understand what she was doing, and they would drive us out after a day or two, until at last we ended up here on the mountain. We have been here for days now. And all the time I have been growing weaker and weaker . . . Why did they have no charity, those villagers? Why did they not try to save me, instead of turning me away with her? I suppose they were afraid of what she might do. For all the time they could see what she was doing to me. How I was growing weaker. . . .

'But now you have come and I shall get well. All I need is rest and food. The monks in Hydra have a special wine, and they did some other things, so that I became well very quickly. But even without their wine and their care, I shall get well in time, if I can only rest. And if that fiend will stay away from me,' he said, his voice quivering with anger and disgust, 'so that the life within me can grow. Watch for her, Anthony, and you, Piers. Watch for her, Roddy. She is not far away, I know, and she will come again. . . .'

And suddenly, as had happened that morning, his eyes closed and he fell asleep.

By now it was early evening and we must make some sort of plan.

'The mayor must be told,' said Roddy.

'He said he would wait.'

'He has already waited a night and a day. We must tell him that we shall be here at least another night, and warn him how difficult it will be to carry Richard down. . . . It may be possible to bind him to one of the mules – but then it could be days before he is strong enough to stand it. . . . But in any case we must speak with the mayor. Courtesy requires it.'

Piers and I nodded.

'But it is important,' Piers said, 'that *two* of us stay here with Richard. In case that woman comes.'

Roddy looked at him with a question in his eye, but seeing how intent was Piers' face, he just nodded in agreement.

'And whoever goes,' said Piers, 'must take care. He must go fast and not linger . . . for anything.'

'It is not far,' said Roddy, 'and there is nothing on this mountain to frighten me. So I had better go.'

'That will be good,' said Piers. 'But remember: *go fast.*'

Roddy gave him another questioning look, but again simply nodded. He rose and made ready to go.

'It is only early evening,' he said. 'I shall be back before dark.'

Richard, disturbed by Roddy's movements, awoke once more.

'Where are you going, Roddy?' he said.

'To speak with friends who have helped us. They are not far.'

'You are going alone?'

'Yes.'

'Take care, Roddy.'

Roddy smiled.

'You needn't worry about me,' he said.

A shadow came into Richard's eyes.

'Lift me to the door,' he said. 'I want to look outside. And to speed Roddy on his way.'

Roddy looked startled, then embarrassed, then deprecating. But Piers signed to me, and together we helped Richard from his bed and supported him to the door. It was the first time we had seen him uncovered by blankets; his clothes were tattered and he smelt abominably. Roddy lifted one of the blankets from the litter on the floor and placed it, like a shawl, round Richard's shoulders and over his chest. Then, having made a vague salute, he started down the steps.

'Wait,' called Richard.

Roddy turned to face us.

'Some say,' said Richard strangely, 'that Zeus was reared on this island. Over in the other mountains to the East.

Others say that his tomb is in those same mountains. The tomb of Zeus . . . But either way, he is strong in this island, and we should pray to him: I for my strength, you for safe passage, and all of us for deliverance.'

Roddy shifted uneasily on the steps.

'It is already evening,' he said, 'I must not wait —'

Richard interrupted him with a movement of his hands. Piers flashed a look at him over Richard's shoulder, a look which said 'pity him and do as he asks.'

'I shall not be long,' Richard said.

So Roddy stood quiet, waiting politely, impatience still stirring in the muscles under his eyes.

Then Richard, leaning on Piers and myself but lifting his voice in a curiously powerful fashion when one considered the low tones in which he had spoken hitherto, called out his prayer to the mountains opposite. He invoked the deity, he asked for the strength to be put back into his limbs, he solicited a safe passage for Roddy, and he requested a good deliverance for us all. The prayer, as he had promised, was brief; and he concluded by asking for a sign.

'Father,' he called out over the mountains, 'send us a sign.'

For a moment no one moved. Then Roddy, saluting once more, began to descend the steps.

'Wait,' called Richard again. And again Roddy turned and stood waiting.

As he turned, a huge black eagle appeared in the sky above us. For a moment it seemed to hover like a hawk, then it swooped down over our heads, so near that the rush of its wings was almost deafening, and soared up again, turning at the same time, till it was once more hovering high above. Again it descended, flying almost into our faces, and again soared up and turned to hover above us. Then it swooped a third time, to ascend, as before, into the sky above our stronghold. And now it hovered, and made as if to swoop yet once more; but before it had come down more than a few yards, it made a wide and beautiful turn and flew away from the declining sun towards the mountains in the East.

'I wouldn't have wanted to miss that,' called Roddy cheerfully. 'Thank you for making me stay.'

He waved gaily. All of us answered his wave, though Richard, who was leaning very hard on the arm I had round him, waved very weakly. Then Roddy turned away; whistling a bar or two of our own regimental march he walked quickly down the graceful steps, turned the corner at the bottom, waved once more as he turned, and was then lost to view. Piers and I made to help Richard inside.

'What did you notice about that eagle?' asked Richard.

'It was a noble bird,' Piers said.

'It was,' said Richard. 'But there are four of us, and the eagle only swooped three times.'

As the evening deepened, Richard slept. Piers and I lit the storm-lantern and sat over it on two large rocks we had carried in from outside.

'Why are you so anxious for Roddy?' I said. 'What danger could there be for him?'

'The same as there could be for us. If that woman came here.'

'And that is . . . ?'

'. . . best not thought about unless it has to be faced.'

I roused myself to press Piers further.

'Piers . . . It is all very well, this fashion of sparing our feelings. But we are adult men, Roddy and I, and we have a right to know what is going on. When you were still in doubt, then you were probably justified in not committing yourself. But there has clearly been no real doubt in your mind for a long while now. And so now, since Roddy and I are sharing in the dangers, we must be allowed to share in your knowledge.'

'I cannot help feeling you have both been slightly obtuse.'

'Myself, possibly. But there is excuse for Roddy. His education has been of an uncomplicated nature.'

Piers looked over at Richard and stirred moodily above the lantern.

'Very well, Anthony,' he said. 'But it is not the sort of thing I can bring myself to explain twice. I will tell you both together when Roddy gets back.'

He rose to look through one of the windows.

'It is nearly dark now,' he said; 'I wonder what is keeping him.'

'The way may be longer than he remembered.'

'Shorter if anything. The storm made it stretch for a

hundred miles.'

'He may be having a difficult time with the mayor and his men. They can hardly be anxious to stay another night.'

'You underrate them. They need never have come in the first place. And I suspect – I know – that it is not only for Richard's sake they have helped us.'

'For what other?'

'For their own. That woman is a danger to all men. To all men and all women too.'

'Then why did they not deal with her themselves?'

'They are afraid of her in a fashion in which they think we cannot be afraid. They believe in her power.'

'But so do you.'

'Yes – and that is one reason why I am not anxious to explain it. But I only believe in part. I share their fear all right. But another side of me, the Western, educated, *Lancaster* side forbids me to be afraid. So I can just make shift to face her.'

The night was down outside, and still Roddy did not come.

'Perhaps the dark overtook him while he was still with the mayor. In which case he might choose to spend the night with him.'

'He would know that we worried for him,' said Piers; 'he would come back.'

'And there can be no question of fear . . .'

'He was brave when you knew him in the Army?'

'Yes. And you can see that he is still brave.'

'But perhaps . . . on the mountain . . . in the night . . .'

'He showed no fear last night,' I said.

'Last night he was fighting a storm, the kind of enemy to which he is accustomed. But now . . .'

'It is the only kind of enemy he acknowledges. If there is another, he does not know of it.'

'He may begin to . . . feel that it is there. So long as he does not realize too late. . . .'

But for some time now Piers' eyelids had been drooping. Each time they nearly closed he had forced them back. But plainly the need for sleep was making him desperate.

'I must sleep for a while,' he now said. 'Can you keep watch, Anthony? Wake me in two hours, and then I will watch for you. It . . . should be all right like that . . . I think . . . unless

. . . But wake me on the instant if you hear any noise at all.'

Without another word he settled himself in a corner and fell asleep.

I took a book from the valise we had brought and began to read in the light of the storm-lantern. The book was heavy to my hands, however, the words drifted in front of my eyes, there was not a flicker of response in my brain. So putting the book down beside me I began to think. I thought of Tyrrel on the night on which everything had started; of Cambridge and of Walter and of Marc Honeydew; of Piers – 'I've seen him three times, Anthony, and each time he was dead'; of how I went to Ludlow to persuade Roddy – 'All that is needed is a little common sense, Anthony, and a lack of superfluous scruple.' I thought of the dinner with Tyrrel before we left, of Penelope's telephone call that night, and of our lighthearted journey across France and Italy; of Venice; of Heraclion with its blind sea-front; of Cnossos and Ratty Arnold . . . 'He likes islands. He likes Crete, but he likes other islands as well, because water is best . . . *αϱιστσν μεν υδωϱ* . . . ariston men hydor . . . ariston men hydor . . . hydor . . . hydor . . .' until I awoke with a start, and this is what I saw.

I saw that the door was half open, and that just inside it was standing a woman, dressed in black trousers and a kind of black tunic above them. She also had on a medium length black cape, which was held together in front by a short gold chain. It was the same woman as we had surprised the night before; but on that occasion she had fled so swiftly, and I had been so numbed by the storm and so dazzled by the white light of the lantern, that I had taken in no detail about her. But now, though newly awoken, I saw with great clarity every detail of her dress and her appearance. That beneath the trousers was a pair of what looked very like Mess Wellingtons, the upper portions of which were concealed under the trouser legs; that on her throat, just above the gold chain which secured her cloak, was a small silver brooch; that her black hair was long and very glossy in appearance for a woman who had just spent a night in the open and many days living in extreme discomfort; that her complexion was white yet healthy, her nose well proportioned, her forehead narrow; that her chin was delicate; and that her eyes were very bright.

It was these bright eyes that were fixed on me now. They were not looking into my own eyes, but just played generally, though seemingly without moving, over my face and the upper part of my body. Sometimes the light caught her brooch and it would flash; sometimes it caught her eyes, which then became brighter than ever. So she stood, while her eyes explored me; and then I realized, not with horror but with a comfortable feeling of resignation, that I could not move. I could shift my gaze, turn my head, even raise a hand; but I could not move my body; and I could not speak. I was not afraid, I was simply numb. I had realized, dimly and without urgency, that I must wake Piers, so I had made to get to my feet and go to him; but my body would not stir. Then I had opened my mouth to call out to him; but no words, not even the faintest sound, would come. I was paralysed; I had made my effort and in a distant, theoretical way regretted my failure: but now I knew, with a kind of grim satisfaction, that I could do nothing more, and I settled with interest and almost with pleasure to watch what happened next.

First of all the woman closed the door. She did not turn; she just moved one arm behind her and pushed it gently home. Then, still letting her eyes play over me, she unfastened her cloak and dropped it on the floor. After this, she walked slowly towards me, smiled with considerable charm, and muttered something in Greek which I did not understand. Taking her eyes off me, she passed on to where Piers was slumped in the corner. I was still fixed to my seat, but as before I could still turn my eyes to follow her. I saw her stand over Piers and regard him with attention. For a while she stood there, playing her eyes over him in the same way as she had done to myself, but all the time muttering in a low, soft voice, a neutral voice, neither of hatred nor desire, but perhaps of incantation. After which she stooped down over him, opened one of his eyes with finger and thumb, looked closely into it, and then let the eyelid drop. I was conscious of faint curiosity: why had she paid so much more attention to Piers, who was safely asleep, than to myself who was at least partially conscious? But the thought, vague and untroubling in any case, soon passed from me. Meanwhile the woman was standing up again, and now, after a last low mutter over Piers, she began to move towards Richard.

When she reached the pathetic shape of clammy blankets, she knelt down on the floor beside them and started to moan softly. She passed her hand over the feet and legs, up over the stomach, stroking and fondling, then on to the chest and throat. At this stage, her moaning struck a higher and more intense key; her caresses were slower and more loving; while her face, of which I could see the right profile, became at once fierce with longing and tender with an effort of love. She stroked Richard's forehead and his cheeks. She passed her fingers lightly over his closed eyes. She smoothed his hair and touched him behind the ears. And then she arched her body and brought her face down over his, being about, as I thought, to kiss him on the lips: but just as her face was almost touching his, she seemed to wrench it to one side; she bared her teeth, until her whole face seemed one hideous grin, and then, with a movement as quick as a snake's, she struck into Richard's naked throat.

And still I could not move or speak; still I felt neither fear nor horror, only interest and the very faintest misgiving. Richard was awake now. I was near enough to see his eyes: into them came a look of utter loneliness and despair; a look which, as he saw my eyes on his, turned to one of pleading and of prayer, and thence, as I continued to regard him without moving, to one of sorrowful reproach. 'Save me,' his eyes had said, 'before the life is drained out of me'; and then, 'You have yielded to her and betrayed your friend.' But still I could do nothing, still I watched with interest and was untouched, in my heart, by the terrible message in those eyes.

Then Richard, seeing that there would be no help from me and knowing that his life was fast leaving him, must have steeled himself to make one final call for help. For the muscles of his face knotted in the desperate summoning of his strength; his eyes bulged and his forehead narrowed and stretched in his agony; and out of his mouth came a great groan of despair and desolation, a call for pity, a call for salvation, a call for love.

The woman, sunk into his throat with lust, did not heed his cry for pity. Myself, lost and paralysed, could interpret but remained indifferent to his plea for salvation. But Piers, whatever the depths to which his sleeping soul had been willed by the woman, awakened to Richard's cry for love. He stirred, sat up, rubbed his eyes and then looked straight at Richard and the woman. His eyes became bright with hatred, brighter than the eyes of the woman had been. He crossed the room in four quick steps; he seized the woman by her shoulders; and with all his strength he wrenched her away from Richard, whose eyes closed, whose head lolled, whose whole body seemed to shrink and sag.

Piers hurled the woman down on the floor. He put one knee on her chest. He placed both hands round her throat and he began to squeeze. He squeezed until the veins and sinews stood out in his neck; until the sweat was running in streams down his face; until his whole body was jerking in spasms, half of rage and half of effort, which struck at him as the multiple lash might strike at a trussed man under the cat. All the time his eyes grew brighter and harder; until at last, after one final and tremendous spasm, which seemed like some supreme and brutish orgasm, he slowly loosened his hands, stood up and back so that I might see what he had done.

'Now are you answered?' he shouted into my face.

On the floor I could see the body of the woman. All of it was limp and easy now. Except for the face: for her mouth was still caught in the hideous grin which she had worn as she struck her face at her victim; and spread over her cheeks and lips, dribbling from the bared white teeth, was the blood wet and shining red, which she had drunk from Richard Fountain's throat.

For a long time I remained without moving. I have a vague recollection of watching Piers drag the body of the woman into a corner and of seeing him busy himself with Richard; but I related none of this to myself or to any kind of reality, for I was still debarred from reality. Gradually, however, I began to come out of my daze, to think and feel as Anthony Seymour, the friend of Piers Clarence and Richard Fountain, and to comprehend the enormity of what I had seen. I put my head between my knees; then rose slowly from the seat of rock, my limbs cramped and bitterly cold, my stomach heaving and contracting with horror and guilt.

'Richard . . . will he be all right?'

'I think so,' said Piers; 'but I only got her in the nick of time.'

'What can I . . . ? Oh, Piers. So sorry . . . I . . .'

Piers got up from beside Richard and smiled at me.

'It wasn't your fault, Anthony. Why do you think I felt so desperately sleepy so very suddenly? I can usually go for days . . . No. You couldn't help it, and Richard of all people will understand why.'

'How did you awake?'

'I don't know. I heard Richard . . . with my soul, I think. His call was too strong for her. But even then she nearly . . . got the better of me. You saw how hard I was . . . trying?'

'Yes.'

'It wasn't anger, Anthony. All that effort, effort of body *and* mind, was really needed. She was a strong woman in more ways than one.'

'And Richard will really be all right?'

'I think so,' he said. 'He's very weak indeed. But when he knows the danger is gone for good . . .'

He paused for a moment.

'Is it gone for good?' he said.

He looked at me very oddly.

'We have gone through too much,' he murmured at last, 'to take any more chances now.'

He went to one corner where Roddy had left a walking stick which he had been shaping, earlier in the day, from a branch he had found.

'Lucky Roddy forgot this,' said Piers softly.

And then, 'You realize, Anthony, that if I am *right* in doing . . . what I am now going to do – and we shall have no way at all of knowing – then there may be . . . consequences for Richard. Even afterwards. Nobody knows really.'

'We must deal with them as and when they arise,' I said, not really understanding.

Piers rummaged in the valise and took out a large clasp knife.

'Take her outside, Anthony.'

I went to the body of the woman and took it by the shoulders. With some difficulty I dragged it to the door, which

Piers opened for me, and then on to the topmost of the wide and graceful steps outside. There was a light cold wind and a trace of dawn.

Piers joined me. He was carrying the storm-lantern and Roddy's stick, which he had sharpened down to a point. He put the lantern down and with great care sawed the stick in two with the knife about nine inches above the sharp end. Then he looked about in the light of the lamp and selected a large, flat-bottomed stone.

'Hold up the lantern, Anthony.'

He knelt down on one knee and placed the point of the stake he had made over the heart of the thing which had been Chriseis.

'Now keep this upright with your other hand.'

I clasped the stake some six inches above the point; and Piers, drawing a deep breath, raised the stone high above his head with both hands, so that he might be able to strike down again with all the strength of his two arms.

GUY DE MAUPASSANT

THE HORLA

translated by Marjorie Laurie

8th May

WHAT A glorious day! I have spent the whole morning lying on the lawn in front of my house, under the spreading plane tree which shelters and shades it entirely. I love this country-side, where I have my roots, those deep-reaching, delicate fibres, which attach a man to the land where his ancestors were born and died, which link him to the local ways of thought, local diet, local idioms, to the intonations of the country-folk, to the odours of the soil, the village, the very atmosphere.

I love this house of mine, in which my childhood was passed. From end to end, my garden skirts the river Seine. I have only to look from my windows across the road to see that great and noble river, covered with the shipping which passes up and down between Rouen and Le Havre.

Yonder on my left lies Rouen, the great slate-roofed city. From it rises a spiky forest of Gothic belfries, too numerous to count. Some are slender, some are massive, and over them towers the iron spire of the Cathedral. Their bells ring out in the misty blue of exquisite mornings. The distant music of clanging iron or sonorous bronze is borne to my ears, varying in volume as the breeze rises or falls.

What a beautiful morning it is!

About eleven o'clock a long convoy of ships moves up-stream, towed by a tug-boat no larger than a fly, which pants and groans under the strain, and vomits out dense clouds of smoke. Next come two English schooners, with their red ensigns fluttering in the breeze, and after them a superb Brazilian three-masted ship, painted white all over and beautifully spick and span. The sight of her gave me so much pleasure that for some reason or other I saluted her.

12th May

I have been feverish for the last few days. I am feeling unwell, or, to be more precise, out of spirits.

What is the source of these mysterious influences which convert our happiness into depression and our confidence into anxiety? It would seem as if the air, the invisible atmosphere, were charged with forces which we can never know, and as if we were subjected to strange effects from their proximity. I sometimes wake in the morning so full of gaiety that I can hardly repress my desire to sing. What is the cause of this access of cheerfulness? Then perhaps I take a walk along the river bank, and in a moment my high spirits have vanished. I turn homewards in a woebegone frame of mind, as though I expected to hear of some misfortune, as soon as I set foot in my house. Why should I feel like this? Is it merely because a cold current of air has breathed upon me, affecting my nerves and throwing a dark shadow over my soul? Have my thoughts been perturbed by the shape of the clouds, the aspect of the day, the ever-varying colours of the objects that pass before my eyes? Who can explain it? Although the mind is unaware, our whole environment, everything we see, everything we brush past without realizing, everything we touch subconsciously, in short all that our senses encounter without discernment, has on ourselves and on our organs and, through the latter, on our ideas and on our soul itself, rapid, astonishing and inexplicable effects.

How profound is the mystery of the invisible! To sound its depths we use in vain our contemptible equipment of senses; our eyes fail to perceive a thing because it is too small or too large, too near or too far. The dwellers in a star are as invisible to our eyes, as the bacteria in a drop of water. Our ears are ever deceptive, because they convert mere atmospheric vibrations into musical tones; they are wizards, who perform this miracle of transmitting mere oscillatory movement into sound, and by this metamorphosis give birth to music, which changes nature's silent vibrations into audible notes. Our sense of smell is feebler than that of a hound. Our sense of taste hardly serves us to decide the age of a wine. Ah! if only we were endowed with other senses, which would perform other wonders for us, how much more widely could we appreciate our surroundings!

16th May

I am not well. There is now no doubt about it. And last month I was in such splendid health. I am dreadfully feverish, or rather, I am suffering from a febrile languor, which affects mind no less than body. I am continually obsessed by a terrifying sensation of menacing danger, of impending disaster or approaching death. These presentiments are doubtless the herald of some evil yet undeclared, which is germinating in my frame.

18th May

I have just returned from a consultation with my doctor, whom I went to see, because I was suffering from sleeplessness. His examination revealed an unduly quick pulse, dilated pupils, and disordered nerves, but there was no indication of anything serious. I am to have a course of shower-baths and take bromide of potassium.

25th May

No change. My condition is certainly curious. As evening approaches, I am possessed by an incomprehensible restlessness, just as if the coming darkness held for me some terrible menace. I hurry through my dinner, after which I try to read a book, but I cannot understand the words, indeed I can hardly distinguish the letters. I pace my drawing-room in all directions; I am under the malign influence of some vague, irresistible fear, which makes me dread not only sleep itself, but even my bed.

I go up to my bedroom at about two in the morning. The moment I enter I double-lock the door, and shoot the bolts. I am afraid . . . but of what? . . . I have never been a timid man . . . but now I open my wardrobe, I look under the bed, I listen . . . listen . . . for what? How strange it is, that a mere indisposition, a defect of the circulation, the irritation of some fibre, a slight congestion, some minute disturbance in the imperfect and delicate mechanism of the body, can afflict the most cheerful of men with melancholy, and convert a brave man into a coward. And, later, when I actually go to bed, I await the coming of sleep, as one would await the arrival of one's executioner. I anticipate its approach with horror. My heart beats faster, my limbs tremble, my whole frame shivers even under the warm blankets, and this lasts, until the moment when I suddenly succumb to sleep. I am plunged into it, as a man is plunged into a pit of stagnant water and drowned. I do not feel myself dozing off as I used to do. The sleep that comes upon me is a perfidious thing. It lurks near me; it watches me like a spy; it is like someone, who is waiting to seize me by the head, to close my eyes, and thrust me into oblivion.

I sleep for an appreciable time, some two or three hours. Then a dream . . . no, a nightmare, strangles me. I am fully aware that I am lying asleep in bed. I not only feel it, but see it. And I feel, too, that there is someone creeping towards me – someone who looks at me, passes his hands over me, climbs up on to the bed, kneels on my chest, grasps my throat with both hands, and squeezes . . . squeezes . . . with all his might, in an effort to strangle me. I struggle and struggle. It is all that I can do. I am bound hand and foot by that horrible impotence, which paralyses us in our dreams. I try to cry out but I cannot make a sound. I endeavour to move, but in vain. I make the most fearful efforts; I strive to turn over and hurl off this being, that is crushing and smothering me. But all my struggles are of no avail. Then suddenly I awake, with my mind distraught and my body bathed in perspiration. I light a candle. But there is nobody there.

This nightly crisis past, I fall into a peaceful slumber, which lasts till dawn.

2nd June

I am getting worse and worse. What can be wrong with me? The bromide has done me no good; the shower-baths have no effect. One day, in order to induce physical fatigue, though I was weary enough already, I went for a walk in the forest of Roumare. At first I believed that the cool woodland air, so pure and balmy with the perfume of leaves and grass, would renew the blood in my veins and imbue my heart with fresh energy. Entering the forest by a great riding avenue, I turned off towards La Bouille, down a narrow path which lay between two ranks of giant trees. Their arching branches formed a green roof, dense and sombre, shutting out the sky. I was suddenly afflicted with a shivering fit, which was not the result of chill, but an inexplicable shudder of apprehension. I felt ill at ease, all alone in the wood, and I hastened my steps. The profound solitude begot in me blind, unreasoning terror. Then all of a sudden the conviction came over me that I was being followed. Someone was treading on my heels, so closely as almost to touch me. I turned sharply. But there was no one there. The wide, straight avenue of towering trees was empty, with an emptiness that daunted me. Behind me, before me, in either direction, it ran on and on, monotonous and terrifying, until it was lost in the distance.

I closed my eyes, I know not why. And I began to spin round on one heel, very quickly, like a teetotum till I nearly fell. When I opened my eyes again, the trees were swaying, the solid ground was undulating. I had to sit down. I could not remember the way I had come. I positively had no idea. An absurd situation! Haphazard, I set off to the right, and presently found myself again in the main avenue, by which I had reached the heart of the forest.

3rd June

A dreadful night. I am going away for a few weeks. A little travelling will doubtless put me right.

2nd July

Home again, and fully restored to health, besides which, I have had a delightful trip. I went to Mont Saint-Michel, a place I had never yet visited. If you arrive at Avranches about sunset, as I did, a vision of beauty rewards you. The town of Avranches is situated on a hill. I was shown the way to the public gardens, which are at one end of the little city, and the view from this point provoked from me a cry of amazement. A prodigiously wide arm of the sea lay before me. On either side of it the coast line stretched out until lost to view in the haze. In the midst of this immense expanse of water, tawny under a cloudless, saffron sky, a weird and sombre hill soared upwards from the sandy shallows. The sun was setting. The silhouette of this fantastic rock, bearing upon its summit a structure not less unearthly, stood out sharply against the flaming sky.

At dawn on the following day I set out for the Mount. The tide was low, as on the previous evening. The nearer I drew, the more impressively did this astonishing Abbey stand out. After a walk of several hours, I reached the enormous congeries of rock with its group of houses and the great church towering above it. I climbed the steep and narrow street and entered the Abbey, the most perfect masterpiece of Gothic architecture ever created for the dwelling-place of God on earth. Great as a city, it has a series of low-pitched halls with massive, vaulted roofs, and lofty galleries supported on slender columns. It is a gigantic jewel, hewn out of granite; yet delicate as a wisp of lace. There are towers everywhere; and winding staircases which lead upwards into slender belfries. Into the azure sky of day, or into the dark firmament of night, these belfries soar. Their grotesque roof-lines bristle with chimaeras, devils, fantastic beasts, prodigious flowers; and each belfry is linked to its neighbour by a graceful arch of wrought stonework.

When I reached the summit, I said to the monk who was acting as my guide:

'Father, you ought surely to be happy here.'

'It is a windy spot, sir,' he replied.

We entered into conversation, while we watched the rising tide course across the sand, covering it with a breastplate of steely blue. The monk told me legend after legend, all old stories of the Mount. One of them specially impressed me. The natives of the place assert that human speech is often heard on the sands at night, and the bleating of two goats, one with a strong voice and the other with a weak one. The incredulous maintain that the sounds are the cries of sea-birds which sometimes resemble the bleating of goats and at other times plaintive human cries. But fishermen, coming home late at night, vow that they have met an old shepherd roaming over the sands at low water and prowling round the little settlement, which has been planted so far away from the world. This ancient shepherd wears his cloak over his head, so that no one has ever seen his face. He walks on ahead, leading his two goats, one of which has the face of a man and the other that of a woman. Both animals have long white hair, and they never cease from talking and wrangling in an unknown tongue, except when they break off to bleat with all their might.

'Do you believe it?' I asked the monk.

'I cannot tell,' he replied.

To this I rejoined:

'If there were really such strange beings on earth, how is it that we have not found out all about them long ago? Wouldn't you and I have seen them?'

'Do you imagine,' he replied, 'that we see the hundred-thousandth part of what exists? Consider for example the wind, which is the greatest of the forces of nature. It knocks men down, demolishes houses, uproots trees, stirs up the sea into mountainous waves, breaks away the cliffs, and drives great ships on to the breakers. The wind whistles, groans, bellows, sometimes it even kills. Have you seen it? Will you ever see it? It exists nevertheless.'

I made no reply to this ingenuous logic. The man might be a sage, or, on the other hand, a fool. Far be it from me to decide. In any case, he succeeded in silencing me, for his remarks agreed closely with certain reflections of my own.

3rd July

I slept badly. I am sure there is a morbid influence at work here. My coachman has had the same symptoms as myself. On my return home I noticed his singular pallor and I asked him:

'What is the matter with you, Jean?'

'Somehow, sir, I can't get to sleep. I have had something hanging over me like a spell ever since you went away.'

The other servants, however, seem in good health. What I am afraid of is a return of the same symptoms in myself.

4th July

There is no doubt about it. It has seized upon me again. My former nightmares have come back. Last night I felt that there was someone squatting on my chest. His mouth was on my mouth and he was drinking my life from between my lips. He was draining my vitality like a leech. Then, when he had had his fill, he rose and left me, and I awoke. I was too prostrate, too crushed and exhausted to move. If this continues I shall go away again.

5th July

Have I lost my reason? The events of last night are so strange that my head reels when I think of them. I had locked my bedroom door, as is now my nightly practice. Being thirsty, I drank half a tumbler of water, and in doing so I happened to notice that my water-bottle had been filled right up to the crystal stopper. When I went to bed, I fell into one of my frightful dreams. Two hours later I was roused by a horror that was even more terrible than the nightmare itself. Imagine the condition of a man, who is being murdered while he sleeps. He awakes with a knife through his lungs, with the death rattle in his throat. He is bathed in blood. He struggles in vain for breath; he is in the very article of death; and yet he understands nothing of what is happening. That was my case. My reasoning powers at last returned to me. Feeling thirsty again, I lit a candle and went towards the table, on which I had put my water-bottle. I lifted it and tilted it over my tumbler. Not a drop came out. It was empty. Absolutely empty. For the moment I was utterly bewildered; but very soon I was conscious of such poignant emotion that I sank, or rather, collapsed into a chair. Then I leaped to my feet and cast a look around me. Aghast with amazement and terror, I sat down in front of the crystal decanter, and gazed at it intently, trying to solve its mystery. My hands were shaking. Someone must have drunk the water. But who? I myself? Yes, surely it must have been I. In that case I was a somnambulist. Unconsciously I was living that mysterious double life which makes us wonder whether there are two selves within us, or whether some alien personality, elusive and invisible, seizes the moment when the soul is heavy with sleep, takes possession of the body, and exacts from it an obedience equal to, or greater than, that which it yields to the rightful owner when awake.

Ah, who can realize my unspeakable anguish? Who can understand the consternation on the part of a man, sane, fully awake, and with all his mental powers about him, gazing at a glass carafe and searching terror-stricken for the water it should contain. I did not dare to go back to bed, but remained sitting where I was until daybreak.

6th July

I must be going mad. Again the contents of my water-bottle have been drunk by someone during the night. Was it I myself? Was it I? Who else could it be? Who indeed? Oh my God! I am going mad. Who will deliver me?

10th July

I carried out some tests, with surprising results. The conclusion that I have come to is that I must be insane. And yet? On the 6th July, before going to bed, I placed on my table the following things: wine, milk, water, bread and strawberries. Somebody, possibly I myself, drank up all the water and a little of the milk. The wine and the strawberries were not touched. On the 7th July I repeated the experiment with the same result. On the 8th July, I omitted the water and the milk. Nothing was touched. And finally on the 9th July I put only water and milk on the table, but I took the precaution of wrapping up both carafes in pieces of white muslin, and tying the stoppers on with string. Then I rubbed my lips, my moustache and my hands with black lead. After this I went to bed. The usual heavy sleep fell upon me, followed presently by the customary, horrible awakening. I had not moved at all. Even the sheets had no trace of the black lead. I untied the string. I was palpitating with terror. All the water had been drunk! And all the milk too! Ah! my God! . . . I am leaving immediately for Paris.

12th July

Paris. Seemingly I was out of my mind those last few days. I must have been the plaything of my sick fancies, unless I am really a somnambulist, or have been subjected to one of those influences, which we know to exist, but cannot yet explain, and which we call suggestions. In any case, although my mental disorder was verging on dementia, twenty-four hours of Paris have sufficed to restore my balance.

Yesterday I did some shopping and paid a few calls, and found my mind greatly vivified and refreshed thereby. In the evening I went to the Théâtre-Français, and saw a play by Alexandre Dumas the younger. My cure was completed by that vivid and commanding genius. Undoubtedly solitude is dangerous for the overwrought intellect. One needs the companionship of men and women, who can both think and express their thoughts. If we are left too long alone, we people the void with phantoms. In excellent spirits, I strolled back by the boulevards to my hotel. Amidst the elbowings of the crowd I could smile ironically at my terrors and fancies of the preceding week, when I had believed, actually believed, that there was an invisible being who shared my house with me. How feeble is our self-control, how quickly we are scared and bewildered when we are brought up against the tiniest manifestation of the unknown! Instead of coming to the obvious conclusion that if one does not understand, it is merely because the cause is hidden, one forthwith imagines terrifying mysteries and the workings of supernatural powers.

14th July

The National Festival. I walked abroad through the streets, and took a childish delight in the fireworks and decorations. Still, it is a silly business, being joyful to order, on a date fixed by Government decree. The public are an imbecile herd, oscillating between patient stupidity and revolutionary ferocity. They are ordered to amuse themselves and they proceed to amuse themselves; to wage war with an adjoining country, and they wage war accordingly; to vote for an Emperor, and forthwith they vote for an Emperor; to vote for a Republic, and, behold, they vote for a Republic.

The leaders of the people are equally besotted, only instead of obeying men, they obey principles, which are *ipso facto* childish, barren and ill-grounded, because, generally speaking, these so-called principles are supposed to be invariable, and this in a world where one can be sure of nothing, where even light is an illusion, and sound itself a fictitious thing.

16th July

Today I witnessed some phenomena which disturbed me greatly. I dined at the house of my cousin Madame Sablé, whose husband commands the 76th Chasseurs at Limoges. The other guests were two ladies and a Doctor Parent, the husband of one of them. Doctor Parent devotes himself to maladies of the nerves and the extraordinary manifestations to which the modern experiments in hypnotism and suggestion give rise. He recounted to us at some length the marvellous results which have been obtained by English investigators and the Nancy Medical School. The incidents he mentioned seemed to me so preposterous that I flatly declared myself incredulous.

'We are,' he proclaimed, 'on the verge of discovering one of the most important of nature's secrets, that is to say, of nature's terrestrial secrets, for there are undoubtedly other mysteries of the stellar universe, which are of the utmost importance. Ever since mankind has learnt to think and to express his thoughts in speech and writing, he has felt the hovering presence of a mystery, which his senses are too gross and imperfect to enable him to divine. He is now endeavouring, through the medium of his intelligence, to make up this deficiency, which is due to the inadequacy of the organs of the senses. As long as man's intelligence remained in its rudimentary stage, these intimations of the invisible manifested themselves in terrifying phenomena of the crudest description. Hence arose the popular belief in the supernatural, the legends of prowling spirits, of fairies, gnomes and ghosts; even I may add, the legend of God, for our conceptions of the unknown Creator, from whatever religion they are derived, are undeniably the most commonplace, the most stupid, the most unconvincing products of the panic-stricken brains of created beings. There was never a truer word than that saying of Voltaire's: "God made man after His own image and man returned the compliment". It is a little more than a century since mankind obtained a first inkling of these new developments. Mesmer and several others have opened out to us an unexpected pathway and we have achieved astonishing results, especially during the past four or five years.'

My cousin, who was as incredulous as myself, smiled sceptically; whereupon Doctor Parent said:

'Would you like me to try to put you to sleep?'

'Yes, certainly.'

She seated herself in an arm-chair, and the doctor proceeded to direct upon her a concentrated and mesmeric gaze. The sight of this induced in me a sudden uneasiness. My heart beat faster, and I felt a constriction of the throat. I saw Madame Sablé's eyes grow heavy; her lips contracted, and her bosom rose and sank. In ten minutes she was asleep.

'Go behind her chair,' said the doctor.

I took a seat behind her. He put into her hands a visiting card.

'This,' he said, 'is a looking-glass. What do you see in it?'

'I see my cousin,' she answered.

'What is your cousin doing?'

'He is twisting his moustache.'

'And now what is he doing?'

'He is taking a photograph out of his pocket.'

'Whose photograph?'

'It is a photograph of himself.'

It was true, and that photograph had been delivered to me only that evening at my hotel.

'Describe the photograph.'

'He is standing up. He is holding his hat in his hand.'

Apparently she saw in this blank card the reflection she would have seen in a mirror.

The other women present were frightened and exclaimed:

'That's enough. That's enough.'

The doctor however continued:

'Tomorrow,' he ordered, 'you will get up at eight o'clock. You will call on your cousin at his hotel, and you will beg him to lend you five thousand francs. Your husband has asked you for this sum and you are to produce it when he returns to Paris.'

Then he awakened her.

On my return to the hotel, my mind was busy with this curious séance. I had no doubt of the absolute and unimpeachable good faith of my cousin, whom I had known like my own sister from childhood. What I did suspect was some trickery on the part of the doctor. Had he held, concealed in the palm of his hand, a mirror and shown it to the sleeping woman simultaneously with the visiting card? Professional conjurers perform feats which are, after their own fashion, quite as extraordinary. I went to bed, and to sleep, and was awakened on the following morning, that is to say, early today, by my valet, who announced that Madame Sablé wanted to see me immediately. I hurriedly dressed myself to receive her.

She seemed in great distress, and did not raise her eyes to mine. Taking a chair, and without lifting her veil, she said:

'My dear cousin, I have a great favour to ask you.'

'What is it?'

'I hate telling you and yet I must. I want five thousand francs. I simply must have them.'

'Surely not for yourself.'

'Yes. It is for myself, or rather for my husband, who has ordered me to get this money for him.'

I was so taken aback that I could hardly speak. I was wondering whether she were in league with Doctor Parent to make fun of me, whether the whole thing was not a hoax, which they had rehearsed beforehand and were now very cleverly acting. But when I looked more closely at my cousin, my doubts vanished. The proceeding was evidently most distasteful to her and was causing her great distress. I could see that she could hardly restrain her tears.

Knowing her to be wealthy, I said:

'It's odd that your husband can't lay hands on five thousand francs. Think again. Are you sure he ordered you to get the money from me?'

She hesitated a few moments as though making a strenuous effort to search her memory. Then she replied:

'Yes. Yes. I'm quite sure.'

'Did he write to you about it?'

Again she hesitated, and tried to remember. I could divine the painful struggle that was going on in her mind. She could not answer my question. All that she knew was that she had to borrow five thousand francs from me on behalf of her husband. She took refuge in a falsehood.

'Yes. He wrote to me.'

'When was that? You didn't mention it yesterday.'

'I got his letter only this morning.'

'Could you let me see it?'

'No, no. There were things in it private, personal things. I . . . I burnt it.'

'I gather that your husband has got into debt.'

'I don't know,' she replied, after some hesitation.

On this I declared abruptly:

'My dear cousin, the fact is that for the moment I haven't five thousand francs available.'

She uttered a cry of anguish.

'Oh, oh, I implore you. Try to get them for me.'

Her agitation was increasing. She clasped her hands as though in prayer. I could hear her voice break. She wept and stammered, tormented and overwhelmed by the irresistible command which had been laid upon her.

'I implore you,' she repeated. 'If you only knew the agony I am suffering. I positively must have the money today.'

I took pity on her.

'I'll let you have it immediately. I give you my word.'

'Oh how can I thank you?' she cried. 'How kind you are.'

'Do you remember,' I asked her, 'what happened yesterday in your house?'

'Yes.'

'Do you remember that Doctor Parent put you to sleep?'

'Yes.'

'Well, Doctor Parent ordered you to come to me this morning and borrow five thousand francs. At this moment you are only obeying his suggestion.'

She considered this for a few moments. Then she replied:

'But don't you understand that it is my husband who wants the money?'

For a good hour I endeavoured to convince her, but my efforts were of no avail. After she had left me, I went at once to see Doctor Parent. He was just going out. He listened to me with a smile.

'Now do you believe?' he asked.

'As if I could help it!'

'Let us go and see Madame Sablé.'

We found my cousin dozing in a *chaise-longue*. She was utterly worn out. The doctor felt her pulse, and looked at her for some time. He held his hand before her eyes, which gradually closed under the irresistible influence of his magnetic power. As soon as she was asleep, he spoke to her:

'Your husband no longer requires the five thousand francs. You may therefore forget that you asked your cousin to lend you the money. If he says anything about it to you, you won't understand.'

Then he awakened her.

I took out my pocket-book.

'Here is the money you asked me for this morning.'

She was so surprised that I could not press the point. I made an effort to recall to her memory what had passed between us, but she denied it vehemently, accused me of making fun of her and ended by showing signs of annoyance.

There it is. I am back in my hotel, so perturbed in mind by this experience that I have not been able to take my luncheon.

19th July

Many persons to whom I have related this incident have laughed at me. What am I to think of it? A wise man would say, 'Who knows?'

21st July

I dined at Bougival and finished the evening at a riverside ball. In the last resort, all depends on place and environment. On the *Ile de la Grenouillière* it seems the height of absurdity to believe in the supernatural; but at the top of Mont Saint-Michel? Or in India? We are terribly susceptible to the influence of our surroundings. Next week I shall return to my own house.

30th July

I came home yesterday. All goes well.

2nd August

Nothing of interest. The weather is superb. I pass my days in watching the Seine flow past.

4th August

My servants are quarrelling with each other. They maintain that someone comes by night and breaks the glassware in the cupboards. The valet accuses the cook and the cook accuses the linen-maid, and the linen-maid puts the blame on the other two. Which of them is the culprit? It will take a clever man to discover.

6th August

This time, at least, I am not mad. I have seen. With my own eyes I have seen. I can no longer doubt. I am still chilled to the very finger tips, panic-stricken to the marrow of my bones. I have seen . . . I have seen . . . At two o'clock, in broad sunshine, I was walking in my rose garden, between the autumn rose trees which are now coming into bloom. I stopped to admire a *géant des batailles,* which had three magnificent blossoms, and I saw, I saw distinctly, quite close to me, the stalk of one of those roses bent as though by an invisible hand. Then it was broken off, as though ghostly fingers had plucked it. The flower was raised into the air in just such a curve as a hand would have described in carrying it to the lips, and there it remained suspended, without visible support, floating in the clear atmosphere, a terrifying patch of red, only a few feet from my eyes. Aghast, I sprang forward to seize it. But my fingers encountered nothing. The rose had vanished. I was seized by furious anger against myself. It was beyond all bounds for a serious and rational man to have such hallucinations. But was it really a hallucination? I went back to look at the stalk and found it immediately. It was between the two roses, which still remained on the tree, and it had been freshly broken. At this my mind was convulsed with horror. I am now convinced that I am haunted by an invisible being. I know it, as surely as I know that night follows day. The incubus absorbs water and milk, it can touch things, grasp them and move them from one place to another. Therefore, although invisible, it is material, and it dwells as I do, under this roof.

7th August

I slept well. My mysterious visitor drank the water in my carafe, but did not disturb my sleep.

I wonder if I am insane. Walking along the river-bank, in the sunshine, I have felt doubts as to my sanity; not merely those vague suspicions that I used to have, but clearly reasoned doubts. I have seen mad people. There were some, who remained intelligent, lucid, and even unusually shrewd in the affairs of life, save on one point only. They would converse on all subjects with acuteness, subtlety and penetration. Then of a sudden their reason would touch upon the reef of their insanity and be battered to pieces, scattered to the winds. They foundered in that raging and terrifying ocean, full of rolling waves, mists, and sudden gusts of storm; the ocean of dementia.

I should have no doubt of my insanity, my absolute insanity, had I not retained full consciousness of my mental plight, had I not probed and analysed it with perfect lucidity. Some unexplained disturbance has taken place within my brain, one of those disturbances which present-day physiologists endeavour to analyse and classify, and this trouble has fixed a deep gulf within my mind and in the logical sequence of my thoughts. Similar phenomena can be noted in dreams, which carry us away into a country of the strangest phantasmagoria, which, however, do not astonish us, for this reason that the verifying apparatus, the controlling power in our brains, is in abeyance, whereas the imaginative faculty is wide awake and functioning actively. Is it not conceivable that one of the notes of my cerebral keyboard is out of action? As the result of some accident, men sometimes lose a portion of their memory; they are unable to recall proper names, or verbs, or numerals, or possibly, dates. It has been established by recent research that all the several departments of the mind are localized in special portions of the brain. What wonder then if my faculty of controlling these hallucinations of mine, should be temporarily paralysed in me. Such were my reflections during my wanderings on the river-bank.

Everything was bathed in sunshine. The sun glorified the face of the waters; it inspired me with the love of all things, of life, of the swallows, whose darting flight is the delight of my eyes, of the riverside plants, whose quivering in the breeze is music to my ears. In spite of this sense of superficial enjoyment, however, I was penetrated by an inexplicable feeling of uneasiness. I could not rid myself of the conviction that some occult force was numbing my faculties, paralysing my will, curtailing my walks, and even drawing me back to the house. I experienced that distressing impulse to return, which haunts one, when some loved one at home is lying on a bed of sickness, and one has a presentiment that an aggravation of his malady has supervened. I turned homewards convinced that some bad news, a letter or telegram, would be awaiting me. But there was nothing of the sort; and I felt even more discomfited and oppressed, than if I had had some new and fantastic vision.

8th August

I have had a frightful night. My visitor does nothing definite, but he hangs about me, watching my movements, obsessing me, dominating me. Working in this hidden way he is more terrible than if he manifested his invisible and persistent presence in supernatural phenomena. Still, I had some sleep.

9th August

Nothing happened. But I am afraid.

10th August

Nothing. But what of tomorrow?

11th August

Still nothing. With these fears and thoughts ever torturing my mind, I cannot stay any longer in this house. I am going away.

12 August, 10 p.m.

The whole day long I have been trying to leave home, and I could not do it. I determined to accomplish this act of liberty, so easy, so simple – to go out of the house, get into my carriage, drive to Rouen. And I found it impossible. Why?

13th August

There are certain maladies that completely destroy the physical elasticity. One's energies are annihilated, one's muscles relaxed, one's bones become as soft as flesh, and one's flesh becomes as fluid as water. Such are the sensations I endure in my moral being, and they work in a strange and devastating fashion. I have lost all strength and courage. I have no dominion over myself; I do not even retain the power of exercising my own faculties. Someone else is in control. I merely carry out his orders.

14th August

I am lost! My mind has become the chattel and serf of some other being; the chattel and serf! There is someone, who orders all my acts, all my movements, all my thoughts. I am reduced to nothing, a servile and terrified spectator of my own actions. If I want to leave the house, I cannot do so, because he will not have it. So I must needs remain at home. He holds me down in my arm-chair! Trembling and distraught, I concentrate on the effort to rise to my feet, so that I am once more my own master. And I cannot do it. I am riveted to my seat, and my seat is riveted to the ground, so that no force can move us. Then, all of a sudden, I feel a compulsion to go to the end of the garden and pick some strawberries. I eat them. Oh, my God, my God! Is there indeed a God? If there be, deliver me, save me, succour me! Pardon! Pity! Grace! Save me. Save me! Oh, what sufferings I endure, what tortures, what horrors!

15th August

It seems to me clear that my poor cousin was under the same sort of domination and possession, when she came to me to borrow five thousand francs. She was subject to an alien will, which entered into her like a second soul, parasitic and tyrannical. Is the world coming to an end? And the despot, who rules me, who is he? I cannot see him, I can know nothing of this prowling stranger of supernatural origin.

If it be true that invisible beings exist, how is it, that, since the origin of the world, these beings have never yet manifested themselves to others in the same definite manner as they have to me? I have never read anything which suggests the events which have occurred in my house. Oh! – if I could only leave it, run away from it, escape, and never come back again. That would save me. But I have not the power to do it.

16th August

I managed to escape today for two hours. I was like a prisoner, who discovers that the door of his dungeon is open. I had suddenly the sensation that I was free; that he was far away. I ordered my carriage to be made ready with all speed and I drove to Rouen.

Oh! what a joy it was to be able to tell the coachman to drive to Rouen, and to have the order obeyed. I stopped at the library to borrow Dr Hermann Herestauss's great treatise on the unknown denizens of the ancient and modern world. And then at the very moment when I was stepping into my carriage, and about to say: 'Drive to the station,' another order came to my lip, and was forced from me in a cry so loud that the passers-by turned to look at me.

'Home!' I shouted, and crazed with misery, I fell back upon the cushions of my carriage. He had tracked me down; I was again his prisoner.

17th August

Ah! what a night! what a night! And yet it seems to me that I have some cause to rejoice. I was able to read, until one o'clock in the morning. Hermann Herestauss, Doctor of Philosophy and Theogony, deals with the history and manifestations of all the invisible beings who haunt the human race or infest our dreams. He describes their origins, their domain, their powers. But not one of them resembles this incubus of mine. His writings suggest to me that ever since man has been able to think, he has had a terrifying presentiment of the coming of a new being, stronger than himself. This being is to be man's successor upon earth. The human race has felt the approach of its master and, unable to foresee his nature, has in its terror created the whole fantastic world of occult beings, vague phantoms, the offspring of man's fears. Having read Herestauss until one in the morning, I went and sat by my open window, in order to freshen my brain in the cool night breeze. The air was balmy and soothing. In happier circumstances, how I should have enjoyed a night like this.

There was no moon. The stars were twinkling in the depths of the dark firmament. Who were the inhabitants of these worlds, I wondered. What forms, what living creatures, what animals, what plants, would one find there? If there are men with the power of thought in those distant spheres, what knowledge have they that is denied to us? What powers that we do not possess? Can they see objects, of which we do not suspect the existence? Some day or other, will not one of those beings traverse space, to appear on this earth, to conquer it, as the Normans once upon a time crossed the sea to conquer weaker races? So feeble, so helpless to protect ourselves, so ignorant, so puny, are we who inhabit this particle of mud, revolving in a drop of water. Thus reflecting I fell asleep, with the cool air of night all about me.

I had been sleeping for about forty minutes when I was awakened by strange, confused emotion. Without stirring, I opened my eyes. At first I saw nothing, but suddenly I had an idea that a page of the Herestauss, which I had left on the table, was turning over of its own accord. There was not a breath of air coming in at the window. I watched in amazement. After about four minutes I saw – yes, with my own eyes I saw – a second page rise, turn over, subside upon the preceding page, exactly as if a human finger had turned the leaf. My arm-chair was to all appearance empty, but I realized that he was there; he, seated in my place, and reading. I made a furious leap, like the spring of a rebellious, wild beast about to disembowel its tamer. I crossed the room; intending to seize him, strangle him, kill him. But before I reached the chair, it was knocked over, as though someone had fled before me. The table rocked, the lamp upset and went out, and the window was closed, as if some robber taken by surprise had hurled himself through it into the darkness, and seizing both sides had slammed them to, behind him.

So then, he had run away. He was afraid, afraid of me. That thing, afraid of me!

Why, then – why, then – tomorrow, or some other day, I might perhaps manage to seize him, and dash him to bits on the ground. Dogs have been known to turn on their masters, bite them and worry them to death.

18th August

All day long I have been thinking, and this is the scheme I have devised. I shall continue to obey all his orders, to do as he directs, act as he wills me. I shall show myself humble, submissive, craven. He is stronger than I. But the hour will come . . .

19th August

Now I know. I know all. I have just read the following paragraph in the *Revue du Monde Scientifique:*

'We have received a curious communication from Rio de Janeiro. At this moment, in the Province of San Paolo, an epidemic of insanity is raging. It resembles the epidemics of contagious dementia, which afflicted the European peoples in the Middle Ages. The inhabitants, driven to distraction, quit their habitations, desert their villages, abandon their work in the fields, declaring that they are pursued, possessed, and tyrannized over, as if they were cattle. Their tormentors are beings, who are tangible but not visible. They are, seemingly, a species of vampire, which sucks the vitality of its sleeping victim. In addition to this, they drink water and milk, but appear to avoid every other form of nourishment. Professor Don Pedro Henriquez, accompanied by several doctors skilled in research, has left for the Province of San Paolo, in order to study on the spot the origins and manifestations of this amazing mania. He will in due course bring before the Emperor proposals for such measures, as are, in his opinion, calculated to restore the stricken population to reason.'

Ah! Ah! Now I remember. I remember that beautiful, Brazilian three-master, which sailed up the Seine on the 8th of May, passing close under my windows. It looked so gay and white and trim. And the Being was on board of her, on his way from Brazil, where his race has its origin. He must have caught sight of me. He must have seen my house, which is white like his ship, and have jumped from the ship on to the bank. Oh, my God! I can now see into the future. The reign of man is over.

He is come; he, whom the early and unsophisticated races of the world associated with their first emotions of terror, he, whom anxious priests exorcized, whom sorcerers invoked in the darkness of the night, though unable as yet to compel his appearance; he, whom the anticipation of the temporary masters of the world invented with every conceivable form, whether monstrous or gracious, as gnome, spirit, genie, fairy, or goblin. The gross imaginings of primitive terror having passed away, men of greater perspicacity arrived at a clearer idea. Mesmer divined it, and medical research discovered and established the nature of the new power, ten years before its advent. This mysterious dominion over the human soul, which is thereby reduced to a state of bondage, is the weapon of our future Lord and Master, and the doctors of medicine have been playing with it, calling it magnetism, hypnotism, suggestion, and what not. I have seen them amusing themselves like reckless children with this horrible power. Woe unto us, woe unto mankind! for he has come, the . . . the . . . what is his name? . . . the . . . I have a feeling that he is calling out his name to me and I cannot catch it . . . yes . . . he is calling it . . . I listen . . . I cannot . . . say it again . . . the . . . Horla . . . yes . . . I have heard it . . . the

Horla . . . it is he, the Horla, . . . he has come.

Alas! the vulture has eaten the dove, the wolf has eaten the sheep, the lion has devoured the sharp-horned buffalo; man has slain the lion with arrow, sword and powder; but the Horla will treat man, as man has treated the horse and the ox. By the mere exercise of his will-power, he will convert man into his chattel, his slave, his food. Woe unto us!

Sometimes, nevertheless, an animal rebels against his tamer and kills him . . . that is my own intention . . . but first I must study him, establish contact with him, see him.

Savants say that the eyes of animals are not as ours and that they have a different method of perception. It is true that my eyes cannot distinguish this newcomer, who lords it over me. Why not, I wonder.

I recall the words of the monk at Mont Saint-Michel. 'Do you imagine that we see the hundred-thousandth part of what exists? Consider for example the wind, which is the greatest of the forces of nature. It knocks men down, it demolishes houses, it uproots trees, it stirs up the sea into mountainous waves, it breaks away the cliffs and drives great ships on to the rocks. The wind whistles, groans, bellows, sometimes it even kills. Have you seen it? It exists nevertheless.'

And I reflected further. The human eye is so feeble and imperfect that it cannot distinguish even solid bodies, if they happen to be transparent. If a glass without a background of tin-foil happens to be in my way, my eyes will betray me, just as a bird, which has flown into a room, will dash its head against the window panes. There are a thousand things besides, which deceive and delude the sight. What wonder then, if my eyes fail to perceive a new body through which the light passes freely?

A new being? Why not? It was inevitable. And if we are unable to distinguish this new being, just as we failed to discern those who were created before us, the reason is that his nature is more perfect than ours, that his body has finer qualities and is more cunningly contrived. The human frame is such a puny thing. Clumsily conceived, it is one mass of organs that are always jaded, that are always collapsing like unduly complicated springs. We live like plants and beasts, deriving our sustenance laboriously from air, vegetation and flesh. Ours is an animal mechanism, subject to maladies, deformities, putrefaction; we are an inadequate machine, unregulated, childish, grotesque, constructed with perverse ingenuity, a work both clumsy and delicate, a mere embryo of a being that might develop into something intelligent and sublime.

There are a certain number of species on this earth, few enough, to be sure, ranging from mollusc to man. Why should not another variation arise after the completion of the period, which separates the successive appearances of the various species? Why not indeed? Why not other trees, with great dazzling blossoms, trees that could fill a whole country-side with their fragrance? Why should there not be other elements, as well as fire, air, earth and water, the parents and fosterers of everything that lives? They are only four in number. What a pity it is! Why should there not be forty, four hundred, four thousand of them?

How poor and paltry and wretched the whole creation! Doled out parsimoniously, contrived without imagination, clumsily constructed. The elephant, the hippopotamus, what grave! The camel, what elegance!

But on the other hand, you will point to the butterfly, that winged blossom. I dream of one as big as a hundred worlds, with wings of such form and beauty, such colour and movement, that I cannot give you even a faint idea of its splendour. But I can see it, as it flits from star to star, while the delicate, rhythmic beating of its pinions diffuses a balmy fragrance. And the dwellers of the stars, in ecstasy and ravishment, watch it fly past.

What has befallen me? It is he, he, it is the Horla who haunts me and fills my mind with these insane imaginings. He lives within me, his soul and my soul are becoming one. But I will kill him.

19th August

I will kill him. I have seen him. I was seated last night by my table, making a pretence of concentrating on what I was writing. I knew that he would come prowling round me, close to me, so close, that I might be able to touch him, or even get him into my clutches. And then I would use every source that a desperate man has at his disposal; hands, knees, chest, head; I would strangle him, crush him, bite and rend him.

With all my senses feverishly excited, I waited and watched. I had lighted two lamps, as well as the eight candles on the mantelpiece, as though the brilliant illumination could reveal him to me. In front of me stood my bed, an old oaken four-poster. On the right was the fireplace, on the left the door, which I had carefully closed, after leaving it open for a sufficient time to attract him to my room. Behind me was a very lofty wardrobe with a glass door. I always shave and dress before this mirror, and lately I had fallen into the habit of stopping whenever I passed it, and examining myself from head to foot.

I knew that the Horla was spying on me, as I on him. To deceive him, I went on making a pretence of writing. Suddenly I became aware, beyond all doubt, that he was looking over my shoulder, reading. I could feel a light contact on my ear.

I rose to my feet and stretched out my hands, turning so quickly that I nearly overbalanced. And what happened then? The room was as bright as daylight. Yet I could not see myself in my mirror. The reflecting surface was blank, clear, deep and shining, but my image was not there, although I was standing right in front of the glass. I scrutinized the gleaming surface from top to bottom. I looked at it aghast. But I durst not go nearer; I feared to make the slightest movement. Although I was conscious that the invisible body, which had annihilated my reflection, was within my reach, I knew that he would again elude my grasp.

My terror was indescribable. And then, gradually, my image began to appear within the mirror, as though breaking through the mist that lies upon a sheet of water, drifting slowly from left to right. Every moment my reflection gained in clearness. It was like the passing of an eclipse. This veil that obscured my reflection, had no sharply defined contours; it was vague, semi-opaque and gradually yielded to complete transparency. Presently I was able to distinguish all the details of my person, as clearly as in everyday life.

I had seen the Horla. The terror of that vision abides with me, and I shudder with the horror of it.

20th August

To kill him. Yes. But how, when I cannot lay hands on him? I might try poison, but he would see me mixing it in the water. And in any case, would our poisons take effect on an imperceptible body? None at all, I fear. Is there no other way?

21st August

I have summoned a locksmith from Rouen. I have ordered him to fit the windows of my room with iron shutters, such as you see on the ground floor of private mansions in Paris, to keep out thieves. He is also making an iron door for me. I shall be taken for a coward, but what do I care?

10th September

Hotel Continental, Rouen. It is done. It is done. But have I really killed him? My mind is utterly overwhelmed by the horrors I have witnessed. Yesterday, after the locksmith had put in the iron door and shutters, I left them open until midnight, although it was getting cold. Then I had a sudden conviction of his presence, and I was filled with joy, a delirium of joy. I rose unconcernedly from my chair and walked carelessly about my room. After I kept this up for some time, so as to avoid arousing his suspicions, I calmly removed my boots and put on a pair of old slippers. Then I closed the iron window-shutters, and lounging with assumed nonchalance across the room, I double-locked the iron door. Then I strolled back to the window, fixed a padlock on it, and put the key in my pocket.

At that moment I had the sudden conviction that the Horla was hovering about me in a state of agitation. It was now his turn to be afraid. He was ordering me to open the door and let him out, and I came within an ace of yielding. However, I withstood him manfully, set my back against the panels and opened it just enough to allow myself to slip out backwards. I am very tall, and the crown of my head touched the lintel of the doorway. I was convinced that he had not had a chance of escaping from the room. And I locked him in, all by himself. Imagine my relief! I had him fast! Then I ran downstairs to the drawing-room which was exactly under my bedroom. I took two lamps and emptied the oil all over the carpet and the furniture. Then I set fire to it, and I escaped from the house, after having double-locked the massive front door. Going to the far end of the garden, I hid myself in a clump of laurels. And then a long time, a very long time elapsed. Everything was dark, silent, motionless. There was not a breath of air, not a star. Overhead were massed great banks of cloud. I could not see them, but I could feel them weighing heavily, heavily, on my soul.

With my eyes fixed on the house, I waited. The delay seemed interminable. By this time I was convinced that the fire had gone out of itself, or that the Horla had extinguished it. At last the fire burst through one of the lower storey windows, and a long tongue of red and yellow flame shot out. Languid, caressing, it glided up the white wall of the house until it licked the roof. The reflection of the flame darted through the tree that shaded the house, illuminating the leaves and the branches, and I will swear that with it came a shudder, a shudder of fear. The birds awoke. A dog began to howl. It was like sunrise.

Presently two other windows fell out, and I could see that the whole lower storey of my house was nothing less than a raging furnace. Then a horrible, shrill shriek rent the air, the shriek of a woman. Two attic windows were thrown open. I had forgotten about my servants. I saw their frantic faces, their arms waving for help. Distraught by this horrible spectacle, I ran towards the village, shouting:

'Help, help! Fire, fire!'

Meeting some men, who were already hurrying from the village, I went back with them to the house, which by this time was simply a pyre, magnificent but horrible, a pyre of monstrous size, illuminating the whole earth, a pyre, in which human beings were being consumed. And with them the Horla! The Horla! My prisoner! The new Being! Man's new master! The Horla!

The roof-beams gave way and the whole roof crashed in. A volcano of flame shot up to heaven. Through the hollow window-frames I saw a raging crater of fire. The Horla is there, I thought. He is in that furnace. He is dead.

Dead? Was that so certain? Might it not be that that transparent body of his was invulnerable by forces that are fatal to the human frame? Suppose he had not been destroyed? It may be that time is the only power that can affect him, that has sway over that invisible and terrible Being. Why should he have been endowed with this transparent, mysterious, ethereal body, if there was any need for him to be afraid of illness, wounds, infirmities, or premature destruction?

Premature destruction? All one's fears for humanity are based on that dreadful possibility. After man, the Horla. After man, who may die any day, any hour, any minute, by any sort of accident, comes that Being, who can die only at the appointed day, hour and minute; who can die on this account alone, that his time-limit has run out.

No. No. I have not killed him. That is a certainty. And it follows, that there is nothing left for me but to kill myself.

E. F. BENSON

MRS AMWORTH

THE VILLAGE of Maxley, where, last summer and autumn, these strange events took place, lies on a heathery and pine-clad upland of Sussex. In all England you could not find a sweeter and saner situation. Should the wind blow from the south, it comes laden with the spices of the sea; to the east high downs protect it from the inclemencies of March; and from the west and north the breezes which reach it travel over miles of aromatic forest and heather. The village itself is insignificant enough in point of population, but rich in amenities and beauty. Half-way down the single street, with its broad road and spacious areas of grass on each side, stands the little Norman church and the antique graveyard long disused: for the rest there are a dozen small, sedate Georgian houses, red-bricked and long-windowed, each with a square of flower garden in front, and an ampler strip behind; a score of shops, and a couple of score of thatched cottages belonging to labourers on neighbouring estates, complete the entire cluster of its peaceful habitations. The general peace, however, is sadly broken on Saturdays and Sundays, for we lie on one of the main roads between London and Brighton and our quiet street becomes a race-course for flying motor-cars and bicycles. A notice just outside the village begging them to go slowly only seems to encourage them to accelerate their speed, for the road lies open and straight, and there is really no reason why they should do otherwise. By way of protest, therefore, the ladies of Maxley cover their noses and mouths with their handkerchiefs as they see a motor-car approaching, though, as the street is asphalted, they need not really take these precautions against dust. But late on Sunday night the horde of scorchers has passed, and we settle down again to five days of cheerful and leisurely seclusion. Railway strikes which agitate the country so much leave us undisturbed because most of the inhabitants of Maxley never leave it at all.

I am the fortunate possessor of one of these small Georgian houses, and consider myself no less fortunate in having so interesting and stimulating a neighbour as Francis Urcombe, who, the most confirmed of Maxleyites, has not slept away from his house, which stands just opposite to mine in the village street, for nearly two years, at which date, though still in middle life, he resigned his Physiological Professorship at Cambridge University, and devoted himself to the study of those occult and curious phenomena which seem equally to concern the physical and the psychical sides of human nature. Indeed his retirement was not unconnected with his passion for the strange uncharted places that lie on the confines and borders of science, the existence of which is so stoutly denied by the more materialistic minds, for he advocated that all medical students should be obliged to pass some sort of examination in mesmerism, and that one of the tripos papers should be designed to test their knowledge in such subjects as appearances at time of death, haunted houses, vampirism, automatic writing, and possession.

'Of course they wouldn't listen to me,' ran his account of the matter, 'for there is nothing that these seats of learning are so frightened of as knowledge, and the road to knowledge lies in the study of things like these. The functions of the human frame are, broadly speaking, known. They are a country, anyhow, that has been charted and mapped out. But outside that lie huge tracts of undiscovered country, which certainly exist, and the real pioneers of knowledge are those who, at the cost of being derided as credulous and superstitious, want to push on into those misty and probably perilous places. I felt that I could be of more use by setting out without compass or knapsack into the mists than by sitting in a cage like a canary and chirping about what was known. Besides, teaching is very very bad for a man who knows himself only to be a learner: you only need to be a self-conceited ass to teach.'

Here, then, in Francis Urcombe, was a delightful neighbour to one who, like myself, has an uneasy and burning curiosity about what he called the 'misty and perilous places'; and this last spring we had a further and most welcome addition to our pleasant little community, in the person of Mrs Amworth, widow of an Indian civil servant. Her husband had been a judge in the North-West Provinces, and after his death in Peshawar she came back to England, and after a year in London found herself starving for the ampler air and sunshine of the country to take the place of the fogs and griminess of town. She had, too, a special reason for settling in Maxley, since her ancestors up till a hundred years ago had long been native to the place, and in the old churchyard, now disused, are many gravestones bearing her maiden name of Chaston. Big and energetic, her vigorous and genial personality speedily woke Maxley up to a higher degree of sociality than it had even known. Most of us were bachelors or spinsters or elderly folk not much inclined to exert ourselves in the expense and effort of hospitality, and hitherto the gaiety of a small tea-party, with bridge afterwards and goloshes (when it was wet) to trip home in again for a solitary dinner, was about the climax of our festivities. But Mrs Amworth showed us a more gregarious way, and set an example of luncheon-parties and little dinners, which we began to follow. On other nights when no such hospitality was on foot, a lone man like myself found it pleasant to know that a call on the telephone to Mrs Amworth's house not a hundred yards off, and an inquiry as to whether I might come over after dinner for a game of piquet before bedtime, would probably evoke a response of welcome. There she would be, with a comrade-like eagerness for companionship, and there was a glass of port and a cup of coffee and a cigarette and a game of piquet. She played the piano, too, in a free and exuberant manner, and had a charming voice and sang to her own accompaniment; and as the days grew long and the light lingered late, we played our game in her garden, which in the course of a few months she had turned from being a nursery for slugs and snails into a glowing patch of luxuriant blossoming. She was always cheery and jolly; she was interested in everything, and in music, in gardening, in games of all sorts was a competent performer. Everybody (with one exception) liked her, everybody felt her to bring with her the tonic of a sunny day. That one exception was Francis Urcombe; he, though he confessed he did not like her, acknowledged that he was vastly interested in her. This always seemed strange to me, for pleasant and jovial as she was, I could see nothing in her that could call forth conjecture or intrigued surmise, so healthy and unmysterious a figure did she present. But of the genuineness of Urcombe's interest there could be no doubt; one could see him watching and scrutinizing her. In matter of age, she frankly volunteered the information that she was forty-five: but her briskness, her activity, her unravaged skin, her coal-black hair, made it difficult to believe that she was not adopting an unusual device, and adding ten years on to her age instead of subtracting them.

Often, also, as our quite unsentimental friendship ripened, Mrs Amworth would ring me up and propose her advent. If I was busy writing, I was to give her, so we definitely bargained, a frank negative, and in answer I could hear her jolly laugh and her wishes for a successful evening of work. Sometimes, before her proposal arrived, Urcombe would already have stepped across from his house opposite for a smoke and a chat, and he, hearing who my intending visitor was, always urged me to beg her to come. She and I should play our piquet, said he, and he would look on, if we did not object, and learn something of the game. But I doubt whether he paid much attention to it, for nothing could be clearer than that, under that penthouse of forehead and thick eyebrows, his attention was fixed not on the cards, but on one of the players. But he seemed to enjoy an hour spent thus, and often, until one particular evening in July, he would watch her with the air of a man who has some deep problem in front of him. She, enthusiastically keen about our game, seemed not to notice his scrutiny. Then came that evening when, as I see in the light of subsequent events, began the first twitching of the veil that hid the secret horror from my eyes. I did not know it then, though I noticed that thereafter, if she rang up to propose coming round, she always asked not only if I was at leisure, but whether Mr Urcombe was with me. If so, she said, she would not spoil the chat of two old bachelors, and laughingly wished me good night. Urcombe, on this occasion, had been with me for some half-hour before Mrs Amworth's appearance, and had been talking to me about the medieval beliefs concerning vampirism, one of those borderland subjects which he declared had not been sufficiently studied before it had been consigned by the medical profession to the dust heap of exploded superstitions. There he sat, grim and eager, tracing, with that pellucid clearness which had made him in his Cambridge days so admirable a lecturer, the history of those mysterious visitations. In them all there were the same general features: one of those ghoulish spirits took up its abode in a living man or woman, conferring supernatural powers of bat-like flight and glutting itself with nocturnal blood-feasts. When its host died it continued to dwell in the corpse, which remained undecayed. By day it rested, by night it left the grave and went on its awful errands. No European country in the Middle Ages seemed to have escaped them; earlier yet, parallels were to be found, in Roman and Greek and in Jewish history.

'It's a large order to set all that evidence aside as being moonshine,' he said. 'Hundreds of totally independent witnesses in many ages have testified to the occurrence of these phenomena, and there's no explanation known to me which covers all the facts. And if you feel inclined to say "Why, then, if these are facts, do we not come across them now?" there are two answers I can make you. One is that there were diseases known in the Middle Ages, such as the black death, which were certainly existent then and which have become extinct since, but for that reason we do not assert that such diseases never existed. Just as the black death visited England and decimated the population of Norfolk, so here in this very district about three hundred years ago there was certainly an outbreak of vampirism, and Maxley was the centre of it. My second answer is even more convincing, for I tell you that vampirism is by no means extinct now. An outbreak of it certainly occurred in India a year or two ago.'

At that moment I heard my knocker plied in the cheerful and peremptory manner in which Mrs Amworth is accustomed to announce her arrival, and I went to the door to open it.

'Come in at once,' I said, 'and save me from having my blood curdled. Mr Urcombe has been trying to alarm me.'

Instantly her vital, voluminous presence seemed to fill the room.

'Ah, but how lovely!' she said. 'I delight in having my blood curdled. Go on with your ghost story, Mr Urcombe. I adore ghost stories.'

I saw that, as his habit was, he was intently observing her.

'It wasn't a ghost story exactly,' said he. 'I was only telling our [illegible] now vampirism was not extinct yet. I was saying that there was an outbreak of it in India only a few years ago.'

There was a more than perceptible pause, and I saw that, if Urcombe was observing her, she on her side was observing him with fixed eye and parted mouth. Then her jolly laugh invaded that rather tense silence.

'Oh, what a shame!' she said. 'You're not going to curdle my blood at all. Where did you pick up such a tale, Mr Urcombe? I have lived for years in India and never heard a rumour of such a thing. Some story-teller in the bazaars must have invented it: they are famous at that.'

I could see that Urcombe was on the point of saying something further, but checked himself.

'Ah! very likely that was it,' he said.

But something had disturbed our usual peaceful sociability that night, and something had damped Mrs Amworth's usual high spirits. She had no gusto for her piquet, and left after a couple of games. Urcombe had been silent too, indeed he hardly spoke again till she departed.

'That was unfortunate,' he said, 'for the outbreak of – of a very mysterious disease, let us call it, took place at Peshawar where she and her husband were. And —'

'Well?' I asked.

'He was one of the victims of it,' said he. 'Naturally I had quite forgotten that when I spoke.'

The summer was unreasonably hot and rainless, and Maxley suffered much from drought, and also from a plague of big black night-flying gnats, the bite of which was very irritating and virulent. They came sailing in of an evening, settling on one's skin so quietly that one perceived nothing till the sharp stab announced that one had been bitten. They did not bite the hands or face, but chose always the neck and throat for their feeding-ground, and most of us, as the poison spread, assumed a temporary goitre. Then about the middle of August appeared the first of those mysterious cases of illness which our local doctor attributed to the long continued heat coupled with the bite of these venomous insects. The patient was a boy of sixteen or seventeen, the son of Mrs Amworth's gardener, and the symptoms were an anaemic pallor and a languid prostration, accompanied by great drowsiness and an abnormal appetite. He had, too, on his throat two small punctures where, so Dr Ross conjectured, one of these great gnats had bitten him. But the odd thing was that there was no swelling or inflammation round the place where he had been bitten. The heat at this time had begun to abate, but the cooler weather failed to restore him, and the boy, in spite of the quantity of good food which he so ravenously swallowed, wasted away to a skin-clad skeleton.

I met Dr Ross in the street one afternoon about this time, and in answer to my inquiries about his patient he said that he was afraid the boy was dying. The case, he confessed, completely puzzled him: some obscure form of pernicious anaemia was all he could suggest. But he wondered whether Mr Urcombe would consent to see the boy, on the chance of his being able to throw some new light on the case, and since Urcombe was dining with me that night, I proposed to Dr Ross to join us. He could not do this, but said he would look in later. When he came, Urcombe at once consented to put his skill at the other's disposal, and together they went off at once. Being thus shorn of my sociable evening, I telephoned to Mrs Amworth to know if I might inflict myself on her for an hour. Her answer was a welcome affirmative, and between piquet and music the hour lengthened itself into two. She spoke of the boy who was lying so desperately and mysteriously ill, and told me that she had often been to see him, taking him nourishing and delicate food. But today – and her kind eyes moistened as she spoke – she was afraid she had paid her last visit. Knowing the antipathy between her and Urcombe, I did not tell her that he had been called into consultation; and when I returned home she accompanied me to my door, for the sake of a breath of night air, and in order to borrow a magazine which contained an article on gardening which she wished to read.

'Ah, this delicious night air,' she said, luxuriously sniffing in the coolness. 'Night air and gardening are the great tonics. There is nothing so stimulating as bare contact with rich mother earth. You are never so fresh as when you have been grubbing in the soil – black hands, black nails, and boots covered with mud.' She gave her great jovial laugh.

'I'm a glutton for air and earth,' she said. 'Positively I look forward to death, for then I shall be buried and have the kind earth all round me. No leaden caskets for me – I have given explicit directions. But what shall I do about air? Well, I suppose one can't have everything. The magazine? A thousand thanks, I will faithfully return it. Good night: garden and keep your windows open, and you won't have anaemia.'

'I always sleep with my windows open,' said I.

I went straight up to my bedroom, of which one of the windows looks out over the street, and as I undressed I thought I heard voices talking outside not far away. But I paid no particular attention, put out my lights, and falling asleep plunged into the depths of a most horrible dream, distortedly suggested, no doubt, by my last words with Mrs Amworth. I dreamed that I woke, and found that both my bedroom windows were shut. Half suffocating I dreamed that I sprang out of bed, and went across to open them. The blind over the first was drawn down, and pulling it up I saw, with the indescribable horror of incipient nightmare, Mrs Amworth's face suspended close to the pane in the darkness outside, nodding and smiling at me. Pulling down the blind again to keep that terror out, I rushed to the second window on the other side of the room, and there again was Mrs Amworth's face. Then the panic came upon me in full blast; here was I suffocating in the airless room, and in whichever window I opened Mrs Amworth's face would float in, like those noiseless black gnats that bit before one was aware. The nightmare rose to screaming point, and with strangled yells I awoke to find my room cool and quiet with both windows open and blinds up and a half-moon high in its course, casting an oblong of tranquil light on the floor. But even when I was awake the horror persisted, and I lay tossing and turning. I must have slept long before the nightmare seized me, for now it was nearly day, and soon in the east the drowsy eyelids of morning began to lift.

I was scarcely downstairs next morning – for after the dawn I slept late – when Urcombe ran up to know if he might see me immediately. He came in, grim and preoccupied, and I noticed that he was pulling on a pipe that was not even filled.

'I want your help,' he said, 'and so I must tell you first of all what happened last night. I went round with the little doctor to see his patient, and found him just alive, but scarcely more. I instantly diagnosed in my own mind what this anaemia, unaccountable by any other explanation, meant. The boy is the prey of a vampire.'

He put his empty pipe on the breakfast table, by which I had just sat down, and folded his arms, looking at me steadily from under his overhanging brows.

'Now about last night,' he said. 'I insisted that he should be moved from his father's cottage into my house. As we were carrying him on a stretcher, whom should we meet but Mrs Amworth? She expressed shocked surprise that we were moving him. Now why do you think she did that?'

With a start of horror, as I remembered my dream that night before, I felt an idea come into my mind so preposterous and unthinkable that I instantly turned it out again.

'I haven't the smallest idea,' I said.

'Then listen, while I tell you about what happened later. I put out all light in the room where the boy lay, and watched. One window was a little open, for I had forgotten to close it, and about midnight I heard something outside, trying apparently to push it farther open. I guessed who it was – yes, it was full twenty feet from the ground – and I peeped round the corner of the blind. Just outside was the face of Mrs Amworth and her hand was on the frame of the window. Very softly I crept close, and then banged the window down, and I think I just caught the tip of one of her fingers.'

'But it's impossible,' I cried. 'How could she be floating in the air like that? And what had she come for? Don't tell me such —'

Once more, with closer grip, the remembrance of my nightmare seized me.

'I am telling you what I saw,' said he. 'And all night long, until it was nearly day, she was fluttering outside, like some terrible bat, trying to gain admittance. Now put together various things I have told you.'

He began checking them off on his fingers.

'Number one,' he said: 'there was an outbreak of disease similar to that which this boy is suffering from at Peshawar, and her husband died of it. Number two: Mrs Amworth protested against my moving the boy to my house. Number three: she, or the demon that inhabits her body, a creature powerful and deadly, tries to gain admittance. And add this, too: in medieval times there was an epidemic of vampirism here at Maxley. The vampire, so the accounts run, was found to be Elizabeth Chaston . . . I see you remember Mrs Amworth's maiden name. Finally, the boy is stronger this morning. He would certainly not have been alive if he had been visited again. And what do you make of it?'

There was a long silence, during which I found this incredible horror assuming the hues of reality.

'I have something to add,' I said, 'which may or may not bear on it. You say that the – the spectre went away shortly before dawn.'

'Yes.'

I told him of my dream, and he smiled grimly.

'Yes, you did well to awake,' he said. 'That warning came from your subconscious self, which never wholly slumbers, and cried out to you of deadly danger. For two reasons, then, you must help me: one to save others, the second to save yourself.'

'What do you want me to do?' I asked.

'I want you first of all to help me in watching this boy, and ensuring that she does not come near him. Eventually I want you to help me in tracking the thing down, in exposing and destroying it. It is not human: it is an incarnate fiend. What steps we shall have to take I don't yet know.'

It was now eleven of the forenoon, and presently I went across to his house for a twelve-hour vigil while he slept, to come on duty again that night, so that for the next twenty-four hours either Urcombe or myself was always in the room where the boy, now getting stronger every hour, was lying. The day following was Saturday and a morning of brilliant, pellucid weather, and already when I went across to his house to resume my duty the stream of motors down to Brighton had begun. Simultaneously I saw Urcombe with a cheerful face, which boded good news of his patient, coming out of his house, and Mrs Amworth, with a gesture of salutation to me and a basket in her hand, walking up the broad strip of grass which bordered the road. There we all three met. I noticed (and saw that Urcombe noticed it too) that one finger of her left hand was bandaged.

'Good morning to you both,' she said. 'And I hear your patient is doing well, Mr Urcombe. I have come to bring him a bowl of jelly, and to sit with him for an hour. He and I are great friends. I am overjoyed at his recovery.'

Urcombe paused a moment, as if making up his mind, and then shot out a pointing finger at her.

'I forbid that,' he said. 'You shall not sit with him or see him. And you know the reason as well as I do.'

I have never seen so horrible a change pass over a human face as that which now blanched hers to the colour of a grey mist. She put up her hand as if to shield herself from that pointing finger, which drew the sign of the cross in the air, and shrank back cowering on to the road. There was a wild hoot from a horn, a grinding of brakes, a shout – too late – from a passing car, and one long scream suddenly cut short. Her body rebounded from the roadway after the first wheel had gone over it, and the second followed. It lay there, quivering and twitching, and was still.

She was buried three days afterwards in the cemetery outside Maxley, in accordance with the wishes she had told me that she had devised about her interment, and the shock which her sudden and awful death had caused to the little community began by degrees to pass off. To two people only, Urcombe and myself, the horror of it was mitigated from the first by the nature of the relief that her death brought; but, naturally enough, we kept our own counsel, and no hint of what greater horror had been thus averted was ever let slip. But, oddly enough, so it seemed to me, he was still not satisfied about something in connexion with her, and would give no answer to my questions on the subject. Then as the days of a tranquil mellow September and the October that followed began to drop away like the leaves of the yellowing trees, his uneasiness relaxed. But before the entry of November the seeming tranquillity broke into hurricane.

I had been dining out one night at the far end of the village, and about eleven o'clock was walking home again. The moon was of an unusual brilliance, rendering all that it shone on as distinct as in some etching. I had just come opposite the house which Mrs Amworth had occupied, where there was a board up telling that it was to let, when I heard the click of her front gate, and next moment I saw, with a sudden chill and quaking of my very spirit, that she stood there. Her profile, vividly illuminated, was turned to me, and I could not be mistaken in my identification of her. She appeared not to see me (indeed the shadow of the yew hedge in front of her garden enveloped me in its blackness) and she went swiftly across the road, and entered the gate of the house directly opposite. There I lost sight of her completely.

My breath was coming in short pants as if I had been running – and now indeed I ran, with fearful backward glances, along the hundred yards that separated me from my house and Urcombe's. It was to his that my flying steps took me, and next minute I was within.

'What have you come to tell me?' he said. 'Or shall I guess?'

'You can't guess,' said I.

'No; it's no guess. She has come back and you have seen her. Tell me about it.'

I gave him my story.

'That's Major Pearsall's house,' he said. 'Come back with me there at once.'

'But what can we do?' I asked.

'I've no idea. That's what we have got to find out.'

A minute later, we were opposite the house. When I had passed it before, it was all dark; now lights gleamed from a couple of windows upstairs. Even as we faced it, the front door opened, and next moment Major Pearsall emerged from the gate. He saw us and stopped.

'I'm on my way to Dr Ross,' he said quickly. 'My wife has been taken suddenly ill. She had been in bed an hour when I came upstairs, and I found her white as a ghost and utterly exhausted. She had been to sleep, it seemed — But you will excuse me.'

'One moment, Major,' said Urcombe. 'Was there any mark on her throat?'

'How did you guess that?' said he. 'There was: one of those beastly gnats must have bitten her twice there. She was streaming with blood.'

'And there's someone with her?' asked Urcombe.

'Yes, I roused her maid.'

He went off, and Urcombe turned to me. 'I know now what we have to do,' he said. 'Change your clothes, and I'll join you at your house.'

'What is it?' I asked.

'I'll tell you on our way. We're going to the cemetery.'

He carried a pick, a shovel, and a screwdriver when he rejoined me, and wore round his shoulders a long coil of rope. As we walked, he gave me the outlines of the ghastly hour that lay before us.

'What I have to tell you,' he said, 'will seem to you now too fantastic for credence, but before dawn we shall see whether it outstrips reality. By a most fortunate happening, you saw the spectre, the astral body, whatever you choose to call it, of Mrs Amworth, going on its grisly business, and therefore, beyond doubt, the vampire spirit which abode in her during life animates her again in death. That is not exceptional – indeed, all these weeks since her death I have been expecting it. If I am right, we shall find her body undecayed and untouched by corruption.'

'But she has been dead nearly two months,' said I.

'If she had been dead two years it would still be so, if the vampire has possession of her. So remember: whatever you see done, it will be done not to her, who in the natural course would now be feeding the grasses above her grave, but to a spirit of untold evil and malignancy, which gives a phantom life to her body.'

'But what shall I see done?' said I.

'I will tell you. We know that now, at this moment, the vampire clad in her mortal semblance is out; dining out. But it must get back before dawn, and it will pass into the material form that lies in her grave. We must wait for that, and then with your help I shall dig up her body. If I am right, you will look on her as she was in life, with the full vigour of the dreadful nutriment she has received pulsing in her veins. And then, when dawn has come, and the vampire cannot leave the lair of her body, I shall strike her with this' – and he pointed to his pick – 'through the heart, and she, who comes to life again only with the animation the fiend gives her, she and her hellish partner will be dead indeed. Then we must bury her again, delivered at last.'

We had come to the cemetery, and in the brightness of the moonshine there was no difficulty in identifying her grave. It lay some twenty yards from the small chapel, in the porch of which, obscured by shadow, we concealed ourselves. From there we had a clear and open sight of the grave, and now we must wait till its infernal visitor returned home. The night was warm and windless, yet even if a freezing wind had been raging I think I should have felt nothing of it, so intense was my preoccupation as to what the night and dawn would bring. There was a bell in the turret of the chapel that struck the quarters of the hour, and it amazed me to find how swiftly the chimes succeeded one another.

The moon had long set, but a twilight of stars shone in a clear sky, when five o'clock of the morning sounded from the turret. A few minutes more passed, and then I felt Urcombe's hand softly nudging me; and looking out in the direction of his pointing finger, I saw that the form of a woman, tall and large in build, was approaching from the right. Noiselessly, with a motion more of gliding and floating than walking, she moved across the cemetery to the grave which was the centre of our observation. She moved round it as if to be certain of its identity, and for a moment stood directly facing us. In the greyness to which now my eyes had grown accustomed, I could easily see her face, and recognize its features.

She drew her hand across her mouth as if wiping it, and broke into a chuckle of such laughter as made my hair stir on my head. Then she leaped on to the grave, holding her hands high above her head, and inch by inch disappeared into the earth. Urcombe's hand was laid on my arm, in an injunction to keep still, but now he removed it.

'Come,' he said.

With pick and shovel and rope we went to the grave. The earth was light and sandy, and soon after six struck we had delved down to the coffin lid. With his pick he loosened the earth round it, and, adjusting the rope through the handles by which it had been lowered, we tried to raise it. This was a long and laborious business, and the light had begun to herald day in the east before we had it out, and lying by the side of the grave. With his screwdriver he loosed the fastenings of the lid, and slid it aside, and standing there we looked on the face of Mrs Amworth. The eyes, once closed in death, were open, the cheeks were flushed with colour, the red, full-lipped mouth seemed to smile.

'One blow and it is all over,' he said. 'You need not look.'

Even as he spoke he took up the pick again, and, laying the point of it on her left breast, measured his distance. And though I knew what was coming, I could not look away. . . .

He grasped the pick in both hands, raised it an inch or two for the taking of his aim, and then with full force brought it down on her breast. A fountain of blood, though she had been dead so long, spouted high in the air, falling with the thud of a heavy splash over the shroud, and simultaneously from those red lips came one long, appalling cry, swelling up like some hooting siren, and dying away again. With that, instantaneous as a lightning flash, came the touch of corruption on her face, the colour of it faded to ash, the plump cheeks fell in, the mouth dropped.

'Thank God that's over,' said he, and without pause slipped the coffin lid back into its place.

Day was coming fast now, and, working like men possessed, we lowered the coffin into its place again, and shovelled the earth over it. . . . The birds were busy with their earliest pipings as we went back to Maxley.

docketed a… fresh information very quickly and accurately in his brain, he seldom made any acknowledgement to the giver. 'I rather fancy we shall know a good deal more about Cheeseman's, Lamberley, before we are through. The letter is, as I had hoped, from Robert Ferguson. By the way, he claims acquaintance with you.'

'With me!'

'You had better read it.'

He handed the letter across. It was headed with the address quoted.

DEAR MR HOLMES (it said) – I have been recommended to you by my lawyers, but indeed the matter is so extraordinarily delicate that it is most difficult to discuss. It concerns a friend for whom I am acting. This gentleman married some five years ago a Peruvian lady, the daughter of a Peruvian merchant, whom he had met in connexion with the importation of nitrates. The lady was very beautiful, but the fact of her foreign birth and of her alien religion always caused a separation of interests and of feelings between husband and wife, so that after a time his love may have cooled towards her and he may have come to regard their union as a mistake. He felt there were sides of her character which he could never explore or understand. This was the more painful as she was as loving a wife as a man could have – to all appearance absolutely devoted.

Now for the point which I will make more plain when we meet. Indeed, this note is merely to give you a general idea of the situation and to ascertain whether you would care to interest yourself in the matter. The lady began to show some curious traits quite alien to her ordinarily sweet and gentle disposition. The gentleman had been married twice and he had one son by the first wife. This boy was now fifteen, a very charming and affectionate youth, though unhappily injured through an accident in childhood. Twice the wife was caught in the act of assaulting this poor lad in the most unprovoked way. Once she struck him with a stick and left a great weal on his arm.

This was a small matter, however, compared with her conduct to her own child, a dear boy just under one year of age. On one occasion about a month ago this child had been left by its nurse for a few minutes. A loud cry from the baby, as of pain, called the nurse back. As she ran into the room she saw her employer, the lady, leaning over the baby and apparently biting his neck. There was a small wound in the neck, from which a stream of blood had escaped. The nurse was so horrified that she wished to call the husband, but the lady implored her not to do so, and actually gave her five pounds as a price for her silence. No explanation was ever given, and for the moment the matter was passed over.

It left, however, a terrible impression upon the nurse's mind, and from that time she began to watch her mistress closely, and to keep a closer guard upon the baby, whom she tenderly loved. It seemed to her that even as she watched the mother, so the mother watched her, and that every time she was compelled to leave the baby alone the mother was waiting to get at it. Day and night the nurse covered the child, and day and night the silent, watchful mother seemed to be lying in wait as a wolf waits for a lamb. It must read most incredible to you, and yet I beg you to take it seriously, for a child's life and a man's sanity may depend upon it.

At last there came one dreadful day when the facts could no longer be concealed from the husband. The nurse's nerve had given way; she could stand the strain no longer, and she made a clean breast of it all to the man. To him it seemed as wild a tale as it may now seem to you. He knew his wife to be a loving wife, and, save for the assaults upon her stepson, a loving mother. Why, then, should she wound her own dear little baby? He told the nurse that she was dreaming, that her suspicions were those of a lunatic, and that such libels upon her mistress were not to be tolerated. Whilst they were talking, a sudden cry of pain was heard. Nurse and master rushed together to the nursery. Imagine his feelings, Mr Holmes, as he saw his wife rise from a kneeling position beside the cot, and saw blood upon the child's exposed neck and upon the sheet. With a cry of horror, he turned his wife's face to the light and saw blood all round her lips. It was she – she beyond all question – who had drunk the poor baby's blood.

So the matter stands. She is now confined to her room. There has been no explanation. The husband is half demented. He knows, and I know, little of Vampirism beyond the name. We had thought it was some wild tale of foreign parts. And yet in the very heart of the English Sussex – well, all this can be discussed with you in the morning. Will you see me? Will you use your great powers in aiding a distracted man? If so, kindly wire to Ferguson, Cheeseman's, Lamberley, and I will be at your rooms by ten o'clock.

Yours faithfully,

ROBERT FERGUSON.

'Yes, you may say so.'

Holmes made a note.

'I fancy,' said he, 'that I may be of more use at Lamberley than here. It is eminently a case for personal investigation. If the lady remains in her room, our presence could not annoy or inconvenience her. Of course, we would stay at the inn.'

Ferguson gave a gesture of relief.

'It is what I hoped, Mr Holmes. There is an excellent train at two from Victoria, if you could come.'

'Of course we could come. There is a lull at present. I can give you my undivided energies. Watson, of course, comes with us. But there are one or two points upon which I wish to be very sure before I start. This unhappy lady, as I understand it, has appeared to assault both the children, her own baby and your little son?'

'That is so.'

'But the assaults take different forms, do they not? She has beaten your son.'

'Once with a stick and once very savagely with her hands.'

'Did she give no explanation why she struck him?'

'None, save that she hated him. Again and again she said so.'

'Well, that is not unknown among stepmothers. A posthumous jealousy, we will say. Is the lady jealous by nature?'

'Yes, she is very jealous – jealous with all the strength of her fiery tropical love.'

'But the boy – he is fifteen, I understand, and probably very developed in mind, since his body has been circumscribed in action. Did he give you no explanation of these assaults?'

'No; he declared there was no reason.'

'Were they good friends at other times?'

'No; there was never any love between them.'

'Yet you say he is affectionate?'

'Never in the world could there be so devoted a son. My life is his life. He is absorbed in what I say or do.'

Once again Holmes made a note. For some time he sat lost in thought.

'No doubt you and the boy were great comrades before this second marriage. You were thrown very close together, were you not?'

'Very much so.'

'And the boy, having so affectionate a nature, was devoted, no doubt, to the memory of his mother?'

'Most devoted.'

'He would certainly seem to be a most interesting lad. There is one point about these assaults. Were the strange attacks upon the baby and the assaults upon your son at the same period?'

'In the first case it was so. It was as if some frenzy had seized her, and she had vented her rage upon both. In the second case it was only Jack who suffered. Mrs Mason had no complaint to make about the baby.'

'That certainly complicates matters.'

'I don't quite follow you, Mr Holmes.'

'Possibly not. One forms provisional theories and waits for time or fuller knowledge to explode them. A bad habit, Mr Ferguson; but human nature is weak. I fear that your old friend here has given an exaggerated view of my scientific methods. However, I will only say at the present stage that your problem does not appear to me to be insoluble, and that you may expect to find us at Victoria at two o'clock.'

It was evening of a dull, foggy November day when, having left our bags at the Chequers, Lamberley, we drove through the Sussex clay of a long winding lane, and finally reached the isolated and ancient farm-house in which Ferguson dwelt. It was a large, straggling building, very old in the centre, very new at the wings, with towering Tudor chimneys and a lichen-spotted, high-pitched roof of Horsham slabs. The doorsteps were worn into curves, and the ancient tiles which lined the porch were marked with the rebus of a cheese and a man, after the original builder. Within, the ceilings were corrugated with heavy oaken beams, and the uneven floors sagged into sharp curves. An odour of age and decay pervaded the whole crumbling building.

There was one very large central room, into which Ferguson led us. Here, in a huge old-fashioned fireplace with an iron screen behind it dated 1670, there blazed and spluttered a splendid log fire.

The room, as I gazed round, was a most singular mixture of dates and places. The half-panelled walls may well have belonged to the original yeoman farmer of the seventeenth century. They were ornamented, however, on the lower part by a line of well-chosen modern water-colours; while above, where yellow plaster took the place of oak, there was hung a fine collection of South American utensils and weapons, which had been brought, no doubt, by the Peruvian lady upstairs. Holmes rose, with that quick curiosity which sprang from his eager mind, and examined them with some care. He returned with his eyes full of thought.

'Hullo!' he cried. 'Hullo!'

A spaniel had lain in a basket in the corner. It came slowly forward towards its master, walking with difficulty. Its hind-legs moved irregularly and its tail was on the ground. It licked Ferguson's hand.

'What is it, Mr Holmes?'

'The dog. What's the matter with it?'

'That's what puzzled the vet. A sort of paralysis. Spinal meningitis, he thought. But it is passing. He'll be all right soon – won't you, Carlo?'

A shiver of assent passed through the drooping tail. The dog's mournful eyes passed from one of us to the other. He knew that we were discussing his case.

'Did it come on suddenly?'

'In a single night.'

'How long ago?'

'It may have been four months ago.'

'Very remarkable. Very suggestive.'

'What do you see in it, Mr Holmes?'

'A confirmation of what I had already thought.'

'For God's sake, what *do* you think, Mr Holmes? It may be a mere intellectual puzzle to you, but it is life and death to me! My wife a would-be murderer – my child in constant danger! Don't play with me, Mr Holmes. It is too terribly serious.'

The big Rugby three-quarter was trembling all over. Holmes put his hand soothingly upon his arm.

'I fear that there is pain for you, Mr Ferguson, whatever the solution may be,' said he. 'I would spare you all I can. I cannot say more for the instant, but before I leave this house I hope I may have something definite.'

'Please God you may! If you will excuse me, gentlemen, I will go up to my wife's room and see if there has been any change.'

He was away some minutes, during which Holmes resumed his examination of the curiosities upon the wall. When our host returned it was clear from his downcast face that he had made no progress. He brought with him a tall, slim, brown-faced girl.

'The tea is ready, Dolores,' said Ferguson. 'See that your mistress has everything she can wish.'

'She verra ill,' cried the girl, looking with indignant eyes at her master. 'She no ask for food. She verra ill. She need doctor. I frightened stay alone with her without doctor.'

Ferguson looked at me with a question in his eyes.

'I should be so glad if I could be of use.'

'Would your mistress see Dr Watson?'

'I take him. I no ask leave. She needs doctor.'

'Then I'll come with you at once.'

I followed the girl, who was quivering with strong emotion, up the staircase and down an ancient corridor. At the end was an iron-clamped and massive door. It struck me as I looked at it that if Ferguson tried to force his way to his wife he would find it no easy matter. The girl drew a key from her pocket and the heavy oaken planks creaked upon their old hinges. I passed in and she swiftly followed, fastening the door behind her.

On the bed a woman was lying who was clearly in a high fever. She was only half conscious, but as I entered she raised a pair of frightened but beautiful eyes and glared at me in apprehension. Seeing a stranger, she appeared to be relieved, and sank back with a sigh upon the pillow. I stepped up to her with a few reassuring words, and she lay still while I took her pulse and temperature. Both were high, and yet my impression was that the condition was rather that of mental and nervous excitement than of any actual seizure.

'She lie like that one day, two day. I 'fraid she die,' said the girl.

The woman turned her flushed and handsome face towards me.

'Where is my husband?'

life. Nurse, I should wish to have a word with you in private.'

He took her aside and spoke earnestly for a few minutes. I only heard the last words, which were: 'Your anxiety will soon, I hope, be set at rest.' The woman, who seemed to be a sour, silent kind of creature, withdrew with the child.

'What is Mrs Mason like?' asked Holmes.

'Not very prepossessing externally, as you can see, but a heart of gold, and devoted to the child.'

'Do you like her, Jack?' Holmes turned suddenly upon the boy. His expressive mobile face shadowed over, and he shook his head.

'Jacky has very strong likes and dislikes,' said Ferguson, putting his arm round the boy. 'Luckily I am one of his likes.'

The boy cooed and nestled his head upon his father's breast. Ferguson gently disengaged him.

'Run away, little Jacky,' said he, and he watched his son with loving eyes until he disappeared. 'Now, Mr Holmes,' he continued, when the boy was gone, 'I really feel that I have brought you on a fool's errand, for what can you possibly do, save give me your sympathy? It must be an exceedingly delicate and complex affair from your point of view.'

'It is certainly delicate,' said my friend, with an amused smile, 'but I have not been struck up to now with its complexity. It has been a case for intellectual deduction, but when this original intellectual deduction is confirmed point by point by quite a number of independent incidents, then the subjective becomes objective and we can say confidently that we have reached our goal. I had, in fact, reached it before we left Baker Street, and the rest has merely been observation and confirmation.'

Ferguson put his big hand to his furrowed forehead.

'For Heaven's sake, Holmes,' he said hoarsely, 'if you can see the truth in this matter, do not keep me in suspense. How do I stand? What shall I do? I care nothing as to how you have found your facts so long as you have really got them.'

'Certainly I owe you an explanation, and you shall have it. But you will permit me to handle the matter in my own way? Is the lady capable of seeing us, Watson?'

'She is ill, but she is quite rational.'

'Very good. It is only in her presence that we can clear the matter up. Let us go up to her.'

'She will not see me,' cried Ferguson.

'Oh, yes, she will,' said Holmes. He scribbled a few lines upon a sheet of paper. 'You at least have the *entrée*, Watson. Will you have the goodness to give the lady this note?'

I ascended again and handed the note to Dolores, who cautiously opened the door. A minute later I heard a cry from within, a cry in which joy and surprise seemed to be blended. Dolores looked out.

'She will see them. She will leesten,' said she.

At my summons Ferguson and Holmes came up. As we entered the room Ferguson took a step or two towards his wife, who had raised herself in the bed, but she held out her hand to repulse him. He sank into an arm-chair, while Holmes seated himself beside him, after bowing to the lady, who looked at him with wide-eyed amazement.

'I think we can dispense with Dolores,' said Holmes. 'Oh, very well, madame, if you would rather she stayed I can see no objection. Now, Mr Ferguson, I am a busy man with many calls, and my methods have to be short and direct. The swiftest surgery is the least painful. Let me first say what will ease your mind. Your wife is a very good, a very loving, and a very ill-used woman.'

Ferguson sat up with a cry of joy.

'Prove that, Mr Holmes, and I am your debtor for ever.'

'I will do so, but in doing so I must wound you deeply in another direction.'

'I care nothing so long as you clear my wife. Everything on earth is insignificant compared to that.'

'Let me tell you, then, the train of reasoning which passed through my mind in Baker Street. The idea of a vampire was to me absurd. Such things do not happen in criminal practice in England. And yet your observation was precise. You had seen the lady rise from beside the child's cot with the blood upon her lips.'

'I did.'

'Did it not occur to you that a bleeding wound may be sucked for some other purpose than to draw the blood from it? Was there not a Queen in English history who sucked such a wound to draw poison from it?'

'Poison!'

'A South American household. My instinct felt the presence of those weapons upon the wall before my eyes ever saw them. It might have been other poison, but that was what occurred to me. When I saw that little empty quiver beside the small bird-bow, it was just what I expected to see. If the child were pricked with one of those arrows dipped in curare or some other devilish drug, it would mean death if the venom were not sucked out.

'And the dog! If one were to use such a poison, would one not try it first in order to see that it had not lost its power? I did not foresee the dog, but at least I understood him and he fitted into my reconstruction.

'Now do you understand? Your wife feared such an attack. She saw it made and saved the child's life, and yet she shrank from telling you all the truth, for she knew how you loved the boy and feared lest it break your heart.'

'Jacky!'

'I watched him as you fondled the child just now. His face was clearly reflected in the glass of the window where the shutter formed a background. I saw such jealousy, such cruel hatred, as I have seldom seen in a human face.'

'My Jacky!'

'You have to face it, Mr Ferguson. It is the more painful because it is a distorted love, a maniacal exaggerated love for you, and possibly for his dead mother, which has prompted his action. His very soul is consumed with hatred for this splendid child, whose health and beauty are a contrast to his own weakness.'

'Good God! It is incredible!'

'Have I spoken the truth, madame?'

The lady was sobbing, with her face buried in the pillows. Now she turned to her husband.

'How could I tell you, Bob? I felt the blow it would be to you. It was better that I should wait and that it should come from some other lips than mine. When this gentleman, who seems to have powers of magic, wrote that he knew all, I was glad.'

'I think a year at sea would be my prescription for Master Jacky,' said Holmes, rising from his chair. 'Only one thing is still clouded, madame. We can quite understand your attacks upon Master Jacky. There is a limit to a mother's patience. But how did you dare to leave the child these last two days?'

'I had told Mrs Mason. She knew.'

'Exactly. So I imagined.'

Ferguson was standing by the bed, choking, his hands outstretched and quivering.

'This, I fancy, is the time for our exit, Watson,' said Holmes in a whisper. 'If you will take one elbow of the too faithful Dolores, I will take the other. There, now,' he added, as he closed the door behind him, 'I think we may leave them to settle the rest among themselves.'

I have only one further note of this case. It is the letter which Holmes wrote in final answer to that with which the narrative begins. It ran thus:

BAKER STREET,
Nov. 21st.

Re Vampires.

SIR,

Referring to your letter of the 19th, I beg to state that I have looked into the inquiry of your client, Mr Robert Ferguson, of Ferguson and Muirhead, tea brokers, of Mincing Lane, and that the matter has been brought to a satisfactory conclusion. With thanks for your recommendation,

I am, Sir,
Faithfully yours,
SHERLOCK HOLMES.

ROBERT BLOCH

THE CLOAK

The sun was dying, and its blood spattered the sky as it crept into its sepulchre behind the hills. The keening wind sent the dry, fallen leaves scurrying toward the west, as though hastening them to the funeral of the sun.

'Nuts!' said Henderson to himself, and stopped thinking.

The sun was setting in a dingy red sky, and a dirty raw wind was kicking up the half-rotten leaves in a filthy gutter. Why should he waste time with cheap imagery?

'Nuts!' said Henderson, again.

It was probably a mood evoked by the day, he mused. After all, this was the sunset of Halloween. Tonight was the dreaded All-hallows Eve, when spirits walked and skulls cried out from their graves beneath the earth.

Either that, or tonight was just another rotten cold fall day. Henderson sighed. There was a time, he reflected, when the coming of this night meant something. A dark Europe, groaning in superstitious terror, dedicated this Eve to the grinning Unknown. A million doors had once been barred against the evil visitants, a million prayers mumbled, a million candles lit. There was something majestic about the idea, Henderson reflected. Life had been an adventure in those times, and men walked in terror of what the next turn of a midnight road might bring. They had lived in a world of demons and ghouls and elementals who sought their souls – and by Heaven, in those days a man's soul meant something. This new scepticism had taken a profound meaning away from life. Men no longer revered their souls.

'Nuts!' said Henderson again, quite automatically. There was something crude and twentieth-century about the coarse expression which always checked his introspective flights of fancy.

The voice in his brain that said 'nuts' took the place of humanity to Henderson – common humanity which would voice the same sentiment if they heard his secret thoughts. So now Henderson uttered the word and endeavoured to forget problems and purple patches alike.

He was walking down this street at sunset to buy a costume for the masquerade party tonight, and he had much better concentrate on finding the costumier's before it closed than waste his time daydreaming about Halloween.

His eyes searched the darkening shadows of the dingy buildings lining the narrow thoroughfare. Once again he peered at the address he had scribbled down after finding it in the phone book.

Why the devil didn't they light up the shops when it got dark? He couldn't make out numbers. This was a poor, run-down neighbourhood, but after all —

Abruptly, Henderson spied the place across the street and started over. He passed the window and glanced in. The last rays of the sun slanted over the top of the building across the way and fell directly on the window and its display. Henderson drew a sharp intake of breath.

He was staring at a costumier's window – not looking through a fissure into hell. Then why was it all red fire, lighting the grinning visages of fiends?

'Sunset,' Henderson muttered aloud. Of course it was, and the faces were merely clever masks such as would be displayed in this sort of place. Still, it gave the imaginative man a start. He opened the door and entered.

The place was dark and still. There was a smell of loneliness in the air – the smell that haunts all places long undisturbed; tombs, and graves in deep woods, and caverns in the earth, and —

'Nuts.'

What the devil was wrong with him, anyway? Henderson smiled apologetically at the empty darkness. This was the smell of the costumier's shop, and it carried him back to college days of amateur theatricals. Henderson had known this smell of moth balls, decayed furs, grease paint and oils. He had played amateur Hamlet and in his hands he had held a smirking skull that hid all knowledge in its empty eyes – a skull, from the costumier's.

Well, here he was again, and the skull gave him the idea. After all, Halloween night it was. Certainly in this mood of his he didn't want to go as a rajah, or a Turk, or a pirate – they all did that. Why not go as a fiend, or a warlock, or a werewolf? He could see Lindstrom's face when he walked into the elegant penthouse wearing rags of some sort. The fellow would have a fit, with society crowds wearing their expensive Elsa Maxwell take-offs. Henderson didn't greatly care for Lindstrom's sophisticated friends anyway; a gang of amateur Noel Cowards and horsy women wearing harnesses of jewels. Why not carry out the spirit of Halloween and go as a monster?

• • • • •

Henderson stood there in the dusk, waiting for someone to turn on the lights, come out from the back room and serve him. After a minute or so he grew impatient and rapped sharply on the counter.

'Say in there! Service!'

Silence. And a shuffling noise from the rear, then – an unpleasant noise to hear in the gloom. There was a banging from downstairs and then the heavy clump of footsteps. Suddenly Henderson gasped. A black bulk was rising from the floor!

It was, of course, only the opening of the trapdoor from the basement. A man shuffled behind the counter, carrying a lamp. In that light his eyes blinked drowsily.

The man's yellowish face crinkled into a smile.

'I was sleeping, I'm afraid,' said the man softly. 'Can I serve you, sir?'

'I was looking for a Halloween costume.'

'Oh, yes. And what was it you had in mind?'

The voice was weary, infinitely weary. The eyes continued to blink in the flabby yellow face.

'Nothing usual, I'm afraid. You see, I rather fancied some sort of monster getup for a par — Don't suppose you carry anything in that line?'

'I could show you masks.'

'No. I mean, werewolf outfits, something of that sort. More of the authentic.'

'So. The *authentic*.'

'Yes.' Why did this old dunce stress the word?

'I might – yes, I might have just the thing for you, sir.' The eyes blinked, but the thin mouth pursed in a smile. 'Just the thing for Halloween.'

'What's that?'

'Have you ever considered the possibility of being a vampire?'

'Like Dracula?'

'Ah – yes, I suppose – Dracula.'

'Not a bad idea. Do you think I'm the type for that, though?'

The man appraised him with that tight smile. 'Vampires are all types, I understand. You would do nicely.'

'Hardly a compliment,' Henderson chuckled. 'But why not? What's the outfit?'

'Outfit? Merely evening clothes, or what you wear. I will furnish you with the authentic cloak.'

'Just a cloak – is that all?'

'Just a cloak. But it is worn like a shroud. It is shroud-cloth, you know. Wait, I'll get it for you.'

The shuffling feet carried the man into the rear of the shop again. Down the trapdoor entrance he went, and Henderson waited. There was more banging, and presently the old man reappeared carrying the cloak. He was shaking dust from it in the darkness.

'Here it is – the genuine cloak.'

'Genuine?'

'Allow me to adjust it for you – it will work wonders, I'm sure.'

The cold, heavy cloth hung draped about Henderson's shoulders. The faint odour rose mustily in his nostrils as he stepped back and surveyed himself in the mirror. The light was poor, but Henderson saw that the cloak effected a striking transformation in his appearance. His long face seemed thinner, his eyes were accentuated in the facial pallor heightened by the sombre cloak he wore. It was a big, black shroud.

'Genuine,' murmured the old man. He must have come up suddenly, for Henderson hadn't noticed him in the glass.

'I'll take it,' Henderson said. 'How much?'

'You'll find it quite entertaining, I'm sure.'

'How much?'

'Oh. Shall we say five dollars?'

'Here.'

The old man took the money, blinking, and drew the cloak from Henderson's shoulders. When it slid away he felt suddenly warm again. It must be cold in the basement – the cloth was icy.

The old man wrapped the garment, smiling, and handed it over.

'I'll have it back tomorrow,' Henderson promised.

'No need. You purchased it. It is yours.'

'But —'

'I am leaving business shortly. Keep it. You will find more use for it than I, surely.'

'But —'

'A pleasant evening to you.'

Henderson made his way to the door in confusion, then turned to salute the blinking old man in the dimness.

Two eyes were burning at him from across the counter – two eyes that did not blink.

'Good night,' said Henderson, and closed the door quickly. He wondered if he were going just a trifle mad.

. . . . .

At eight, Henderson nearly called up Lindstrom to tell him he couldn't make it. The cold chills came the minute he put on the cloak, and when he looked at himself in the mirror his blurred eyes could scarcely make out the reflection.

But after a few drinks he felt better about it. He hadn't eaten, and the liquor warmed his blood. He paced the floor, attitudinizing with the cloak – sweeping it about him and scowling in what he thought was a ferocious manner. He was going to be a vampire all right! He called a cab, went down to the lobby. The driver came in, and Henderson was waiting, black cloak furled.

'I wish you to drive me,' he said, in a low voice.

The cabman took one look at him in the cloak and turned pale.

'Whazzat?'

'I ordered you to come,' said Henderson gutturally, while he quaked with inner mirth. He leered ferociously and swept the cloak back.

'Yeah, yeah. OK.'

The driver almost ran outside. Henderson stalked after him.

'Where to, boss – I mean, sir?'

The frightened face didn't turn as Henderson intoned the address and sat back.

The cab started with a lurch that set Henderson to chuckling deeply, in character. At the sound of the laughter the driver got panicky and raced his engine up to the limit set by the governor. Henderson laughed loudly, and the impressionable driver fairly quivered in his seat. It was quite a ride, but Henderson was entirely unprepared to open the door and find it slammed after him as the cabman drove hastily away without collecting a fare.

'I must look the part,' he thought complacently, as he took the elevator up to the penthouse apartment.

There were three or four others in the elevator; Henderson had seen them before at other affairs Lindstrom had invited him to attend, but nobody seemed to recognize it. It rather pleased him to think how his wearing of an unfamiliar cloak and an unfamiliar scowl seemed to change his entire personality and appearance. Here the other guests had donned elaborate disguises – one woman wore the costume of a Watteau shepherdess, another was attired as a Spanish ballerina, a tall man dressed as Pagliacci, and his companion had donned a toreador outfit. Yet Henderson recognized them all; knew that their expansive habiliments were not truly disguises at all, but merely elaborations calculated to enhance their appearance. Most people at costume parties gave vent to suppressed desires. The women showed off their figures, the men either accentuated their masculinity as the toreador did, or clowned it. Such things were pitiful; these conventional fools eagerly doffing their dismal business suits and rushing off to a lodge, or amateur theatrical, or mask ball in order to satisfy their starving imaginations. Why didn't they dress in their garish colours on the street? Henderson often pondered the question.

Surely, these society folk in the elevator were fine-looking men and women in their outfits – so healthy, so red-faced, and full of vitality. They had such robust throats and necks. Henderson looked at the plump arms of the woman next to him. He stared, without realizing it, for a long moment. And then he saw that the occupants of the car had drawn away from him. They were standing in the corner, as though they feared his cloak and scowl, and his eyes fixed on the woman.

Their chatter had ceased abruptly. The woman looked at him, as though she were about to speak, when the elevator doors opened and afforded Henderson a welcome respite.

What the devil was wrong? First the cab driver, then the woman. Had he drunk too much?

Well, no chance to consider that. Here was Marcus Lindstrom, and he was thrusting a glass into Henderson's hand.

'What have we here? Ah, a bogeyman!' It needed no second glance to perceive that Lindstrom, as usual at such affairs, was already quite bottle-dizzy. The fat host was positively swimming in alcohol.

'Have a drink, Henderson, my lad! I'll take mine from the bottle. That outfit of yours gave me a shock. Where'd you get the make-up?'

'Make-up? I'm not wearing any make-up.'

'Oh. So you're not. How . . . silly of me.'

Henderson wondered if he were crazy. Had Lindstrom really drawn back? Were his eyes actually filled with a certain dismay?

'I'll . . . I'll see you later,' babbled Lindstrom, edging away and quickly turning to the other arrivals. Henderson watched the back of Lindstrom's neck. It was fat and white. It bulged over the collar of his costume and there was a vein in it. A vein in Lindstrom's fat neck. Frightened Lindstrom.

Henderson stood alone in the ante-room. From the parlour beyond came the sound of music and laughter; party noises. Henderson hesitated before entering. He drank from the glass in his hand – Bacardi rum, and powerful. On top of his other drinks it almost made the man reel. But he drank, wondering. What was wrong with him and his costume? Why did he frighten people? Was he unconsciously acting his vampire role? That crack of Lindstrom's about make-up, now —

Acting on impulse, Henderson stepped over to the long panel mirror in the hall. He lurched a little, then stood in the harsh light before it. He faced the glass, stared into the mirror, and saw nothing.

He looked at himself in the mirror, and there was no one there!

Henderson began to laugh softly, evilly, deep in his throat. And as he gazed into the empty, unreflecting glass, his laughter rose in black glee.

'I'm drunk,' he whispered. 'I must be drunk. Mirror in my apartment made me blurred. Now I'm so far gone I can't see straight. Sure I'm drunk. Been acting ridiculously, scaring people. Now I'm seeing hallucinations – or not seeing them, rather. Visions. Angels.'

His voice lowered. 'Sure, angels. Standing right in back of me, now. Hello, angel.'

'Hello.'

Henderson whirled. There she stood, in the dark cloak, her hair a shimmering halo above her white, proud face; her eyes celestial blue, and her lips infernal red.

'Are you real?' asked Henderson, gently. 'Or am I a fool to believe in miracles?'

'This miracle's name is Sheila Darrly, and it would like to powder its nose if you please.'

'Kindly use this mirror through the courtesy of Stephen Henderson,' replied the cloaked man, with a grin. He stepped backwards, eyes intent.

The girl turned her head and favoured him with a slow, impish smile. 'Haven't you ever seen powder used before?' she asked.

'Didn't know angels indulged in cosmetics,' Henderson replied. 'But then there's a lot I don't know about angels. From now on I shall make them a special study of mine. There's so much I want to find out. So you'll probably find me following you around with a notebook all evening.'

'Notebooks for a vampire!'

'Oh, but I'm a very intelligent vampire – not one of those backwoods Transylvanian types. You'll find me charming, I'm sure.'

'Yes, you look like the sure type,' the girl mocked. 'But an angel and a vampire – that's a queer combination.'

'We can reform one another,' Henderson pointed out. 'Besides, I have a suspicion that there's a bit of the devil in you. That dark cloak over your angel costume; dark angel, you know. Instead of heaven you might hail from my home town.'

Henderson was flippant, but, underneath his banter, cyclonic thoughts whirled. He recalled discussions in the past; cynical observations he had made and believed.

derson had declared that there was no such th... at first sight, save in books or plays where such a dra... vice served to speed up action. He asserted that people le... d about romance from books and plays and accordingly adopted a belief in love at first sight when all one could possibly feel was desire.

And now this Sheila – this blonde angel – had to come along and drive out all thoughts of morbidity, all thoughts of drunkenness and foolish gazings into mirrors, from his mind; had to send him madly plunging into dreams of red lips, ethereal blue eyes and slim white arms.

Something of his feelings had swept into his eyes, and as the girl gazed up at him she felt the truth.

'Well,' she breathed, 'I hope the inspection pleases.'

'A miracle of understatement, that. But there was something I wanted to find out particularly about divinity. Do angels dance?'

'Tactful vampire! The next room?'

Arm in arm they entered the parlour. The merry-makers were in full swing. Liquor had already pitched gaiety at its height, but there was no dancing any longer. Boisterous little grouped couples laughed arm in arm about the room. The usual party gagsters were forming their antics in corners. The superficial atmosphere, which Henderson detested, was fully in evidence.

It was reaction which made Henderson draw himself up to full height and sweep the cloak about his shoulders. Reaction brought the scowl to his pale face, caused him to stalk along in brooding silence. Sheila seemed to regard this as a great joke.

'Pull a vampire act on them,' she giggled, clutching his arm. Henderson accordingly scowled at the couples, sneered horrendously at the women. And his progress was marked by the turning of heads, the abrupt cessation of chatter. He walked through the long room like Red Death incarnate. Whispers trailed in his wake.

'Who is that man?'

'We came up with him in the elevator, and he —'

'His eyes —'

'Vampire!'

'Hello, Dracula!' It was Marcus Lindstrom and a sullen-looking brunette in Cleopatra costume who lurched towards Henderson. Host Lindstrom could scarcely stand, and his companion in cups was equally at a loss. Henderson liked the man when sober at the club, but his behaviour at parties had always irritated him. Lindstrom was particularly objectionable in his present condition – it made him boorish.

'M' dear, I want you t' meet a very dear friend of mine, Yessir, it being Halloween and all, I invited Count Dracula here, t'gether with his daughter. Asked his grandmother, but she's busy tonight at the Black Sabbath – along with Aunt Jemima. Ha! Count, meet my little playmate.'

The woman leered up at Henderson.

'Oooh Dracula, what big eyes you have! Oooh, what big teeth you have! Ooooh —'

'Really, Marcus,' Henderson protested. But the host had turned and shouted to the room.

'Folks, meet the real goods – only genuine living vampire in captivity! Dracula Henderson, only existing vampire with false teeth.'

In any other circumstances Henderson would have given Lindstrom a quick, efficient punch on the jaw. But Sheila was at his side, it was a public gathering; better to humour the man's clumsy jest. Why not be a vampire?

Smiling quickly at the girl, Henderson drew himself erect, faced the crowd, and frowned. His hands brushed the cloak. Funny, it still felt cold. Looking down he noticed for the first time that it was a little dirty at the edges; muddy or dusty. But the cold silk slid through his fingers as he drew it across his breast with one long hand. The feeling seemed to inspire him. He opened his eyes wide and let them blaze. His mouth opened. A sense of dramatic power filled him. And he looked at Marcus Lindstrom's soft, fat neck with the vein standing in the whiteness. He looked at the neck, saw the crowd watching him, and then the impulse seized him. He turned, eyes on that creasy neck – that wabbling, creasy neck of the fat man.

Hands darted out. Lindstrom squeaked like a frightened rat. He was a plump, sleek white rat, bursting with blood. Vampires liked blood. Blood from the rat, from the neck of the rat, from the vein in the neck of the squeaking rat.

'Warm blood.'

The deep voice was Henderson's own.

The hands were Henderson's own.

The hands that went round Lindstrom's neck as he spoke, the hands that felt the warmth, that searched out the vein. Henderson's face was bending for the neck, and, as Lindstrom struggled, his grip tightened. Lindstrom's face was turning purple. Blood was rushing to his head. That was good. Blood!

Henderson's mouth opened. He felt the air on his teeth. He bent down towards that fat neck, and then —

'Stop! That's plenty!'

The voice, the cooling voice of Sheila. Her fingers on his arm. Henderson looked up, startled. He released Lindstrom, who sagged with open mouth.

The crowd was staring, and their mouths were all shaped in the instinctive O of amazement.

Sheila whispered, 'Bravo! Served him right – but you frightened him!'

Henderson struggled a moment to collect himself. Then he smiled and turned.

'Ladies and gentlemen,' he said, 'I have just given a slight demonstration to prove to you what our host said of me was entirely correct. I *am* a vampire. Now that you have been given fair warning, I am sure you will be in no further danger. If there is a doctor in the house I can, perhaps, arrange for a blood transfusion.'

The O's relaxed and laughter came from startled throats. Hysterical laughter, in part, then genuine. Henderson had carried it off. Marcus Lindstrom alone still stared with eyes that held utter fear. *He* knew.

And then the moment broke, for one of the gagsters ran into the room from the elevator. He had gone downstairs and borrowed the apron and cap of a newsboy. Now he raced through the crowd with a bundle of papers under his arm.

'Extra! Extra! Read all about it. Big Halloween Horror! Extra!'

Laughing guests purchased papers. A woman approached Sheila, and Henderson watched the girl walk away in a daze.

'See you later,' she called, and her glance sent fire through his veins. Still, he could not forget the terrible feeling that came over him when he had seized Lindstrom. Why?

Automatically, he accepted a paper from the shouting, pseudo newsboy. 'Big Halloween Horror,' he had shouted. What was that?

Blurred eyes searched the paper.

Then Henderson reeled back. That headline! It was an *Extra* after all. Henderson scanned the columns with mounting dread.

'Fire in costumier's . . . shortly after 8 pm firemen were summoned to the shop of . . . flames beyond control . . . completely demolished . . . damage estimated at . . . peculiarly enough, name of proprietor unknown . . . skeleton found in —'

'No!' gasped Henderson aloud.

He read, re-read *that* closely. The skeleton had been found in a box of earth in the cellar beneath the shop. The box was a coffin. There had been two other boxes, empty. The skeleton had been wrapped in a cloak, undamaged by the flames —

And in the hastily penned box at the bottom of the column were eyewitness comments, written up under scareheads of heavy black type. Neighbours had feared the place. Hungarian neighbourhood, hints of vampirism, of strangers who entered the shop. One man spoke of a cult believed to have held meetings in the place. Superstition about things sold there – love philters, outlandish charms and weird disguises.

Weird disguises – vampires – cloaks – his eyes!

'This is an authentic cloak.'

'I will not be using this much longer. Keep it.'

Memories of these words screamed through Henderson's brain. He plunged out of the room and rushed to the panel mirror.

A moment, then he flung one arm before his face to shield his eyes from the image that was not there – the missing reflection. *Vampires have no reflections.*

No wonder he looked strange. No wonder arms and necks invited him. He had wanted Lindstrom. Good God!

The cloak had done that, the dark cloak with the stains. The stains of earth, grave-earth. The wearing of the cloak, the cold cloak, had given him the feelings of a true vampire.

It was a garment accursed, a thing that had lain on the body of one undead. The rusty stain along one sleeve was blood.

Blood. It would be nice to see blood. To taste its warmth, its red life, flowing.

No. That was insane. He was drunk, crazy.

'Ah! My pale friend the vampire.'

It was Sheila again. And above all horror rose the beating of Henderson's heart. As he looked at her shining eyes, her warm mouth shaped in red invitation, Henderson felt a wave of warmth. He looked at her white throat rising above her dark, shimmering cloak, and another kind of warmth arose. Love, desire, and a – hunger.

. . . . .

She must have seen it in his eyes, but she did not flinch. Instead her own gaze burned in return.

Sheila loved him, too!

With an impulsive gesture, Henderson ripped the cloak from about his throat. The icy weight lifted. He was free. Somehow, he hadn't wanted to take the cloak off, but he had to. It was a cursed thing, and in another minute he might have taken the girl in his arms, taken her for a kiss and remained to —

But he dared not think of that.

'Tired of masquerading?' she asked. With a similar gesture she, too, removed her cloak and stood revealed in the glory of her angel robe. Her blonde, statuesque perfection forced a gasp to Henderson's throat.

'Angel,' he whispered.

'Devil,' she mocked.

And suddenly they were embracing. Henderson had taken her cloak in his arm with his own. They stood with lips seeking rapture until Lindstrom and a group moved noisily into the ante-room.

At the sight of Henderson the fat host recoiled.

'You —' he whispered. 'You are —'

'Just leaving,' Henderson smiled. Grasping the girl's arm, he drew her towards the empty elevator. The door shut on Lindstrom's pale, fear-filled face.

'Were we leaving?' Sheila whispered, snuggling against his shoulder.

'We were. But not for earth. We do not go down into my

realm, but up – into yours.'

'The roof garden?'

'Exactly, my angelic one. I want to talk to you against the background of your own heavens, kiss you amidst the clouds, and —'

Her lips found his as the car rose.

'Angel and devil. What a match!'

'I thought so, too,' the girl confessed. 'Will our children have halos or horns?'

'Both, I'm sure.'

They stepped out on to the deserted rooftop. And once again it was Halloween.

Henderson felt it. Downstairs it was Lindstrom and his society friends, in a drunken costume party. Here it was night, silence, gloom. No light, no music, no drinking, no chatter which made one party identical with another; one night like all the rest. This night was individual here.

The sky was not blue but black. Clouds hung like the grey beards of hovering giants peering at the round orange globe of the moon. A cold wind blew from the sea, and filled the air with tiny murmurings from afar.

It was also quite cold.

'Give me my cloak,' Sheila whispered. Automatically, Henderson extended the garment, and the girl's body swirled under the dark splendour of the cloth. Her eyes burned up at Henderson with a call he could not resist. He kissed her, trembling.

'You're cold,' the girl said. 'Put on your cloak.'

Yes, Henderson, he thought to himself. Put on your cloak while you stare at her throat. Then, the next time you kiss her you will want her throat and she will give it in love and you will take it in – hunger.

'Put it on, darling – I insist,' the girl whispered. Her eyes were impatient, burning with an eagerness to match his own.

Henderson trembled.

Put on the cloak of darkness? The cloak of the grave, the cloak of death, the cloak of the vampire? The evil cloak, filled with a cold life of its own that transformed his face, transformed his mind?

'Here.'

The girl's slim arms were about him, pushing the cloak

on to his shoulders. Her fingers brushed his neck, caressingly, as she linked the cloak about his throat.

Then he felt it – through him – that icy coldness turning to a more dreadful heat. He felt himself expanded, felt the sneer across his face. This was Power!

And the girl before him, her eyes taunting, inviting. He saw her ivory neck, her warm slim neck, waiting. It was waiting for him, for his lips.

For his teeth.

No – it couldn't be. He loved her. His love must conquer this madness. Yes, wear the cloak, defy its power, and take her in his arms as a man, not as a fiend. He must. It was the test.

'Sheila, I must tell you this.'

Her eyes – so alluring. It would be easy!

'Sheila, please. You read the paper tonight.'

'Yes.'

'I . . . I got my cloak there. I can't explain it. You saw how I took Lindstrom. I wanted to go through with it. Do you understand me? I meant to . . . to bite him. Wearing this thing makes me feel like one of those creatures. But I love you, Sheila.'

'I know.' Her eyes gleamed in the moonlight.

'I want to test it. I want to kiss you, wearing this cloak. I want to feel that my love is stronger than this – thing. If I weaken, promise me you'll break away and run, quickly. But don't misunderstand. I must face this feeling and fight it; I want my love for you to be that pure, that secure. Are you afraid?'

'No.' Still she stared at him, just as he stared at her throat. If she knew what was in his mind!

'You don't think I'm crazy? I went to this costumier's – he was a horrible little old man – and he gave me the cloak. Actually told me it was a real vampire's. I thought he was joking, but tonight I didn't see myself in the mirror, and I wanted Lindstrom's neck, and I want you. But I must test it.'

The girl's face mocked. Henderson summoned his strength. He bent forward, his impulses battling. For a moment he stood there under the ghastly orange moon, and his face was twisted in struggle.

And the girl lured.

Her odd, incredibly red lips parted in a silvery, chuckly laugh as her white arms rose from the black cloak she wore to circle his neck gently. 'I know – I knew when I looked in the mirror. I knew you had a cloak like mine – got yours where I got mine —'

Queerly, her lips seemed to elude his as he stood frozen for an instant of shock. Then he felt the icy hardness of her sharp little teeth on his throat, a strangely soothing sting, and an engulfing blackness rising over him.

NICOLAI GOGOL

VIY[1]

Translated by Constance Garnett

As soon as the rather musical seminary bell which hung at the gate of the Bratsky Monastery rang out every morning in Kiev, schoolboys and students hurried thither in crowds from all parts of the town. Students of grammar, rhetoric, philosophy and theology, trudged to their classrooms with exercise books under their arms. The grammarians were quite small boys: they shoved each other as they went along and quarrelled in a shrill alto; they almost all wore muddy or tattered clothes, and their pockets were full of all manner of rubbish, such as knucklebones, whistles made of feathers, or a half-eaten pie, sometimes even little sparrows, one of whom suddenly chirruping at an exceptionally quiet moment in the classroom would cost its owner some sound whacks on both hands and sometimes a thrashing. The rhetoricians walked with more dignity; their clothes were often quite free from holes; on the other hand, their countenances almost all bore some decoration, after the style of a figure of rhetoric; either one eye had sunk right under the forehead, or there was a monstrous swelling in place of a lip, or some other disfigurement. They talked and swore among themselves in tenor voices. The philosophers conversed an octave lower in the scale; they had nothing in their pockets but strong, cheap tobacco. They laid in no stores of any sort, but ate on the spot anything they came across; they smelt of pipes and vodka to such a distance that a passing workman would sometimes stop a long way off and sniff the air like a setter dog.

As a rule the market was just beginning to stir at that hour, and the women with bread-rings, rolls, melon seeds,

[1] Viy (pronounced vee-y) is a colossal creation of the popular imagination. It is the name among the Little Russians of the chief of the gnomes, whose eyelids droop down to the earth. This whole story is a peasant tradition. I was unwilling to change it, and I tell it almost in the simple words in which I heard it. (*Author's Note.*)

and poppy cakes would tug at the skirts of those whose coats were of fine cloth or some cotton material.

'This way, young gentlemen, this way!' they kept saying from all sides: 'here are bread-rings, poppy cakes, twists, good white rolls; they are really good! Made with honey! I baked them myself.'

Another woman lifting up a sort of long twist made of dough would cry: 'Here's a bread-stick! Buy my bread-stick, young gentlemen!'

'Don't buy anything off her; see what a horrid woman she is, her nose is nasty and her hands are dirty. . . .'

But the women were afraid to worry the philosophers and the theologians, for the latter were fond of taking things to taste and always a good handful.

On reaching the seminary, the crowd dispersed to their various classes, which were held in low-pitched but fairly large rooms, with little windows, wide doorways, and dirty benches. The classroom was at once filled with all sorts of buzzing sounds: the 'auditors' heard their pupils repeat their lessons; the shrill alto of a grammarian rang out, and the window-pane responded with almost the same note; in a corner a rhetorician, whose mouth and thick lips should have belonged at least to a student of philosophy, was droning something in a bass voice, and all that could be heard at a distance was 'Boo, boo, boo . . .' The 'auditors', as they heard the lesson, kept glancing with one eye under the bench, where a roll or a cheese-cake or some pumpkin seeds were peeping out of a scholar's pocket.

When this learned crowd managed to arrive a little too early, or when they knew that the professors would be later than usual, then by general consent they got up a fight, and everyone had to take part in it, even the monitors whose duty it was to maintain discipline and look after the morals of all the students. Two theologians usually settled the arrangements for the battle: whether each class was to defend itself individually, or whether all were to be divided into two parties, the bursars and the seminarists. In any case the grammarians first began the attack, and as soon as the rhetoricians entered the fray, they ran away and stood at points of vantage to watch the contest. Then the devotees of philosophy, with long black moustaches, joined in, and finally those of theology, very thick in the neck and attired in shocking trousers, took part. It commonly ended in theology beating all the rest, and the philosophers, rubbing their ribs, were forced into the classroom and sat down on the benches to rest. The professor, who had himself at one time taken part in such battles, could, on entering the class, see in a minute from the flushed faces of his audience that the battle had been a good one, and while he was caning a rhetorician on the fingers, in another classroom another professor would be smacking philosophy's hands with a wooden bat. The theologians were dealt with in quite a different way: they received, to use the expression of a professor of theology, 'a peck of peas apiece,' in other words a liberal drubbing with short leather thongs.

On holidays and ceremonial occasions the bursars and the seminarists went from house to house as mummers. Sometimes they acted a play, and then the most distinguished figure was always some theologian, almost as tall as the belfry of Kiev, who took the part of Herodias or Potiphar's wife. They received in payment a piece of linen, or a sack of millet or half a boiled goose, or something of the sort. All this crowd of students – the seminarists as well as the bursars, with whom they maintain an hereditary feud – were exceedingly badly off for means of subsistence, and at the same time had extraordinary appetites, so that to reckon how many dumplings each of them tucked away at supper would be utterly impossible, and therefore the voluntary offerings of prosperous citizens could not be sufficient for them. Then the 'senate' of the philosophers and theologians dispatched the grammarians and rhetoricians, under the supervision of a philosopher (who sometimes took part in the raid himself), with sacks on their shoulders to plunder the kitchen gardens – and pumpkin porridge was made in the bursars' quarters. The members of the 'senate' ate such masses of melons that next day their 'auditors' heard two lessons from them instead of one, one coming from their lips, another muttering in their stomachs. Both the bursars and the seminarists wore long garments resembling frock-coats, 'prolonged to the utmost limit,' a technical expression signifying below their heels.

The most important event for the seminarists was the

coming of the vacation: it began in June, when they usually dispersed to their homes. Then the whole high road was dotted with philosophers, grammarians and theologians. Those who had nowhere to go went to stay with some comrade. The philosophers and theologians took a situation, that is, undertook the tuition of the children in some prosperous family, and received in payment a pair of new boots or sometimes even a coat. The whole crowd trailed along together like a gipsy encampment, boiled their porridge, and slept in the fields. Everyone hauled a long sack in which he had a shirt and a pair of leg-wrappers. The theologians were particularly careful and precise: to avoid wearing out their boots, they took them off, hung them on sticks and carried them on their shoulders, particularly if it was muddy; then, tucking their trousers up above their knees, they splashed fearlessly through the puddles. When they saw a village they turned off the high road and, going up to any house which seemed a little better looking than the rest, stood in a row before the windows and began singing a chant at the top of their voices. The master of the house, some old Cossack villager, would listen to them for a long time, his head propped on his hands, then he would sob bitterly and say, turning to his wife: 'Wife! What the scholars are singing must be very deep; bring them fat bacon and anything else that we have.' And a whole bowl of dumplings was emptied into the sack, a good sized piece of bacon, several flat loaves, and sometimes a trussed hen would go into it too. Fortified with such stores, the grammarians, rhetoricians, philosophers and theologians went on their way again. Their numbers lessened, however, the further they went. Almost all wandered off towards their homes, and only those were left whose parental abodes were further away.

Once, at the time of such a migration, three students turned off the high road in order to replenish their store of provisions at the first homestead they could find, for their sacks had long been empty. They were the theologian, Halyava; the philosopher, Homa Brut; and the rhetorician, Tibery Gorobets.

The theologian was a well-grown, broad-shouldered fellow; he had an extremely odd habit – anything that lay within his reach he invariably stole. In other circumstances, he was of an excessively gloomy temper, and when he was drunk he used to hide in the rank grass, and the seminarists had a lot of trouble to find him there.

The philosopher, Homa Brut, was of a cheerful temper, he was very fond of lying on his back, smoking a pipe; when he was drinking he always engaged musicians and danced the trepak. He often had a taste of the 'peck of peas,' but took it with perfect philosophical indifference, saying that there is no escaping what has to be. The rhetorician, Tibery Gorobets, had not yet the right to wear a moustache, to drink vodka, and to smoke a pipe. He only wore a curl round his ear, and so his character was as yet hardly formed; but, judging from the big bumps on the forehead, with which he often appeared in class, it might be presumed that he would make a good fighter. The theologian, Halyava, and the philosopher, Homa, often pulled him by the forelock as a sign of their favour, and employed him as their messenger.

It was evening when they turned off the high road; the sun had only just set and the warmth of the day still lingered in the air. The theologian and the philosopher walked along in silence smoking their pipes; the rhetorician, Tibery Gorobets, kept knocking off the heads of the wayside thistles with his stick. The road ran between scattered groups of oak and nut trees standing here and there in the meadows. Sloping uplands and little hills, green and round as cupolas, were interspersed here and there about the plain. The cornfields of ripening wheat, which came into view in two places, showed that some village must soon be seen. It was more than an hour, however, since they had passed the cornfields, yet they had come upon no dwelling. The sky was now completely wrapped in darkness, and only in the west there was a pale streak left of the glow of sunset.

'What the devil does it mean?' said the philosopher, Homa Brut. 'It looked as though there must be a village in a minute.'

The theologian did not speak, he gazed at the surrounding country, then put his pipe back in his mouth, and they continued on their way.

'Upon my soul!' the philosopher said, stopping again, 'not a devil's fist to be seen.'

'Maybe some village will turn up further on,' said the

theologian, not removing his pipe.

But meantime night had come on, and a rather dark night. Small storm-clouds increased the gloom, and by every token they could expect neither stars nor moon. The students noticed that they had lost their way and for a long time had been walking off the road.

The philosopher, after feeling about with his feet in all directions, said at last, abruptly: 'I say, where's the road?'

The theologian did not speak for a while, then after pondering, he brought out: 'Yes, it is a dark night.'

The rhetorician walked off to one side and tried on his hands and knees to feel for the road, but his hands came upon nothing but foxes' holes. On all sides of them there was the steppe, which, it seemed, no one had ever crossed.

The travellers made another effort to press on a little, but there was the same wilderness in all directions. The philosopher tried shouting, but his voice seemed completely lost on the steppe, and met with no reply. All they heard was, a little afterwards, a faint moaning like the howl of a wolf.

'I say, what's to be done?' said the philosopher.

'Why, halt and sleep in the open!' said the theologian, and he felt in his pocket for flint and tinder to light his pipe again. But the philosopher could not agree to this: it was always his habit at night to put away a quartern loaf of bread and four pounds of fat bacon, and he was conscious on this occasion of an insufferable sense of loneliness in his stomach. Besides, in spite of his cheerful temper, the philosopher was rather afraid of wolves.

'No, Halyava, we can't,' he said. 'What, stretch out and lie down like a dog, without a bite or a sup of anything? Let's make another try for it; maybe we shall stumble on some dwelling-place and get at least a drink of vodka for supper.'

At the word 'vodka' the theologian spat to one side, and brought out: 'Well, of course, it's no use staying in the open.'

The students walked on, and to their intense delight caught the sound of barking in the distance. Listening which way it came from, they walked on more boldly and a little later saw a light.

'A village! It really is a village!' said the philosopher.

He was not mistaken in his supposition; in a little while they actually saw a little homestead consisting of only two cottages looking into the same farm yard. There was a light in the windows; a dozen plum trees stood up by the fence. Looking through the cracks in the paling-gate the students saw a yard filled with carriers' wagons. Stars peeped out here and there in the sky at the moment.

'Look, mates, don't let's be put off! We must get a night's lodging somehow!'

The three learned gentlemen banged on the gates with one accord and shouted, 'Open!'

The door of one of the cottages creaked, and a minute later they saw before them an old woman in sheepskin.

'Who is there?' she cried, with a hollow cough.

'Give us a night's lodging, granny; we have lost our way; a night in the open is as bad as a hungry belly.'

'What manner of folks may you be?'

'Oh, harmless folks: Halyava, a theologian; Brut, a philosopher; and Gorobets, a rhetorician.'

'I can't,' grumbled the old woman. 'The yard is crowded with folk and every corner in the cottage is full. Where am I to put you? And such great hulking fellows, too! Why, it would knock my cottage to pieces if I put such fellows in it. I know these philosophers and theologians; if one began taking in these drunken fellows, there'd soon be no home left. Be off, be off! There's no place for you here!'

'Have pity on us, granny! How can you let Christian souls perish for no rhyme or reason? Put us where you please; and if we do aught amiss or anything else, may our arms be withered, and God only knows what befall us – so there!'

The old woman seemed somewhat softened.

'Very well,' she said, as though reconsidering, 'I'll let you in, but I'll put you all in different places; for my mind won't be at rest if you are all together.'

'That's as you please; we'll make no objection,' answered the students.

The gate creaked and they went into the yard.

'Well, granny,' said the philosopher, following the old woman, 'how would it be, as they say . . . upon my soul I feel as though somebody were driving a cart in my stomach: not a morsel has passed my lips all day.'

'What next will he want!' said the old woman. 'No, I've nothing to give you, and the oven's not been heated today.'

'But we'd pay for it all,' the philosopher went on, 'tomorrow morning, in hard cash. Yes!' he added in an undertone, 'the devil a bit you'll get!'

'Go in, go in! and you must be satisfied with what you're given. Fine young gentlemen the devil has brought us!'

Homa the philosopher was thrown into utter dejection by these words; but his nose was suddenly aware of the odour of dried fish; he glanced towards the trousers of the theologian who was walking at his side, and saw a huge fish tail sticking out of his pocket. The theologian had already succeeded in filching a whole carp from a wagon. And as he had done this from no interested motive but simply from habit, and, quite forgetting his carp, was already looking about for anything else he could carry off, having no mind to miss even a broken wheel, the philosopher slipped his hand into his friend's pocket, as though it were his own, and pulled out the carp.

The old woman put the students in their several places: the rhetorician she kept in the cottage, the theologian she locked in an empty closet, the philosopher she assigned a sheep's pen, also empty.

The latter, on finding himself alone, instantly devoured the carp, examined the hurdle-walls of the pen, kicked an inquisitive pig that woke up and thrust its snout in from the next pen, and turned over on his right side to fall into a sound sleep. All at once the low door opened, and the old woman bending down stepped into the pen.

'What is it, granny, what do you want?' said the philosopher.

But the old woman came towards him with outstretched arms.

'Aha, ha!' thought the philosopher. 'No, my dear, you are too old!'

He turned a little away, but the old woman unceremoniously approached him again.

'Listen, granny!' said the philosopher. 'It's a fast time now; and I am a man who wouldn't sin in a fast for a thousand golden pieces.'

But the old woman opened her arms and tried to catch him without saying a word.

The philosopher was frightened, especially when he

noticed a strange glitter in her eyes. 'Granny, what is it? Go – go away – God bless you!' he cried.

The old woman said not a word, but tried to clutch him in her arms.

He leapt on to his feet, intending to escape; but the old woman stood in the doorway, fixed her glittering eyes on him and again began approaching him.

The philosopher tried to push her back with his hands, but to his surprise found that his arms would not rise, his legs would not move, and he perceived with horror that even his voice would not obey him; words hovered on his lips without a sound. He heard nothing but the beating of his heart. He saw the old woman approach him. She folded his arms, bent his head down, leapt with the swiftness of a cat upon his back, and struck him with a broom on the side; and he, prancing like a horse, carried her on his shoulders. All this happened so quickly that the philosopher scarcely knew what he was doing. He clutched his knees in both hands, trying to stop his legs from moving, but to his extreme amazement they were lifted against his will and executed capers more swiftly than a Circassian racer. Only when they had left the farm, and the wide plain lay stretched before them with a forest black as coal on one side, he said to himself: 'Aha! she's a witch!'

The waning crescent of the moon was shining in the sky. The timid radiance of midnight lay mistily over the earth, light as a transparent veil. The forests, the meadows, the sky, the dales, all seemed as though slumbering with open eyes; not a breeze fluttered anywhere; there was a damp warmth in the freshness of the night; the shadows of the trees and bushes fell on the sloping plain in pointed wedge shapes like comets. Such was the night when Homa Brut, the philosopher, set off galloping with a mysterious rider on his back. He was aware of an exhausting, unpleasant, and at the same time, voluptuous sensation assailing his heart. He bent his head and saw that the grass which had been almost under his feet seemed growing at a depth far away, and that above it there lay water, transparent as a mountain stream, and the grass seemed to be at the bottom of a clear sea, limpid to its very depths; anyway, he saw clearly in it his own reflection with the old woman sitting on his back. He saw shining there a sun instead of the moon; he heard the bluebells ringing as they bent their little heads; he saw a water-nymph float out from behind the reeds, there was the gleam of her leg and back, rounded and supple, all brightness and shimmering. She turned towards him and now her face came nearer, with eyes clear, sparkling, keen, with singing that pierced to the heart; now it was on the surface, and shaking with sparkling laughter it moved away; and now she turned on her back, and her cloud-like breasts, dead white like unglazed china, gleamed in the sun at the edges of their white, soft and supple roundness. Little bubbles of water like beads bedewed them. She was all quivering and laughing in the water....

Did he see this or did he not? Was he awake or dreaming? But what was that? The wind or music? It is ringing and ringing and eddying and coming closer and piercing to his heart with an insufferable thrill....

'What does it mean?' the philosopher wondered, looking down as he flew along, full speed. The sweat was streaming from him. He was aware of a fiendishly voluptuous feeling, he felt a stabbing, exhaustingly terrible delight. It often seemed to him as though his heart had melted away, and with terror he clutched at it. Worn out, desperate, he began trying to recall all the prayers he knew. He went through all the exorcisms against evil spirits, and all at once felt somewhat refreshed; he felt that his step was growing slower, the witch's hold upon his back seemed feebler, thick grass touched him, and now he saw nothing extraordinary in it. The clear, crescent moon was shining in the sky.

'Good!' the philosopher Homa thought to himself, and he began repeating the exorcisms almost aloud. At last, quick as lightning, he sprang from under the old woman and in his turn leapt on her back. The old woman, with a tiny tripping step, ran so fast that her rider could scarcely breathe. The earth flashed by under him; everything was clear in the moonlight, though the moon was not full; the ground was smooth, but everything flashed by so rapidly that it was confused and indistinct. He snatched up a piece of wood that lay on the road and began whacking the old woman with all his might. She uttered wild howls; at first they were angry and menacing, then they grew fainter, sweeter, clearer, then rang out gently like delicate silver bells that stabbed him to the heart; and the thought flashed through his mind: was it really an old woman?

'Oh, I can do no more!' she murmured, and sank exhausted on the ground.

He stood up and looked into her face (there was the glow of sunrise, and the golden domes of the Kiev churches were gleaming in the distance): before him lay a lovely creature with luxuriant tresses all in disorder and eyelashes as long as arrows. Senseless she tossed her bare white arms and moaned, looking upwards with eyes full of tears.

Homa trembled like a leaf on a tree; he was overcome by pity and a strange emotion and timidity, feelings he could not himself explain. He set off running, full speed. His heart throbbed uneasily as he went, and he could not account for the strange new feeling that had taken possession of it. He did not want to go back to the farm; he hastened to Kiev, pondering all the way on this incomprehensive adventure.

There was scarcely a student left in the town. All had dispersed about the countryside, either to situations, or simply without them; because in the villages of Little Russia they could get dumplings, cheese, sour cream, and puddings as big as a hat without paying a kopeck for them. The big rambling house in which the students were lodged was absolutely empty, and although the philosopher rummaged in every corner, and even felt in all the holes and cracks in the roof, he could not find a bit of bacon or even a stale roll such as were commonly hidden there by the students.

The philosopher, however, soon found means to improve his lot: he walked whistling three times through the market, finally winked at a young widow in a yellow bonnet who was selling ribbons, shot and wheels – and was that very day regaled with wheat dumplings, a chicken . . . in short, there is no telling what was on the table laid for him in a little mud house in the middle of a cherry orchard.

That same evening the philosopher was seen in a tavern: he was lying on the bench, smoking a pipe as his habit was, and in the sight of all he flung the Jew who kept the house a gold coin. A mug stood before him. He looked at all that came in and went out with eyes full of cool satisfaction, and thought no more of his extraordinary adventure.

Meanwhile rumours were circulating everywhere that the daughter of one of the richest Cossack *sotniks*,[1] who lived nearly forty miles from Kiev, had returned one day from a walk, terribly injured, hardly able to crawl home to her father's house, was lying at the point of death, and had expressed a wish that one of the Kiev seminarists, Homa Brut, should read the prayers over her and the psalms for three days after her death. The philosopher heard of this from the rector himself, who summoned him to his room and informed him that he was to set off on the journey without any delay, that the noble *sotnik* had sent servants and a carriage to fetch him.

The philosopher shuddered from an unaccountable feeling which he could not have explained to himself. A dark presentiment told him that something evil was awaiting him. Without knowing why, he bluntly declared that he would not go.

'Listen, Domine Homa!' said the rector. (On some occasions he expressed himself very courteously with those under his authority.) 'Who the devil is asking you whether you want to go or not? All I have to tell you is that if you go on jibbing and making difficulties, I'll order you such a whacking with a young birch tree, on your back and the rest of you, that there will be no need for you to go to the bath after.'

The philosopher, scratching behind his ear, went out without uttering a word, proposing at the first suitable opportunity to put his trust in his heels. Plunged in thought he went down the steep staircase that led into a yard shut in by poplars, and stood still for a minute, hearing quite distinctly the voice of the rector giving orders to his butler and someone else – probably one of the servants sent to fetch him by the *sotnik*.

'Thank his honour for the grain and the eggs,' the rector was saying: 'and tell him that as soon as the books about which he writes are ready I will send them at once. I have already given them to a scribe to be copied, and don't forget, my good man, to mention to his honour that I know there

[1] An officer in command of a company of Cossacks, consisting originally of a hundred, but in later times of a larger number. (*Translator's Note*.)

are excellent fish at his place, especially sturgeon, and he might on occasion send some; here in the market it's bad and dear. And you, Yavtuh, give the young fellows a cup of vodka each, and bind the philosopher or he'll be off directly.'

'There, the devil's son!' the philosopher thought to himself. 'He scented it out, the wily long-legs!' He went down and saw a covered chaise, which he almost took at first for a baker's oven on wheels. It was, indeed, as deep as the oven in which bricks are baked. It was only the ordinary Cracow carriage in which Jews travel fifty together with their wares to all the towns where they smell out a fair. Six healthy and stalwart Cossacks, no longer young, were waiting for him. Their tunics of fine cloth, with tassels, showed that they belonged to a rather important and wealthy master; some small scars proved that they had at some time been in battle, not ingloriously.

'What's to be done? What is to be must be!' the philosopher thought to himself, and turning to the Cossacks, he said aloud: 'Good day to you, comrades!'

'Good health to you, master philosopher,' some of the Cossacks replied.

'So I am to get in with you? It's a goodly chaise!' he went on, as he clambered in, 'we need only hire some musicians and we might dance here.'

'Yes, it's a carriage of ample proportions,' said one of the Cossacks, seating himself on the box beside the coachman, who had tied a rag over his head to replace the cap which he had managed to leave behind at a pot-house. The other five and the philosopher crawled into the recesses of the chaise and settled themselves on sacks filled with various purchases they had made in the town. 'It would be interesting to know,' said the philosopher, 'if this chaise were loaded up with goods of some sort, salt for instance, or iron wedges, how many horses would be needed then?'

'Yes,' the Cossack, sitting on the box, said after a pause, 'it would need a sufficient number of horses.'

After this satisfactory reply the Cossack thought himself entitled to hold his tongue for the remainder of the journey.

The philosopher was extremely desirous of learning more in detail, who this *sotnik* was, what he was like, what had been heard about his daughter who in such a strange way returned home and was found on the point of death, and whose story was now connected with his own, what was being done in the house, and how things were there. He addressed the Cossacks with inquiries, but no doubt they too were philosophers, for by way of a reply they remained silent, smoking their pipes and lying on their backs. Only one of them turned to the driver on the box with a brief order. 'Mind, Overko, you old booby, when you are near the tavern on the Tchuhraylovo road, don't forget to stop and wake me and the other chaps, if any should chance to drop asleep.'

After this he fell asleep rather audibly. These instructions were, however, quite unnecessary, for as soon as the gigantic chaise drew near the pot-house, all the Cossacks with one voice shouted: 'Stop!' Moreover, Overko's horses were already trained to stop of themselves at every pot-house.

In spite of the hot July day, they all got out of the chaise and went into the low-pitched dirty room, where the Jew who kept the house hastened to receive his old friends with every sign of delight. The Jew brought from under the skirt of his coat some ham sausages, and, putting them on the table, turned his back at once on this food forbidden by the Talmud. All the Cossacks sat down round the table; earthenware mugs were set for each of the guests. Homa had to take part in the general festivity, and, as Little Russians infallibly begin kissing each other or weeping when they are drunk, soon the whole room resounded with smacks. 'I say, Spirid, a kiss.' 'Come here, Dorosh, I want to embrace you!'

One Cossack with grey moustaches, a little older than the rest, propped his cheek on his hand and began sobbing bitterly at the thought that he had no father nor mother and was all alone in the world. Another one, much given to moralizing, persisted in consoling him, saying: 'Don't cry; upon my soul, don't cry! What is there in it . . . ? The Lord knows best, you know.'

The one whose name was Dorosh became extremely inquisitive, and turning to the philosopher Homa, kept asking him: 'I should like to know what they teach you in the college. Is it the same as what the deacon reads in church, or something different?'

'Don't ask!' the sermonizing Cossack said emphatically:

'let it be as it is, God knows what is wanted, God knows everything.'

'No, I want to know,' said Dorosh, 'what is written there in those books? Maybe it is quite different from what the deacon reads.'

'Oh my goodness, my goodness!' said the sermonizing worthy, 'and why say such a thing, it's as the Lord wills. There is no changing what the Lord has willed!'

'I want to know all that's written. I'll go to college, upon my word, I will. Do you suppose I can't learn, I'll learn it all, all!'

'Oh my goodness . . . !' said the sermonizing Cossack, and he dropped his head on the table, because he was utterly incapable of supporting it any longer on his shoulders. The other Cossacks were discussing their masters and the question why the moon shone in the sky. The philosopher, seeing the state of their minds, resolved to seize his opportunity and make his escape. To begin with he turned to the grey-headed Cossack who was grieving for his father and mother.

'Why are you blubbering, uncle?' he said, 'I am an orphan myself! Let me go in freedom, lads! What do you want with me?'

'Let him go!' several responded, 'why, he is an orphan, let him go where he likes.'

'Oh my goodness, my goodness!' the moralizing Cossack articulated, lifting his head. 'Let him go!'

'Let him go where he likes!'

And the Cossacks meant to lead him out into the open air themselves, but the one who had displayed his curiosity stopped them, saying: 'Don't touch him. I want to talk to him about college: I am going to college myself. . . .'

It is doubtful, however, whether the escape could have taken place, for when the philosopher tried to get up from the table his legs seemed to have become wooden, and he began to perceive such a number of doors in the room that he could hardly discover the real one.

It was evening before the Cossacks bethought themselves that they had further to go. Clambering into the chaise, they trailed along the road, urging on the horses and singing a song of which nobody could have made out the words or the sense. After trundling on for the greater part of the night, continually straying off the road, though they knew every inch of the way, they drove at last down a steep hill into a valley, and the philosopher noticed a paling or hurdle that ran alongside, low trees and roofs peeping out behind it. This was a big village belonging to the *sotnik*. By now it was long past midnight; the sky was dark, but there were little stars twinkling here and there. No light was to be seen in a single cottage. To the accompaniment of the barking of dogs, they drove into the courtyard. Thatched barns and little houses came into sight on both sides; one of the latter, which stood exactly in the middle opposite the gates, was larger than the others, and was apparently the *sotnik's* residence. The chaise drew up before a little shed that did duty for a barn, and our travellers went off to bed. The philosopher, however, wanted to inspect the outside of the *sotnik's* house; but though he stared his hardest, nothing could be seen distinctly; the house looked to him like a bear; the chimney turned into the rector. The philosopher gave it up and went to sleep.

When he woke up, the whole house was in commotion: the *sotnik's* daughter had died in the night. Servants were running hurriedly to and fro; some old women were crying; an inquisitive crowd was looking through the fence at the house, as though something might be seen there. The philosopher began examining at his leisure the objects he could not make out in the night. The *sotnik's* house was a little, low-pitched building, such as was usual in Little Russia in old days; its roof was of thatch; a small, high, pointed gable with a little window that looked like an eye turned upwards, was painted in blue and yellow flowers and red crescents; it was supported on oak posts rounded above and hexagonal below, with carving at the top. Under this gable was a little porch with seats on each side. There were verandas round the house resting on similar posts, some of them carved in spirals. A tall pyramid pear tree, with trembling leaves, made a patch of green in front of the house. Two rows of barns for storing grain stood in the middle of the yard, forming a sort of wide street leading to the house. Beyond the barns, close to the gate, stood facing each other two three-cornered storehouses, also thatched. Each triangular wall was painted in various designs and had a little door in it. On one of them was depicted a Cossack sitting on a barrel, holding a mug above his head with the inscription: 'I'll drink it all!' On the other, there was a bottle, flagons, and at the sides, by way of ornament, a horse upside down, a pipe, a tambourine, and the inscription: 'Wine is the Cossack's comfort!' A drum and brass trumpets could be seen through the huge window in the loft of one of the barns. At the gates stood two cannons. Everything showed that the master of the house was fond of merrymaking, and that the yard often resounded with the shouts of revellers. There were two windmills outside the gate. Behind the house stretched gardens, and through the tree-tops the dark caps of chimneys were all that could be seen of cottages smothered in green bushes. The whole village lay on the broad sloping side of a hill. The steep side, at the very foot of which lay the courtyard, made a screen from the north. Looked at from below, it seemed even steeper, and here and there on its tall top uneven stalks of rough grass stood up black against the clear sky; its bare aspect was somehow depressing; its clay soil was hollowed out by the fall and trickle of rain. Two cottages stood at some distance from each other on its steep slope; one of them was overshadowed by the branches of a spreading apple tree, banked up with soil and supported by short stakes near the root. The apples, knocked down by the wind, were falling right into the master's courtyard. The road, coiling about the hill from the very top, ran down beside the courtyard to the village. When the philosopher scanned its terrific steepness and recalled their journey down it the previous night, he came to the conclusion that either the *sotnik* had very clever horses or that the Cossacks had very strong heads to have managed, even when drunk, to escape flying head over heels with the immense chaise and baggage. The philosopher was standing on the very highest point in the yard. When he turned and looked in the opposite direction he saw quite a different view. The village sloped away into a plain. Meadows stretched as far as the eye could see; their brilliant verdure was deeper in the distance, and whole rows of villages looked like dark patches in it, though they must have been more than fifteen miles away. On the right of the meadowlands was a line of hills, and a hardly perceptible streak of flashing light and darkness showed where the Dnieper ran.

'Ah, a splendid spot!' said the philosopher, 'this would be the place to live, fishing in the Dnieper and the ponds, bird-catching with nets, or shooting king-snipe and little bustard. Though I do believe there would be a few great bustards too in those meadows! One could dry lots of fruit, too, and sell it in the town, or, better still, make vodka of it, and there's no drink to compare with fruit-vodka. But it would be just as well to consider how to slip away from here.'

He noticed outside the fence a little path completely over-grown with weeds; he was mechanically setting his foot on it with the idea of simply going first out for a walk, and then stealthily passing between the cottages and dashing out into the open country, when he suddenly felt a rather strong hand on his shoulder.

Behind him stood the old Cossack who had on the previous evening so bitterly bewailed the death of his father and mother and his own solitary state.

'It's no good your thinking of making off, Mr Philosopher!' he said: 'this isn't the sort of establishment you can run away from; and the roads are bad, too, for anyone on foot; you had better come to the master: he's been expecting you this long time in the parlour.'

'Let us go! To be sure . . . I'm delighted,' said the philosopher, and he followed the Cossack.

The *sotnik*, an elderly man with grey moustaches and an expression of gloomy sadness, was sitting at a table in the parlour, his head propped on his hands. He was about fifty; but the deep despondency on his face and its wan pallor showed that his soul had been crushed and shattered at one blow, and all his old gaiety and noisy merrymaking had gone for ever. When Homa went in with the old Cossack, he removed one hand from his face and gave a slight nod in response to their low bows.

Homa and the Cossack stood respectfully at the door.

'Who are you, where do you come from, and what is your calling, good man?' said the *sotnik*, in a voice neither friendly nor ill-humoured.

'A bursar, student in philosophy, Homa Brut. . . .'

'Who was your father?'

'I don't know, honoured sir.'

'Your mother?'

'I don't know my mother either. It is reasonable to suppose, of course, that I had a mother; but who she was and where she came from, and when she lived – upon my soul, good sir, I don't know.'

The old man paused and seemed to sink into a reverie for a minute.

'How did you come to know my daughter?'

'I didn't know her, honoured sir, upon my word, I didn't. I have never had anything to do with young ladies, never in my life. Bless them, saving your presence!'

'Why did she fix on you and no other to read the psalms over her?'

The philosopher shrugged his shoulders. 'God knows how to make that out. It's a well-known thing, the gentry are for ever taking fancies that the most learned man couldn't explain, and the proverb says: "The devil himself must dance at the master's bidding." '

'Are you telling the truth, philosopher?'

'May I be struck down by thunder on the spot if I'm not.'

'If you had but lived one brief moment longer,' the *sotnik* said to himself mournfully, 'I should have learned all about it. "Let no one else read over me, but send, father, at once to Kiev Seminary and fetch the bursar, Homa Brut; let him pray three nights for my sinful soul. He knows . . . !" But what he knows, I did not hear; she, poor darling, could say no more before she died. You, good man, are no doubt well known for your holy life and pious works, and she, maybe, heard tell of you.'

'Who? I?' said the philosopher, stepping back in amazement. 'I — holy life!' he articulated, looking straight in the *sotnik's* face. 'God be with you, sir! What are you talking about! Why – though it's not a seemly thing to speak of – I paid the baker's wife a visit on Maundy Thursday.'

'Well . . . I suppose there must be some reason for fixing on you. You must begin your duties this very day.'

'As to that, I would tell your honour . . . Of course, any man versed in holy scriptures may, as far as in him lies . . . but a deacon or a sacristan would be better fitted for it. They are men of understanding, and know how it is all done; while I . . . Besides I haven't the right voice for it, and I myself am good for nothing. I'm not the figure for it.'

'Well, say what you like. I shall carry out all my darling's wishes, I will spare nothing. And if for three nights from today you duly recite the prayers over her, I will reward you, if not . . . I don't advise the devil himself to anger me.'

The last words were uttered by the *sotnik* so vigorously that the philosopher fully grasped their significance.

'Follow me!' said the *sotnik*.

They went out into the hall. The *sotnik* opened the door into another room, opposite the first. The philosopher paused a minute in the hall to blow his nose and crossed the threshold with unaccountable apprehension.

The whole floor was covered with red cotton stuff. On a high table in the corner under the holy images lay the body of the dead girl on a coverlet of dark blue velvet adorned with gold fringe and tassels. Tall wax candles, entwined with sprigs of guelder rose, stood at her feet and head, shedding a dim light that was lost in the brightness of daylight. The dead girl's face was hidden from him by the inconsolable father, who sat down facing her with his back to the door. The philosopher was impressed by the words he heard:

'I am grieving, my dearly beloved daughter, not that in the flower of your age you have left the earth, to my sorrow and mourning, without living your allotted span; I grieve, my darling, that I know not him, my bitter foe, who was the cause of your death. And if I knew the man who could but dream of hurting you, or even saying anything unkind of you, I swear to God he should not see his children again, if he be as old as I, nor his father and mother, if he be of that time of life, and his body should be cast out to be devoured by the birds and beasts of the steppe! But my grief it is, my wild marigold, my birdie, light of my eyes, that I must live out my days without comfort, wiping with the skirt of my coat the trickling tears that flow from my old eyes, while my enemy will be making merry and secretly mocking at the feeble old man. . . .'

He came to a standstill, due to an outburst of sorrow, which found vent in a flood of tears.

The philosopher was touched by such inconsolable sadness; he coughed, uttering a hollow sound in the effort to clear his throat. The *sotnik* turned round and pointed him to a place at the dead girl's head, before a small lectern with books on it.

'I shall get through three nights somehow,' thought the philosopher: 'and the old man will stuff both my pockets with gold pieces for it.'

He drew near, and, clearing his throat once more, began reading, paying no attention to anything else and not venturing to glance at the face of the dead girl. A profound stillness reigned in the apartment. He noticed that the *sotnik* had withdrawn. Slowly he turned his head to look at the dead, and . . .

A shudder ran through his veins: before him lay a beauty whose like had surely never been on earth before. Never, it seemed, could features have been formed in such striking yet harmonious beauty. She lay as though living: the lovely forehead, fair as snow, as silver, looked deep in thought; the even brows – dark as night in the midst of sunshine – rose proudly above the closed eyes; the eyelashes, that fell like arrows on the cheeks, glowed with the warmth of secret desires; the lips were rubies, ready to break into the laugh of bliss, the flood of joy. . . . But in them, in those very features, he saw something terrible and poignant. He felt a sickening ache stirring in his heart, as though, in the midst of a whirl of gaiety and dancing crowds, someone had begun singing a funeral dirge. The rubies of her lips looked like blood surging up from her heart. All at once he was aware of something dreadfully familiar in her face. 'The witch!' he cried in a voice not his own, as, turning pale, he looked away and fell to repeating his prayers. It was the witch that he had killed!

When the sun was setting, they carried the corpse to the church. The philosopher supported the coffin swathed in black on his shoulder, and felt something cold as ice on it. The *sotnik* walked in front, with his hand on the right side of the dead girl's narrow resting home. The wooden church, blackened by age and overgrown with green lichen, stood disconsolately, with its three cone-shaped domes, at the very end of the village. It was evident that no service had been performed in it for a long time. Candles had been lighted before almost every image. The coffin was set down in the centre opposite the altar. The old *sotnik* kissed the dead girl once more, bowed down to the ground, and went out together with the coffin-bearers, giving orders that the philosopher should have a good supper and then be taken to the church. On reaching the kitchen all the men who had carried the coffin began putting their hands on the stove, as the custom is with Little Russians, after seeing a dead body.

The hunger, of which the philosopher began at that moment to be conscious, made him for some minutes entirely oblivious of the dead girl. Soon all the servants began gradually assembling in the kitchen, which in the *sotnik's* house was something like a club, where all the inhabitants of the yard gathered together, including even the dogs, who, wagging their tails, came to the door for bones and slops. Wherever anybody might be sent, and with whatever duty he might be charged, he always went first to the kitchen to rest for at least a minute on the bench and smoke a pipe. All the unmarried men in their smart Cossack tunics lay there almost all day long, on the bench, under the bench, or on the stove – anywhere, in fact, where a comfortable place could be found to lie on. Then everybody invariably left behind in the kitchen either his can or a whip to keep stray dogs off or some such thing. But the biggest crowd always gathered at supper-time, when the drover who had taken the horses to the paddock, and the herdsman who had brought the cows in to be milked, and all the others who were not to be seen during the day, came in. At supper, even the most taciturn tongues were moved to loquacity. It was then that all the news was talked over: who had got himself new breeches, and what was hidden in the bowels of the earth, and who had seen a wolf. There were witty talkers among them; indeed, there is no lack of them anywhere among the Little Russians.

The philosopher sat down with the rest in a big circle in the open air before the kitchen door. Soon a peasant woman in a red bonnet popped out, holding in both hands a steaming bowl of dumplings, which she set down in their midst. Each pulled out a wooden spoon from his pocket, or for lack of a spoon, a wooden stick. As soon as their jaws began moving more slowly, and the wolfish hunger of the whole party was somewhat assuaged, many of them began talking. The conversation naturally turned on the dead maiden.

'Is it true,' said a young shepherd who had put so many

buttons and copper discs on the leather strap on which his pipe hung that he looked like a small haberdasher's shop, 'is it true that the young lady, saving your presence, was on friendly terms with the Evil One?'

'Who? The young mistress?' said Dorosh, a man our philosopher already knew, 'why, she was a regular witch! I'll take my oath she was a witch!'

'Hush, hush, Dorosh,' said another man, who had shown a great disposition to soothe the others on the journey, 'that's no business of ours, God bless it! It's no good talking about it.'

But Dorosh was not at all inclined to hold his tongue; he had just been to the cellar on some job with the butler, and, having applied his lips to two or three barrels, he had come out extremely merry and talked away without ceasing.

'What do you want? Me to be quiet?' he said, 'why, I've been ridden by her myself! Upon my soul, I have!'

'Tell us, uncle,' said the young shepherd with the buttons, 'are there signs by which you can tell a witch?'

'No, you can't,' answered Dorosh, 'there's no way of telling: you might read through all the psalm-books and you couldn't tell.'

'Yes, you can, Dorosh, you can; don't say that,' the former comforter objected; 'it's with good purpose God has given every creature its peculiar habit; folks that have studied say that a witch has a little tail.'

'When a woman's old, she's a witch,' the grey-haired Cossack said coolly.

'Oh! you're a nice set!' retorted the peasant woman, who was at that instant pouring a fresh lot of dumplings into the empty pot; 'regular fat hogs!'

The old Cossack, whose name was Yavtuh and nickname Kovtun, gave a smile of satisfaction seeing that his words had cut the old woman to the quick; while the herdsman gave vent to a guffaw, like the bellowing of two bulls as they stand facing each other.

The beginning of the conversation had aroused the philosopher's curiosity and made him intensely anxious to learn more details about the *sotnik's* daughter, and so, wishing to bring the talk back to that subject, he turned to his neighbour with the words: 'I should like to ask why all the folk sitting at supper here look upon the young mistress as a witch? Did she do a mischief to anybody or bring anybody to harm?'

'There were all sorts of doings,' answered one of the company, a man with a flat face strikingly resembling a spade. 'Everybody remembers the dog-boy Mikita and the . . .'

'What about the dog-boy Mikita?' asked the philosopher.

'Stop! I'll tell about the dog-boy Mikita,' said Dorosh.

'I'll tell about him,' said the drover, 'for he was a great crony of mine.'

'I'll tell about Mikita,' said Spirid.

'Let him, let Spirid tell it!' shouted the company.

Spirid began: 'You don't know Mikita, Mr Philosopher Homa. Ah, he was a man! He knew every dog as well as he knew his own father. The dog-boy we've got now, Mikola, who's sitting next but one from me, isn't worth the sole of his shoe. Though he knows his job, too, but beside the other he's trash, slops.'

'You tell the story well, very well!' said Dorosh, nodding his head approvingly.

Spirid went on: 'He'd see a hare quicker than you'd wipe the snuff from your nose. He'd whistle: "Here, Breaker! here, Swiftfoot!" and he in full gallop on his horse; and there was no saying which would outrace the other, he the dog, or the dog him. He'd toss off a mug of vodka without winking. He was a fine dog-boy! Only a little time back he began to be always staring at the young mistress. Whether he had fallen in love with her, or whether she had simply bewitched him, anyway the man was done for, he went fairly silly; the devil only knows what he turned into . . . pfoo! No decent word for it. . . .'

'That's good,' said Dorosh.

'As soon as the young mistress looks at him, he drops the bridle out of his hand, calls Breaker Bushybrow, is all of a fluster and doesn't know what he's doing. One day the young mistress comes into the stable where he is rubbing down a horse.

'"I say, Mikita," says she, "let me put my foot on you." And he, silly fellow, is pleased at that. "Not your foot only," says he, "you may sit on me altogether." The young mistress lifted her foot, and as soon as he saw her bare, plump, white leg, he went fairly crazy, so he said. He bent his back, silly fellow, and clasping her bare leg in his hands, ran galloping like a horse all over the countryside. And he couldn't say where he was driven, but he came back more dead than alive, and from that time he withered up like a chip of wood; and one day when they went into the stable, instead of him they found a heap of ashes lying there and an empty pail; he had burnt up entirely, burnt up of himself. And he was a dog-boy such as you couldn't find another all the world over.'

When Spirid had finished his story, reflections upon the rare qualities of the deceased dog-boy followed from all sides.

'And haven't you heard tell of Sheptun's wife?' said Dorosh, addressing Homa.

'No.'

'Well, well! You are not taught with too much sense, it seems, in the seminary. Listen, then. There's a Cossack called Sheptun in our village – a good Cossack! He is given to stealing at times, and telling lies when there's no occasion, but . . . he's a good Cossack. His cottage is not so far from here. Just about the very hour that we sat down this evening to table, Sheptun and his wife finished their supper and lay down to sleep, and as it was fine weather, his wife lay down in the yard, and Sheptun in the cottage on the bench; or no . . . it was the wife lay indoors on the bench and Sheptun in the yard. . . .'

'Not on the bench, she was lying on the floor,' put in a peasant woman, who stood in the doorway with her cheek propped in her hand.

Dorosh looked at her, then looked down, then looked at her again, and after a brief pause, said: 'When I strip off your petticoat before everybody, you won't be pleased.'

This warning had its effect; the old woman held her tongue and did not interrupt the story again.

Dorosh went on: 'And in the cradle hanging in the middle of the cottage lay a baby a year old – whether of the male or female sex I can't say. Sheptun's wife was lying there when she heard a dog scratching at the door and howling fit to make you run out of the cottage. She was scared, for women are such foolish creatures that, if towards evening you put your tongue out at one from behind a door, her heart's in her mouth. However, she thought: "Well, I'll go and give that damned dog a whack on its nose, and maybe it will stop howling," and taking the oven-fork she went to open the door. She had hardly opened it when a dog dashed in between her legs and straight to the baby's cradle. She saw that it was no longer a dog, but the young mistress, and if it had been the young lady in her own shape as she knew her, it would not have been so bad. But the peculiar thing is that she was all blue and her eyes glowing like coals. She snatched up the child, bit its throat, and began sucking its blood. Sheptun's wife could only scream: "Oh, horror!" and rushed towards the door. But she sees the door's locked in the passage; she flies up to the loft and there she sits all of a shake, silly woman; and then she sees the young mistress coming up to her in the loft; she pounced on her, and began biting the silly woman. When Sheptun pulled his wife down from the loft in the morning she was bitten all over and had turned black and blue; and next day the silly woman died. So you see what uncanny and wicked doings happen in the world! Though it is of the gentry's breed, a witch is a witch.'

After telling this story, Dorosh looked about him complacently and thrust his finger into his pipe, preparing to fill it with tobacco. The subject of the witch seemed inexhaustible. Each in turn hastened to tell some tale of her. One had seen the witch in the form of a haystack come right up to the door of his cottage; another had had his cap or his pipe stolen by her; many of the girls in the village had had their hair cut off by her; others had lost several quarts of blood sucked by her.

At last the company pulled themselves together and saw that they had been chattering too long, for it was quite dark in the yard. They all began wandering off to their several sleeping places, which were either in the kitchen, or the barns, or the middle of the courtyard.

'Well, Mr Homa! now it's time for us to go to the deceased lady,' said the grey-haired Cossack, addressing the philosopher; and together with Spirid and Dorosh they set off to the church, lashing with their whips at the dogs, of which there were a great number in the road, and which gnawed at their sticks angrily.

Though the philosopher had managed to fortify himself with a good mugful of vodka, he felt a fearfulness creeping stealthily over him as they approached the lighted church. The stories and strange tales he had heard helped to work upon his imagination. The darkness under the fence and trees grew less thick as they came into the more open place. At last they went into the church enclosure and found a little yard, beyond which there was not a tree to be seen, nothing but open country and meadows swallowed up in the darkness of night. The three Cossacks and Homa mounted the steep steps to the porch and went into the church. Here they left the philosopher with the best wishes that he might carry out his duties satisfactorily, and locked the door after them, as their master had bidden them.

The philosopher was left alone. First he yawned, then he stretched, then he blew into both hands, and at last he looked about him. In the middle of the church stood the black coffin; candles were gleaming under the dark images; the light from them only lit up the ikon-stand and shed a faint glimmer in the middle of the church; the distant corners were wrapped in darkness. The tall old-fashioned ikon-stand showed traces of great antiquity; its carved fret-work, once gilt, only glistened here and there with splashes of gold; the gilt had peeled off in one place, and was completely tarnished in another; the faces of the saints, blackened by age, had a gloomy look. The philosopher looked round him again. 'Well,' he said, 'what is there to be afraid of here? No living man can come in here, and to guard me from the dead and ghosts from the other world I have prayers that I have but to read aloud to keep them from laying a finger on me. It's all right!' he repeated with a wave of his hand, 'let's read.' Going up to the lectern he saw some bundles of candles. 'That's good,' thought the philosopher; 'I must light up the whole church so that it may be as bright as by daylight. Oh, it is a pity that one must not smoke a pipe in the temple of God!'

And he proceeded to stick up wax candles at all the cornices, lecterns and images, not stinting them at all, and soon the whole church was flooded with light. Only overhead the darkness seemed somehow more profound, and the gloomy ikons looked even more sullenly out of their antique carved frames, which glistened here and there with specks of gilt. He went up to the coffin, looked timidly at the face of the dead – and could not help closing his eyelids with a faint shudder: such terrible, brilliant beauty!

He turned and tried to move away; but with the strange curiosity, the self-contradictory feeling, which dogs a man especially in times of terror, he could not, as he withdrew, resist taking another look. And then, after the same shudder, he looked again. The striking beauty of the dead maiden certainly seemed terrible. Possibly, indeed, she would have overwhelmed him with such panic fear if she had been a little less lovely. But there was in her features nothing faded, tarnished, dead; her face was living, and it seemed to the philosopher that she was looking at him with closed eyes. He even fancied that a tear was oozing from under her right eyelid, and when it rested on her cheek, he saw distinctly that it was a drop of blood.

He walked hastily away to the lectern, opened the book, and to give himself more confidence began reading in a very loud voice. His voice smote upon the wooden church walls, which had so long been deaf and silent; it rang out, forlorn, unechoed, in a deep bass in the absolutely dead stillness, and seemed somehow uncanny even to the reader himself. 'What is there to be afraid of?' he was saying meanwhile to himself. 'She won't rise up out of her coffin, for she will fear the word of God. Let here lie there! And a fine Cossack I am, if I should be scared. Well, I've drunk a drop too much – that's why it seems dreadful. I'll have a pinch of snuff. Ah, the good snuff! Fine snuff, good snuff!' However, as he turned over the pages, he kept taking sidelong glances at the coffin, and an involuntary feeling seemed whispering to him: 'Look, look, she is going to get up! See, she'll sit up, she'll look out from the coffin!'

But the silence was deathlike; the coffin stood motionless; the candles shed a perfect flood of light. A church lighted up at night with a dead body in it and no living soul near is full of terror!

Raising his voice, he began singing in various keys, trying to drown the fears that still lurked in him, but every minute he turned his eyes to the coffin, as though asking, in spite of himself: 'What if she does sit up, if she gets up?'

But the coffin did not stir. If there had but been some sound! some living creature! There was not so much as a cricket churring in the corner! There was nothing but the faint splutter of a faraway candle, the light tap of a drop of wax falling on the floor.

'What if she were to get up . . . ?'

She was raising her head. . . .

He looked at her wildly and rubbed his eyes. She was, indeed, not lying down now, but sitting up in the coffin. He looked away, and again turned his eyes with horror on the coffin. She stood up . . . she was walking about the church with her eyes shut, moving her arms to and fro as though trying to catch someone.

She was coming straight towards him. In terror he drew a circle round him; with an effort he began reading the prayers and pronouncing the exorcisms which had been taught him by a monk who had all his life seen witches and evil spirits.

She stood almost on the very line; but it was clear that she had not the power to cross it, and she turned livid all over like one who has been dead for several days. Homa had not the courage to look at her; she was terrifying. She ground her teeth and opened her dead eyes; but, seeing nothing, turned with fury – that was apparent in her quivering face – in another direction, and flinging her arms, clutched in them each column and corner, trying to catch Homa. At last she stood still, holding up a menacing finger, and lay down again in her coffin.

The philosopher could not recover his self-possession, but kept gazing at the narrow dwelling-place of the witch. At last the coffin suddenly sprang up from its place and with a hissing sound began flying all over the church, zigzagging through the air in all directions.

The philosopher saw it almost over his head, but at the same time he saw that it could not cross the circle he had drawn, and he redoubled his exorcisms. The coffin dropped down in the middle of the church and stayed there without moving. The corpse got up out of it, livid and greenish. But at that instant the crow of the cock was heard in the distance; the corpse sank back in the coffin and closed the lid.

The philosopher's heart was throbbing and the sweat was streaming down him, but, emboldened by the cock's crowing, he read on more rapidly the pages he ought to have read through before. At the first streak of dawn the sacristan came to relieve him, together with old Yavtuh, who was at that time performing the duties of a beadle.

On reaching his distant sleeping-place, the philosopher could not for a long time get to sleep; but weariness gained the upper hand at last and he slept on till dinner-time. When he woke up, all the events of the night seemed to him to have happened in a dream. To keep up his strength he was given at dinner a mug of vodka.

Over dinner he soon grew lively, made a remark or two, and devoured a rather large sucking pig almost unaided; but some feeling he could not have explained made him unable to bring himself to speak of his adventures in the church, and to the inquiries of the inquisitive he replied: 'Yes, all sorts of strange things happened.' The philosopher was one of those people who, if they are well fed, are moved to extraordinary benevolence. Lying down with his pipe in his teeth he watched them all with a honied look in his eyes and kept spitting to one side.

After dinner the philosopher was in excellent spirits. He went round the whole village and made friends with almost everybody; he was kicked out of two cottages, indeed; one good-looking young woman caught him a good smack on the back with a spade when he took it into his head to try her shift and skirt, and inquire what stuff they were made of. But as evening approached the philosopher grew more pensive. An hour before supper almost all the servants gathered together to play *kragli* – a sort of skittles in which long sticks are used instead of balls, and the winner has the right to ride on the loser's back. This game became very entertaining for the spectators; often the drover, a man as broad as a pancake, was mounted on the swineherd, a feeble little man, who was nothing but wrinkles. Another time it was the drover who had to bow his back, and Dorosh, leaping on it, always said: 'What a fine bull!' The more dignified of the company sat in the kitchen doorway. They looked on very gravely, smoking their pipes, even when the young people roared with laughter at some witty remark from the drover or Spirid. Homa tried in vain to give himself up to this game; some gloomy thought stuck in his head like a nail. At supper, in spite of his efforts to be merry, terror grew within him as the darkness spread over the sky.

'Come, it's time to set off, Mr Seminarist!' said his friend, the grey-headed Cossack, getting up from the table, together with Dorosh; 'let us go to our task.'

Homa was taken to the church again in the same way; again he was left there alone and the door was locked upon him. As soon as he was alone, fear began to take possession of him again. Again he saw the dark ikons, the gleaming frames, and the familiar black coffin standing in menacing stillness and immobility in the middle of the church.

'Well,' he said to himself, 'now there's nothing marvellous to me in this marvel. It was only alarming the first time. Yes, it was only rather alarming the first time, and even then it wasn't so alarming; now it's not alarming at all.'

He made haste to take his stand at the lectern, drew a circle round him, pronounced some exorcisms, and began reading aloud, resolving not to raise his eyes from the book and not to pay attention to anything. He had been reading for about an hour and was beginning to cough and feel rather tired; he took his horn out of his pocket and, before putting the snuff to his nose, stole a timid look at the coffin. His heart turned cold; the corpse was already standing before him on the very edge of the circle, and her dead, greenish eyes were fixed upon him. The philosopher shuddered, and a cold chill ran through his veins. Dropping his eyes to the book, he began reading the prayers and exorcisms more loudly, and heard the corpse again grinding her teeth and waving her arms trying to catch him. But with a sidelong glance out of one eye, he saw that the corpse was feeling for him where he was not standing, and that she evidently could not see him. He heard a hollow mutter, and she began pronouncing terrible words with her dead lips; they gurgled hoarsely like the bubbling of boiling pitch. He could not have said what they meant; but there was something fearful in them. The philosopher understood with horror that she was making an incantation.

A wind blew through the church at her words, and there was a sound as of multitudes of flying wings. He heard the beating of wings on the panes of the church windows and on the iron window-frames, the dull scratching of claws upon the iron, and an immense troop thundering on the doors and trying to break in. His heart was throbbing violently all this time; closing his eyes, he kept reading prayers and exorcisms. At last there was a sudden shrill sound in the distance; it was a distant cock crowing. The philosopher, utterly spent, stopped and took breath.

When they came in to fetch him, they found him more dead than alive; he was leaning with his back against the wall, while with his eyes almost staring out of his head, he stared at the Cossacks as they came in. They could scarcely get him along and had to support him all the way back. On reaching the courtyard, he pulled himself together and bade them give him a mug of vodka. When he had drunk it, he stroked down the hair on his head and said: 'There are lots of foul things of all sorts in the world! And the panics they give one, there. . . .' With that the philosopher waved his hand in despair.

The company sitting round him bowed their heads, hearing such sayings. Even a small boy, whom everybody in the servants' quarters felt himself entitled to depute in his place when it was a question of cleaning the stables or fetching water, even this poor youngster stared open-mouthed at the philosopher.

At that moment the old cook's assistant, a peasant woman, not yet past middle age, a terrible coquette, who always found something to pin to her cap – a bit of ribbon, a pink, or even a scrap of coloured paper, if she had nothing better – passed by, in a tightly girt apron, which displayed her round, sturdy figure.

'Good day, Homa!' she said, seeing the philosopher. 'Aie, aie, aie! what's the matter with you?' she shrieked, clasping her hands.

'Why, what is it, silly woman?'

'Oh, my goodness! Why, you've gone quite grey!'

'Aha! why, she's right!' Spirid pronounced, looking attentively at the philosopher. 'Why, you have really gone as grey as our old Yavtuh.'

The philosopher, hearing this, ran headlong to the kitchen, where he had noticed on the wall a fly-blown triangular bit of looking-glass before which were stuck forget-me-nots, periwinkles and even wreaths of marigolds, testifying to its importance for the toilet of the finery-loving coquette. With horror he saw the truth of their words: half of his hair had in fact turned white.

Homa Brut hung his head and abandoned himself to reflection. 'I will go to the master,' he said at last. 'I'll tell him all about it and explain that I cannot go on reading. Let him send me back to Kiev straight away.'

With these thoughts in his mind he bent his steps towards the porch of the house.

The *sotnik* was sitting almost motionless in his parlour. The same hopeless grief which the philosopher had seen in his face before was still apparent. Only his cheeks were more sunken. It was evident that he had taken very little food, or perhaps had not eaten at all. The extraordinary pallor of his face gave it a look of stony immobility.

'Good day,' he pronounced on seeing Homa, who stood, cap in hand, at the door. 'Well, how goes it with you? All satisfactory?'

'It's satisfactory, all right; such devilish doing, that one can but pick up one's cap and take to one's heels.'

'How's that?'

'Why, your daughter, your honour . . . Looking at it reasonably, she is, to be sure, of noble birth, nobody is going to gainsay it; only, saving your presence, God rest her soul. . . .'

'What of my daughter?'

'She had dealings with Satan. She gives one such horrors that there's no reading scripture at all.'

'Read away! read away! She did well to send for you; she took much care, poor darling, about her soul and tried to drive away all evil thoughts with prayers.'

'That's as you like to say, your honour; upon my soul, I cannot go on with it!'

'Read away!' the *sotnik* persisted in the same persuasive voice, 'you have only one night left; you will do a Christian deed and I will reward you.'

'But whatever rewards . . . Do as you please, your honour, but I will not read!' Homa declared resolutely.

'Listen, philosopher!' said the *sotnik*, and his voice grew firm and menacing. 'I don't like these pranks. You can behave like that in your seminary; but with me it is different.

When I flog, it's not the same as your rector's flogging. Do you know what good leather whips are like?'

'I should think I do!' said the philosopher, dropping his voice; 'everybody knows what leather whips are like: in a large dose, it's quite unendurable.'

'Yes, but you don't know yet how my lads can lay them on!' said the *sotnik*, menacingly, rising to his feet, and his face assumed an imperious and ferocious expression that betrayed the unbridled violence of his character, only subdued for the time by sorrow.

'Here they first give a sound flogging, then sprinkle with vodka, and begin over again. Go along, go along, finish your task! If you don't – you'll never get up again. If you do – a thousand gold pieces!'

'Oho, ho! he's a stiff one!' thought the philosopher as he went out: 'he's not to be trifled with. Wait a bit, friend; I'll cut and run, so that you and your hounds will never catch me.'

And Homa made up his mind to run away. He only waited for the hour after dinner when all the servants were accustomed to lie about in the hay in the barns and to give vent to such snores and wheezing that the backyard sounded like a factory.

The time came at last. Even Yavtuh closed his eyes as he lay stretched out in the sun. With fear and trembling, the philosopher stealthily made his way into the pleasure garden, from which he fancied he could more easily escape into the open country without being observed. As is usual with such gardens, it was dreadfully neglected and overgrown, and so made an extremely suitable setting for any secret enterprise. Except for one little path, trodden by the servants on their tasks, it was entirely hidden in a dense thicket of cherry trees, elders and burdock, which thrust up their tall stems covered with clinging pinkish burs. A network of wild hop was flung over this medley of trees and bushes of varied hues, forming a roof over them, clinging to the fence and falling mingled with wild bell-flowers, from it in coiling snakes. Beyond the fence, which formed the boundary of the garden, there came a perfect forest of rank grass and weeds, which looked as though no one cared to peep enviously into it, and as though any scythe would be broken to bits trying to mow down the stout stubbly stalks.

When the philosopher tried to get over the fence, his teeth chattered and his heart beat so violently that he was frightened at it. The skirts of his long coat seemed to stick to the ground as though someone had nailed them down. As he climbed over, he fancied he heard a voice shout in his ears with a deafening hiss: 'Where are you off to?' The philosopher dived into the long grass and fell to running, frequently stumbling over old roots and trampling upon moles. He saw that when he came out of the rank weeds he would have to cross a field, and that beyond it lay a dark thicket of blackthorn, in which he thought he would be safe. He expected after making his way through it to find the road leading straight to Kiev. He ran across the field at once and found himself in the thicket.

He crawled through the prickly bushes, paying a toll of rags from his coat on every thorn, and came out into a little hollow. A willow with spreading branches went down almost to the earth. A little brook sparkled pure as silver. The first thing the philosopher did was to lie down and drink, for he was insufferably thirsty. 'Good water!' he said, wiping his lips; 'I might rest here!'

'No, we had better go straight ahead; they'll be coming to look for you!'

These words rang out above his ears. He looked round – before him was standing Yavtuh. 'Curse Yavtuh!' the philosopher thought in his wrath; 'I could take you and fling you . . . And I could batter in your ugly face and all of you with an oak post.'

'You needn't have gone such a long way round,' Yavtuh went on, 'you'd have done better to keep to the road I have come by, straight by the stable. And it's a pity about your coat. It's good cloth. What did you pay a yard for it? But we've walked far enough; it's time to go home.'

The philosopher trudged after Yavtuh, scratching himself. 'Now the cursed witch will give it to me!' he thought. 'Though, after all, what am I thinking about? What am I afraid of? Am I not a Cossack? Why, I've been through two nights, God will succour me the third also. The cursed witch committed a fine lot of sins, it seems, since the Evil One makes such a fight for her.'

Such were the reflections that absorbed him as he walked into the courtyard. Keeping up his spirits with these thoughts, he asked Dorosh, who thought the patronage of the butler sometimes had access to the cellars, to pull out a keg of vodka; and the two friends, sitting in the barn, put away not much less than half a pailful, so that the philosopher, getting on to his feet, shouted: 'Musicians! I must have musicians!' and without waiting for the latter fell to dancing a jig in a clear space in the middle of the yard. He danced till it was time for the afternoon snack, and the servants who stood round him in a circle, as is the custom on such occasions, at last spat on the ground and walked away, saying: 'Good gracious, what a time the fellow keeps it up!' At last the philosopher lay down to sleep on the spot, and a good sousing of cold water was needed to wake him up for supper. At supper he talked of what it meant to be a Cossack, and how he should not be afraid of anything in the world.

'Time is up,' said Yavtuh, 'let us go.'

'A splinter through your tongue, you damned hog!' thought the philosopher, and getting to his feet he said: 'Come along.'

On the way the philosopher kept glancing from side to side and made faint attempts at conversation with his companions. But Yavtuh said nothing; and even Dorosh was disinclined to talk. It was a hellish night. A whole pack of wolves was howling in the distance, and even the barking of the dogs had a dreadful sound.

'I fancy something else is howling; that's not a wolf,' said Dorosh. Yavtuh was silent. The philosopher could find nothing to say.

They drew near the church and stepped under the decaying wooden domes that showed how little the owner of the place thought about God and his own soul. Yavtuh and Dorosh withdrew as before, and the philosopher was left alone.

Everything was the same, everything wore the same sinister familiar aspect. He stood still for a minute. The horrible witch's coffin was still standing motionless in the middle of the church.

'I won't be afraid; by God, I will not!' he said, and, drawing a circle around himself as before, he began recalling all his spells and exorcisms. There was an awful stillness; the candles spluttered and flooded the whole church with light. The philosopher turned one page, then turned another and noticed that he was not reading what was written in the book. With horror he crossed himself and began chanting. This gave him a little more courage; the reading made progress, and the pages turned rapidly one after the other.

All of a sudden . . . in the midst of the stillness . . . the iron lid of the coffin burst with a crash and the corpse rose up. It was more terrible than the first time. Its teeth clacked horribly against each other, its lips twitched convulsively, and incantations came from them in wild shrieks. A whirlwind swept through the church, the ikons fell to the ground, broken glass came flying down from the windows. The doors were burst from their hinges and a countless multitude of monstrous beings trooped into the church of God. A terrible noise of wings and scratching claws filled the church. All flew and raced about looking for the philosopher.

All trace of drink had disappeared, and Homa's head was quite clear now. He kept crossing himself and repeating prayers at random. And all the while he heard the unclean horde whirring round him, almost touching him with their loathsome tails and the tips of their wings. He had not the courage to look at them; he only saw a huge monster, the whole width of the wall, standing in the shade of its matted locks as of a forest; through the tangle of hair two eyes glared horribly with eyebrows slightly lifted. Above it something was hanging in the air like an immense bubble with a thousand claws and scorpion-stings stretching from the centre; black earth hung in clods on them. They were all looking at him, seeking him, but could not see him, surrounded by his mysterious circle. 'Bring Viy! Fetch Viy!' he heard the corpse cry.

And suddenly a stillness fell upon the church; the wolves' howling was heard in the distance, and soon there was the thud of heavy footsteps resounding through the church. With a sidelong glance he saw they were bringing a squat, thick-set bandy-legged figure. He was covered all over with black earth. His arms and legs grew out like strong sinewy roots. He trod heavily, stumbling at every step. His long eyelids hung down to the very ground. Homa saw with horror that his face was of iron. He was supported under the arms and led straight to the spot where Homa was standing.

'Lift up my eyelids. I do not see!' said Viy in a voice that seemed to come from underground – and all the company flew to raise his eyelids.

'Do not look!' an inner voice whispered to the philosopher. He could not restrain himself, and he looked.

'There he is!' shouted Viy, and thrust an iron finger at him. And all pounced upon the philosopher together. He fell expiring to the ground, and his soul fled from his body in terror.

There was the sound of a cock crowing. It was the second cock-crow; the first had been missed by the gnomes. In panic they rushed pell-mell to the doors and windows to fly out in utmost haste; but they could not; and so they remained there, stuck in the doors and windows.

When the priest went in, he stopped short at the sight of this defamation of God's holy place, and dared not serve the requiem on such a spot. And so the church was left for ever, with monsters stuck in the doors and windows, was overgrown with forest trees, roots, rough grass and wild thorns, and no one can now find the way to it.

When the rumours of this reached Kiev, and the theologian, Halyava, heard at last the fate of the philosopher Homa, he spent a whole hour plunged in thought. Great changes had befallen him during that time. Fortune had smiled on him; on the conclusion of his course of study, he was made bellringer of the very highest belfry, and he was almost always to be seen with a damaged nose, as the wooden staircase to the belfry had been extremely carelessly made.

'Have you heard what has happened to Homa?' Tibery Gorobets, who by now was a philosopher and had a newly-grown moustache, asked, coming up to him.

'Such was the lot God sent him,' said Halyava the bell-ringer. 'Let us go to the pot-house and drink to his memory!'

The young philosopher, who was beginning to enjoy his privileges with the ardour of an enthusiast, so that his full trousers and his coat and even his cap reeked of spirits and coarse tobacco, instantly signified his readiness.

'He was a fine fellow, Homa!' said the bellringer, as the lame innkeeper set the third mug before him. 'He was a fine man! And he came to grief for nothing.'

'I know why he came to grief: it was because he was afraid; if he had not been afraid, the witch could not have done anything to him. You have only to cross yourself and spit just on her tail, and nothing will happen. I know all about it. Why, all the old women who sit in our market in Kiev are all witches.'

To this the bellringer bowed his head in token of agreement. But, observing that his tongue was incapable of uttering a single word, he cautiously got up from the table, and, lurching to right and to left, went to hide in a remote spot in the rough grass; from the force of habit, however, he did not forget to carry off the sole of an old boot that was lying about on the bench.

E. C. TUBB

FRESH GUY

SAMMY WAS playing knucklebones on The Tombstone when the vampire arrived. As a vampire he obviously had a lot to learn. Sammy had heard him, recognized him for what he was and had dismissed him as a possible danger before the stranger stumbled into the light of the tiny fire which Sammy tended. Even when he finally arrived Sammy paid him no attention, concentrating instead on his game, rolling the five scraps of bone with easy familiarity.

He was good at the game, having had much time in which to practise, and he took a quiet pride in the skilful manner he tossed and snatched, flipped and caught, spun and held the knucklebones. He ended the game by throwing them high into the air, catching them on the back of his hand. It was a broad, shovel-like hand with stubby fingers, thick, strong nails and well-developed muscles.

'Not bad, eh?' Sammy flipped the bones again, letting them bounce down the back of his hand and trapping them neatly between his fingers. He looked up, grinning at the stranger.

'What?' The vampire, a pale, distraught young character, was obviously out of his depth. He wore a faded khaki shirt and pants, a pair of cracked and mildewed boots and a baffled expression. 'What did you say?'

'I said "Not bad, eh?"' Sammy rolled the bones lovingly between his palms. 'I bet you couldn't handle them like that.'

'I don't suppose I could,' admitted the stranger. He ran the tip of his tongue over his lips. 'Do you mind if I join you?'

'Help yourself.' Sammy waved to a spot opposite him across the fire. 'Glad of company.' He rolled his bones again and stared moodily into the fire.

The stranger stared too. He seemed to be struggling with some private burden for twice he attempted to speak and changed his mind at the last moment. He squinted towards Sammy but the fire was low and the light was bad and all he could make out was a formless blur. Finally he coughed and got to the heart of what was worrying him.

'Look,' he said. 'My name is Smith, Edward Smith, and I seem to be in some sort of trouble. I wonder if you could help me?'

'Everyone's in some sort of trouble,' said Sammy feelingly. 'What's your particular brand?'

'Well,' said Smith urgently, 'something seems to have happened to me.' He passed a wavering hand across his forehead. 'This may sound crazy to you but I seem to be living in some weird kind of dream.'

'Do tell,' said Sammy, he was interested. Casually he flipped the knucklebones into a pocket of the tattered old jacket he wore. 'What makes you think that?'

'Everything.' Smith frowned as he tried to collect his thoughts. 'I was sick, I remember that well enough what with Uncle screaming about doctor's bills and the price of medicine and how he was having trouble getting in the harvest because I couldn't help him and how he'd have to hire a man and who was going to pay for it?' Smith took a deep breath.

Sammy nodded, picking idly at his teeth. 'I follow.'

'I was as sick as a dog,' corrected Smith feelingly. 'I guess I would have died if it hadn't been for some queer old coot of a doctor Uncle dug up from somewhere or other. He was cheap, I guess, otherwise I wouldn't have had him but he had a smell like he'd been out in the rain and hadn't dried off properly.'

'And he only came after dark,' said Sammy. 'Right?'

'How did you know?' Smith blinked in surprise. 'Maybe you know him, is that it?'

'I could take a guess,' said Sammy. He picked his teeth again. 'Then what happened?'

'I don't know.' Smith was genuinely baffled. 'I must have passed out, I guess, because the next thing I know I was in a hole in the ground on the other side of a hill. I had cramp something cruel so I yelled for help but no one could have heard me because no one came to see what was wrong.' He frowned again. 'And that's another queer thing. When I finally managed to get out of the hole and take a look round I couldn't find a thing. The farm was gone, the road all grown over, everything had changed.' He shook his head and stared bleakly into the fire. 'So I'm either dreaming or crazy.'

'You might be crazy,' said Sammy. 'I wouldn't argue about that, not knowing you well enough to form an opinion, but you're not dreaming, that's for sure.'

'I must be,' said Smith, he didn't seem to like the idea that he was crazy. 'All this is a stupid mixed-up nightmare. It must be.'

Sammy didn't bother to argue. He merely reached out and gently pinched Smith on the thigh. Smith screamed and rolled beside the fire, nursing his leg and whimpering with pain.

'Still think that you're dreaming?' asked Sammy pleasantly.

'No,' said Smith wildly. 'But if I'm not dreaming then I'm crazy. I'm just a poor, crazy madman, that's what.'

'Crazy you might be but a man you are not,' said Sammy. Smith jerked up his head.

'Not a man?' His voice rose a little. 'Then what am I?'

'A vampire.'

'A *what*!'

'A vampire.'

'Now I know who is crazy.' Smith forgot about his leg. 'All that guff is for the birds. Superstitious rubbish! Old wives' tales! Nonsense, all of it!'

Sammy shrugged.

'Well, it is,' insisted Smith weakly. He brooded for a long time. 'All right,' he said finally. 'I'll ride along with what you say. So I'm a vampire.' He leaned forward, triumph glinting in his eyes. 'But if I'm a vampire what does that make you?'

'A ghoul,' said Sammy. He threw some dried twigs on the fire, blinking in the sudden flare of light.

'Satisfied?' Sammy sucked reflectively at a tooth as the light died.

'I don't know.' Smith had been shaken by the sight. 'You're either the most deformed human I've ever seen or you aren't human at all.'

'I'm not human,' admitted Sammy patiently. 'I told you that. I'm a ghoul.'

'Incredible!' Smith shook his head. 'I simply can't believe it.'

Sammy grunted and rolled over on his back. His ears twitched a little, he was listening to the sounds of something moving in the woods.

'It's not that I'm calling you a liar,' said Smith. 'I wouldn't want you to think that, but the whole thing's so crazy!' He shook his head as if it hurt a little. 'And another thing. I must have walked for miles; if I hadn't seen your fire I'd have stumbled around all night, and in all that time I haven't seen or heard a soul. Not even a dog. Where is everyone?'

'Around,' said Sammy vaguely. He suddenly caught on to what Smith meant. 'Oh, you mean *humans*!' He stabbed a finger downwards towards the overgrown concrete slab of The Tombstone. 'At a guess I'd say they are about half a mile down.'

'All of them?'

'All that are left. In this part of the world anyway, I wouldn't know about over the oceans.' He stared at the young man's expression. 'Didn't you know?'

'No.' Smith was breathing fast from the top of his chest. 'What happened?'

'The Big Bang.' Sammy grimaced. 'The thing everyone knew would happen, said they didn't want to happen, yet made happen anyway.' Speculation narrowed his eyes. 'Say, just when were you buried, anyway?'

'I fell sick in 1960,' said Smith, dodging the leading question. Sammy pursed his lips in a soundless whistle.

'That accounts for it. The Big Bang came a couple of years later and they certainly made a good job of it. A better job than the embalmer did on you or you wouldn't be sitting there now.'

'Embalmer?' Smith looked blank. 'I don't get you. Are you sure that you know what you're talking about?'

'Listen,' snapped Sammy, he was getting annoyed. 'I may look a little odd, to you at least, but I'm no dumbbell. I can read fifteen languages and speak twenty more and once I went to school; spent most of a year there before I had to leave.'

'Why?'

'It was a medical school,' said Sammy shortly. 'What I'm getting at is that I know what happened to you. If the embalmer had done a better job you would have died for real. And even then you were lucky; your folks must have cut corners when they planted you. Otherwise you wouldn't have been washed out at the right time.'

'Uncle Silas was always a tight wad,' admitted Smith. 'He fancied himself at carpentry too.' He fell silent, thinking. 'I guess that all this must be real then.' He chuckled. 'Me, a vampire! Well, what do you know?' A sudden thought wiped the smile from his face. 'Say! If you're a ghoul —' He swallowed. 'What I mean is that ghouls are supposed to – well, aren't they?'

'Forget it,' said Sammy. 'We've a Gentleman's Agreement, neither touches the other.'

'Well!' Smith dabbed at his forehead. 'That's a relief. You had me worried for a while about that.'

Sammy didn't answer, he was busy listening to the stealthy approach of a visitor. Smith, now that the sounds were loud enough for even his dull hearing to catch, stiffened in sudden alarm.

'Say, what's that?'

'Relax,' said Sammy, setting an example. 'It's just one of the boys.'

'Who?' Smith seemed anxious.

'Who?' Sammy gave a grin. 'Well, now,' he said deliberately. 'At a guess I'd say it was your pappy.' He was always one for a joke.

Boris was of the old school, a tall, thin, cadaverous vampire who believed that the old traditions should be maintained. He came striding out of the woods, his cloak swirling around him, his monocle gleaming red in the reflected light. He sat beside the fire, warming his thin, almost transparent hands, then nodded to Smith.

'Who's the new one?'

Sammy chuckled. He had seen the expression on Smith's face and now awaited the denouement.

'I know you,' suddenly blurted Smith. 'You're the doctor who attended me when I was sick.'

'That's right,' said Sammy. 'Boris, meet your son. Smith, meet your Pop.'

'He's not my father,' denied Smith. 'Anyway, my old man died way back in a car crash.'

'Your new father for your new rebirth,' explained Sammy. 'Boris infected you when he snitched your blood. If it hadn't been for him you wouldn't be here now so, in a way, he's your Pop.' He became serious. 'It's the only way vampires can breed, you know, they depend on their victims to perpetuate their race.'

'And ghouls?' said Smith shrewdly. 'What about them?'

'Like humans,' said Sammy shortly. He didn't want to talk about it. Neither, it appeared, did Boris want to discuss his new offspring.

'Lupe here yet?' He shivered a little and drew closer to the fire. Sammy shook his head.

'He'll be along.'

'I hope we have better luck this time.' Boris sucked at his bloodless lips. 'Seven years now we've been waiting and still no sign of them coming out.' He looked suddenly panic-stricken. 'Could they all be dead?'

'Lupe said that he could hear sounds the last time,' reminded Sammy. 'And we know they took care to stock up well on supplies.'

'But something could have happened.' Boris was a natural pessimist. 'Maybe something went wrong with their water supply, or they took a bug down there with them and it wiped them out.' He began to chew at his nails as he thought about it. 'And they're the only ones we know of.'

'Take it easy,' said Sammy, he was becoming infected with the other's doubts. 'They'll be all right, I know they will.' He changed the subject. 'Anything new?'

'Nothing.' Boris hunched closer to the fire, his evening dress, dirt-stained but still retaining a traditional dignity, giving him the appearance of an old and slightly moth-eaten aristocrat. 'I've covered a pretty wide area and haven't seen a thing. I guess that we're the last, Sammy, you and me and Lupe, and we're not going to last much longer unless they come out from under The Tombstone pretty soon.'

'Don't forget me, Pop,' said Smith. 'I'm one of the boys now.' He grinned at Boris's expression. 'What's the matter, Pop? Touch you on the raw?'

'I am not used to being addressed as "Pop",' said Boris with simple dignity. 'And don't kid yourself that you are something special. Why, I remember the time when young pups like you were ten a penny. And a lot of trouble they caused too, back in the old days. Made life very hectic for a while.'

'That's because you weren't organized,' said Smith brusquely. 'Now, take me. I'm modern with modern ideas of how to go about things. You've got to be organized to get anywhere in this world.' He stared disdainfully at Boris's garments. 'Take you now, dressed up like a Continental Count playing a bit part in some crummy production.'

'I am a Count,' said Boris in a strangled voice.

'Maybe you were,' said Smith airily, 'but who wants Counts? What counts now is the front you put on. Dress like big money, talk like big money and, brother, you'll get big money.' He beamed in self-satisfaction. 'Believe me, I know.'

'What's the good of money,' said Sammy from the shadows. 'It can't buy you anything, not now.'

'It will.' Smith was confident in his own knowledge of the human race. 'And the smart ones are those who get in on the ground floor.'

Boris grunted in disgust; he was a quiet old vampire who believed in keeping himself to himself and not making enemies. It was a system of life which had stood him in good stead in the past and he saw no reason to change just because some young squirt thought he knew it all. He gave a dry laugh at the prospect of deflating the young vampire. Sammy spoilt his fun.

'Better tell Smith what he has to know,' he said. 'After all, you owe it to him in a way.'

'I owe him nothing,' snorted the old vampire. 'What has he ever done for me?'

'You want me to answer that?' Smith grew annoyed as he thought about it. It wasn't that he objected too much to his new status but the principle behind it annoyed him. He was firm in his belief of the paradox of free enterprise and the sanctity of property, especially private property, and Boris had successfully pulled off a very personal theft. And there was nothing he could do about it.

'Tell him, Boris,' said Sammy again. 'You owe it to the lad.'

'You don't have to tell me anything,' snapped Smith. He expanded his chest. 'I've read a bit and I know what the score is. I know what to eat and know that I've to return to my grave before dawn.' Suddenly he looked haggard. "My grave! Hell! I'd never be able to find it again in a month of Sundays!'

Boris snorted with amused contempt. 'That's for the comic books,' he said. 'All that guff about returning to our graves before dawn, I mean. All that's necessary is that you stay out of sunlight; the actinic rays will trigger off skin cancers. Artificial light's all right but nothing containing ultra violet.'

'That so?' Smith looked relieved. 'Anything else you should tell me while you're at it?'

'Only to respect your elders,' snapped Boris. 'And don't get careless or you'll wind up with a stake through the heart or a bullet through the ribs. And it needn't be a silver bullet either.' He broke off as an animal howled from the darkness.

'Here's Lupe,' said Sammy happily, and threw more twigs on the fire.

A big, sleek Alsatian-like dog loped into the firelight, sat down and promptly changed into a man. Even in human form he retained a slightly wolf-like air. He nodded to the others.

'Hi! How's tricks?'

'I'm starving,' grumbled Boris.

'So am I.' Sammy belched wind and rubbed his stomach. 'I've been living off my fat for so long now that soon I'll be too weak to take a bit if I had the chance.' He looked hopefully at the werewolf. 'Any news?'

'Wife's had a new litter,' said Lupe proudly. 'Three boys and two girls.' He beamed at their congratulations. 'Things aren't as easy as they might be but I'm making out.' He lifted a foot and scratched himself behind one ear. He noticed Smith's boggle-eyed stare. 'New boy?'

'Just born,' said Sammy. 'Boris was responsible for him.'

'Congratulations,' said Lupe politely to the old vampire. 'How's he shaking down?'

'Well, he hasn't gone crazy on us yet,' said Sammy thoughtfully. Boris changed what was, to him, obviously a painful subject.

'Any other news?'

'The rabbits are getting more plentiful,' said Lupe.

'Rabbits!' Boris screwed up his mouth. Sammy echoed his sentiments.

'Rabbits might be good eating for you, Lupe, but not for us. Anything else?'

'I don't think so.' The werewolf frowned. 'There was just one more thing now I come to think about it but it's slipped my mind.' He waved a hand. 'Never mind, I guess it'll come back if it was important.' He returned to the subject closest to his heart. 'I wish you could see the youngsters; fine kids all of them.'

'You're breeding fast,' said Sammy enviously. 'Sure you aren't going a little too fast?'

'I don't think so.' Lupe scratched the other ear. 'I'm keeping the litters down as low as I can but we daren't get too low. Anyway, all our troubles will be over when they come out.'

'You can say that again,' said Sammy with real feeling. He smacked his lips. 'Hell, I never thought that I'd miss humans so much.'

'Nor me,' said Boris fervently. 'Why, once in the old days when they were pressing close I even wished a plague on them.' He sighed. 'Right now I could do with the old days, stakes, garlic, silver bullets and all. Modern times were a gift, sure, but look how things wound up!'

They nodded, even Smith, all agreeing that the human race had hardly played fair.

'When they come out,' said Sammy thoughtfully, 'we'll have to take things easy. Treat them gently and give them a chance to breed.'

'That's right,' agreed Lupe. 'Build up the supply before we can let loose the demand. Personally, though, I'm not worried too much. My guess is that they wouldn't have taken many dogs down under The Tombstone with them or, if they did, then they'd have to restrict them to the limit. Anyway, they'd welcome a change.' He bared his teeth, concentrated, and changed into a handsome pseudo-Alsatian. He was grinning as he resumed human form. 'See what I mean?'

'Humans were always suckers for dogs,' said Boris enviously. 'I've often wondered why you just didn't move right in and take over.'

'Why should we?' Lupe shook his head at the vampire's

ignorance. 'No need to kill the goose, you know. They never suspected us, not after the Middle Ages, and many a human has worked himself silly to support us in luxury.' He scowled. 'When I think of how many of us got caught in the Big Bang —!'

'We all got caught in it.' Sammy kicked at the fire.

The rest nodded, agreeing with Sammy all the way. Smith didn't say anything. He was still a little confused and more than inclined to think he was in a dream. But fantastic as everything seemed it all made a peculiar kind of sense. Ghouls, vampires and werewolves were, obviously, very real. Divergent branches of human stock, perhaps, ultra specialists who had become utterly dependent on the human race for their sustenance. Lupe and his kind had adapted best of all but, in the final essence, they were all parasites. He too, now he came to think of it; and suddenly he was very conscious of their concern over the survival of the few humans left beneath The Tombstone.

Parasites cannot live without a host.

Lupe stretched himself, yawned, and rose to his feet. 'Well,' he said, 'I guess that we'd better get on with it.' Changing to animal form he began to run over the cracked, overgrown expanse of the slab of cadmium concrete which was The Tombstone. Nose to the ground, tail waving, he looked every inch a splendid specimen of the canine species. Even Smith, who knew better, had to restrain a desire to call to him so that he could pat his head.

'What's he doing?' he asked.

'Checking up,' said Sammy. 'Lupe's got sharper senses than we have and he's finding out whether or not they are still moving around down there.' He held up his hand for silence. 'Watch him!'

Lupe looked over his shoulder, grinned, then vanished behind a clump of scrub. When he reappeared he was in human shape.

'I think I've got something,' he called. 'Scent's pretty strong by this ventilator.'

'They coming out?' Sammy sprang to his feet, his strong legs carrying him over to the werewolf. 'Are they?'

'Can't tell.' Lupe altered his shape again and sniffed around some more, finally cocking his head and resting one furry ear against a fairly visible crack in the concrete. He concentrated so hard that even his tail stopped wagging.

'Dawn'll be here soon,' whispered Boris. He shivered and drew his ragged cloak around him. 'Another day in the mud.'

'How do you arrange it?' said Smith. Like Boris he kept his voice low. 'I guess that you could just cover yourself with that cloak and you'd be safe. Is that why you wear it?'

'It has its uses,' said Boris ambiguously. He glared at the young vampire with an active dislike. 'Listen,' he warned, 'just because I was responsible for you being here doesn't mean that I've got to wet-nurse you. Life's tough enough without that.'

'Who wants you to wet-nurse anyone?' Smith returned the glare. 'From what I can see you're just an old-fashioned has-been. Walking around with that cloak as if you were some Count or something. Why didn't you get a plastic cover like they used to cover automobiles with? You could fold that up small and have a regular tent at daytimes.'

'Smart guy,' sneered Boris. 'That's the trouble with you young pups, always think you know better than your elders. I'd look fine walking about with a tent on my back now, wouldn't I? Maybe you'd better learn that people like us have to practise camouflage all the time. One slip and —!' He made a suggestive gesture. 'It's happened before, you know.'

'In comic books,' admitted Smith. 'But who believes in vampires now?'

'And what's the reason for that?' Boris tightened his thin mouth. 'Camouflage, of course, what else? Same as humans don't believe in Sammy and his kind, but how long would it take them to figure it out? So maybe they'd think you was sick in the head and lock you away in an asylum, but what then? They wouldn't feed you the right diet and they'd keep you there for a long, long time. And you'd die there, make no mistake about that.' He shuddered. 'It happened to a friend of mine.'

'Old fashioned, that's what you are.' Smith appealed to Sammy. 'You can see that, can't you? You're educated and —'

'Pipe down,' interrupted Sammy. He felt all on edge as he

always did when Lupe came to make one of his periodic checkups. His hunger had mounted until it was a fire in his stomach and his nerves were like harp strings. Restlessly he got to his feet and wandered over to where the werewolf was sniffing the ground.

'They're still alive,' said Lupe. He'd changed again and stood, breathing deeply, his chest and forehead covered with sweat. 'Hell, I'm all in!'

'Come and sit down.' Sammy led the way back to the fire, knowing of the demands that shape-changing made on Lupe's energy sources. The werewolf sagged as he slumped beside the blaze.

'I could smell them,' he said after a while. 'Scent's stronger than it was and it's my guess that they are moving upwards.'

'On their way out?' Hope flamed in the old vampire's eyes. 'Is that it, Lupe?'

'Could be.' Lupe relaxed still more. 'From the sounds I'd say that they are moving heavy equipment towards the surface. Maybe one of their tunnels got blocked and they have to clear it. That or they aren't too sure what conditions are like up here and don't want to take any chances.' He grinned. 'Anyway, they're still safe.'

The others grinned with him.

'You know,' said Smith thoughtfully, 'this needs careful planning.' He threw another twig on the fire. '*Very* careful planning.'

'Meaning?' Sammy stared dully into the fire. Lupe had gone; he'd rested for a short while and then, resuming animal form for fast travel, had loped off back to his wife and new litter. Sammy felt more depressed than usual after he had gone. It must be nice to be able to return back to a family. He wished he had one of his own.

'Well,' said Smith, 'if Lupe knows his business then the humans are on their way out. When they do finally come out we'll have to contact them, right?'

'That's right.' Sammy fought down the hunger which thought of all those humans living and dying down below always aroused. Once he had tried digging down towards them but had had to give up in despair. That had been during one of his desperate periods.

'So who is going to be the contact.' Smith glanced at Sammy. 'You?'

'Why not?' Boris was quick to defend his friend.

'Why not?' Smith shrugged. 'Look at him, that's why not.'

'Sammy's held down jobs with humans before.'

'In the old days, maybe, but there were plenty of freaks walking around then. Those days are over.'

'Let's not get personal about this,' snapped Sammy. 'What's on your mind?'

'I'm a modern man,' said Smith. 'At least, I was a modern man and I know how they think. Those humans down there know that the surface was blasted with radiation. If Sammy turns up they'll think that he's a mutation or something. They've bred true down there and they aren't going to want mutations around at any price. So they'll shoot him.' He spread his hands. 'Well,' he said defensively. 'How can you argue about it? Sammy doesn't look human, does he?'

'Go on,' gritted Sammy. He clamped his teeth together, hating Smith for the first time. Fresh guy!

'So that rules out Sammy,' continued Smith. It was obvious that he had given the matter some thought. 'That leaves me and Boris.' He shrugged. 'I guess that we needn't even consider Boris.'

'Why not?' The old vampire was hurt.

'Because you look a freak too, that's why.' Smith was brutally frank. 'Let's face it, fellows, neither of you would get to first base.'

'And you would, I suppose?' Sammy was sarcastic.

'Sure.' Smith had an iron hide, sarcasm didn't reach him. 'I'm young and I know what the score is. I could talk my way into their confidence and be accepted.'

'And what about us?'

'Oh, I'd take care of you somehow.' Smith didn't meet Sammy's eyes. 'I'd try to sneak Boris here a drink or two and fix it so that you got something to eat now and again. Things will be hard at first, naturally, but I'll do my best.'

'Fresh young pup!' Boris ground his teeth in anger. 'No respect for your elders at all! Why I —'

'Hold it!' Sammy sprang to his feet, then relaxed as Lupe bounded into the firelight. 'Trouble?'

'No.' Lupe grunted as he forced his tired body back into

human shape. 'Wish that I didn't have to do this every time I wanted to talk.' He looked at Sammy. 'It's just that I remembered what it was I had to tell you. I bumped into someone you'd be interested in a short while ago. She's living in a cave way south of here, in a place where they used to hang their dead, the humans, I mean. You know it?'

'I know it.' Sammy felt excitement warm his blood. 'I thought that area had been cleared out long ago.'

'Maybe it was, but she's there now and from what I could see she's making out fine.' Lupe winked. 'I told her about you and she's interested. Young too.' He dropped to all fours. 'And lonely.' He began to change shape. 'Well, just thought that you'd be interested.' Abruptly he was gone, a sleek shape bounding through the brush.

Sammy stared after him, too thrilled to shout his thanks. A girl ghoul! Almost he had given up hope of ever finding a female of his own kind but, if Lupe was telling the truth, and he was, then there was something to be gained in life even yet. He sagged at a sudden thought.

The caves were a long way away and he hadn't eaten for too long. Travel took energy and he just didn't have the energy. Smith looked enviously at the ghoul as he slumped beside the fire.

'Lucky devil,' he said. 'I wish I could get a girl.'

'You have to make your own,' said Sammy dully. Boris frowned.

'What's wrong with you, Sammy? That was good news. You're going, of course?'

'How can I?' Sammy sighed from the pit of his stomach. 'Radiations sterilize, remember, and I can't eat sterile food. Around here it wasn't so bad, that's how I've managed to live this long, but I can't hope to pick up anything decent to eat on so long a journey.' He slumped still more. 'I'm too weak to chance it.' He sighed again. 'If I could only get one really decent meal to set me up I'd be off like a shot. Just one good meal.'

'Tough,' said Smith carelessly. 'Still, maybe she'll wait.'

'Hold your tongue!' snapped Boris. He glanced at Sammy, then at Smith, then at Sammy again. Nervously he wet his lips. 'There's one way,' he said suggestively.

'There's the Agreement,' reminded Sammy. He'd already

thought of what Boris had in mind and dismissed it because of that.

'We're a quorum,' pointed out Boris. 'We could agree to suspend the Agreement for just this once.' He became urgent. 'Be sensible, Sammy. The way things are the two of us wouldn't stand a chance to survive until they come out. From what Lupe said it might take another year and those Red Cross stocks are mostly smashed and useless. And when they do come out, what then?'

'Geometrical progression,' said Sammy understandingly. 'Two makes four and four makes eight and —'

'He's young,' said Boris. 'That means that he'll have a hell of an appetite. He won't be able to use discretion, he hasn't had the experience. And you heard what he said about contacting them. What's the betting that he just cuts us out?'

'What are you talking about?' Smith glanced from one to the other. They ignored him.

'I'm not sure,' said Sammy slowly. 'We've got to stick together now or we'll all be sunk.'

'We'll be sunk anyway,' said Boris. 'He'll foul things up for sure.' His hand closed pleadingly on Sammy's arm. 'Please, Sammy. Just for this once.'

'What are you two freaks talking about?' snapped Smith again. Youth and confidence in his superiority made him contemptuous of these old has-beens. Sitting beside the fire he had made his own plans and they didn't include either of the others. He lost both confidence and contempt as he read Sammy's expression. 'No!' he screamed, understanding hitting like a thunderbolt. 'No! You wouldn't! You couldn't! You —'

He rose together with Sammy and, turning, raced into the dark safety of the woods. He didn't get far.

Fresh guys rarely do.

LUIGI CAPUANA

A VAMPIRE

translated by Gillian Riley

'IT'S NO laughing matter!' said Lelio Giorgi.

'Why shouldn't I laugh?' replied Mongeri. '*I* don't believe in ghosts.'

'Neither did I, once . . . and I'd still rather not,' went on Giorgi. 'That's why I've come to see you. You might be able to explain whatever it is that's making my life a misery and wrecking my marriage.'

'*Whatever it is?* You mean whatever you *imagine* it is. You're not well. It's true that a hallucination is itself a fact, but what it represents has no reality outside yourself. Or, to put it better, it's the externalization of a sensation, a sort of projection of yourself, so that the eye sees what it in fact does not see, and the ear hears sounds that were never made. Previous impressions, often stored up unconsciously, project themselves rather like events in dreams. We still don't know how or why. We dream, and that's the right word, with our eyes wide open. But one has to distinguish between split-second hallucinations which don't necessarily indicate any organic or psychic disturbance, and those of a more persistent nature. . . . But of course that's not the case with you.'

'But it *is*, with me *and* my wife.'

'You don't understand. What we scientists call persistent hallucinations are those experienced by the insane. I don't have to give you an example. . . . The fact that you both suffer the same hallucinations is just a case of simple induction. You probably must have influenced your wife's nervous system.'

'No. She was the first.'

'Then you mean that your nervous system, having a greater receptivity, was the one to be influenced. And don't turn up your poetical nose at what you please to call my scientific jargon. It has its uses.'

'If you would just let me get a word in edgeways. . . .'

'Some things are best let well alone. Do you want a scientific explanation? Well, the answer is that for the moment you wouldn't get anything of the sort. We are in the realm of hypotheses. One today, a different one tomorrow, and a different one the day after. You are a curious lot, you artists! When you feel like it you make fun of Science, you undervalue the whole business of experiment, research and hypothesis that makes it progress; then when a case comes along that interests you personally you want a clear, precise and categorical answer. And there are scientists who play the game, out of conviction or vanity. But I'm not one of them. You want the plain truth? Science is the greatest proof of our own ignorance. To calm you down I can talk of hallucinations, of induction, receptivity. Words! Words! the more I study the more I despair of ever knowing anything for certain. It seems to happen on purpose, no sooner do scientists get a kick out of some new law they've discovered than along comes some new fact, some discovery, that upsets the lot. You need to take it easy, just let life flow by; what's happened to you and your wife has happened to so many others. It will pass. Why must you try and find out how and why it happened? Are you scared of dreams?'

'If you'd just let me tell you. . . .'

'Go on then, tell me, if you want to get it off your chest. But I warn you, it can only make matters worse. The only way to get over it, is to busy yourself with other things, get away from it. Find a new devil to drive out the old – it's a good saying.'

'We did all that. It wasn't any good. The first signs . . . the first manifestations, happened in the country, in our villa at Foscolara. We ran away from it, but the very night that we came back to town. . . .'

'It's natural. What distraction could you find in your own house? You ought to travel, stay in hotels, one day here, another day there; spend the whole day sightseeing, looking at churches, museums, go to the theatre, come back late at night, tired out. . . .'

'We did all that too, but . . .'

'Just the two of you, on your own. You should have been with a friend, a party. . . .'

'But we were, it wasn't any good.'

'It all depends on the party!'

'But they were a lively crowd. . . .'

'Selfish, you mean, and there you were, isolated, I know. . . .'

'But we were lively too, when we were with them. But you can hardly expect them to have come and slept with us. . . .'

'Then you *were* asleep? Really I don't know what you mean any more, dreams or hallucinations. . . .'

'To hell with your dreams and hallucinations. We were wide awake and completely sound in mind and body, just as I am now, if you would only let me get a word in edgeways. . . .'

'As you wish.'

'Well, you could at least let me give you the facts.'

'I know. I can imagine it all. The books are full of them. There could be small differences in detail . . . but they don't count. The essentials are the same.'

'Can't I even have the satisfaction of . . .'

'You can. Hundreds of them. You are one of those who seem to want to lay up troubles for themselves, even make them worse . . . I'm sorry, that's stupid! But if it would please you. . . .'

'Quite frankly, you seem to me to be scared.'

'Scared of what? A nice idea!'

'Scared of having to change your mind. You've just said, "I do not believe in ghosts." And what if I force you to believe in them?'

'All right then. It would be a blow. What do you expect? We scientists are like that, we're men after all. When our way of seeing things, of judging them, takes a knock, the intellect refuses to follow the senses. Even intelligence is a matter of habit. But now you have me with my back to the wall. All right then. Let's hear your precious facts.'

'Well,' said Lelio Giorgi with a sigh, 'you know already the unhappy background to my years in America. Luisa's parents were against our marrying – and they may well have been right, they were thinking above all of the economic situation of their future son-in-law – they had no faith in my abilities, and were doubtful about my future as a poet.

That slim volume of early verse was my worst enemy. I haven't even written, let alone published, any more from that day to this, yet even now you called me "poetical". The label stuck. Oh well.'

'Just like you writers to go right back to the remote beginning.'

'Don't get impatient. Listen. I had no news of Luisa for the three years I was in Buenos Aires. Then came that rich uncle's will, after he had nothing to do with me while he was alive. I came back to Europe, hurried to London, and flew here with £200,000 in my pocket, only to find that Luisa had been married for six months! And I was as much in love with her as ever. The poor girl must have given in to family pressure. At that time I might have done anything.... All these details are important.... I was stupid enough, however, to write her a letter full of violent reproaches. I never thought that it could have fallen into the hands of her husband. The next day he turned up at my house, having realized the folly of my behaviour, and determined to persuade me to calm down. He was calm himself.

' "I have come to give you your letter back," he said. "I opened it by mistake, not out of inquisitiveness; and it's just as well I did. I am assured that you are a gentleman. I have every respect for your distress, but I do trust you have no intention of needlessly disturbing the peace of a family. If you can bring yourself to think things over you will realize that nobody wished to harm you intentionally. It was pure misfortune. You must see now where your duty lies, and I can tell you quite plainly that I am determined to defend my domestic happiness at all costs."

'He was pale as he spoke, and his voice trembled.

' "I must apologize for my indiscretion," I replied, "and to reassure you I can add that tomorrow I shall be leaving for Paris." I must have been even paler than him, the words would hardly come. I held out my hand, he shook it. And I kept my word. Six months later I received a telegram from Luisa: "I am a widow. I still love you. And you?" Her husband had been dead for two months.'

'Such is life, it's an ill wind....'

'And that's what I somewhat selfishly thought; but it isn't always true. I had never been so happy in my life as I was on my wedding night and during the following months. We both of us avoided any mention of *him*. Luisa had destroyed every trace. Not out of ingratitude, for he had done everything to make her happy, but because she was afraid that even the slightest memory would have upset me. And she was right. Sometimes the thought that someone else, however legitimately, had once possessed her, made me tremble from head to foot. I could scarcely hide it from her. Often she must have sensed this, and her lovely eyes were clouded with tears. But how radiant she looked on the day she felt sure enough to tell me of the expected arrival of a child. I remember it clearly, we were drinking coffee, I was standing and she was sitting down, with a look of touching weariness. And that was the first time she had ever made any reference to the past: "How glad I am that this didn't happen *then*!" she exclaimed.

'A loud crash was heard at the door, as if someone had struck it a blow with their fist. We leapt up. I rushed out to see what had happened, imagining it was one of the servants, but the adjoining room was empty.'

'It could have been one of the beams in the house shrinking in the heat.'

'That was how I explained it to Luisa, seeing how upset she was, but I was not convinced myself. I felt somehow disturbed. We waited some minutes, nothing happened. But from then onwards I noticed that Luisa avoided being left on her own; she was still upset, though she would not admit it and I dared not question her.'

'And now I see how you were both influencing each other, without realizing it.'

'Not at all. A few days later I was laughing at the whole episode, and thought that Luisa's agitated state of mind was due to her condition. Then even she seemed to calm down. Eventually the child was born. After a few months, however, I noticed that the old feeling of fear and terror had returned. At night, all of a sudden, she would cling to me, cold and trembling. "What is it? Are you ill?" I would ask anxiously. "I'm frightened, didn't you hear?" "No." "Don't you hear?" she insisted the following night. "No." Though this time I had heard the sound of footsteps in the room, pacing up and down, by the bed: I said "no" so as not to frighten her any more. I raised my head and looked around, "It must be a mouse in the room. . . ." "I'm afraid! . . . I'm afraid! . . ." And for several nights, at the same time, the same shuffling, the same uncanny coming and going, up and down, by the bed. We lay and waited for it.'

'And your jangling nerves did the rest.'

'You know me, I'm not the sort to get worked up easily. I put up a brave show, because of Luisa; I tried to explain things: echoes of distant sounds, accidental resonances in the structure of the villa. . . . We went back to town. But that very night the phenomena turned up again worse than before. Twice the bedstead was shaken violently. I peered out. "It's he! It's he!" stammered Luisa, huddled under the bedclothes.'

'If you don't mind my saying so,' interrupted Mongeri, '*I* wouldn't marry a widow for all the gold in the world! Something of the dead husband always remains with her, in spite of everything. Your wife wasn't seeing his ghost. "It's *he*" is the "he" of the sensations he left behind him, purely physiological. . . .'

'Well, maybe so,' replied Lelio Giorgi. 'But in that case where do *I* come in?'

'Suggestion. Now it seems perfectly plain.'

'Suggestion only at specified times in the middle of the night?'

'Just waiting for it to happen would be enough.'

'Well then, how can the phenomena vary every time when my imagination isn't working at all?'

'That's what you think; the Unconscious at work.'

'Do let me go on. Keep your explanations until I've finished. Just note that the following morning we were able to discuss the matter with relative calm. Luisa described her impressions and I told her of mine, in such a way that I was convinced that it could not have been an unpleasant trick played on us by our over-excited imaginations; the same blow on the bedstead, the same tugging at the sheets in the same circumstances, when I was trying to comfort her with a kiss and prevent her from crying, as if this itself had provoked the malice of the invisible person. Then one night Luisa flung her arms round my neck and whispered in my ear in a voice that made me shudder: "He spoke!" "What did he say?" "I couldn't hear. Now! He said: You're mine!" And as I held her closer I felt her being dragged violently away from me by two powerful hands, and I had to give way in spite of her resistance.'

'What resistance could she offer to what must have been her own behaviour?'

'All right. . . . But I felt it too, a something trying to stop her coming into contact with me. . . . I saw her flung back with a jolt . . . then she tried to get to her feet, to go to the child, who was sleeping in the cot at the foot of the bed. Then we heard the cot wheels squeaking and saw it tossed across the room, blankets flying in all directions; that wasn't a hallucination. We picked things up, made up the cot, and soon they were flying through the air again and the child was whimpering with fear. Three nights later it was even worse. Luisa seemed drawn completely under *his* evil spell. She seemed unaware of me when I spoke to her, as if I were no longer there. She seemed to be talking to *him* and I could tell from her replies what he was saying to her. "But can it be his fault that you are dead?" "No, no, no, how could you think So? *I*, poison you? That's monstrous!" "And what can the child have done to harm you?" "But why are you unhappy? I have prayed for you. . . ." "Why don't you want my prayers? You want *me*, but how can you, you're dead!" I tried without success to shake her from the trance. Then she came to. "Did you hear that?" she said. "He says I poisoned him. *You* wouldn't believe that of me. . . . O God! What about the child? He'll kill him. Did you hear?" I heard nothing, but I was well aware that Luisa was not raving. She wept, clutching the child to her. "What shall we do? What shall we do?"'

'But the child was all right. That must have reassured her.'

'What can you expect? This sort of thing would upset even the most strong-minded. I myself am not superstitious, but I'm not a free-thinker either. I just don't have much time for religion. But in a case like this, and with my wife saying "I'll pray for you", I naturally thought of calling in a priest.'

'You had him exorcize it?'

'No, but I had a blessing said in the house, with a fine sprinkling of holy water . . . as much to influence poor Luisa, if it really were a case of nerves, as anything. Luisa is a religious person. You can laugh, I'd like to have seen what you would have done in my place.'

'What about the holy water?'

'Useless. No effect at all.'

'Not a bad idea though. Some nervous diseases can be cured that way. We had a case of a man who thought his nose was being stretched. The doctor went through all the motions of an operation, without actually doing anything, and the man was cured.'

'But the holy water in fact made things worse. The next night . . . My God! I can't bear to think of it. This time *he* seemed to be taking everything out on the child . . . it was awful. When Luisa saw . . .'

'Or thought she saw. . . .'

'Saw, man, saw. . . . And *I* saw too, almost. She couldn't get near the cot, something was holding her back. There she was, stretching out her hands to the child, while that *thing* – she described it to me – bent over the baby and did something horrible, its lips pressed to his mouth, sucking his blood. . . . For three nights this ghastly process has been repeated, and the poor little thing . . . you wouldn't recognize him. . . . He used to be so plump and rosy, and now . . . in only three nights . . . he's wasted away. This can't be imagination. Come and see for yourself.'

'So it could really be? . . .'

Mongeri thought for a few minutes, frowning. The sarcastic and somewhat pitying smile with which he had listened to Lelio Giorgi had vanished all of a sudden. Then he looked up and said:

'So it could really be? . . . Listen. I can't explain anything because I'm convinced there *is* no explanation. One can't be more sceptical than that. But I could give you some advice, which might make you laugh, coming from me. . . . Anyway, that's up to you.'

'I'll do as you suggest, at once.'

'You would need several days for what you have to do. I'll help you to cut it as short as possible. I don't doubt the facts you've put before me. And I ought to add that since Science has come to examine this kind of problem, it, too, has been less sceptical. It has now become a question of trying to see this sort of thing as a natural phenomena; but a physical problem, not a spiritual one. That's not our province, we leave that to priests or spiritualists. We are concerned with the flesh, blood and bone that go to make an individual and disintegrate into their original elements when he dies. But then the question arises, does this disintegration, this cessation of organic function, end instantaneously with death, annulling all individuality, or does this persist, in some cases, for any amount of time after death? One is beginning to suspect that this could be the case. And Science is on the verge of coming round to popular beliefs. I have been studying for three years now the empirical remedies of "old wives" and witches and I am coming to the conclusion that they are in fact the remnants of the ancient secret sciences and also, even more likely, of the instincts we can still observe in animals. When man was closer to animals he knew instinctively the medicinal value of certain herbs, but as he evolved away from them he lost this primitive use of certain faculties, and the tradition died out. Only the honest peasant women, in whom it was more deeply-rooted, preserved some of these natural medicines; and I think that Science should study them, for every superstition contains something more than mere popular error. I'm sorry about this digression.... What scientists now admit, that the existence of an individual does not cease at death, but only when actual decomposition of the body has taken place, popular superstition has already acknowledged through the belief in vampires, and has even offered a remedy. Vampires are individuals, rare but not unheard of, who persist after death. You may look surprised, but this is a case, and not the only one, where science and popular superstition, or rather, primitive intuition, find themselves at one. And what is the only defence against this evil thing, this disembodied individual sucking the blood and life-force from healthy individuals? The complete destruction of its former body. Where vampires have been known to occur the victims have run to the grave, dug up the body and burned it; then the vampire really does die, and the visitations cease. Now you were saying that your child ...'

'Come and see him, you wouldn't recognize him. Luisa is going crazy. And I'm not far off myself. I keep saying to myself that it can't be true, it couldn't possibly happen, I even think: "Well, if she did poison him, it was for my sake, it shows how much she loves me...." But it won't work, the thought repels me, *she* repels me even . . . all *his* doing! And the reproaches go on, I can tell by her replies, "What? Poison you? . . . How can you believe such a thing?" Life has become impossible, for months now we have gone on like this. You are the first person I have dared to confide in. I'm desperate, I need help. . . . And we would have put up with everything if it weren't for the child.'

'As a friend and as a scientist, I give you this advice: Have the body cremated. Your wife will easily get permission, and I will help you to speed up the formalities. And Science herself would not be ashamed to have recourse to somewhat empirical methods, trying out a remedy which might well be a superstition in appearance only, seeking out the truth by unconventional methods. Cremate the body. Seriously,' he added, seeing from the look in his friend's eye that he feared he was being treated like one of the ignorant populace.

'But what about the child?' cried Lelio Giorgi, wringing his hands.

'One night I lost my temper and threw myself at him yelling "Get out! For God's sake get out!" But I was stopped dead in my tracks, unable to move, mumbling, with the words drying up in my throat. You can't imagine . . .'

'Would you allow me to accompany you tonight?'

'I hardly dared to ask you such a favour.... But perhaps it would upset him even more, would you leave it until tomorrow?'

But the next day he returned in such shattered state that Mongeri really wondered if he had gone out of his mind.

'He knows!' stammered Lelio Giorgi. 'God, what a night! He swore he would do the most terrible things if we dared to . . .'

'All the more reason for daring,' replied Mongeri.

'If you had seen the cot tossed about! I don't know how the poor child survived! Luisa had to get down on her knees to him, weeping. "I *will* be yours, all yours, only please don't hurt the child!" And I felt at that moment that every link with her was broken, that she belonged to *him* again and not to me.'

'Calm down! We shall get rid of him. Let me come round tonight.'

Mongeri went, thinking, convinced that his presence would keep the vampire away. 'It's always the case, a neutral, indifferent force will counteract the unknown thing. We don't yet know how or why, but continued observation and study will show.'

And in the early hours of the night this seemed to be the case. Luisa looked anxiously around but nothing happened. The child slept untroubled in his cot, pale and wan. Lelio Giorgi did his best to conceal his worry, but kept glancing fearfully from his wife to the complacent Mongeri.

They kept up a conversation on various topics. Mongeri was describing some highly amusing incident on one of his holidays; he was a good talker, without any of his professional pomposity, and he hoped to distract the attention of both of them, so that if the phenomenon did occur he could observe it uninterrupted, when suddenly, as he glanced at the cot, he noticed a slight movement, which could not have been caused by either of the parents, since they were sitting at the other side of the room. He stopped, and they leapt to their feet. By the time they had followed his gaze to the cot it was rocking with some violence. Luisa cried 'O heavens, my poor child!' and rushed towards the cot, but was stopped short and sank back on to the couch. Pale as death, she rolled her eyes in terror and muttered something unintelligible, on the point of suffocating.

'It's nothing!' said Mongeri, rising himself, and grasping the hand of Lelio who was shaken with terror. Then Luisa, with a violent shudder, returned to her normal self though with her attention fixed on some invisible person, listening to words they could not hear but at which they could guess from the sense of her replies.

'Why do you say that I keep on wanting to hurt you? . . . But I've prayed for you . . . No, I can't do anything about it, you're dead . . . But how can you say I've poisoned you if you are not dead? . . . That I was plotting it with him? . . . That he sent me the poison? . . . But how can you? I kept my promise! ... I did! It's absurd! ... All right, I won't say you are dead any more ... no, no more....'

'This is a case of spontaneous trance!' said Mongeri. 'Leave it to me.'

He took Luisa by the wrists and said in a loud voice: 'Come now!' At the sound of the robust, angry and masculine voice with which she replied Mongeri was taken aback. She had drawn herself up with such a hard, truculent expression that she seemed another person. Her gentle, timid beauty had completely vanished.

'What do you want? Why must you interfere?'

Mongeri pulled himself together. The habitual reserve of the scientist might have made him fear that he too had come under the influence of an overheated imagination, but for the sight of the cot rocking to and fro and this sudden uncanny phenomenon of the personification of the fantasma. He drew himself up, angry for having been startled by the harsh masculine voice, and said sharply: 'Stop that! Stop it at once!'

There was such a note of command in his voice, enough to dominate, as he thought, the young woman's mind, that he was surprised at the sardonic laugh with which she replied.

'Stop that! At once!' he replied in stronger tones.

'Aha! Another poisoner! You were in on this too?'

'That's a damned lie!'

Mongeri could not prevent himself from replying as if to a living person. His mind, already troubled, in spite of his efforts to remain calm and impartial, received another shock when he felt himself struck twice on the shoulder by an invisible fist, and turning towards the lamp, saw silhouetted against the light a greyish, wasted hand that seemed almost like smoke from the candle.

'You see? You see?' cried Giorgi with a sob in his voice.

Suddenly everything stopped. Luisa came out of her trance and looked around her as if waking from a natural sleep, questioning her husband and Mongeri with a pathetic movement of the head. They too were amazed and gazed around, speechless, overcome by the sense of peace and serenity. No one dared to break the silence. Only a slight sound of moaning from the cot made them turn in that direction. The baby whimpered and struggled under the pressure that was forcing something against his mouth ... Then without warning that, too, stopped, and nothing more happened.

The next morning, on his way home, Mongeri was thinking not only about the folly of scientists who fail to examine cases which coincide with popular superstition, but also of what he had said to his friend two days previously: *I wouldn't marry a widow for all the gold in the world.*

As a scientist he had acquitted himself well, carrying out the experiment to its logical conclusion, without considering the humiliating consequences of failure if the experiment (the cremation of the body of Luisa's first husband) had failed. But notwithstanding the fact that the experiment had confirmed a popular superstition, and that from the day of the cremation the visitations had stopped completely, to the great relief of the good Lelio Giorgi and his Luisa, in his report, not yet published, he did not write with complete sincerity. He could not say, The facts are such, and such is the result of the remedy: popular superstition has triumphed over the narrow-mindedness of science; the vampire died as soon as the body was cremated. No, he restricted his narrative with so many 'if's' and 'but's' and confused it with so many 'hallucinations,' 'suggestions' and 'inductions,' simply to confirm what he had already admitted: that even intelligence is a matter of habit, and that having to change his mind had shaken him.

And what is even more curious, his own life became somewhat incoherent, for he who had once sworn that he would not marry a widow for all the gold in the world, married one for far less, a pension of a mere £7,000! And when his friend Lelio Giorgi ingenuously remarked 'What? You!' he replied, 'But her husband has been dead for the past seven years, not a scrap of him remains,' without realizing that in so saying, he was contradicting that author of the learned paper: *A case of alleged vampirism*, namely, himself.

RAY BRADBURY

THE MAN UPSTAIRS

HE REMEMBERED how carefully and expertly Grandmother would fondle the cold cut guts of the chicken and withdraw the marvels therein; the wet shining loops of meat-smelling intestine, the muscled lump of heart, the gizzard with the collection of seeds in it. How neatly and nicely Grandma would slit the chicken and push her fat little hand in to deprive it of its medals. These would be segregated, some in pans of water, others in paper to be thrown to the dog later, perhaps. And then the ritual of taxidermy, stuffing the bird with watered, seasoned bread, and performing surgery with a swift, bright needle, stitch after pulled-tight stitch.

This was one of the prime thrills of Douglas's eleven-year-old life span.

Altogether, he counted twenty knives in the various squeaking drawers of the magic kitchen table from which Grandma, a kindly, gentle-faced, white-haired old witch, drew paraphernalia for her miracles.

Douglas was to be quiet. He could stand across the table from Grandmama, his freckled nose tucked over the edge, watching, but any loose boy-talk might interfere with the spell. It was a wonder when Grandma brandished silver shakers over the bird, supposedly sprinkling showers of mummy-dust and pulverized Indian bones, muttering mystical verses under her toothless breath.

'Grammy,' said Douglas at last, breaking the silence. 'Am I like that inside?' He pointed at the chicken.

'Yes,' said Grandma. 'A little more orderly and presentable, but just about the same....'

'And more *of* it!' added Douglas, proud of his guts.

'Yes,' said Grandma. 'More of it.'

'Grandpa has lots more'n me. His sticks out in front so he can rest his elbows on it.'

Grandma laughed and shook her head.

Douglas said, 'And Lucie Williams, down the street, she...'

'Hush, child!' cried Grandma.

'But she's got . . .'

'Never you mind what she's got! That's different.'

'But why is *she* different?'

'A darning-needle dragon-fly is coming by some day and sew up your mouth,' said Grandma firmly.

Douglas waited, then asked, 'How do you know I've got insides like that, Grandma?'

'Oh, go 'way, now!'

The front-door bell rang.

Through the front-door glass as he ran down the hall, Douglas saw a straw hat. The bell jangled again and again. Douglas opened the door.

'Good morning, child, is the landlady at home?'

Cold grey eyes in a long, smooth, walnut-coloured face gazed upon Douglas. The man was tall, thin, and carried a suit-case, a brief-case, an umbrella under one bent arm, gloves rich and thick and grey on his thin fingers, and wore a horribly new straw hat.

Douglas backed up. 'She's busy.'

'I wish to rent her upstairs room, as advertised.'

'We've got ten boarders, and it's already rented; go away!'

'Douglas!' Grandma was behind him suddenly. 'How do you do?' she said to the stranger. 'Never mind this child.'

Unsmiling, the man stepped stiffly in. Douglas watched them ascend out of sight up the stairs, heard Grandma detailing the conveniences of the upstairs room. Soon she hurried down to pile linens from the linen closet on Douglas and send him scooting up with them.

Douglas paused at the room's threshold. The room was changed oddly, simply because the stranger had been in it a moment. The straw hat lay brittle and terrible upon the bed, the umbrella leaned stiff against one wall like a dead bat with dark moist wings folded.

Douglas blinked at the umbrella.

The stranger stood in the centre of the changed room, tall, tall.

'Here!' Douglas littered the bed with supplies. 'We eat at noon sharp, and if you're late coming down the soup'll get cold. Grandma fixes it so it will, every time!'

The tall strange man counted out ten new copper pennies

and tinkled them in Douglas's blouse pocket. 'We shall be friends,' he said, grimly.

It was funny, the man having nothing but pennies. Lots of them. No silver at all, no dimes, no quarters. Just new copper pennies.

Douglas thanked him glumly. 'I'll drop these in my dime bank when I get them changed into a dime. I got six dollars and fifty cents in dimes all ready for my camp trip in August.'

'I must wash now,' said the tall strange man.

Once, at midnight, Douglas had wakened to hear a storm rumbling outside – the cold hard wind shaking the house, the rain driving against the window. And then a lightning bolt had landed outside the window with a silent, terrific concussion. He remembered that fear of looking about at his room, seeing it strange and awful in the instantaneous light.

So it was, now, in this room. He stood looking up at the stranger. This room was no longer the same, but changed indefinably because this man, quick as a lightning bolt, had shed his light about it. Douglas backed up slowly as the stranger advanced.

The door closed in his face.

The wooden fork went up with mashed potatoes, came down empty. Mr Koberman, for that was his name, had brought the wooden fork and wooden knife and spoon with him when Grandma called lunch.

'Mrs Spaulding,' he had said, quietly, 'my own cutlery; please use it. I will have lunch today, but from tomorrow on, only breakfast and supper.'

Grandma bustled in and out, bearing steaming tureens of soup and beans and mashed potatoes to impress her new boarder, while Douglas sat rattling his silverware on his plate, because he had discovered it irritated Mr Koberman.

'I know a trick,' said Douglas. 'Watch.' He picked a fork-tine with his fingernail. He pointed at various sectors of the table, like a magician. Wherever he pointed, the sound of the vibrating fork-tine emerged, like a metal elfin voice. Simply done, of course. He pressed the fork handle on the table-top, secretly. The vibration came from the wood, like a sounding board. It looked quite magical. 'There, there, and *there*!' exclaimed Douglas, happily plucking the fork again. He pointed at Mr Koberman's soup and the noise came from it.

Mr Koberman's walnut-coloured face became hard and firm and awful. He pushed the soup bowl away violently, his lips twisting. He fell back in his chair.

Grandma appeared. 'Why, what's wrong, Mr Koberman?'

'I cannot eat this soup.'

'Why?'

'Because I am full and can eat no more. Thank you.'

Mr Koberman left the room, glaring.

'What did you do, just then?' asked Grandma at Douglas, sharply.

'Nothing. Grandma, why does he eat with *wooden* spoons?'

'Yours not to question! When do you go back to school, anyway?'

'Seven weeks.'

'Oh, my land!' said Grandma.

Mr Koberman worked nights. Each morning at eight he arrived mysteriously home, devoured a very small breakfast, and then slept soundlessly in his room all through the dreaming hot daytime, until the huge supper with all the other boarders at night.

Mr Koberman's sleeping habits made it necessary for Douglas to be quiet. This was unbearable. So, whenever Grandma visited down the street, Douglas stomped up and downstairs beating a drum, bouncing golf balls, or just screaming for three minutes outside Mr Koberman's door, or flushing the toilet seven times in succession.

Mr Koberman never moved. His room was silent, dark. He did not complain. There was no sound. He slept on and on. It was very strange.

Douglas felt a pure white flame of hatred burn inside himself with a steady, unflickering beauty. Now that room was Koberman Land. Once it had been flowery bright when Miss Sadlowe lived there. Now it was stark, bare, cold, clean, everything in its place, alien and brittle.

Douglas climbed upstairs on the fourth morning.

Half-way to the second floor was a large sun-filled window,

framed by six-inch panes of orange, purple, blue, red and burgundy glass. In the enchanted early mornings when the sun fell through to strike the landing and slide down the stair banister, Douglas stood entranced at this window peering at the world through multicoloured windows.

Now a blue world, a blue sky, blue people, blue street-cars and blue trotting dogs.

He shifted panes. Now – an amber world! Two lemonish women gliding by, resembling the daughters of Fu Manchu! Douglas giggled. This pane made even the sunlight more purely golden.

It was 8 am. Mr Koberman strolled by below, on the sidewalk, returning from his night's work, his cane looped over his elbow, straw hat glued to his head with patent oil.

Douglas shifted panes again. Mr Koberman was a red man walking through a red world with red trees and red flowers and – something else.

Something about – Mr Koberman.

Douglas squinted.

The red glass *did* things to Mr Koberman. His face, his suit, his hands. The clothes seemed to melt away. Douglas almost believed, for one terrible instant, that he could see *inside* Mr Koberman. And what he saw made him lean wildly against the small red pane, blinking.

Mr Koberman glanced up just then, saw Douglas, and raised his cane-umbrella angrily, as if to strike. He ran swiftly across the red lawn to the front door.

'Young man!' he cried, running up the stairs. 'What were you doing?'

'Just looking,' said Douglas, numbly.

'That's all, is it?' cried Mr Koberman.

'Yes, sir. I look through all the glasses. All kinds of worlds. Blue ones, red ones, yellow ones. All different.'

'All kinds of worlds, is it!' Mr Koberman glanced at the little panes of glass, his face pale. He got hold of himself. He wiped his face with a handkerchief and pretended to laugh. 'Yes. All kinds of worlds. All different.' He walked to the door of his room. 'Go right ahead; play,' he said.

The door closed. The hall was empty. Mr Koberman had gone in.

Douglas shrugged and found a new pane.

'Oh, everything's violet!'

Half an hour later, while playing in his sandbox behind the house, Douglas heard the crash and the shattering tinkle. He leaped up.

A moment later, Grandma appeared on the back porch, the old razor strop trembling in her hand.

'Douglas! I told you time and again never fling your basketball against the house! Oh, I could just cry!'

'I been sitting right here,' he protested.

'Come see what you've done, you nasty boy!'

The great coloured window-panes lay shattered in a rainbow chaos on the upstairs landing. His basketball lay in the ruins.

Before he could even begin telling his innocence, Douglas was struck a dozen stinging blows upon his rump. Wherever he landed, screaming, the razor strop struck again.

Later, hiding his mind in the sandpile like an ostrich, Douglas nursed his dreadful pains. He knew who'd thrown that basketball. A man with a straw hat and a stiff umbrella and a cold, grey room. Yeah, yeah, yeah. He dribbled tears. Just wait. Just *wait*.

He heard Grandma sweeping up the broken glass. She brought it out and threw it in the trash bin. Blue, pink, yellow meteors of glass dropped brightly down.

When she was gone, Douglas dragged himself, whimpering, over to save out three pieces of the incredible glass. Mr Koberman disliked the coloured windows. These – he clinked them in his fingers – would be worth saving.

Grandfather arrived from his newspaper office each night, shortly ahead of the other boarders, at five o'clock. When a slow, heavy tread filled the hall, and a thick, mahogany cane thumped in the cane-rack, Douglas ran to embrace the large stomach and sit on Grandpa's knee while he read the evening paper.

'Hi, Grampa!'

'Hello, down there!'

'Grandma cut chickens again today. It's fun watching,' said Douglas.

Grandpa kept reading. 'That's twice this week, chickens.

She's the chickenist woman. You like to watch her cut 'em, eh? Cold-blooded little pepper! Ha!'

'I'm just curious.'

'You are,' rumbled Grandpa, scowling. 'Remember that day when that young lady was killed at the rail station. You just walked over and looked at her, blood and all.' He laughed. 'Queer duck. Stay that way. Fear nothing, ever in your life. I guess you get it from your father, him being a military man and all, and you so close to him before you came here to live last year.' Grandpa returned to his paper.

A long pause. 'Gramps?'

'Yes?'

'What if a man didn't have a heart or lungs or stomach but still walked around, alive?'

'That,' rumbled Gramps, 'would be a miracle.'

'I don't mean a – a miracle. I mean, what if he was all *different* inside. Not like me.'

'Well, he wouldn't be quite human then, would he, boy?'

'Guess not, Gramps. Gramps, you got a heart and lungs?'

Gramps chuckled. 'Well, tell the truth, I don't *know*. Never seen them. Never had an X-ray, never been to a doctor. Might as well be potato-solid for all I know.'

'Have *I* got a stomach?'

'You certainly have!' cried Grandma from the parlour entry. ' 'Cause I feed it! And you've lungs, you scream loud enough to wake the crumblees. And you've dirty hands, go wash them! Dinner's ready. Grandpa, come on. Douglas, git!'

In the rush of boarders streaming downstairs, Grandpa, if he intended questioning Douglas further about the weird conversation, lost his opportunity. If dinner delayed an instant more, Grandma and the potatoes would develop simultaneous lumps.

The boarders, laughing and talking at the table – Mr Koberman silent and sullen among them – were silenced when Grandfather cleared his throat. He talked politics a few minutes and then shifted over into the intriguing topic of the recent peculiar deaths in the town.

'It's enough to make an old newspaper editor prick up his

ears,' he said, eyeing them all. 'That young Miss Larson, lived across the ravine, now. Found her dead three days ago for no reason, just funny kinds of tattoos all over her, and a facial expression that would make Dante cringe. And that other young lady, what was her name? Whitely? She disappeared and *never did* come back.'

'Them things happen alla time,' said Mr Bitz, the garage mechanic, chewing. 'Ever peek inna Missing Peoples Bureau file? It's *that* long.' He illustrated. 'Can't tell *what* happens to most of 'em.'

'Anyone want more dressing?' Grandma ladled liberal portions from the chicken's interior. Douglas watched, thinking about how that chicken had had two kinds of guts – God-made and Man-made.

Well, how about *three* kinds of guts?

Eh?

Why not?

Conversation continued about the mysterious death of so-and-so, and, oh, yes, remember a week ago, Marion Barsumian died of heart failure, but maybe that didn't connect up? or did it? you're crazy! forget it, why talk about it at the dinner table? So.

'Never can tell,' said Mr Britz. 'Maybe we got a vampire in town.'

Mr Koberman stopped eating.

'In the year 1927?' said Grandma. 'A vampire? Oh, go on, now.'

'Sure,' said Mr Britz. 'Kill 'em with silver bullets. Anything silver for that matter. Vampires *hate* silver. I read it in a book somewhere, once. Sure, I did.'

Douglas looked at Mr Koberman who ate with wooden knives and forks and carried only new copper pennies in his pocket.

'It's poor judgment,' said Grandpa, 'to call anything by a name. We don't know what a hobgoblin or a vampire or a troll is. Could be lots of things. You can't heave them into categories with labels and say they'll act one way or another. That'd be silly. They're people. People who do things. Yes, that's the way to put it: people who *do* things.'

'Excuse me,' said Mr Koberman, who got up and went out for his evening walk to work.

The stars, the moon, the wind, the clock ticking, and the chiming of the hours into dawn, the sun rising, and here it was another morning, another day, and Mr Koberman coming along the sidewalk from his night's work. Douglas stood off like a small mechanism whirring and watching with carefully microscopic eyes.

At noon, Grandma went to the store to buy groceries.

As was his custom every day when Grandma was gone, Douglas yelled outside Mr Koberman's door for a full three minutes. As usual, there was no response. The silence was horrible.

He ran downstairs, got the pass-key, a silver fork, and the three pieces of coloured glass he had saved from the shattered window. He fitted the key to the lock and swung the door slowly open.

The room was in half light, the shades drawn. Mr Koberman lay atop his bedcovers, in slumber clothes, breathing gently, up and down. He didn't move. His face was motionless.

'Hello, Mr Koberman!'

The colourless walls echoed the man's regular breathing.

'Mr Koberman, hello!'

Bouncing a golf ball, Douglas advanced. He yelled. Still no answer. 'Mr Koberman!'

Bending over Mr Koberman, Douglas picked the tines of the silver fork in the sleeping man's face.

Mr Koberman winced. He twisted. He groaned bitterly.

Response. Good. Swell.

Douglas drew a piece of blue glass from his pocket. Looking through the blue glass fragment he found himself in a blue room, in a blue world different from the world he knew. As different as was the red world. Blue furniture, blue bed, blue ceiling and walls, blue wooden eating utensils atop the blue bureau, and the sullen dark blue of Mr Koberman's face and arms and his blue chest rising, falling. Also . . .

Mr Koberman's eyes were wide, staring at him with a hungry darkness.

Douglas fell back, pulled the blue glass from his eyes.

Mr Koberman's eyes were shut.

Blue glass again – open. Blue glass away – shut. Blue glass again – open. Away – shut. Funny. Douglas experimented, trembling. Through the glass the eyes seemed to peer hungrily, avidly through Mr Koberman's closed lids. Without the blue glass they seemed tightly shut.

But it was the rest of Mr Koberman's body. . . .

Mr Koberman's bedclothes dissolved off him. The blue glass had something to do with it. Or perhaps it was the clothes themselves, just being *on* Mr Koberman. Douglas cried out.

He was looking through the wall of Mr Koberman's stomach, right *inside* him!

Mr Koberman was solid.

Or, nearly so, anyway.

There were strange shapes and sizes within him.

Douglas must have stood amazed for five minutes, thinking about the blue worlds, the red worlds, the yellow worlds side by side, living together like glass panes around the big white stair window. Side by side, the coloured panes, the different worlds; Mr Koberman had said so himself.

So this was why the coloured window had been broken.

'Mr Koberman, wake up!'

No answer.

'Mr Koberman, where do you work at night? Mr Koberman, where do you work?'

A little breeze stirred the blue window shade.

'In a red world or a green world or a yellow one, Mr Koberman?'

Over everything was a blue glass silence.

'Wait there,' said Douglas.

He walked down to the kitchen, pulled open the great squeaking drawer and picked out the sharpest, biggest knife.

Very calmly he walked into the hall, climbed back up the stairs again, opened the door to Mr Koberman's room, went in, and closed it, holding the sharp knife in one hand.

Grandma was busy fingering a piecrust into a pan when Douglas entered the kitchen to place something on the table.

'Grandma, what's this?'

She glanced up briefly, over her glasses. 'I don't know.'

It was square, like a box, and elastic. It was bright orange in colour. It had four square tubes, coloured blue, attached to it. It smelled funny.

'Ever see anything like it, Grandma?'

'No.'

'That's what *I* thought.'

Douglas left it there, went from the kitchen. Five minutes later he returned with something else. 'How about *this*?'

He laid down a bright pink linked chain with a purple triangle at one end.

'Don't bother me,' said Grandma. 'It's only a chain.'

Next time he returned with two hands full. A ring, a square, a triangle, a pyramid, a rectangle, and – other shapes. All of them were pliable, resilient, and looked as if they were made of gelatine. 'This isn't all,' said Douglas, putting them down. 'There's more where this came from.'

Grandma said, 'Yes, yes,' in a far-off tone, very busy.

'You were wrong, Grandma.'

'About what?'

'About all people being the same inside.'

'Stop talking nonsense.'

'Where's my piggy-bank?'

'On the mantel, where you left it.'

'Thanks.'

He tromped into the parlour, reached up for his piggy-bank.

Grandpa came home from the office at five.

'Grandpa, come upstairs.'

'Sure, son. Why?'

'Something to show you. It's not nice; but it's interesting.'

Grandpa chuckled, following his grandson's feet up to Mr Koberman's room.

'Grandma mustn't know about this; she wouldn't like it,' said Douglas. He pushed the door wide open. 'There.'

Grandfather gasped.

Douglas remembered the next few hours all the rest of his life. Standing over Mr Koberman's naked body, the coroner and his assistants. Grandma, downstairs, asking somebody, 'What's going on up there?' and Grandpa saying, shakily, 'I'll take Douglas away on a long vacation so he can forget this whole ghastly affair. Ghastly, ghastly affair!'

Douglas said, 'Why should it be bad? I don't see anything bad. I don't feel bad.'

His assistant sweated. 'Did you see those *things* in the pans of water and in the wrapping paper?'

'Oh, my God, my God, yes, I saw them.'

'Christ.'

The coroner bent over Mr Koberman's body again. 'This better be kept secret, boys. It wasn't murder. It was a mercy the boy acted. God knows what might have happened if he hadn't.'

'What was Koberman? A vampire? A monster?'

'Maybe. I don't know. Something – not human.' The coroner moved his hands deftly over the suture.

Douglas was proud of his work. He'd gone to much trouble. He had watched Grandmother carefully and remembered. Needle and thread and all. All in all, Mr Koberman was as neat a job as any chicken ever popped into hell by Grandma.

'I heard the boy say that Koberman lived even after all those *things* were taken out of him.' The coroner looked at the triangles and chains and pyramids floating in the pans of water. 'Kept on *living*. God.'

'Did the boy say that?'

'He did.'

'Then, what *did* kill Koberman?'

The coroner drew a few strands of sewing thread from their bedding.

'This. . . .' he said.

Sunlight blinked coldly off a half-revealed treasure trove; six dollars and seventy cents' worth of silver dimes inside Mr Koberman's chest.

'I think Douglas made a wise investment,' said the coroner, sewing the flesh back up over the 'dressing' quickly.

BRAM STOKER

THE DEATH OF DRACULA

from *Dracula*

JONATHAN HARKER'S JOURNAL

4th November, evening. – The accident to the launch has been a terrible thing for us. Only for it we should have overtaken the boat long ago; and by now my dear Mina would have been free. I fear to think of her, off on the wolds near that horrid place. We have got horses, and we follow on the track. I note this whilst Godalming is getting ready. We have our arms. The Szgany must look out if they mean fight. Oh, if only Morris and Seward were with us. We must only hope! If I write no more Good-bye, Mina! God bless and keep you.

DR SEWARD'S DIARY

5th November. – With the dawn we saw the body of Szgany before us dashing away from the river with their leiter-wagon. They surrounded it in a cluster, and hurried along as though beset. The snow is falling lightly and there is a strange excitement in the air. It may be our own excited feelings, but the depression is strange. Far off I hear the howling of wolves; the snow brings them down from the mountains, and there are dangers to all of us, and from all sides. The horses are nearly ready, and we are soon off. We ride to death of someone. God alone knows who, or where, or what, or when, or how it may be....

DR VAN HELSING'S MEMORANDUM

5th November, afternoon. – I am at least sane. Thank God for that mercy at all events, though the proving it has been dreadful. When I left Madam Mina sleeping within the Holy circle, I took my way to the castle. The blacksmith hammer which I took in the carriage from Veresti was useful; though the doors were all open I broke them off the rusty hinges, lest some ill-intent or ill-chance should close them, so that being entered I might not get out. Jonathan's bitter experience served me here. By memory of his diary I found my way to the old chapel, for I knew that here my work lay. The air was oppressive; it seemed as if there was some sulphurous fume, which at times made me dizzy. Either there was a roaring in my ears or I heard afar off the howl of wolves. Then I bethought me of my dear Madam Mina, and I was in terrible plight. The dilemma had me between his horns. Her, I had not dare to take into this place, but left safe from the Vampire in that Holy circle; and yet even there would be the wolf! I resolve me that my work lay here, and that as to the wolves we must submit, if it were God's Will. At any rate it was only death and freedom beyond. So did I choose for her. Had it but been for myself the choice had been easy; the maw of the wolf were better to rest in than the grave of the Vampire! So I make my choice to go on with my work.

I knew that there were at least three graves to find – graves that are inhabit; so I search, and search, and I find one of them. She lay in her Vampire sleep, so full of life and voluptuous beauty that I shudder as though I have come to do murder. Ah, I doubt not that in old time, when such things were, many a man who set forth to do such a task as mine, found at the last his heart fail him, and then his nerve. So he delay, and delay, and delay, till the mere beauty and the fascination of the wanton Un-Dead have hypnotize him; and he remain on, and on, till sunset come, and the Vampire sleep be over. Then the beautiful eyes of the fair woman open and look love, and the voluptuous mouth present to a kiss – and man is weak. And there remains one more victim in the Vampire fold; one more to swell the grim and grisly ranks of the Un-Dead! . . .

There is some fascination, surely, when I am moved by the mere presence of such an one, even lying as she lay in a tomb fretted with age and heavy with the dust of centuries, though there be that horrid odour such as the lairs of the Count have had. Yes, I was moved – I, Van Helsing, with all my purpose and with my motive for hate – I was moved to a yearning for delay which seemed to paralyse my faculties and to clog my very soul. It may have been that the need of natural sleep, and the strange oppression of the air were beginning to overcome me. Certain it was that I was lapsing into sleep, the open-eyed sleep of one who yields to a sweet fascination, when there came through the snow-stilled air a long, low wail, so full of woe and pity that it woke me like the sound of a clarion. For it was the voice of my dear Madam Mina that I heard.

Then I braced myself again to my horrid task, and found by wrenching away tomb-tops one other of the sisters, the other dark one. I dared not pause to look on her as I had on her sister, lest once more I should begin to be enthral; but I go on searching until, presently, I find in a high great tomb as if made to one much beloved that other fair sister which, like Jonathan, I had seen to gather herself out of the atoms of the mist. She was so fair to look on, so radiantly beautiful, so exquisitely voluptuous, that the very instinct of man in me, which calls some of my sex to love and to protect one of hers, made my head whirl with new emotion. But, God be thanked, that soul-wail of my dear Madam Mina had not died out of my ears; and, before the spell could be wrought further upon me, I had nerved myself to my wild work. By this time I had searched all the tombs in the chapel, so far as I could tell; and as there had been only three of these Un-Dead phantoms around us in the night, I took it that there were no more of active Un-Dead existent. There was one great tomb more lordly than all the rest; huge it was, and nobly proportioned. On it was but one word

DRACULA

This then was the Un-Dead home of the King-Vampire, to whom so many more were due. Its emptiness spoke eloquent to make certain what I knew. Before I began to restore these women to their dead selves through my awful work, I laid in Dracula's tomb some of the Wafer, and so banished him from it, Un-Dead, for ever.

Then began my terrible task, and I dreaded it. Had it been but one, it had been easy, comparative. But three! To begin twice more after I had been through a deed of horror; for if it was terrible with the sweet Miss Lucy, what would it not be with these strange ones who had survived through centuries and who had been strengthened by the passing of the years; who would, if they could, have fought for their foul lives. . . .

Oh, my friend John, but it was butcher work; had I not been nerved by thoughts of other dead, and of the living over whom hung such a pall of fear, I could not have gone on. I tremble and tremble even yet, though till all was over, God be thanked, my nerve did stand. Had I not seen the repose in the first face, and the gladness that stole over it just ere the final dissolution came, as realization that the soul had been won, I could not have gone further with my butchery. I could not have endured the horrid screeching as the stake drove home; the plunging of writhing form, and lips of bloody foam. I should have fled in terror and left my work undone. But it is over! And the poor souls, I can pity them now and weep, as I think of them placid each in her full sleep of death, for a short moment ere fading. For, friend John, hardly had my knife severed the head of each, before the whole body began to melt away and crumble into its native dust, as though the death that should have come centuries agone had at last assert himself and say at once and loud 'I am here!'

Before I left the castle I so fixed its entrances that never more can the Count enter there Un-Dead.

When I stepped into the circle where Madam Mina slept, she woke from her sleep, and, seeing me, cried out in pain that I had endured too much.

'Come!' she said, 'come away from this awful place! Let us go to meet my husband, who is, I know, coming towards us.' She was looking thin and pale and weak; but her eyes were pure and glowed with fervour. I was glad to see her paleness and her illness, for my mind was full of the fresh horror of that ruddy Vampire sleep.

And so with trust and hope, and yet full of fear, we go eastward to meet our friends – and *him* – whom Madam Mina tell me that she *know* are coming to meet us.

MINA HARKER'S JOURNAL

6th November. – It was late in the afternoon when the Professor and I took our way towards the east whence I knew

Jonathan was coming. We did not go fast, though [illegible] was steeply down-hill, for we had to take heavy rugs and wraps with us; we dared not face the possibility of being left without warmth in the cold and the snow. We had to take some of our provisions too, for we were in a perfect desolation, and, as far as we could see through the snowfall, there was not even the sign of a habitation. When we had gone about a mile, I was tired with the heavy walking and sat down to rest. Then we looked back and saw where the clear line of Dracula's castle cut the sky; for we were so deep under the hill whereupon it was set that the angle of perspective of the Carpathian mountains was far below it. We saw it in all its grandeur, perched a thousand feet on the summit of a sheer precipice, and with seemingly a great gap between it and the steep of the adjacent mountain on any side. There was something wild and uncanny about the place. We could hear the distant howling of wolves. They were far off, but the sound, even though coming muffled through the deadening snowfall, was full of terror. I knew from the way Dr Van Helsing was searching about that he was trying to seek some strategic point, where we would be less exposed in case of attack. The rough roadway still led downwards; we could trace it through the drifted snow.

In a little while the Professor signalled to me, so I got up and joined him. He had found a wonderful spot, a sort of natural hollow in a rock, with an entrance like a doorway between two boulders. He took me by the hand and drew me in: 'See!' he said, 'here you will be in shelter; and if the wolves do come I can meet them one by one.' He brought in our furs, and made a snug nest for me, and got out some provisions and forced them upon me. But I could not eat; to even try to do so was repulsive to me, and, much as I would have liked to please him, I could not bring myself to the attempt. He looked very sad, but did not reproach me. Taking his field-glasses from the case, he stood on the top of the rock, and began to search the horizon. Suddenly he called out:

'Look! Madam Mina, look! look!' I sprang up and stood beside him on the rock; he handed me his glasses and pointed. The snow was now falling more heavily, and swirled about fiercely, for a high wind was beginning to blow. However, there were times when there were pauses between the snow-flurries, and I could see a long way round. From the height where we were it was possible to see a great distance; and far off, beyond the white waste of snow, I could see the river lying like a black ribbon in kinks and curls as it wound its way. Straight in front of us and not far off – in fact so near that I wondered we had not noticed before – came a group of mounted men hurrying along. In the midst of them was a cart, a long leiter-wagon which swept from side to side, like a dog's tail wagging, with each stern inequality of the road. Outlined against the snow as they were, I could see from the men's clothes that they were peasants or gipsies of some kind.

On the cart was a great square chest. My heart leaped as I saw it, for I felt that the end was coming. The evening was now drawing close, and well I knew that at sunset the Thing, which was till then imprisoned there, would take new freedom and could in any of many forms elude all pursuit. In fear I turned to the Professor; to my consternation, however, he was not there. An instant later, I saw him below me. Round the rock he had drawn a circle, such as we had found shelter in last night. When he had completed it he stood beside me again, saying:

'At least you shall be safe here from *him*!' He took the glasses from me, and at the next lull of the snow swept the whole space below us. 'See,' he said, 'they come quickly; they are flogging the horses, and galloping as hard as they can.' He paused and went on in a hollow voice:

'They are racing for the sunset. We may be too late. God's will be done!' Down came another blinding rush of driving snow, and the whole landscape was blotted out. It soon passed, however, and once more his glasses were fixed on the plain. Then came a sudden cry:

'Look! Look! Look! See, two horsemen follow fast, coming up from the south. It must be Quincey and John. Take the glass. Look, before the snow blots it all out!' I took it and looked. The two men might be Dr Seward and Mr Morris. I knew at all events that neither of them was Jonathan. At the same time I *knew* that Jonathan was not far off; looking around I saw on the north side of the coming party two other men, riding at break-neck speed. One of them I knew was Jonathan, and the other I took, of course, to be Lord Godalming. They, too, were pursuing the party with the cart. When I told the Professor he shouted in glee like a schoolboy, and, after looking intently till a snowfall made sight impossible, he laid his Winchester rifle ready for use against the boulder at the opening of our shelter. 'They are all converging,' he said. 'When the time comes we shall have the gipsies on all sides.' I got out my revolver ready to hand, for whilst we were speaking the howling of wolves came louder and closer. When the snowstorm abated a moment we looked again. It was strange to see the snow falling in such heavy flakes close to us, and beyond, the sun shining more and more brightly as it sank down towards the far mountain tops. Sweeping the glass all around us I could see here and there dots moving singly and in twos and threes and larger numbers – the wolves were gathering for their prey.

Every instant seemed an age whilst we waited. The wind came now in fierce bursts, and the snow was driven with fury as it swept upon us in circling eddies. At times we could not see an arm's length before us; but at others as the hollow-sounding wind swept by us, it seemed to clear the air-space around us so that we could see afar off. We had of late been so accustomed to watch for sunrise and sunset, that we knew with fair accuracy when it would be; and we knew that before long the sun would set.

It was hard to believe that by our watches it was less than an hour that we waited in that rocky shelter before the various bodies began to converge close upon us. The wind came now with fiercer and more bitter sweeps, and more steadily from the north. It seemingly had driven the snow-clouds from us, for, with only occasional bursts, the snow fell. We could distinguish clearly the individuals of each party, the pursued and the pursuers. Strangely enough those pursued did not seem to realize, or at least to care, that they were pursued; they seemed, however, to hasten with redoubled speed as the sun dropped lower and lower on the mountain tops.

Closer and closer they drew. The Professor and I crouched down behind our rock, and held our weapons ready; I could see that he was determined that they should not pass. One and all were quite unaware of our presence.

All at once two voices shouted out to 'Halt!' One was my Jonathan's, raised in a high key of passion; the other, Mr Morris's strong resolute tone of quiet command. The gipsies may not have known the language, but there was no mistaking the tone, in whatever tongue the words were spoken. Instinctively they reined in, and at the instant Lord Godalming and Jonathan dashed up at one side and Dr Seward and Mr Morris on the other. The leader of the gipsies, a splendid-looking fellow, who sat his horse like a centaur, waved them back, and in a fierce voice gave to his companions some word to proceed. They lashed the horses, which sprang forward; but the four men raised their Winchester rifles, and in an unmistakable way commanded them to stop. At the same moment Dr Van Helsing and I rose behind the rock and pointed our weapons at them. Seeing that they were surrounded, the men tightened their reins and drew up. The leader turned to them and gave a word, at which every man of the gipsy party drew what weapon he carried, knife or pistol, and held himself in readiness to attack. Issue was joined in an instant.

The leader, with a quick movement of his rein, threw his horse out in front, and pointing first to the sun – now close down on the hill-tops – and then to the castle, said something which I did not understand. For answer, all four men of our party threw themselves from their horses and dashed towards the cart. I should have felt terrible fear at seeing Jonathan in such danger, but that the ardour of battle must have been upon me as well as the rest of them; I felt no fear, but only a wild, surging desire to do something. Seeing the quick movement of our parties, the leader of the gipsies gave a command; his men instantly formed round the cart in a sort of undisciplined endeavour, each one shouldering and pushing the other in his eagerness to carry out the order.

In the midst of this I could see that Jonathan on one side of the ring of men, and Quincey on the other, were forcing a way to the cart; it was evident that they were bent on finishing their task before the sun should set. Nothing seemed to stop or even to hinder them. Neither the levelled weapons nor the flashing knives of the gipsies in front, or the howling of the wolves behind, appeared to even attract their attention. Jonathan's impetuosity, and the manifest singleness of his purpose, seemed to overawe those in front of him; instinctively they cowered aside and let him pass. In an instant he had jumped upon the cart, and, with a strength which seemed incredible, raised the great box, and flung it over the wheel to the ground. In the meantime, Mr Morris had had to use force to pass through his side of the ring of Szgany. All the time I had been breathlessly watching Jonathan I had, with the tail of my eye, seen him pressing desperately forward, and had seen the knives of the gipsies flash as he won a way through them, and they cut at him. He parried with his great bowie knife, and at first I thought that he too had come through in safety; but as he sprang beside Jonathan, who had by now jumped from the cart, I could see that with his left hand he was clutching at his side, and that the blood was spurting through his fingers. He did not delay notwithstanding this, for as Jonathan, with desperate energy, attacked one end of the chest, attempting to prise off the lid with his great Kukri knife, he attacked the other frantically with his bowie. Under the efforts of both men the lid began to yield; the nails drew with a quick screeching sound, and the top of the box was thrown back.

By this time the gipsies, seeing themselves covered by the Winchesters, and at the mercy of Lord Godalming and Dr Seward, had given in and made no further resistance. The sun was almost down on the mountain tops, and the shadows of the whole group fell long upon the snow. I saw the Count lying within the box upon the earth, some of which the rude falling from the cart had scattered over him. He was deathly pale, just like a waxen image, and the red eyes glared with the horrible vindictive look which I knew too well.

As I looked, the eyes saw the sinking sun, and the look of hate in them turned to triumph.

But, on the instant, came the sweep and flash of Jonathan's great knife. I shrieked as I saw it shear through the throat; whilst at the same moment Mr Morris's bowie knife plunged into the heart.

It was like a miracle; but before our very eyes, and almost

in the drawing of a breath, the whole body crumbled into dust and passed from our sight.

I shall be glad as long as I live that even in that moment of final dissolution there was in the face a look of peace, such as I never could have imagined might have rested there.

NOTES

Page 9

THE VAMPIRES OF HUNGARY AND SURROUNDING COUNTRIES

This is an extract from *Dissertation sur les apparitions des esprits et sur les vampires et revenants,* which was published in 1749. Dom Augustin Calmet (1672–1757) was a learned Benedictine whose works included a *Dictionnaire historique, critique, chronologique, géographique et littéral de la Bible* in 4 volumes, which was published in Paris in 1720–1.

Page 23

CARNIVAL

When he was asked what reasons had led Pursewarden, one of the characters in the *Alexandrian Quartet,* to be interested in vampires, the author replied with a pun on the word *sangsue,* meaning a leech: '. . . because Pursewarden had read a great deal about "sangsuel" women in the works of Laforgue, and always called himself "un homme moyen sangsuel" like Baudelaire. Perhaps it was the assassination of ideas? Who knows? L. D.'

Page 33

CARMILLA

This famous story was included in the collection *In a Glass Darkly,* first published in 1872, the year before the author died. It provided the theme for Roger Vadim's film *Et Mourir de Plaisir.* Another story from the same collection had already given Carl Theodor Dreyer the idea for his famous film *The Vampire.*

Page 96

THE BEAUTIFUL VAMPIRE

First published (*La Morte Amoureux*) in the *Chronique de Paris,* June 23rd–26th, 1836.

Théophile Gautier, like Edgar Allan Poe, Gérard de Nerval and Villiers de l'Isle-Adam, who were all intrigued by life beyond the grave, lost the woman he loved when he was very young. It is curious to note that in his tales dealing with macabre lovers Gautier nearly always takes the names of his heroes from Hoffman, who had been his literary model during his youth.

Page 125

BERENICE

This story was first published in the *Southern Literary Mesenger*, Richmond, Virgina, USA, in March, 1835. Baudelaire's translation was published in France in 1857.

As Marie Bonaparte has shown, the successive losses of his mother, then of the women he loved (and he loved them preferably when they were wasting away) turned Poe into a necrophile and a sublimated thanatophile.

Page 134

CHRISEIS

Chapter 9 from *Doctors Wear Scarlet*, first published in London in 1960.

Page 149

THE HORLA

First published in Paris in 1887.

An earlier version had appeared in the periodical *Gil Blas* during the previous year, but this second one was amplified and enriched by extremely realistic details, including whole pages of a scientific or para-scientific nature, allusions to studies of the school of Charcot, travel notes made by Maupassant on the spot during his visit to the Mont Saint-Michel and the description of a house on the banks of the Seine, which was none other than Flaubert's house at Diessard. As for the name *Horla*, he probably made it up, as Pierre Castex has supposed, basing it on the word *horzain* which is used in Normandy to describe a stranger.

The story had a great success and in the *Figaro* (July 16th, 1887) Maupassant mentioned a trip he had been invited to make in a balloon which had been called 'the Horla' in his honour.

Between 1885 and 1887 more than sixty works were published in France dealing with neurosis, hypnotism and suggestion. Maupassant himself had become a regular visitor to the Salpêtrière hospital, seizing every opportunity to build up documentation on the subject of magnetism and on psychiatry in general. The stories written during the last ten years of his life illustrate the increasing intensity of his mental illness. Maupassant underwent the same fate as the narrator in his story, for his obsession with death drove him to the grave.

Page 225

VIY

Gogol wrote this story in 1835. It was highly praised by Mérimée and other continental critics, while in his *Treatise on Tales of Horrors* (1944) Edmund Wilson describes it as 'one of the most terrific things of its kind ever written'.

Page 264

FRESH GUY

This was chosen by Judith Merrill as one of the best science fiction stories published during 1958.

Page 279

A VAMPIRE

This story by Luigi Capuana (1839–1915) was first published in Rome in 1907. The writer, who belonged to the Italian naturalist school, dedicated the story to the famous psychiatrist and criminologist Cesare Lombroso, whose *Studies in Hypnotism* in particular had caused a sensation at the end of the nineteenth century.